Titles by Christine Feehan

VIPER GAME	DEADLY GAME
SAMURAI GAME	CONSPIRACY GAME
RUTHLESS GAME	NIGHT GAME
STREET GAME	MIND GAME
MURDER GAME	SHADOW GAME
PREDATORY GAME	

HIDDEN CURRENTS	DANGEROUS TIDES
TURBULENT SEA	OCEANS OF FIRE
SAFE HARBOR	

LEOPARD'S PREY	BURNING WILD
SAVAGE NATURE	WILD RAIN
WILD FIRE	

AIR BOUND
SPIRIT BOUND
WATER BOUND

DARK BLOOD	DARK SECRET
DARK WOLF	DARK DESTINY
DARK LYCAN	DARK MELODY
DARK STORM	DARK SYMPHONY
DARK PREDATOR	DARK GUARDIAN
DARK PERIL	DARK LEGEND
DARK SLAYER	DARK FIRE
DARK CURSE	DARK CHALLENGE
DARK HUNGER	DARK MAGIC
DARK POSSESSION	DARK GOLD
DARK CELEBRATION	DARK DESIRE
DARK DEMON	DARK PRINCE

VIPER GAME

CHRISTINE FEEHAN

JOVE BOOKS, NEW YORK

THE BERKLEY PUBLISHING GROUP
Published by the Penguin Group
Penguin Group (USA) LLC
375 Hudson Street, New York, New York 10014

USA • Canada • UK • Ireland • Australia • New Zealand • India • South Africa • China

penguin.com

A Penguin Random House Company

VIPER GAME

A Jove Book / published by arrangement with the author

Jove Books are published by The Berkley Publishing Group.
JOVE® is a registered trademark of Penguin Group (USA) LLC.
The "J" design is a trademark of Penguin Group (USA) LLC.

For information, address: The Berkley Publishing Group,
a division of Penguin Group (USA) LLC,
375 Hudson Street, New York, New York 10014.

ISBN: 978-0-515-15554-9

PUBLISHING HISTORY
Jove mass-market edition / February 2015

PRINTED IN THE UNITED STATES OF AMERICA

10 9 8 7 6 5 4 3 2 1

Cover art by Dan O'Leary.

*For my daughter Manda, and not because
she gave birth to Shylah, which she did,
along with Skyler, both girls being the joy in
my life, but because* Manda *always makes me
proud, makes me laugh and I can count on
her no matter what. Much love!*

For My Readers

Be sure to go to christinefeehan.com/members/ to sign up for my *private* book announcement list and download the free ebook of *Dark Desserts*. Join my community and get firsthand news, enter the book discussions, ask your questions and chat with me. Please feel free to email me at Christine@christinefeehan.com. I would love to hear from you.

Acknowledgments

No book can be written without a little help along the way. I would like to thank my wonderful power-hour sisters: C. L. Wilson, Kathie Firzlaff, Susan Edwards and Karen Rose! Also a huge shout-out to my power-hour writing son, Brian, for always making me feel that little edge of competition. Oh, yeah, what did that little note you sent to me say??? You were kicking *whose* booty for that hour???? WHAT??? WHAT??? I DON'T think so!!! As always, Domini, thank you for your help when I need that extra research done *right now*, and to Brian Feehan for brainstorming to activate the brain cells in a crunch. You all are the best!

The GhostWalker Symbol Details

SIGNIFIES
shadow

SIGNIFIES
protection against
evil forces

SIGNIFIES
the Greek letter *psi*, which is
used by parapsychology
researchers to signify ESP or
other psychic abilities

SIGNIFIES
qualities of a knight—
loyalty, generosity,
courage and honor

SIGNIFIES
shadow knights who protect
against evil forces using
psychic powers, courage
and honor

nox noctis est nostri

The GhostWalker Creed

We are the GhostWalkers, we live in the shadows
The sea, the earth, and the air are our domain
No fallen comrade will be left behind
We are loyalty and honor bound
We are invisible to our enemies
and we destroy them where we find them
We believe in justice and we protect our country
and those unable to protect themselves
What goes unseen, unheard, and unknown
are GhostWalkers
There is honor in the shadows and it is us
We move in complete silence whether
in jungle or desert
We walk among our enemy unseen and unheard
Striking without sound and scatter to the winds
before they have knowledge of our existence
We gather information and wait with endless patience
for that perfect moment to deliver swift justice
We are both merciful and merciless
We are relentless and implacable in our resolve
We are the GhostWalkers and the night is ours

CHAPTER 1

Wyatt Fontenot tied up his airboat, but stood in it in the dark, listening to the familiar sounds of the bayou. He'd grown up in these swamps, hearing the bullfrogs, the bellow of the alligator and the plop of snakes sliding from the cypress trees into the dark waters. The constant drone of insects had been his lullaby. The soft fall of rain didn't bring the cold, rather just ratcheted up the heat, wrapping one up in a blanket of humidity and the strange perfume of the swamp.

He let his breath out slowly, just drinking in the sights around him. He'd always felt at home in the bayou. He'd never really much liked going other places, but now, he wasn't certain it was the smartest thing in the world for him to be back . . . yet. He couldn't breathe in cities, yet now that he'd come home, he found his chest was tight and his famous Cajun temper had settled into a slow boil in the pit of his stomach.

"You all right, Wyatt?" Malichai Fortunes asked softly. He stood just to the left of Wyatt, in the deeper shadows of the sweeping cypress, impossible to see until he moved.

Wyatt glanced at him. Malichai was a big man, all roped muscle and cool, with strange, almost golden eyes. He looked into a man, cutting straight through to who and what he was. Wyatt had learned to trust him implicitly. They were both bone weary. Exhausted. Four months and over four hundred rescue operations, most conducted in the "hot" zones of war. The last had gone to hell and them with it.

"Yeah, I'm all right. Just breathing in home," he replied.

The scent of pipe tobacco drifted to him. The slight wind rustled through the trees, swaying the branches in a macabre fashion. He'd always enjoyed taking his city friends out into the swamp at night and scaring the hell out of them before taking them to one of the backwoods bars where they could get drunk and fight with anyone who looked at them wrong.

He could fish with a string or a knife. He could kill a gator with a knife or gun. He was one of the best hunters in the swamps. Few of the boys who knew him ever challenged him to a fight. His word was gold all over the swamp and bayous. He'd studied long and hard to be a doctor, a surgeon, one that could come home and be of great use here in the bayou. It wasn't that he couldn't have left— he hadn't wanted to leave. There was a huge difference.

He let out his breath again and scrubbed his hand down his face, wishing he could wipe his memories of his own damn foolishness away so easily.

"Did you tell your *grand-mere* we were coming with you?" Ezekiel Fortunes, Malichai's brother, asked softly. Too softly. His voice was almost a rolling purr in the night, like that of a cat waiting for prey.

Wyatt glanced at the third man on the airboat, the man to his right. Ezekiel was an inch or so shorter than either of the other two, but he had the same roped muscles and solid build. His eyes, a strange amber color, glowed in the dark just as Wyatt's and Malichai's did. All three could see as easily at night as they could during the day, which gave them a decided advantage in night combat situations.

"Nonny's expecting all three of us," Wyatt said. "And you two had better be on your best behavior. She's good at grabbing ears and twisting if you get out of line." He rubbed his ear, a little grin slowly finding its way to his mouth at the memory of quite a few of those ear-pulling incidents. "War wounds aren' goin' to save you."

"She's a good cook?" Malichai asked. "Because I'm starving."

Wyatt and Ezekiel both laughed. "You're always starving."

"We never get to eat. Someone's always trying to kill us," Malichai complained. He looked around him. "I'll bet there's good hunting here."

Wyatt nodded slowly. "We're resting, boys. Resting and relaxing. Not hunting. These people are my neighbors. They'll want to drink with you and fight with you, but you don't get to kill them."

"You sure do know how to take the fun out of a party," Ezekiel groused.

Wyatt stepped off the airboat to the solid wooden pier. The last time he'd been home, he'd fixed the rotting boards and it was still in fine shape. He'd been afraid his grandmother would have tried to repair the dock in spite of her age and failing health. That would be just like her. It was the last thing he'd done for her before he'd left—in the dead of night—without a word. Skulking away like some sulking child just because he got his heart ripped out. No, because he *thought* he got his heart ripped out, which was infinitely worse.

He just stood there another minute, reluctant to walk up to the house, knowing his grandmother would welcome him with open arms, and not one hint of censure, but he felt guilty. He kept trying to think of what to say to her. There were no words. None at all. She would know the moment she saw him, the moment she looked into his eyes and saw what he'd done, that he'd been changed for all time—just as his brother Raoul had been.

"What is it, Wyatt?" Malichai asked again. His voice was pitched low and he used that same purring tone of the hunter Ezekiel had used.

"She'll know. Nonny. The minute she lays eyes on me, she'll know what I am."

Ezekiel looked out over the bayou, avoiding his gaze.

Malichai shook his head. "No, she won't, Wyatt. She'll know you're different in some way, but she won't know what you are."

"I left a doctor, a healer." Wyatt looked down at his hands. "I came back a killer. You tell me how she isn't going to know that."

"We don't have to stay," Ezekiel reminded, his tone noncommittal. "We can turn around and get the hell out of here if that makes you feel any better."

"She asked me to come home," Wyatt said. "She doesn't ever ask for much. She said she needed help, and my other brothers are out of the country at the moment. I had leave comin' and knew I had to face her sooner or later. It's been a while, but the bayou still feels like home."

Malichai looked around him slowly. "It feels like a hunting ground to me."

The Fontcnot home was old, even for the bayou, but kept in very good shape. Iron gates and a large fence kept the property private with its own pier off the river. Nonny's hunting dogs had set up a cry when the airboat had first arrived, but Wyatt had sent them a quick, silent command and they'd ceased baying immediately.

There were two large buildings, the house and a garage. The garage had double pull-down doors and a single, smaller entrance, all locked with padlocks. The house was two stories, with a balcony and a wraparound deck.

"This is nice, Wyatt," Malichai said. "A sweet setup."

"It started out as a frame house, very traditional," Wyatt

said. "One and a half stories, with a *galerie* raised on pillars to keep it from the soggy ground. We've got good frontage on the bayou, which allowed us good access to the waterways. We have plenty of woods to hunt, and we harvested trees to help build this. We have fields for growin', and Grand-mere had the touch when it came to plantin'. We did all right." There was pride in his voice. "We built the house, my brothers and me, for Nonny."

"It's amazing, Wyatt. What a place to grow up in," Malichai said. He glanced at his brother. "We could have done some damage here."

"We'd have been able to eat once in a while," Ezekiel said, with another slow look around him. "You wouldn't need much more than this place."

"There's always plenty to eat here," Wyatt assured and stepped back, waving them forward. "Seriously, with four big boys to feed, Nonny was trappin' and huntin' and fishin' every day. She wanted us all in school to get an education. Then she had a heart attack and Raoul—Gator, we call him here in the bayou—he snuck away from school and helped out with supplyin' us with food. 'Course when the rest of us did it, Gator beat the crap out of us." Wyatt laughed at the memory.

"We know about beating the crap out of people," Malichai said, "That's usually how we got our food."

Ezekiel nodded. "We got real good at it."

"Grand-mere is in her eighties with a bad heart. Don' go makin' her cut down a switch to use on either of you," Wyatt warned, half teasing, but more serious. "Because she would if you don' mind your manners."

Ezekiel glanced uneasily toward the house. "Wyatt, we've never had a family. It's always been the three of us. Malichai, Mordichai, and me. We're not exactly civilized. Are you certain you want to bring us into your home?"

"I'm certain. Nonny will be happy for the company. There's no other place to just relax and rest. The moment she knows you both were wounded, expect to be spoiled. She cracks the whip when we need it, but she's always been the glue that holds our family together. You're going to love her."

Ezekiel took a long slow look around. "Mordichai would love it here. He's hanging with Joe, making sure he pulls through, then he plans to join us. This is his kind of place."

"Damn straight, it is," Malichai agreed.

"Wyatt. Boy, come on in and stop swappin' lies out there. There's been a couple of gators gettin' all frisky lately on the lawn. I wouldn' want you to run into them. And the Rougarou has been a visitin' folks up and down these parts lately. Wouldn't want you or your friends to be caught out in the open." Grand-mere's voice cut through the night. Clear. Crisp. Welcoming.

Wyatt smiled for the first time. Just the sound of her voice settled the knots in his gut. "You're smokin' that pipe again, Nonny. I thought the doc told you to stop."

What the hell is Rougarou? Malichai asked, using telepathic communication.

Local legend mainly used to scare the crap out of wayward boys to keep them out of the swamps and bayous at night, Wyatt answered with a quick grin. *Not that the tactic was particularly successful.*

"Doc's not even wet behin' the ears yet, Wyatt," his grandmother said. "I ben smokin' this pipe nigh onto seventy years now. I'm not about to quit now."

She was sitting in an old sturdy, hand-carved rocking chair on the verandah, pipe in one hand and a shotgun close to the other. Wyatt frowned when he saw the gun. He took the pier in several long strides, covered the circular drive and the lawn in a few leaps and landed on the porch in a crouch beside his grandmother.

She was very small and fragile looking, the shotgun nearly as big as she was, but her hands were rock steady.

She wore her silver white hair braided and looped in a bun at the back of her head. Her skin was thin and pale, but her eyes were clear and just as steady as her hands.

"What the hell's goin' on, Nonny? Did someone threaten' you?"

She took the pipe from her mouth. "Greet me properly, boy. I been a missin' you for a long while now."

"I'm sorry. You worried me holdin' that shotgun so close." He leaned in to kiss her on both cheeks. "You smell like home. Spicy pipe tobacco, gumbo and fresh-baked bread. I'm never home until I get close to you, Nonny."

Nonny blinked back pleased tears and turned her face away from him. "Since when did you learn to leap around like a jungle cat, Wyatt? They teach you such things in the service?"

Wyatt's heart jumped. He hadn't thought about using his enhancements in front of his grandmother. "I learned to run fast right here in the bayou tryin' to get away from that switch of yours." At least that wasn't a lie.

She gave a little sniff as she looked past Wyatt to the two men who followed him much more slowly. Her sharp eyes couldn't help but notice that the taller of the two was limping and the shorter one had dropped back behind him, almost as if he were a little reluctant to come here, but clearly he was really looking out for the other one, his gaze sweeping the bayou and surrounding buildings constantly.

She stepped up to the porch column, studying both men. "Are you hurt too, Wyatt? It seems the lot of you are all injured in some way."

"We took some fire," Wyatt admitted. "Helicopter went down and we were trapped behind enemy lines, but we made it out. Each of us took a hit or two, but we're good. We've come to help you out with your problem and maybe get a little rest and recoup."

"Just what does 'a hit or two' mean in terms of injuries,

Wyatt?" There was a note in his grandmother's voice warning him she wanted information.

Wyatt sighed. Sometimes there was no getting around his grandmother. She could be stubborn and tough when she wanted to be. "Malichai took a hit in the leg. It was pretty bad, but I was able to repair the damage right there. Ezekiel took both of us down, protecting us when someone lobbed a mortar in our direction. His back took the brunt of the fire. And I had a couple of smaller injuries, a ricochet when the helicopter first took fire and a stab wound just below my heart. Joe, our pilot got the worst of it, but Mordichai, Zeke and Malichai's brother, is with him, seein' to him."

Nonny closed her eyes for a moment and hugged the pillar tighter. She swallowed hard and then took a deep breath and nodded. "Thank the good Lord none of you were killed."

"It wasn' even close, Grand-mere," Wyatt lied, and kissed her cheek. "I want you to meet my good friends."

The two men made it to the stairs and halted. Neither took a step closer. There was no denying the way their eyes glowed like a cat's in the dark. His grandmother had been hunting all her life. She wouldn't fail to notice such a detail, but she simply smiled at them both.

"Any friend of Wyatt's is welcome here. I expect you're both hungry. There's always food on the stove. Simple, but nourishin'."

"Nonny, this is Ezekiel and Malichai Fortunes. My *grand-mere*, Grace Fontenot. Nonny." Wyatt introduced.

He couldn't keep the notes of love and of pride out of his voice. His grandmother had raised four big Cajun boys, pretty much on her own, and they'd been wild. In truth, he'd brought Ezekiel and Malichai home with him not only because they were his best friends, but because he felt both of them could use a good dose of his grandmother. They needed to know what home and family really was. The cat in them was always seeking to get the upper hand with its need to hunt.

"Thank you for having us, Mrs. Fontenot," Malichai said, his tone very formal.

"Call me Nonny. Everyone around here does," she said. "And Ezekiel, thank you for shieldin' my grandson when you were takin' such good care of your brother."

Ezekiel ducked his head, embarrassed.

"Yes, ma'am—Nonny," Malichai murmured, and came up the stairs as if there might be a hidden mine under each step. He held out his hand. "I'm Malichai. Ezekiel is my older brother."

Her faded eyes shifted to the man standing so utterly still at the bottom of the stairs. He was so still, he nearly faded into the night. "Good Christian names," she commented.

The two brothers exchanged a long look. "Not so much, ma'am," Malichai said. "There's very little Christian about us." He nodded his head toward the shotgun. "That's how we read people from the good book."

"There aren't any gators close, ma'am," Ezekiel said. "Are you worried about squirrels or some other varmint?"

Nonny smiled at him. "Human varmints, boy, that's what this old squirrel gun is for. Human varmints and the Rougarou."

"Hell of a squirrel gun, Nonny," Wyatt said, picking up the gun. It was clean and oiled and fully loaded. "It looks new to me."

"Gator gave it to me for my birthday. I told him not to remember such things, but once I saw how beautiful it was, I was fine with him givin' it to me." She waved them inside.

The moment Wyatt was in the house, he was glad he'd come home. There was something always welcoming and peaceful about Grand-mere's house. Shame shouldn't have kept him away for so long. There were pictures of his brothers and him, all young, along the stairway. They got older in the photographs toward the bottom of the stairs, but all had the same thick, wavy black hair and laughing eyes.

Wyatt swallowed hard, keeping his face forward and his expression clear. He didn't have those laughing eyes anymore and it was through his own stupidity. He was going to have to talk to Nonny—to confess what he'd done. Knowing her, she'd box his ears and tell him no woman was worth it—and he'd agree with her on that. He'd learned his lesson the hard way.

A hand-carved chest sat at the bottom of the stairs with a marriage quilt over it. Two more chests were lined up, both with marriage quilts over the top of them. The fourth—his brother Gator's—was gone now. He remembered how his brother's wife, Flame, had cried and clutched the marriage quilt to her that Nonny had made long ago. Each of the boys had one on top of their ornately carved chests. So, okay, his sister-in-law was the exception to the women-weren't-worth-it rule. They'd keep her in the family.

He knew Nonny longed for babies. She'd hoped Flame and Gator would provide them for her, but Flame couldn't have children. Nonny loved her dearly, but she prayed for a miracle and wasn't quiet about her praying. Often, she glared at Wyatt as if he needed to pull babies out of a hat for their family. He avoided the subject at all costs. He glanced back at Malichai and Ezekiel. He should have warned them what a force Nonny was and how she could get you promising things you never considered.

Both men were looking around the house with wide, almost shocked eyes. Wyatt looked too. He knew what they saw. When they were growing up, the Fontenots weren't the richest family in the bayou, not by a long shot, but there was love in the house. You couldn't walk indoors without feeling it.

The smell of fresh bread and gumbo permeated the house. He lifted his head and found himself smiling. She'd made his favorite dessert as well. That was Nonny, she did the little things that mattered.

"I called ahead, but you didn't tell me you felt so threatened you needed to sit outside your home with a shotgun," Wyatt said, heading toward the kitchen.

"Best not to mention things like that right off," Nonny replied with a shrug of her bony shoulders. "You might not have been able to come and then you woulda felt bad. There's no need of that."

Of course there wasn't. Grand-mere would never want one of her boys feeling bad for her or even feeling concern. She humbled him sometimes with her generous spirit.

The pot of gumbo was right there where it always was. He couldn't remember a time when he had come home and not found something simmering on the stove. He reached up into the cupboard to pull down the bowls.

"You're in for a treat, boys."

"You're not goin' to show them around the house first?" Nonny asked. There was laughter in her voice.

"Eatin' is on our minds, Grand-mere," Wyatt admitted.

"He's been talking so much about your cooking, ma'am," Malichai added, "that all we've been thinking about is food."

"That's good," Nonny said, and sank into her familiar chair at the kitchen table.

Wyatt couldn't help but think about all the times he'd sat at the table with his brothers as laughter and conversation had flowed. There was a part of him that wanted to go back to those carefree days when living on the bayou was enough—was everything.

When all three men had a bowl of gumbo, warm fresh bread and hot *café*, Wyatt glanced at his grandmother.

"Tell me what's going on around here that has you packin' a shotgun, Nonny."

She leaned back in her chair and looked at him with her faded blue eyes, eyes still as sharp as ever. "There's been a coupla strange things happenin', Wyatt. I know you don' believe in the Rougarou, and in truth, I never much believed either, but there's been things in the swamp there's no accountin' for."

She paused dramatically. Malichai and Ezekiel both paused as well, the spoons halfway to their mouths. Wyatt kept shoveling food in. He was used to his grandmother's storytelling abilities. She could hold an audience spellbound. She'd used it more than once to keep the boys from wolfing their food.

"Food disappearin', clothes stolen right off the line."

"Sounds like someone hungry, Nonny, a homeless person maybe."

At the word "hungry," both Malichai and Ezekiel resumed eating.

"Maybe," Nonny conceded. "But the food was taken from *inside* the houses. Sometimes the clothes as well. The houses were locked."

"No one locks houses on the bayou," Wyatt said.

"They do now with all the thievin' goin' on. I keep a pot of somethin' simmerin' on the stove at all times, Wyatt. You know that. Neighbors drop by. Sometimes Flame comes unexpectedly when Gator's out doin' whatever it is he does. I lock up, and I've got the dogs. Twice I let them in the house with me, but every third or fourth mornin' the food was gone out of that pot, even with the dogs inside."

"Someone entered the house while you were sleepin'?" Wyatt demanded, his temper beginning to do a slow boil.

Nonny nodded. "Yep. I couldn' even figger how they got in. When food disappeared here, I started puttin' a package out with little bits I thought might help. Food, clothes, even a blanket or two. Each time I put somethin' out, it was gone the next mornin', but three mornin's in a row after that, I had fresh fish on my table waitin'. Dogs didn't bark. The doors were locked. I couldn't tell how they got in, but it made me a mite uncomfortable knowin' the Rougarou was in my house."

"Why the Rougarou and not a person, ma'am?" Malichai asked.

"Delmar Thibodeaux seen it himself, with his own two eyes. It was movin' fast through the brush, so fast he could barely track it."

"Delmar Thibodeaux owns the Huracan Club, where liquor flows in abundance," Wyatt explained to the others.

"He swore he wasn't drinkin' when he saw it."

Wyatt sighed. "What else is goin' on around here, Nonny? That shotgun wasn't out for the Rougarou. You wouldn't kill it."

"I might," the old lady insisted. "If it threatened me."

Wyatt lifted his eyebrow at her. "Animals don' threaten you, Nonny. Everyone in the bayou knows that. Even the alligators leave you alone."

The boys were fairly certain they'd inherited their psychic abilities from their grandmother, although she never admitted to anything.

Nonny let out a resigned sigh. Clearly she wanted the shapeshifting legend to be true. "Do you remember that old hospital that burned down a couple of years back? There were whispers about that place, some madman owned it and held a girl prisoner there and she set the whole thing on fire to escape."

Wyatt nodded reluctantly. There were always rumors in the bayou—superstition melding with truth. The bayous and swamps were places where myth or legend often was rooted in reality. In this case, he knew the whispers were true.

Dr. Whitney, the previous owner of the hospital, was truly a madman. He had dedicated his life to creating a supersoldier. Those soldiers were known as GhostWalkers, because they owned the night. Few saw them, or heard them as they carried out their missions. Few knew that their DNA had been tampered with and they were all psychically as well as physically enhanced.

Now they were getting into classified things—things he couldn't discuss with his grandmother. He kept his head down while he ate.

"I remember it," he admitted.

"Some big shot bought up the land right away and cleaned it all up. They built a long, ugly building with few windows and walls at least a foot thick, all concrete. Not a single man or woman on the river was employed."

There was no denying the little sneer in her voice. It was considered an insult for a large company to come into the bayou and not hire the locals who needed work. Most of the families living on the river would have taken it the same way. The "big shot" hadn't made any friends with his decision to give work to outsiders, but he hadn't broken any laws either.

"Who owns the land now, Nonny?" he asked.

Whitney Trust had owned it, and Lily, Whitney's daughter, had sold it the moment she realized her father had used the facilities to experiment on a child. Wyatt didn't look at either of the Fortunes brothers. Like him, they were fairly new in the GhostWalker force, but he had information they didn't on the founder and creator of the program.

"They have a big sign up on their fourteen-foot-high chain-link fence with razor wire rolled up along on the top and men with guns patrolling with dogs," Nonny said in disgust. "Like they're afraid everyone in the bayou wants to know their business."

Wyatt couldn't stop the grin. "Nonny, everyone in the bayou *does* want to know their business."

She threw back her head and laughed, the sound adding to the feeling of home.

"Ma'am," Malichai interrupted. "Do you mind if I have another bowl of this very good gumbo? I've never tasted anything like it."

"It's authentic gumbo, a traditional recipe that's been in my family for generations," Nonny said, looking pleased.

"Dive right in, that's what it's there for. We always have somethin' cookin' on the stove for you when you come in hungry."

"I'm always hungry," Malichai admitted.

"You're a big man and it takes a might of food to keep you satisfied," she said.

"If you don't mind me saying, ma'am," Ezekiel said, "he's got some kind of hollow leg that's plain impossible to fill. I ought to know, I tried for years."

"He broke into a grocery store once," Malichai said, "you know, back when we were kids," he added hastily when Wyatt shot him a look. "The kind that has the hot chicken roasting and already-cooked food. Our brother Mordichai and I feasted all night and we were still hungry in the morning. Ezekiel said it was impossible to keep up with our stomachs."

"He's like a starved wolf, ma'am," Ezekiel said. "Never gains an ounce of fat, but he gorges on food when we've got it. Our other brother is the same way."

Nonny's eyebrows drew together in a frown. "You boys had no one lookin' after you when you were young? Not anyone?"

Malichai shrugged. "We did a pretty good job of it, ma'am. We had each other's backs. We grew up in a city, and we knew every building and alley there was." He scooped a hefty amount of gumbo into his bowl and caught up a generous amount of bread before taking his seat.

"The older we got, the easier it was," Ezekiel added. "We got a reputation for fighting and the others left us alone."

Nonny shook her head. "You boys. You'll fit right in with my boys. They do like to fight." She sat back in her chair with a feigned little slump. "I should put in a call to Delmar and warn him you might be visitin' his place and not to let the three of you in."

"The Delmar that saw the Rougarou," Malichai clarified.

"That's the one," Wyatt said. "His place, the Huracan

Club, is the best place on the bayou to go for drinks, women and fights. Well, for drinks and fights. Or just plain fights," Wyatt said to the Fortunes brothers. He laughed and raised his eyebrow at his grandmother. "That would just be mean, Nonny. We're all grown up now and we don' get into trouble like we used to."

She gave a little unladylike snort. "I'm expectin' lightnin' to strike you any minute now, boy."

"Why the shotgun, Nonny?" Wyatt persisted quietly, slipping the question back in casually. He slathered butter on the bread and took a bite. Pure heaven. Evidently Ezekiel and Malichai felt the same. They were making short work of the three loaves his *grand-mere* had baked.

"That fence is right along that swamp area where my plants I need for medicinal purposes grow. I was there harvestin' the other day and some kind of ruckus broke out in that buildin', with alarms shriekin' and voices on loudspeakers. Dogs were goin' crazy, and the guards got all panicked. Now that's none of my business. My plants was my business, Wyatt."

Wyatt put down his spoon and sat back, giving her his full attention.

"All of a sudden, these men surround me, trampin' through my plants and swearin' like they was gunna kill me. I had to raise my hands, and one of them put his hands on me, so I kicked him where it counts."

Wyatt felt the familiar surge of heat rushing through his body, threatening to boil over. He had a temper, he knew that, but his enhancement had made it worse, much more difficult to control, and the thought of a man putting his hands on his grandmother made his blood swirl hotly. Beneath the table his fists clenched and under his feet, the floor shivered.

Both Ezekiel and Malichai put down their spoons as well, heads up alertly, suddenly listening just as closely to what Nonny had to say.

"Explain puttin' his hands on you, Grand-mere," Eze-kiel said, his voice deadly quiet.

"Now don' go gettin' all riled, boys. I can handle myself, I'm not that old yet. He was pattin' me down for weapons. Took my best knife too. Still has that knife, and I want it back. They told me they knew where I lived and called me by name. Ms. Fontenot, they said. The big one said he'd be comin' by my house and settin' his dog on me if I didn' keep my nose out their business and keep my mouth shut 'bout what I seen and heard."

"What did you see and hear?"

"That's the thing, Wyatt." Nonny sounded annoyed. "I was workin' and had my contraption in my ear, the one you got me for Christmas with all the music. I wasn' lis-tenin' or lookin' until those sirens went off." Clearly she was deeply disappointed she hadn't seen whatever it was they didn't want her to see. "I got me the idea that they're making dirty bombs."

Wyatt worked hard to keep the smile from his face. He found the idea that his petite grandmother even knew what a dirty bomb was both unsettling and a little funny. She glared at him, so he didn't make the mistake of actually grinning.

"Dirty bomb?" he echoed. "Where did you come up with that?"

"I listen to the news," she replied with great dignity. "I know what goes on in the world, and those men are up to no good." She leaned close. "When they go to the Huracan Club, they don' talk to nobody. Not even Delmar. They jist keep to themselves and glower at everyone. Even when the boys push them a bit, they don' want to fight and that's jist not natural. Delmar says they don' drink anythin' but beer and never more than two apiece."

"Maybe the bayou doesn' give them a powerful thirst like it does the rest of us. Are they city boys?" Wyatt asked.

"They don' look like city boys, Wyatt, except for a cou-ple of the suits that come and go on occasion."

"So you do keep an eye on the place," he said, using his mildest tone.

His tone didn't matter. She gave him a look that had withered him as a boy and still left the pit of his stomach unsettled.

"Everyone keeps an eye on them. I'm tellin' you, somethin's not right there."

"Well, you know, Grand-mere, I think it best you stop your harvestin' until I check it out. Which man put his hands on you? Do you have a description for me?"

"I can do better than that, Wyatt. I took his picture with that newfangled camera Flame got me. She calls it a cell and it rings now and then, but I don' know how to answer it so I just take pictures with it."

Wyatt shook his head. "You don' answer your phone, Nonny?"

"Who wants to be talkin' when they should be workin'?"

"She's got a point," Malichai said. "Can we see this picture?" He glanced at Wyatt. Clearly he couldn't imagine a man patting down Nonny and then intimidating her by threatening to come to her home. "I'm glad you have that shotgun, ma'am."

"I may have to use it if you keep callin' me ma'am," Nonny said. "My boys call me Grand-mere or Nonny. You're here in my home and I'm claimin' you as my own."

"Yes, ma'am," Ezekiel said. "Thank you. We've never been claimed before."

Wyatt snorted derisively. "Don' be so happy about it. That means she'll take a switch to you if you give her any trouble," Wyatt said.

"He sounds like he got the switch a lot, Nonny," Malichai said.

"He *should* have gotten the switch," Nonny said, "but he and his brothers were far too charmin'." She sounded proud—and loving.

Wyatt could hear the love in her voice. He almost

couldn't remember the reason he'd been so reluctant to return to the bayou. He loved it there, everything about it, especially his grandmother. After hearing about the men guarding the new plant, he was more than happy he'd come back home. Still, what man wanted to come home and admit to the woman he respected and admired most, just what a blind ass he'd been?

"Did you go back there, Nonny?" he asked suspiciously.

"I'm fixin' to. They trampled my plants, and I've spent years puttin' them all in that one spot in the swamp so I could gather them easier. I'm too old to be gallivantin' around the swamp lookin' for the right plants to make medicine when the *traiteur* calls for it."

"*Traiteur*?" Malichai asked.

"Our local healer," Wyatt supplied.

"I'll go look after your plants for you, ma'am," Ezekiel said. At her swift look he cleared his throat. "Grand-mere, I mean. I'll be more than happy to read anyone from the good book who comes looking to step on those plants again."

"You're a fine boy, Ezekiel. You may not have had much parentin' but you probably are one of those boys who just figgurs it out on your own," Nonny said.

Wyatt sent Ezekiel a sharp glance. All three of them were enhanced physically and psychically. Unfortunately, their cat DNA gave them a need for hunting. Wyatt felt sometimes as if his mind was always at war. The healer side of him versus the killer instinct that the cat had. Ezekiel already had been an aggressive, dominant male. He didn't fight for fun in the way Wyatt and his brothers did—Malichai, Mordichai and Ezekiel had fought from birth to stay alive. The new mixture of DNA into their already explosive make-up could be hazardous under the wrong circumstances.

You can't kill in my grand-mere's *backyard.* He used telepathic communication.

Ezekiel didn't look up from mopping up the gumbo with the bread.

What did you plan on doing, Wyatt? Malichai asked. *Shaking hands with them and thanking them politely for patting down your* grand-mere?

Your sarcasm is not appreciated. I plan on a little recon before I go to bed. I want to check out this building and who owns it. I can get word back to Mordichai and see if he can dig anything up on them for us while he's lookin' after Joe.

Wyatt hadn't been too surprised when his ability to speak telepathically with his team had been so easy—he'd always heard others in his head—catching random thoughts now and then—which was how he caught the love of his life cheating on him. At least at the time he'd thought she was the love of his life, now, after much soul searching, he realized he was just a damned fool with a white knight complex.

Beneath his hands the table trembled slightly, just enough for both Malichai and Ezekiel to frown at him.

What's wrong? We'll get these bastards, Ezekiel said. *No one's going to hurt your grandmother, not with us here.*

What could he say? That he couldn't bear thinking about what an idiot he'd been because he'd thought some woman ripped out his heart, stomped on it and then told him what she really thought of him—none of it good. He thought he loved her from the time he was five years old, when he'd first laid eyes on her at a neighborhood *fais do-do.* He'd devoted himself to her, although they didn't date in school. She appeared too fragile and always turned to him when she broke up with her latest boyfriend.

He hadn't ever let himself believe, not for one minute, in spite of Nonny warning him a time or two, that Joy Chassion was playing him, using him until someone came along who could get her out of the bayou. He hadn't wanted to know—to believe—to even consider for one moment that his judgment could be that bad.

He'd never had that kind of hurt before and he sure as hell never wanted to experience it again. He'd sworn off women. They were unreliable and untrustworthy. He'd be damned if he ever went down that road again. And worse, he couldn't trust his own judgment. Joy hadn't been worth it, and the sad truth was, he'd never really been in love with her, only with his own fantasy. He'd made a damn fool of himself and he'd have to live with the consequences for the rest of his life—and so would his family. Nonny was going to have to look elsewhere for babies.

The funny thing was, he must have known all along that Joy couldn't be trusted. She wanted money and a different life. He had the ability to give her both, but he never told her. Never wanted her to know. She had to love him for who he was, not what he could do for her.

Wyatt shook his head. "Grand-mere, I've been braggin' to Malichai and Ezekiel that there's nothin' quite like our *café* and beignets. They've never had them before."

Nonny looked both shocked and horrified. "Never?"

She got up immediately and went to the warmer, where she removed a large platter of beignets. She placed it squarely between the two men and marched back to get the hot black coffee for them.

Wyatt waited until she was seated again and his two friends were covered in powdered sugar. He leaned toward his grandmother, holding out his hand to her. "Your phone, Nonny. I want to see what these men look like."

She pulled the small cell phone from the pocket of her sweater. "I took several. Those are the men who trampled my plants. The one with the dog tried to scare me, but I whispered to it and it stopped showin' me its teeth. He wasn' too happy and I was afraid I mighta gotten the dog in trouble."

Malichai and Ezekiel both put down their beignets to

study the series of photographs on her phone. Most were quite clear in spite of the fact that she was taking them on the sly.

"Which one put his hands on you?" Ezekiel asked.

"You sound jist like my boys. No sense in gettin' everyone riled up. My dress and jeans came out clean and I woulda had to wash them anyway."

Wyatt stiffened. "What does that mean? You fell?" he demanded. "Did you fall down? Did they *push* you?"

"I said they put their hands on me and I kicked one where it counts," she reiterated. "He didn't like it much, 'specially when his friends all laughed at him."

This time the table actually shook. It was no slight tremor. Wyatt got up and paced across the floor trying to rid himself of restless energy—energy that could easily get out of hand with his kind of temper.

"He *shoved* you into the swamp?" He managed to get each word out between his teeth. He glared at Malichai, who had begun eating the beignets again. "He *shoved* her and you're eating?"

Malichai's eyebrow shot up. "Fuel, my man. One of us has to be efficient when the two of you are hotheads. Nonny, out of curiosity, were you aware you raised a hothead?"

She nodded thoughtfully. "I did, Malichai. I did. I thought he might grow out of it, but like his brothers, he's got that Cajun temper and it just grew up right along with all of them."

"You should have told me *immediately* that these men pushed you down, Nonny," Wyatt said. "It's no laughin' matter. I thought maybe they got a little overzealous tryin' to guard their plant when somethin' went wrong, and that was bad enough but . . ."

He raked both hands through his hair and his eyes glittered like a hungry cat hunting prey. "Shovin' you? Pattin' you down? Threatnin' you? No, that's intolerable. I think I need to have a little friendly chat with these men."

Ezekiel rose and pushed back his chair, reaching for the plates. "Thank you for such a fine meal. I'll just do up the dishes, Grand-mere, and then we'll go see about reading from the good book along with Wyatt."

Malichai shoved both chairs back into the table and helped gather the bowls. "Magnificent meal, Nonny. I'm actually full . . . for the time being."

"Leave the dishes, boys," Nonny said. "I'll get them done. You boys don' be out too late, and Malichai, there'll be somethin' hot on the stove when you come back in."

CHAPTER 2

"We're goin' to take the pirogue so we can go in quiet," Wyatt announced as he stepped off the porch. "Neither of you has to come with me. I'm goin' in soft, just a recon to see what I'm up against."

"Like hell we're going to let you go alone," Malichai said. "I ate a lot. I need a little exercise before going to sleep." *And I don't believe for one minute you're going in soft. I'll just tag along and make certain you behave yourself.*

Wyatt sent him an innocent look.

Ezekiel nudged his brother. "You just want to walk off the dinner so you can eat more. I swear, Malichai, you should weigh five hundred pounds."

"I got all the good genes," Malichai said, and stepped onto the pirogue. "What the hell is this contraption? Are you certain it's safe?"

He peered into the black water. Hanging like great ropes, vines of moss dangled from the cypress trees, sweeping the water with thin, feathery arms, creating a macabre effect. The humidity was extremely high, so that everything in the night seemed to move slow and easy, and even the air seemed to enter lungs slow and lazy.

Ezekiel studied the small, flat-bottomed wooden craft that appeared to be made from a tree trunk. The last thing he wanted to do was to find himself in the dark water with snapping turtles, snakes and alligators.

Wyatt leaned on a long pole. "The water's shallow. If you can't stay balanced, no worries. You'll only go up to your thighs. Or waist. Unless we hit a pocket where the bottom falls out."

Ezekiel shot him a glare. "I'm armed, you cretin."

Wyatt laughed. "If you prefer, you can hang out here and Grand-mere will keep you safe with that shotgun of hers."

Ezekiel stepped carefully onto the pirogue. "That's one hell of a woman. Do they even make them like that anymore?"

Wyatt pushed off carefully using the long pole. Malichai picked up the other one to help. He watched Wyatt and then mimicked his movements.

"I think my brother Gator got the last one," he admitted. "She carries a big-ass knife and isn't afraid to use it. The first time I ever saw her, she broke into our home, crept up on Gator and stuck a knife to his throat. He stole her motorcycle, and she took my Jeep. It was a really interestin' relationship."

"My kind of woman," Ezekiel said.

"She's one of us," Wyatt added. "A GhostWalker."

"I figured she'd have to be if she managed to get the drop on your brother," Malichai said. "He's got a badass reputation."

He took a careful look around him. It was dark and eerie in the bayous. The network of canals was hidden from one another by tall reeds and strips of land with weeping cypress trees.

"A man could get lost around here," he observed. "I've never had trouble in jungles or desert, but this is something altogether different."

"I grew up here, Malichai," Wyatt assured him. "This was my play yard. We hunted and fished here. We had crab and crawfish traps we attended to daily before we ever went to school. We used a rowboat to take us to the French Quarter where we caught the buses to school."

"What did you hunt?" Ezekiel asked.

"Anything we could eat. We couldn't afford ammo, so every single bullet had to count. We didn't miss."

"Did Grand-mere teach you to shoot?" Malichai asked.

Wyatt nodded. "With guns, knives and a bow and arrow. We all had chores. Once a year we collected the moss from the cypress trees and laid it all out to dry. It was a big job. There were five of us and we used the moss to stuff our mattresses. We needed a lot of it. That's what we slept on."

"I noticed a lot of the furniture was thick and sturdy and carved out of wood," Malichai said. "Whoever did the furniture making was good."

Wyatt smiled at him. "We got good. After a few chairs collapsed and we broke the sofa once, we learned if we wanted a chair to sit in, or a table to eat at, we'd better do a good job. We offered to buy Nonny all new furniture after we were grown and a little more successful, but she loves the things we made. She's very sentimental."

"I wouldn't give it up either," Ezekiel said. "I thought the table and chairs were unique and quite comfortable. Did you carve those chests in the hall by the stairs?"

"Each of us carved one. They're marriage chests. Nonny wanted us to have them for our brides. Gator took his, and Flame was particularly happy about it. She didn't have a family and I think the chest and things inside it made her feel connected, really part of our family—which she is."

"Did Grand-mere make those quilts?" Malichai asked.

Wyatt glanced at him and then away. There was a note of longing in Malichai's voice, one Wyatt was certain he wouldn't want anyone to notice. Growing up poor in the bayou had been a struggle, but they hadn't realized they were poor. Nonny made them feel lucky and very loved. He knew his brothers felt the same as he did about their home.

"Yours was a good childhood," Ezekiel commented.

"Yeah," Wyatt agreed. "The best. We worked hard but we played just as hard." He held up his hand for silence and indicated for Malichai to put his pole down.

Sound travels on these waters like you wouldn't believe. No noise. Ezekiel, can you do your thing with the insects? If they go silent, the guards are goin' to know. We want the alligators to bellow and the frogs to croak.

Ezekiel, even as a boy, could manipulate the insects, calling them to him, sending them away. None of the team knew how he did it, but the ability was an asset unlike any other. He could move without detection through any type of terrain and protect his entire team while doing it. Since his enhancement, Ezekiel's ability had grown into a powerful instrument. He could flood the entire compound with swarms of insects, snakes and frogs should he want to do such a thing.

No problem. Give me a minute to connect. Ezekiel was all business. Once on the hunt, he wasn't a man who joked around like some of the other members on the team— Wyatt included.

We're close then? Malichai asked.

We've got a little tramp through the swamp. It's dangerous. There're a few spongy places in this direction.

Wyatt used the pole carefully, each movement slow and easy, so that even the pole moving through the water made no splash as he used it to push off the bottom and propel them forward through the shallow water toward the shore. The pirogue easily ran onto the ground and all three stepped off.

Gator slide right at your feet, Malichai. Move to your left. You don' want to meet that big boy tonight. He's been around for a long while and he's a wily one. He's eaten more than one huntin' dog for dinner.

That's why you have all those dogs at your place. You use them for hunting, Malichai said.

We also like Nonny to have them around when all of us are gone.

Malichai slid his knife from his boot and stepped away from the muddy slide where clearly a large alligator moved from land to water on a regular basis. The moment they stepped onto land, all three changed subtly, lifting their faces to the air for information.

The five o'clock shadow on their faces along with the small hair on their bodies acted like sonar, a radar to give them precise information on their surroundings. They could tell if a small space was enough to slide their bodies through or if the branches of a tree could support their weight. They knew the location of every animal close to them. They each had allowed their hair to grow longer, believing it aided them in gathering more information as well as keeping them in tune to their surroundings and danger.

Can we use the trees? Malichai asked.

Once we're closer to the compound. We can move fairly quickly through here. There're only a few spots that are dangerous. Watch for snakes.

I'll keep the snakes away, Ezekiel assured.

Wyatt led the way. On land, they made no noise, slipping through the thick brush and reeds easily, their bodies fluid, the roped muscles and flexible spines giving them an advantage as they made their way toward the part of the swamp Nonny had spent years transplanting her medicinal herbs and plants in.

We're right at the edge of Grand-mere's field. The local traiteur has used Nonny's concoctions for years. Wyatt didn't bother to try to keep the pride from his voice.

He remembered as a little boy, coming to this part of the swamp with his grandmother. She carried plants, carefully wrapped to transplant. One by one. She found them in other places throughout the vast swamp land, dug them up in the heat and humidity with mosquitos biting her and tramped through dangerous swamp to transfer them to this section.

Why? Ezekiel asked, surveying the acre of plants.

She told me that we all get old and havin' them in one spot where we could watch over them and take care of them would ensure our families would always have medicine if they couldn't afford modern medicine. Remember she's in her eighties. She was the local pharmacist for years. When the traiteur *needed a medicine, she would experiment with plants and herbs until she found the best one that worked. That's what all this is. It's the bayou's pharmacy.*

Grand-mere is quite a woman, Malichai reiterated.

Wyatt felt pride in his grandmother and was pleased at the admiration of his friend for her. Nonny wore old clothes and smoked a pipe. She was very traditional in a lot of ways and some people just didn't take to her. He was glad his friends didn't view her at face value.

Malichai and Ezekiel were two of the toughest men Wyatt knew—and he knew plenty of hard-asses. As a rule the brothers kept to themselves. It had taken hundreds of missions before the two had included Wyatt in their small circle of absolute trusted friends.

He had hoped his grandmother would work her spell on them both, but on Ezekiel in particular. His nature, shaped on the streets of Detroit, was already savage. Adding cat DNA made him far more aggressive and dangerous. Grand-mere was a stabilizing influence no matter what. He couldn't imagine anyone resisting her down-home wisdom and the sheer welcome she gave to complete strangers. It helped that already, he could tell, she had their respect.

Dogs, Ezekiel warned. *Up ahead and to the left of us.*

That would be the corner of Nonny's pharmaceutical field. They spread out, each moving independently of the other, heading for the thick growth of trees outside the tall chain-link fence.

Nonny was right. The fence was overkill for whatever they were keeping hidden from the world. Wyatt caught sight of the sign. *Wilson Plastics.* Now that was a load of crap, but they'd claim they were researching and needed the security to keep out rival companies. He'd have to send Joe the name of the company and find out who owned it and what they actually did.

Rolls of razor wire had been strung all along the top of the fence. The three-story building was a good forty feet from the fence with no ground cover.

Are they keepin' us out, or somethin' in? Wyatt asked the others.

Good question, Malichai replied. *I'd say there's a good chance it's both.*

Maybe they really are making dirty bombs in there, just like Nonny said, Ezekiel added. *We've got a guard and dog approaching at six o'clock, Wyatt, and I think he's the one that shoved Grand-mere.*

Wyatt studied the big man. He moved easily, fluidly. Too easily. The large semiautomatic cradled in his arms looked a part of him.

Something's not right here, Ezekiel said. *That's no private security. He knows his way around a gun. And that dog is skilled. He's not for show.*

Maybe, but more likely ex-military private security. He just doesn't feel enhanced to me. Good, but not Whitney kind of soldier, Wyatt said.

The dog looked out toward the trees where the three of them were concealed, alerting for just a moment before Ezekiel could calm him.

Dog smells big cats and doesn't like it. He's difficult to control. If I push too hard I could hurt him, Ezekiel warned. *You're better with mammals, Wyatt. You try. I'll save my energy for reptiles.*

The handler was skilled as well. He didn't dismiss the dog's seeming confusion. He stopped immediately and shone his light all along the ground leading to the fence on the inside, not the outside. That told Wyatt there was something inside they didn't want out.

*You need the practice, Ezekiel, and the dog's listenin'
to you.* Wyatt wanted to save every bit of energy for dealing with the man who'd shoved his grandmother. He knew
he wasn't 100 percent healed, but he wasn't going to wait
to give the man a beating.

The guard checked the fence itself next. He stepped up
to it with his light and carefully examined all along the
chain link, even up to the razor wire. He was thorough in
his inspection, taking his time, another mark of a professional. When he was finished, he crouched beside the dog,
scratching its ears and talking low while he examined the
ground on the other side of the fence.

What the hell is he lookin' for? Wyatt asked.

Not us, Malichai said. *It hasn't even occurred to him yet
that he might have someone out here watchin' him.*

The guard spoke into his radio softly. Wyatt's hearing
had always been extremely acute and was even more so
from both his psychic and physical enhancements. With
the feline DNA, he found he could hear higher pitches far
better than he'd ever been able to before.

Did you make out what he said, Wyatt? Malichai asked.

*He asked someone inside to check the cells. Cells, not
rooms. And I don' think he's enhanced. He's been a soldier at one time, but he's not a GhostWalker.*

Wyatt's warning radar was beginning to give him a few
prickles. He took a long slow look around, careful not to
rustle a single leaf in the tree.

*I don' think we're alone out here, boys. You feelin'
anythin'?*

There was a long silence while both brothers stretched
their senses to encompass as much of their surroundings as
possible.

I don't see or hear anything at all, Ezekiel said, *but the
dog is getting harder to control. I think we're going to
have to get out of here for tonight and rethink our plan of
reading to that man from the good book.*

That wasn't happening. *You go on ahead and I'll meet you at the pirogue.*

Wyatt stared hard at the man who had shoved his grandmother into the swamp. He'd patted her down and pushed her. She could easily have broken a hip, and the guard had known it but hadn't cared.

The guard brought the dog twice up to one of the gates and stood waiting, as if he'd receive a signal to let the animal loose. The dog barked, baring its teeth, looking out behind Malichai.

He's feeling something I can't, Ezekiel said.

Fall back, Wyatt told them. *He's goin' to come out and investigate.*

Not alone, he's not, Malichai said.

As the guard opened the gate, two other guards ran up to join him. Neither of the others had a dog, but they were heavily armed. They came outside the fence and immediately spread out, keeping about five feet apart as they moved toward the grove of trees where Wyatt and the Fortunes brothers had taken up residence.

That dog has the scent of something, Ezekiel said. *And it isn't us.*

Wyatt inhaled deeply, taking in the odors of the night. Jasmine hung heavy in the air, mixing with the smell of the swamp, the moss hanging in ropes from the cypress groves and the mix of wild flowers. The pharmaceutical field had its own perfume from hundreds of varieties of herbs and flowering plants, some poisonous, some not, but all with their individual scents.

He caught the odor of the alligator. A bobcat lurked close. Somewhere a little farther off was a small herd of deer. Raccoons caught fish near the riverbank and a family of opossum trailed through the vegetation seeking dinner. Nutrias, originally from South America, traveled in a small group as well, wandering around destroying the plants as they devoured the stems and roots.

The wind shifted just a fraction and he caught the same scent the dog had. Elusive. Beckoning. Mysterious. Impossible to identify, but there. It made every hair on his body stand up. His heart beat faster and blood ran hot through his veins. He felt an itch between his shoulder blades as if someone had a scope and a rifle with their centers on him.

The dog burst from the gate and, slipping its collar, sprang away from his handler, rushing across the clearing and low-level plants straight into the cypress grove. He made no noise at all, but he moved fast with purpose. His handler raced after him, calling his name, clearly alarmed at the dog being off the leash. What was out there that might harm his dog? The other two men moved much more cautiously, exchanging a quick signal with one another before they followed into the grove, maintaining a five-foot spread from one another.

Wyatt ran lightly along a heavy branch that nearly touched another tree next to the one he was in. He leapt for the tree, landing lightly and quickly moving to the next. He used the branches as a highway above the swamp, following the three guards. He knew their exact positions but he couldn't always see them through the thick vines and foliage.

Someone shouted—the dog handler, he was certain. The guard fired his gun in short bursts. The dog yelped. In the distance, through the tree branches, Wyatt caught a glimpse of something moving fast—too fast for anything human. It was small, no more than a foot or so tall. It ran, zigzagging as the guard fired at it.

Movement drew Wyatt's gaze back to the guard as something hit the dog handler hard in the back, knocking him forward and down. For a moment, Wyatt thought he might actually be catching his first glimpse of the Rougarou—shapeshifter of the bayous and swamps—but this was no tall creature with a wolf's head. It was small in comparison to the guard, but not tiny like the first creature. He was fairly certain whoever had struck the guard was human.

He moved carefully, knowing he would draw fire from

the other guards if they spotted him in the trees. By the time he was able to see again, whoever it was had smashed the guard's gun into pieces against the trunk of a tree. The dog hurled itself on the smaller figure, driving it to the ground. Animal and human rolled for a moment and then, to his astonishment, the dog went flying backward with such force that when it landed, the blow was strong enough to knock the wind from the animal.

Whatever it was that had attacked the guard ran in the direction of the much smaller creature, just as fast, with blurring speed, leaping over fallen logs and yet never once running into an obstacle in spite of the speed.

The other two guards laid down fire, spraying the swamp with bullets, but none appeared to strike their target. The two small creatures, one no more than a foot and a half tall and the other maybe hitting five feet or an inch or two above, ran through the dense vegetation without hesitation or a hitch in their strides.

None of the guards gave chase, and that was significant as well. The guards, as armed and as well trained as they were, didn't want to follow the two figures into the swamp at night. They were afraid.

One of the guards reached down to help the dog handler from the ground. He immediately rushed over to kneel by the dog.

"Is he alive, Larry?"

"Yeah." The dog handler sounded grim. "She didn't kill him, but his rib might be cracked. We were lucky."

"You shouldn't have let him loose, Larry."

"Go to hell, Blake, he slipped his leash." The dog handler gathered the animal into his arms and lifted him gently.

Wyatt liked him better for that. Still, the man was due a good beating, and he wasn't getting out of that.

"Gentlemen, put down your guns," he advised softly. "I'm only goin' to tell you once. If you don' comply, I'll shoot you in the leg. If you still don' comply, it will be the other leg. We'll just keep goin' until you run out of blood or I run out of bullets."

"Don't you worry, my friend," Malichai said, his voice coming out of the night low and purring. "I've got enough ammo to keep on shooting long after you're out."

"And then I'll start," Ezekiel added.

Surrounded, the guards put their weapons on the ground, stepped back away from them and linked their fingers behind their heads.

"You're making a mistake," the one named Blake said.

"No, I think you're the ones who made the mistake." Wyatt leapt from the tree, landing in a crouch on the balls of his feet, right beside Blake's gun. He tossed it up into the tree where Ezekiel was concealed and then threw the second one to him as well.

"Put the dog down. I don' want to hurt an animal, so if he's protective of you, leash him and hand the leash to one of your friends. They can just make themselves comfortable while you and I settle our score." Wyatt pinned the other two with a serious gaze. "Don' make the mistake of thinkin' you can go for your holdout guns or your other weapons. I know you have 'em and I just plain don' give a damn. That's how angry you've made me. So know my two friends will shoot you down the moment you make one wrong move."

Larry set the dog near the third guard, clearly not trusting Blake. He snapped the leash back on him and handed the end to his friend. "Don't let him loose, Jim," he cautioned, and then turned slowly. "Who the hell are you and why do you have such a hard-on for me?"

"You know that sweet old lady you thought you'd shove into the swamp? The one you threatened? The one you told you'd come by her home and take care of her?" Deliberately, and making a show of it, Wyatt placed his gun a distance from them and walked within feet of Larry. "That's my *grand-mere*, and I don' take to anyone threatenin' her or puttin' hands on her."

"It wasn't personal," Larry said with a small shrug. "I was doing my job. We don't want anyone coming around, not only for our protection but theirs as well."

"It's very personal to me," Wyatt said. "So let's get to this."

"You swamp rats are all alike. We go to that shack you call a club and everyone wants to fight us to prove what men you are," Larry accused, shaking his head.

The other two guards laughed. "This ought to be fun."

"No, we're not alike," Wyatt said quietly. "That's where you're wrong. The boys at the Huracan are out for fun and they were invitin' you to join in. No animosity and nothin' to prove, just a good Saturday night *bataille*. Me, I'm dead serious about teachin' you some manners, there's no funnin' in my mind at all. Swamp rats know how to treat women, and apparently you need to learn that lesson."

"You're going to be one sorry rat," Larry said, and circled Wyatt, his hands coming up in the classic boxer's stance. "I'm so sick of all of you, thinking you're so tough just because you grew up around alligators. I'll bet that's what they call you around these parts—*Gator*." He said the name in a sneering taunt.

"No, that would be my brother, and you should be damn glad he's not here. He wouldn' be quite so gentle as I'm goin' to be." Wyatt nodded at the man's boot. "If you think you're goin' to make your try for that holdout gun, all bets are off."

Larry scowled at him. "I won't need a gun for this." He stepped in close and fired off three rapid punches at Wyatt's face.

Wyatt blocked all three, and delivered a hard right to the man's belly, punching deep, driving the air from his lungs and letting him know it was a punishment, not a dance. The breath exploded out of Larry and he stumbled back, doubling over. Wyatt slammed an elbow on his back, driving him straight to the ground. He stepped back.

"The thing you should know comin' into a neighborhood, Larry," he said, his voice gentle, as if he was a mother instructing a child, "you treat the people decent. That's all, just decent. And you don' ever put your hands on old ladies or any woman for that matter. It just isn' done."

Larry got to his feet slowly, this time looking at Wyatt warily. His two friends stopped laughing, watching as he staggered a little. All traces of amusement and contempt were gone from Larry's face.

Wyatt let him get his feet under him and set himself back in his warrior's stance. He exploded into action, gliding in, hitting Larry hard with two straight rights to the left eye, both shockingly hard, knocking Larry's head back rapidly. The third punch was a left roundhouse to the jaw. Larry's body shuddered. His legs turned to rubber and he went down. Wyatt stepped back a second time. He wasn't even breathing hard and he hadn't broken a sweat.

"You might want to drop by Grand-mere's house and apologize. She's hell on wheels with a gun, but if you come by all sorry, with your tail tucked between your legs, she'll feed you and forgive you, because that's what we do here." The soft voice changed. "Get up. We're not nearly finished."

Larry rolled over and stared up at the night sky. "You hit like a damn jackhammer." His left eye was already swollen shut. "I've never been punched that hard in my life. I didn't know anyone could hit that hard."

"Swamp rats learn how to punch on the way outa their mama's womb. Stand up. And for the record, I'm takin' it easy on you."

Larry held up his hand. "I'm done, man. I get it. I'll apologize. The place was crazy that day and she was just in the way."

Wyatt reached down and yanked him off the ground with one hand as he struck three more times in the mouth with the other. He dragged Larry close to him, looking eye to eye. "This is our land. You don' own anythin' beyond that fence. Those acres of plants belong to the people of the bayou. We use them for medicine. You don' come onto our land and dictate to us when we can harvest them. She wasn' in *your* way. You were in *her* way."

Wyatt released Larry's shirt and the man dropped again to ground. The earth beneath them shivered. It was a small tremor, but it was there, indicating Wyatt's temper was rising, not diminishing.

"Wyatt, don't get all crazy on us," Malichai warned. "You don't want to bring their house down."

"I want Nonny's knife. That knife is important to her, you thief."

Larry rolled over, glaring with his one good eye. Blood bubbled around his split lip and inside his mouth. "You want her knife?" He yanked the knife from his boot and stood up, staggering a little. "Come and get it."

"Oh, now that's just downright stupid," Wyatt said softly. "Real stupid. How do you think we killed the food we ate? Do you really think we had the money for bullets? I cut my teeth on knives, killin' game, fightin' with my friends and protectin' our property. You really don' learn, do you? That's called bein' too stupid to live. You don' choose a man's weapon and then expect to live through the fight."

Wyatt circled Larry, watching his eyes. He definitely couldn't see out of his left eye, so he moved to Larry's left, forcing him to turn to keep him in sight at all times. The man spit blood out several times, and twice he looked as if he might fall, but he didn't drop the knife.

Wyatt moved in with blinding speed, for the first time using his enhanced cat reflexes. He caught the man's wrist in a brutal grip, controlling the knife as he stepped back behind Larry, taking the arm with him. Larry went flying down, screaming at the pressure on his arm. Wyatt held him there, removed the knife from his hand and slipped it into his own boot and then casually stuck the boot in Larry's throat.

"You're damn lucky I don' break your arm. This is me not bein' angry. You don' want to ever make me come for you again because I won't spank you sweetly like I've done.

I'll shove a knife down your throat and toss your body to the gators. I expect you'll be by to tell Grand-mere how bad you feel for shovin' her into the swamp."

There was no let up on the arm at all. Wyatt made it clear that he could break the bone at any time. The pressure on the throat remained just as steady. "Our people will be here to replant the plants you trampled on. You aren' goin' to give them trouble. Not you and not any of your friends. I don' really give a damn what you're doin' behind that fence, but you don' get to come onto our land and treat anyone like you own it all. Do we have an understandin'?"

"I think we do," Blake said. "Let him up."

"I need him to say it," Wyatt said quietly. "It's been a long day and I'm damn tired. Get it done or I'll end it for you."

"I understand," Larry bit out between his teeth.

Wyatt released him immediately and stepped back. He moved into the shadows of the trees, keeping his gaze on all three men.

Blake and Jim hurried over to Larry to help him stand. The dog remained standing, not looking toward Wyatt or the two men concealed in the trees. Wyatt knew that meant Ezekiel had control of the animal.

"Our guns?" Jim asked quietly.

"We'll leave them for you outside the gate," Wyatt replied. "We wouldn't want anyone to lose his temper and do somethin' stupid. It seems you don' have any more sense than you do manners."

Blake shot him a look that said he'd be more than happy to lose his temper, but all three men turned back toward the compound, Larry between the other two.

Wyatt waited until they were all the way inside with the gate closed before he moved.

"That was you being nice," Malichai said. "Impressive. You didn't even break a sweat."

"We grew up fightin' in the bayou, no rules, just gettin' it done," Wyatt said. "What idiot would pull a knife on me?"

Malichai leapt from the tree and landed easily on the balls of his feet. "Not me, bayou badass. I'm all for going back home and seeing what Grand-mere has left on the stove. Watching you expend all that energy just helped me work up an appetite."

"Not quite yet," Wyatt said. "I think we need to figure out just what spooked those boys tonight."

"Grand-mere's Rougarou, is my guess," Ezekiel said as he jumped from the tree. "Those guards were scared. All three of them. And the dog too."

"I wonder why. They were armed to the teeth," Wyatt mused, looking toward the swamp where the fast-moving figure had disappeared.

"Does the Rougarou have babies?" Malichai asked. "Because there was a little scary thing running faster than possible and disappearing into the swamp. I swear the damned thing glowed."

"I saw it too," Ezekiel admitted. "But I wasn't going to say anything."

"At night, the swamp can get you all mixed up," Wyatt admitted.

His gaze drifted back to the compound and the three men limping their way to the building. He didn't trust them not to come running back with automatic weapons—but then he wasn't a trusting man.

"As far back as I can remember, I've heard tales of monsters in the swamps. They say we don' have panthers here, but I've seen 'em. They say a lot of things, but the truth is, no one knows what's true and what's not. I don' believe in the Rougarou, but it was fun as a child to be scared. I think we're chasin' something else, but what it is, I have no idea," Wyatt said with a small shrug.

He was used to chasing myths in the swamps, and it didn't bother him in the least. Screams and strange noises abounded. Sometimes the swamp went eerily quiet. It didn't matter. It was home to him. He thrived there. Felt alive. The humidity. The heat. The insects. The way of life. It was home. If that included a monster or two, well, that just provided unexpected excitement.

"The guards are inside," Wyatt announced. "Let's move."

He was already leading the way, heading toward the spot in the swamp where he'd last seen the blurred images. The three of them cast around for signs and scents of the mysterious intruders.

"Over here, Wyatt," Ezekiel said. "I've got a partial track, but it looks like a baby's bare footprint. Am I looking at a bear cub? A really small one?"

Wyatt crouched down to examine the small smear of a footprint in the muddy leaves. He brushed the debris from the track, but there was only a heel mark and what had to be the ball of a foot. But it was tiny. Far too small to be a bear, even a cub.

"There's blood over here," Malichai informed them. "It's splashed on the leaves and there are a couple of spots on the ground. The guards sprayed bullets over this entire area and they must have hit something."

"If the guards actually did hit something, the wound didn't slow it down," Wyatt said. "I was watching it run, although it was so fast and smooth, I honestly couldn't see an image, just a blur, but if they were hit, the body didn't even jerk and they didn't miss a step."

"It's a lot of blood, Wyatt," Malichai said, moving through the brush.

"It's the adult, not the infant," Ezekiel added.

Wyatt frowned. Could whatever have been moving that fast be human? He doubted it. They were enhanced, all three of them, with animal DNA, and they could move with blurring speed, but no way could he have caught that entity, not the way it was moving.

He surveyed the brush and leaves. Malichai was right. Whatever it was had been shot and had lost a great deal of blood. They followed the blood trail deeper into the interior of the swamp. There was a spot where the creature had halted and the smaller one had joined it. There were no more tracks, but a few broken limbs on the bushes gave them away.

"Uh-oh," Wyatt said aloud. "I think the smaller one was hit too."

"That doesn't surprise me," Malichai replied. "They must have sprayed two hundred rounds into the swamp."

"The blood trail ends here," Ezekiel pointed out. "Whatever it is, it's adept at hiding itself. I can't even catch a scent."

Wyatt sighed. "We'll come back at daylight and see if we can pick anything up."

"Good idea," Malichai said with a huge grin. "Grandmere's cooking is calling."

CHAPTER 3

Wyatt used sheer muscle to power the pirogue quickly through the shallow waters of the bayou back toward his grandmother's property. The moon was no more than a sliver in the dark skies. Charcoal-painted clouds roiled above their heads and the water appeared an inky black surrounding them.

"Storm's comin' in," Wyatt announced softly, and redoubled his efforts.

The wind picked up and the branches of the cypress trees, knobby knees in the water, swayed, setting the long trails of moss swinging macabrely. The long vines of moss swept the surface of the water and looked, in the wind, like hundreds of spidery arms reaching for them.

Ezekiel grinned at his brother. "This is living, Malichai. I could get used to this."

Malichai shoved with the long pole, helping Wyatt to move the pirogue around the finger of land choked with tall reeds and back into the canal that would take them home.

"That's because you're sitting on your ass watching me work," Malichai replied.

Ezekiel nodded. "I had noticed that unusual detail. But then, you'll want a good appetite when we hit Grandmere's kitchen."

Wyatt ignored the byplay. He knew when the heavens opened up, a torrent of rain would come down and the water would rise fast. The swamps and marshes were already at full capacity. He pushed himself harder, feeling the unease building in the bayou. It was always that way, subtle, but easy for one to feel if you were tuned to it.

As he neared the pier, he glanced up to the two-story house that had been his home for much of his life. The familiar light was on in Nonny's bedroom. When her "boys" came home for visits, she didn't go to sleep until they were all safe under the roof. That light meant home to him, it always had—a loving welcome even when sometimes the words weren't spoken aloud.

The parlor light was on, unusual for that time of night. Nonny rarely had more than one light on in the house, especially if she was alone. He shoved with the pole, scooting them up the center of the canal, nearing the pier. That brought the entire house into his vision. A third light was on in the kitchen. *Three* lights. With anyone else, that might seem natural. No possible way with his grandmother.

They had no money in the early days and very little as they grew up. Things like electricity cost money and were never used unless absolutely necessary. Nonny still used candles in the house and sometimes gas lanterns, but never *three* electric lights.

Adrenaline hit hard, flooding his system. The water churned beneath the pirogue and the Fortunes brothers gripped the sides and stared at him, faces suddenly grim, waiting for him to let him know what was wrong.

Stay quiet. Nonny's in trouble. Before the dogs could catch their scent, Wyatt sent them a silent message to remain silent.

Neither man asked questions. They knew him. Trusted him. They'd served hundreds of rescue missions together under heavy fire and they knew he was as steady as a rock. If he said Nonny was in trouble, she was. Wyatt never wanted to take that kind of solidarity and trust for granted. Both of his friends were ready when he drew the pirogue next to the dock in the deepest shadows of the cypress trees lining the waters.

Ezekiel stepped off first, staying low to prevent sky-lining himself just in case anyone was watching. He tied up the boat fast and moved back into the shadows. Malichai followed, splitting off to make his way around to the back of the house. Wyatt pointed up toward Nonny's window, indicating to Ezekiel to go high. He was going straight in the front door.

Once Ezekiel gained the balcony, Wyatt stepped out of the shadows and began to saunter up to the porch as if he didn't have a care in the world. There was no vehicle to indicate Larry and his friends had reached the house before him, but it was possible. Wyatt and the Fortunes brothers had lingered in the swamp to examine the tracks of the Rougarou. That might have given the guards enough time to get to his *grand-mere*'s home. Still, Larry needed some tending, and the chances that his friends had taken care of him that fast were slim.

Wyatt walked right up the stairs and pulled open the door to the sitting room. It was the one room Nonny kept formal—at least as formal as she was able to be with all her years in the bayou. It was their entertaining room. Nothing fancy, but their best. It was empty. He gave it a quick once-over. One of his gifts was his ability to see every detail in a single sweep of his gaze—the smallest detail registered. He was certain no intruder had been in this room.

There was no sound in the house, almost as if the walls held their breath. He felt Ezekiel's entrance as well as Malichai's, one from above and one from the back of the house. Both were absolutely silent, but their presence sent a small shimmer of awareness through the old wood and he felt it.

Wyatt inhaled and instantly smelled blood. His heart stuttered and he forced himself under control, but fear for his grandmother took hold. He breathed it away, and kept his body loose, palming his knife, laying the blade up along his wrist out of sight. He strode into the parlor, knowing his grandmother was in there and she wasn't alone.

He stopped abruptly in the doorway. His grandmother's tiny body shielded someone else. There was an arm curved around her neck and the hand held a knife. Bowls of water were lined up on the small coffee table he'd made for Nonny himself. Three bowls. All hand-painted by Nonny's mother and cherished by the entire family. One bowl was still steaming, which meant they'd used extremely hot water. The water was bloody. There was a cloth in the second bowl of water. The third held plants mixed into medicine.

"What the hell's goin' on in here, Nonny?" he demanded, shifting a few inches to get a better angle on his grandmother's assailant. Nonny was small, so whoever was using her as a shield wasn't any bigger.

Something else moved in the room. On the pile of blankets in the corner. His heart jumped. His breath caught in his lungs. A child sat up, a small girl with a mop of dark, wavy hair, thick, but not long, curled in little whorls all over her head. She couldn't have been much more than a year, two at the very most. One little arm was bandaged, and he recognized his grandmother's work.

"Nothin' wrong here, Wyatt. Don' be worried about me. I'm jist helpin' out some friends."

Nonny didn't move a muscle. Neither did the knife. A shiver of awareness went through him. Most GhostWalkers could feel one another. Psychic energy surrounded them and immediately identified them to one another, although there were a rare few whose psychic energy was so contained the others couldn't feel them. Those same individuals could shield the teams from everyone else as well.

His heart jumped hard in his chest and suspicion

mounted. That knife never wavered, not one inch, and whoever held it was just that little bit too still to be a normal human being. He let out his breath slowly. Nonny didn't appear to be afraid, but if this was the Rougarou that had moved with astonishing, blurring speed, he wasn't happy about her being in his home.

"I'm not okay with the knife. I'm not goin' to hurt anyone, but I can't abide someone holdin' a knife to Grandmere's throat. If you want to get out of this room alive, put it down and back off," Wyatt said. "I'm damn tired of people threatenin' Nonny."

He was too. *Damn* tired of it. The floor beneath his feet trembled. The walls expanded and contracted. The light overhead swayed. The child's eyes grew large and round. She looked to the one standing behind his grandmother.

"I can take down the house. You're fast. I know you're fast, but you're not goin' to be able to save the kid. You take somethin' of mine, lady, and I'm gonna take somethin' you love."

The scent, not the blood scent, but the other, the one he'd smelled in the swamp was getting to him. Flooding his lungs. Doing something to the chemistry of his body, so that he felt alive in every cell, with every breath. He told himself it was adrenaline, but he knew it was far more than that, and it was dangerous. Just the beckoning, exotic scent of her, like a mixture of jasmine and silken sheets.

The little girl stood up, and the floor trembled, throwing her back to the ground. Behind Nonny, the woman gave a small cry and tossed the knife to the floor. His grandmother didn't move, but remained standing in front of the woman, clearly protecting her.

"That was unnecessary, Wyatt. She wouldn't have hurt me. She was protectin' her child. Both of them were shot by the same men who pushed me down in the swamp. I'm of a mind to go huntin' them with my squirrel gun."

He ignored the warning note in his grandmother's

voice. She didn't know what she was dealing with. This was no ordinary woman and child. He couldn't feel the psychic energy, that was true, but they were both enhanced and that didn't bode well for anyone in the room—especially his grandmother.

"Step out from behind Grand-mere. I want to see your hands."

The room had settled. He kept an eye on the child. She was no ordinary toddler, that was for certain. She'd stayed too still. She hadn't made a sound, not even when the ground shook and she'd been frightened. Her reactions seemed more animal than human to him. She would be unpredictable and he wasn't dismissing the possibility that she was dangerous—not after seeing the reactions of the guards at the Wilson Plastics compound.

The woman took one step to her right—toward the baby. She didn't look at the child, but he had the feeling she communicated with her. The woman was small, but she had all the curves a woman should have and then some. Her hair was thick and dark, like a pelt, woven into some intricate braid, but what was most unusual were the strange dark patterns stamped into the mass of nearly blue black hair.

For one moment, his entire being focused wholly on her. His heart did a curious somersault and his cock stirred in spite of the circumstances. She was built for long, lazy nights on the bayou, and images of her naked and writhing beneath him came out of nowhere.

Her eyes were unusual. Large. Framed with heavy black lashes. The color was difficult to define. One moment they looked normal to him, a deep nearly purple violet, nearly as rich as her hair, but there was a diamond ring around the dark center that spread through the darker color like a starburst. She was small, curvy and compact. Even from where he was standing, he could see the defined muscles in her slender arms and shapely legs—and he'd seen her run with a bullet wound in her.

He hadn't been with a woman in a long time and he'd always been careful to stay away from the wild ones, because he knew himself. He was jealous and mean and wouldn't be able to keep his hands off them once he got started. He'd sworn off women and he had no heart. He was blaming the momentary lapse on the knife. Bayou men loved women with knives—at least those in his family.

"How bad is it?" he asked, to break the tension and distract her—and himself. "And please don' grab the baby like you're thinkin' and dive out the window. I don' want to be fixin' the damn thing tonight, and Grand-mere would have my hide for scarin' you."

Le Poivre, more simply called Pepper, tried not to stare at the mouthwatering man who had interrupted Nonny cleaning and binding their wounds. She had seen him in the swamp, just earlier, casually giving a guard a beating. He'd fascinated her with his fluid movement, the sheer savagery of his attack, the casual way he kept at the guard. He'd been breathtaking. Poetry in motion. Fascinating.

He'd walked into his grandmother's parlor knowing she was there, but he'd entered with supreme confidence anyway. He dominated the room. Commanded it. She was used to men thinking they were in control, but none of those men had Nonny's grandson's command. Or his sheer sexual pull.

Everything about him screamed sensuality, from his dark, wavy hair to his hooded, intense eyes and a mouth that told her he could kiss the socks off a woman. She knew a dangerous man when she saw one, and this one looked like an avenging angel. She wondered, for just one moment, how it would feel to have a man like that charging to her rescue as he so clearly was doing with his grandmother.

He moved, a subtle almost imperceptible step, gliding just a little closer to the baby. Her baby. She needed to get to the child and run for it. Disappear into the swamp. No one would be able to get to them there. No one. Not even this man.

Wyatt studied the beautiful face of the woman. She

looked as if she'd stepped out of a picture frame. She didn't belong in the swamp, a bloody shoulder marring that perfect skin. The baby inched closer to the woman. He took another couple of steps toward his grandmother.

Hold off comin' in, boys. Let me get this under control. His grandmother was still far too close to the woman and he'd seen her move. He didn't want Ezekiel and Malichai to spook her into doing anything stupid.

I can feel the threat to you, Wyatt, Ezekiel said. *That woman is dangerous and so is the kid.*

"I'm warnin' you now, ma'am," Wyatt said. "I'm not alone. I know you're fast, but you're wounded and so is the baby. You know what I am. I know you do. My two friends are like me, and there's no way we can't track you. I don' want to hurt you or the kid. I just want to talk for a minute."

Wyatt took another step that successfully put him closer to the child, almost between them. The baby let out a small hissing sound, somewhere between a baby's cry and the hiss of a snake. The little toddler launched herself at him, running the couple of steps it took to the coffee table, leapt up on it and flung herself into the air.

The woman gave a horrified cry. *"No ne mordent pas, bébé, ne mordent pas."* She threw herself between Wyatt and the child.

The baby bit into the woman's arm, biting hard with her tiny baby teeth. At once she lifted her head, looking up at the woman with strange, too-old eyes—horrified at what she'd done. There were tears swimming in the baby's eyes, but she didn't cry aloud. She stayed perfectly still. Utterly still. For some reason, looking at the two of them broke Wyatt's heart.

"Take the baby, please, Ms. Fontenot," the woman instructed calmly. Too calmly. "Ginger, you go with Grand-mere." Her tone changed to one of sternness. "You are not to bite for any reason, do you understand?"

Wyatt heard the subtle change in the woman's breathing.

He caught her arm, his heart pounding hard. "Wait, Nonny. Don' touch that child." He turned the woman's arm over and examined the wounds. "She's venomous, isn't she?"

The woman nodded reluctantly. "She's just a baby. She doesn't mean to hurt anyone. She doesn't bite out of meanness. She was afraid." The woman stayed calm, although he felt her accelerated pulse. "Please allow your grandmother to hold her and comfort her. She knows what she did was wrong and she won't do it again."

Wyatt glanced down at the child. Tears trickled down her face. It felt obscene to be looking at a baby who was so completely alone.

"Her name is Ginger. She's only seventeen months old and her life has been hell. She's afraid of everyone but me. Please, please take care of her."

"I'm not afraid, Wyatt," Nonny insisted. "Come here, baby." She held out her arms to the child.

The woman leaned over to brush a kiss on the baby's forehead. "It's all right. Go with her, Ginger. They aren't going to hurt you. Remember, I told you about the nice lady who left us food and the blanket for you?" She lifted her head to look at Nonny, avoiding Wyatt's gaze. "She can't stay warm unless she's in the sun. You have to keep her warm."

"No. Don' you touch that child, Nonny." Much to his consternation, his voice came out a snarling command. Fear could do that to one. He took a breath and tried again. "She's dangerous. Her bite is dangerous. Trust me on this, Grandmere, she's as dangerous as the snakes here in the bayou."

Nonny made a single sound and all three pairs of eyes immediately went to her. He'd heard that sound a few times when he'd been a young boy, mainly when he was out of control and she was about to come down hard on him.

"This is still my home, Wyatt Fontenot, and I still make my own decisions. Tha's a baby, and in this house, as long as I own it, we take care of the children. Snakes and alligators don' bother me. I'm not afraid of her. She's terrified.

Can' you see that? Someone shot an *enfant*. Tha's who you should save your anger for."

"I can' take the chance of you gettin' hurt, Nonny," Wyatt said, much quieter. He knew that tone, the set of her shoulders. She was not going to back down. He was fighting a losing battle.

"It isn' your choice," Nonny said firmly. She held out her arms to the child. "Come here to me, Ginger. I'll keep you safe."

The child looked to the woman, who nodded slowly.

"I'll take good care of her," Nonny assured. "We're goin' to sit right here on the couch, wrapped in blankets, and Wyatt will take care of your mommy. He's a *traiteur*, baby. A very good one and he won't let your mama die."

Wyatt had no choice. He went to the woman and helped her over to a chair. Retaining possession of her arm, he held it below her heart. "What's your name?" Raising his voice, he called out to his friend. "Ezekiel, I need clean soapy water. Warm, not hot."

"Pepper. Just Pepper."

Wyatt was astonished at how calm she was. The toxin was fast acting. Already her eyelids were drooping. She was showing signs of eye weakness, of facial paralysis. The venom was acting on her nervous system fast.

"I'm a doctor. I can help you. Just stay calm. I want you to sit down slowly. We have to keep the wound below your heart. What venom? Which snake?" He already feared he knew.

"Cobra." Pepper looked past him to Nonny. "Please, I don't have much time, although I won't die. I won't. Ginger, I'm going to be fine. It will hurt for a little while, I'll be sick, you know that, but I'll be fine tomorrow or the next day."

"Don' tell her that if it's a cobra," Wyatt said.

Pepper ignored his warning, her gaze clinging to his. "She's a good girl. You can't let them take her back to the laboratory. They were going to kill her. I had to get her out. You have to promise me you'll hide her. You'll take care of her . . ."

"Stop talkin'," Wyatt ordered. "Are you able to slow your heart down? Has she bitten you before?" There were older bite marks on her arm in three places.

She ignored him. "Please. Promise me if something goes wrong this time, you'll look after her."

"Damn it, woman. Shut the hell up. Your heart is racin'. You need to slow it down. You know I'm like you. You have to know that."

She shook her head. "We're not like you. You're the perfect ones. The ones they want to keep. We're their mistakes, the ones they have to get rid of. She can't see this. The baby. I'm going to get very sick fast and she can't see."

There was something almost mesmerizing about her voice. A kind of velvet seduction even in the dire circumstances and that shook him almost as much as the fact that his grandmother was cooing to a baby who had a venomous bite.

"Are *all* these bite marks from her?"

"They forced her to bite me—and others. She didn't want to. She isn't dangerous, not like you're thinking. They were going to terminate her." The calm façade was fading, to be replaced by desperation.

"You said that. Stay calm. Were they using you to develop an antidote, or trying to make you immune to the bite?"

She nodded slowly. "Yes. There were doctors there and they took care of it."

He knew it wasn't that simple. A bite from a cobra or other venomous snakes was serious. Life threatening. In any case, she wasn't exactly answering his questions.

"Malichai." He raised his voice again. "I need my medical field kit. The new snakebite spray is inside the snakebite kit. Hurry."

He tried a slow, charming smile to ease her mind. He didn't want her to think he was a mad scientist—because he was certain she'd been exposed to more than one. "I'm going to try a relatively new product on you. There isn't time to get you to a hospital and they wouldn't have the antivenom for this snakebite here. You know that."

She had known and she'd known the bite could be fatal—even to her—yet she'd still stepped in front of him, protecting him at a very real risk to her own life.

Pepper raised her eyes to Wyatt's face. She wasn't going to die, she already knew that, not unless something went very wrong. It wasn't the cobra venom she feared. That wasn't going to kill her or make her all that sick. If it was just that . . .

She didn't want him to drag the baby from his grandmother, and if he knew exactly how venomous she really was, he would be like all the others—the ones who had created her—he would kill her.

She didn't understand the pull of his man, or why his face was so familiar. Why her heart sang when he was close. The scent of him enveloped her and she actually felt safe instead of threatened. She'd never been safe, and she certainly wasn't now.

"Here's the water, Wyatt," Ezekiel said.

Ezekiel's gaze was on the child, not the woman or Wyatt. He watched her in the way a hunter watched his prey, eyes fixed and wholly focused. The baby buried her face against Nonny's bony shoulder with a small little shudder of fear.

"Set the water down and quit tryin' to intimidate a baby," Wyatt said.

Ezekiel did as Wyatt asked slowly, for the first time turning his head to look at the woman. He put out his hand, toward her arm, her bare skin, as if he had to feel that it was as soft as it appeared. Wyatt actually felt the impact of her go right through Ezekiel's gut. His breathing hitched. Instantly flames burned in Wyatt's belly, igniting like a firestorm, hot and all encompassing.

"Walk away, Zeke," he said quietly. "Step back and walk away."

Ezekiel blinked rapidly, as if trying to come out of some hypnotic trance. He stood, almost mesmerized by the woman, unable to look away. "Holy crap, Wyatt." There was awe in his voice.

Wyatt fought the urge to pull his grandmother's knife out of his boot and slice him from his belly to his chest.

"Step back, Zeke," he repeated, and this time he put command in his voice.

Ezekiel obeyed out of respect for rank. He stepped back, still blinking rapidly. Wyatt knew they were all in trouble. This woman was dangerous to all of them. She could tear them apart without even trying—and what would happen if she tried?

He began to wash the wound carefully. Her skin had gone clammy. She was very pale. He tried not to notice that her skin was softer than anything he'd ever felt in his life.

"I don't have a lot of time before I get very sick. Give me your word you'll protect her."

Again he had to shake off the seductive sound of her voice. He seemed particularly susceptible to it, although when he glanced at Ezekiel, he noticed the man was still staring at Pepper as if he might devour her.

"Why would you believe me? You just put a knife to *ma grand-mere*'s throat," Wyatt said. He had no idea why he was so affected by her calm demeanor, by her insistence they save the child that had put her life in jeopardy, but he was. He wanted to save this woman. She was worth it. He didn't know how he knew that, or why he felt it, but the need was the strongest emotion he'd ever felt.

"Where the hell is that snakebite kit, Malichai?" He kept the urgency he was feeling out of his voice.

"Because you're a Fontenot. I've been in the bayou a little while now, and you have a reputation for keeping your word." She coughed. Her eyes drooped more.

The venom was moving quickly through her system in spite of the fact that she had slowed her heart rate. She had tremendous control.

"Ginger can't see this," Pepper reiterated. "She's been traumatized enough. Take me out of here."

It wasn't prudent to move her around. "Malichai! Where the hell are you?" Wyatt glanced at his grandmother. Did he dare leave her alone with a child who could kill with one bite? A baby who didn't know what she was doing?

"She's extremely intelligent. Her emotions are baby emotions, but she understands . . ." Pepper coughed. Tried to clear her voice. "I'm feeling nauseous."

"You know that's just one of the symptoms." Wyatt poured a soothing note into his voice. He'd always been gifted with a voice that could mesmerize if he needed it—although hers had his beat by a mile. When she spoke in that soft, husky, barely there tone, he felt her moving right through his body.

He'd always been particularly careful of using his gift—especially after he was enhanced. He used it now. "We'll get through this."

"There're two more. Two babies." She coughed, tried to clutch her throat. "God, it's going to be bad this time."

He kept possession of her arm to keep her from raising it above her heart. "Stop talkin'. Just stay calm." She was becoming a little agitated, another symptom.

She tried to talk. The words came out garbled. Her eyes went wider than ever. She shook her head and tried again.

Wyatt had to take control or he was going to lose her. "Look at me, Pepper. Only at me." He poured command into his voice. "Eyes to me, *now*." He waited until the strange, dark purple eyes jumped to his face. He could see the fear finally. It was there in her eyes. This wasn't going to be a picnic. She'd been through it before and knew what was coming.

"I'll get you through this. We'll take care of the little one, that's a promise. Nonny's goin' to find a bottle and give her somethin' warm to help her sleep. And then she'll be right in the other room rockin' her."

Pepper nodded. She didn't try to talk. Her face was

slowly becoming paralyzed. He could see the evidence. Her breathing was very shallow.

"Malichai will find the kit. The nasal spray is new, but it works. In the meantime, I'm goin' to try somethin' else." He explained, keeping his voice low and gentle. "You're goin' to feel me inside you. Open your mind to mine as best you can."

He laid his hand over the wound, not quite touching, but only a paper width from the bite marks. He had healed this way before, but wounds of the flesh, wounds that needed repairing from the inside out. He'd never tried to stop a fast-acting toxin from attacking the nervous system.

He knew he would leave a little part of himself behind in her—and take a part of her with him. Mind merging was intimate and far different from telepathy. One was a phone call. The other was . . .

He forced his mind to the problem at hand. Letting go was the most difficult part. He had things to hide. He wasn't a perfect man. No one wanted anyone to see who or what they were deep inside. Still staring into her eyes, he poured himself into her mind. He felt her shock. Resistance. He pushed past the barriers and immersed himself in her.

There was terror. Sheer terror. But she had nerves of steel. She didn't flinch or fight. She waited. His hands grew warm. Hot. His arms. His body. He felt the familiar fire, the one that had consumed him from the time he was a child when he'd needed to heal. It was a gift—a great gift.

He "saw" the venom moving like a slow lava through her body, extending toward her heart, but branching out to reach for her brain, her lungs, her throat. The venom was the enemy. To him, it appeared a white, thick stream. She stayed very still, not trying to hide from him, and he was aware she saw what he did. Just as he felt her terror, she felt his determination to save her, and that steadied her.

His hands followed the path of the venom, that stream he visualized in her body. Neurotoxins disrupted the function of the nervous system as well as the brain. He couldn't allow that to happen. The venom could cause lack of muscle control and paralysis, as well as interrupting the signals sent between neurons and muscles.

He didn't close his eyes as he normally would have done, instead he fell into hers. The strange midnight purple eyes with fantastic diamond starbursts that took him in, until he felt as if he might be free-falling through space.

He wasn't alone. She was right there with him, and he knew he would never feel alone as long as she was close. They could ride through the stars, into the galaxies and visit the Milky Way, but they wouldn't be alone ever again. They were tied together now, by the scorching heat he transferred to her body, by the way the merging of their minds made them one.

He had always felt different from those around him. He was a little wild and he knew it. He needed the bayou and the outlet of the waterways and swamps. Now, with his psychic enhancement and the cocktail of DNA he'd been given to make him into a supersoldier, he felt edgier than ever, more alone. Until this moment. Until this woman.

The heat he generated slowly turned the toxin from a white, almost crystalline stream to a glowing orange. The toxin began to separate into individual strands. Strands he could deal with. Strands he understood. He worked at incinerating each component, choosing the deadliest first. Neurotoxins were working to bind themselves at a rapid rate to the receptors in her muscles, preventing the muscles from contracting.

Even as he poured the healing energy against the neurotoxins, he became aware that Pepper's blood contained molecules that worked to neutralize the cobra venom. While the receptors on her muscles appeared the same, they weren't—at least not all of them, some of them contained an amino acid that differed from the rest. She was feeling the effects of the cobra bite, but the receptors the neurotoxins sought were covered with a bulky sugar molecule, preventing the neurotoxin from attaching itself.

"I've got the snakebite kit, Wyatt," Malichai announced. "Do you want me to use the nasal spray on her?"

Wyatt heard the voice as if in the distance. He was completely caught up in the way her body was fighting off the effects of the bite. She'd been enhanced with a cocktail of DNA, and clearly someone had tried to use her body to develop an antidote for snake venom—and it wasn't only cobra.

He pulled his mind from hers and immediately felt the loss. He had never felt so empty or alone. He sank back on his heels and lifted his hand for the spray. For some reason it was important to him that he care for Pepper himself. Malichai put the canister in his hand.

Malichai was staring at Pepper with the same stunned look on his face that his brother had. His breathing changed subtly and his eyes swept over her almost possessively. Wyatt stepped between them, trying not to snarl. This woman was going to get someone killed. Her scent was potent, yet it shouldn't be. She should smell of sweat and blood and toxins, not jasmine and rain.

"Malichai, I need some room to work," he said, gritting his teeth.

With an effort, Malichai stepped back.

"Pepper, this works. Several of the soldiers have tried it after being bitten," Wyatt said, using his most soothing voice to reassure her. She was shaking and her skin had gone grayish. Grayish, but still soft as silken sheets. No, even softer. He cursed under his breath. She was getting to him and he already knew what she was, how she was enhanced. He'd been in her mind. He knew her every secret and yet he still wanted to kill his friends to keep them away from her.

She nodded, her gaze clinging to his. He wondered if she felt as empty and lost as he did without her. He crouched down beside her, wrapped one hand around her wrist and sprayed her with the other.

Her fingers moved weakly against his hand. He immediately enveloped her fingers in his much larger hand. "We'll need some blankets and a clean bowl."

"I'll get them," Malichai said. "I saw a linen closet in the hall when I was looking for your bag."

Wyatt forgot he'd tossed his duffel bag into his bedroom just before they left to find the men who had assaulted his grandmother. No wonder it had taken Malichai a few minutes to find his medical kit.

"She said there were more babies?" Ezekiel questioned. "Did I hear that right? What son of a bitch would do this to a baby?"

"There are rumors, Ezekiel, a lot of them. We joined up after the founder of the program had disappeared, but I heard he took babies from orphanages and used them for experiments." Wyatt wasn't going to reveal his brother's wife's information to anyone. She was family. She was sacred. Her past was hers alone, and their family would protect her from everyone.

Pepper's hand tightened for a fraction of a second, and his heart gave a funny jump. It was difficult to be so close to her physically and not want to feel her merged with him once more. He'd never felt so starkly alone as he did in the moment—not even after Joy Chaisson had left him and he'd realized what a true jackass he'd been, pining for something that had never been real in the first place.

"Do you think that's what Wilson Plastics is hiding, then?" Ezekiel said. "It's really a laboratory where they experiment on children?"

Pepper shook her head, or rather tried to. Wyatt felt the movement. Her eyes were wide open and clung to his face. The impact of her eyes on him astonished him. It almost felt like a solid punch to his gut. His chest burned. His heart shifted. Hot blood flooded his veins and pooled low and mean in his groin. The woman was very ill and she still had this much effect on him. Disaster. She was definitely going to be a disaster.

You're capable of telepathy. I know you talk to the little one.

There was a moment of silence, as if it took her a moment to process. *Sorry. Brain's not working. Hurts like hell. Everything feels slow and hazy.*

He closed his eyes briefly, trying not to feel the intensity of the intimacy between them. Initiating telepathic communication with her was clearly a mistake. She crawled into his mind, into his body and wrapped herself tight. *Stay with me, Pepper. Stay alert. I need to know what's happenin'.*

The facility is used to house the rejects. The ones they can't use in the field or are deemed too dangerous to continue with, she explained.

The babies?

In vitro. All three have killed with their bites. They're too intelligent for their age, and too difficult for their handlers. No one would take care of them but me. When I found out they were going to terminate them, I escaped, but the other two were caught when we broke out. They were both hurt.

Do you think they've killed them already?

No. They wouldn't dare, not with me out. Those two are the only leverage they have to get me to come back.

He felt the sudden urgency in her and immediately helped her into a half-sitting position, holding her with one arm and the bowl in place with the other. She was horribly sick, again and again. He was grateful her digestive system worked enough to allow her to be sick. She wasn't going to die, thanks to the antivenom already built up in her system.

He wondered just how many times she'd been bitten and how many times she'd had to go through this. At seventeen months, the babies would still be getting teeth. Their mouths would hurt. If something scared them, the snake in them would want to strike out with a bite just as Ginger had done.

He sighed. He knew damn well he was going to have to get those babies out of there. What was he going to do with three little vipers? Well, technically they weren't really vipers, they were elapids, but vipers sounded more . . . *female*. He couldn't leave them with Grand-mere, although if anyone could handle them it would be her.

He'd been steadfastly avoiding his brother Gator. Facing him after all Gator had revealed to him about the infamous Dr. Whitney, who had started genetic dosing to make supersoldiers, would be difficult. Gator wouldn't be too happy with Wyatt's choices. The truth was, Wyatt knew he hadn't been making good decisions from the moment Joy had left him. He'd been a childish idiot, and that didn't sit well with him.

He handed the bowl off to Ezekiel and took the blankets Malichai brought, tucking them around Pepper's shivering body. "The light is hurting her eyes, can you get rid of it?" If Malichai kept staring at her, he wasn't certain what he would do, but he had to get himself under control.

She was slipping away from him now, drifting in a sea of pain. "You two may as well go to bed," he said to his teammates—his friends. He needed them gone. He needed just for a few minutes to allow himself to think about what she was and how he was going to handle her. "I'll stay with her."

Both Ezekiel and Malichai were trained medics, but Wyatt was a doctor—a surgeon as well as a natural gifted healer. He told himself Wyatt was the logical man for the job, but he knew he wouldn't have turned it over to either of the other two. He didn't want to leave her. He couldn't leave her, especially not with another man.

"Tell Nonny to put the baby to bed, Ezekiel. They both need sleep. I think the baby will understand if you tell her Pepper is doing fine and she'll be okay soon."

Ezekiel raked both hands through his hair. "There's a part of me that wants to go into that place and kill them all for this. The idea that someone would do such a thing to a baby sickens me. On the other hand, I have this need to take out threats to my family, and that includes you, Wyatt. That child in there is a ticking bomb. We both know that." He gestured toward Pepper. "And this one. She's pure poison. I can feel her working us all against each other."

"Zeke." Wyatt sighed and sank down onto the floor, his back to the low-slung couch Pepper rested on. "You could no more kill a baby than you could kill Malichai. Nor could you kill a helpless woman. You're tired. I'm tired. This is all one hell of a mess."

"Yeah. I know. But that baby is a little freaky. On the other hand, I just wanted to pick her up myself after I heard what the woman said, and hold her close. That's not like me."

Malichai nudged his brother with his foot. "You used to hold Mordichai and me at night and rock us back and forth and tell us stories."

"I did not," Ezekiel denied hotly. "I told you to shut up and go to sleep."

Malichai handed his brother a cup of coffee. "There's a pot of some kind of fish stew on the stove and it's good. Don't listen to him, Wyatt. He's a master storyteller. He can do all the voices and make the stories come alive. He'll be a great babysitter."

"Go to hell, Malichai. I never told you a story in my life."

Wyatt grinned at him, suddenly knowing things were going to be all right between him and the others, even with Pepper sitting between them all. "Ezekiel. The big bad wolf. You did. You did tell him stories. I always know when someone's lyin', and you're lyin' your ass off right now."

"Yeah, well, both of you can go to hell," Ezekiel snapped.

"Boys." Nonny raised her voice from the next room. "This young'un is still awake and can hear your foul words. I have a bar of soap ready and waitin'."

Ezekiel went to the door and peered into the darkened

room. "Sorry, Grand-mere. I have a problem when someone starts harming babies. I feel like I have this rage inside of me and there's nowhere for it to go."

"Don' you worry, none, Ezekiel," Nonny said. "You and my boy will get those other babies out of that place and when they're safe, I have no doubt you'll go back there and read 'em all from the good book."

Ezekiel studied the small child curled up in Nonny's arms. She was very small with her mop of wavy dark hair and fair skin. Her eyes were different, yet almost familiar to him. He was certain he could see a hint of the snake—and something else—something that pulled at him.

He turned back to Wyatt. "I didn't think, when I signed up for the psychic enhancement program, how they ever arrived at the engineering. The experiments that would have had to go before us."

"We were told it would make us enhanced, better soldiers as well as stronger psychics," Malichai said. "We skimmed a bit over the genetic parts of it, mainly because that's not our field of expertise."

Wyatt didn't have that excuse—and worse—he hadn't considered the experiments either. How had they come up with the perfect cocktail to enhance muscles, hearing, eyesight and to make them so much stronger and faster? No one ever got it right the first time. There were always mistakes.

What had Pepper said? She denied being like him. She was one of the mistakes. The children had been slated for termination. Had she been as well? Was that what Wilson Plastics really was? A disposal site? They could do their last experiments out in the swamp, kill whatever had been created and use the ocean and swamp to get rid of the bodies. A thought struck him. If they cremated the bodies on site, they wouldn't even have the issue of hiding their tracks.

"We're goin' to have to get inside that compound," he told Ezekiel and Malichai. "We need to see for ourselves what's goin' on."

CHAPTER 4

He was dreaming. He had to be. The night sky was strewn with a million stars and he floated through them, drifting with the scent of jasmine filling his lungs. Candles flickered among the stars and the stars spun until they became small, fragrant flowers, thousands of them, falling on his face and bare skin.

He turned over, a slow, lazy roll that had him against the softest skin he'd ever felt in his life. She was there, smiling at him. Sultry. Sensual. Her long hair sliding over his body, inflaming it more as she crawled over top of him, her full breasts teasing the muscles of his chest.

She was hot. So hot. He wanted her more than he'd ever wanted anything in his life. He would have done anything to have her. She leaned close, her mouth nearly on his. He could feel the warmth of her breath.

"Are you awake?"

Of course he wasn't awake. Hot, sexy women didn't crawl all over him, teasing with hands and teeth and tongue.

"Wyatt?" Her teeth nipped his earlobe. Her tongue dipped into it. "Wake up."

Hell no. He wasn't waking up. He caught at her waist, her small, tucked-in waist fit perfectly into his large hands. His hands came together, and she was gone.

"Wyatt? Are you awake?"

Her soft voice came out of the night and moved over his skin like the caress of fingers. His body reacted with an instant savage ache, reminding him it had been a very long time since he'd been with a woman. It didn't help that she'd haunted his dreams with that body of hers. And her voice. He'd always been susceptible to a certain type of voice. When Joy sang, most any man would follow her anywhere. He had to admit, although he didn't want to, that Pepper's voice was even more enthralling.

He rolled over and stared up at the ceiling, breathing deep to rid himself of the giant hard-on for a woman who had been snake bit. She'd held a knife to his grandmother's throat. She was one of Whitney's experiments—*failed* experiments at that. She was too much of a lure not to be all about sex. That meant she wasn't a prize by any means. He was just that damned hard up. "Yep." And he'd proba-bly be for the rest of the night thanks to her.

"I can't seem to slow my heart down. This part always scares me."

Damn the woman anyway. Now he felt like a first-class jerk. She was suffering real pain and his foul temper had kicked in just because she could stir him up with three lit-tle words—"Are you awake?" Now that would conjure up erotic images for any man. That voice. The knife. Her body. What the hell did one expect? He wasn't a saint. It hadn't helped that he'd been dreaming about her.

"Breathe slow." He nearly groaned aloud. Great advice. *Breathe slow.* What kind of a doctor was he? She was reaching out to him, needing help, and he couldn't move because if he did, his body, still as hard as a rock, might shatter into a million pieces.

He tried not to think about what she'd look like without

clothes. Or what she'd feel like, skin to skin. What the hell was wrong with him? He detested women. They were sultry creatures bent on a man's destruction. She was just proving to him that he'd been right about them all along.

He didn't want to talk to her and soothe her, he wanted to strike out at her. She was going to be a handful. He knew that. He knew every man in the bayou was going to be panting after her. Damn her to hell, he knew what was coming. "You sing, don' you? Your voice, you can use it to seduce, right?"

There was a small silence. His tone had been harsh. Accusing even. He took a breath and let it out, willing his body to stop. Willing his mind to forget everything Joy had said to him. Willing himself not to hear those sensual notes in Pepper's voice.

"Yes."

He hadn't expected her soft admission. Or the way he felt the small confession slip inside of him, spreading through him like bubbles from the finest champagne. "So what? You were engineered to be the secret sexual weapon? The one used to lure the enemy close so you could stab them through the heart? That's why you have that skin? That body? And that voice? Nature and a fuckin' scientist gave them to you?"

Again a small silence. He felt his own heart accelerate. He stared up at the ceiling, his cat's eyes able to count every knot in the wood.

"Yes."

His lungs filled and refused to continue. He ached. Everywhere. It was all he could do not to open his jeans and find some kind of relief. "What went wrong? Why did they change their mind and start usin' you for snake bait?"

He was being a bastard. An utter and complete bastard. He knew it, he just couldn't stop himself. He wanted to punish her for being a seductive woman—one that could put a spell on a man without even trying. He wanted to punish her for his own weakness.

"They overlooked one important detail," Pepper replied softly. "One serious flaw in their plans for me."

"I can't see any mistakes," he admitted.

"They gave me the body, the voice, and even the sexual need. It's like a hunger that won't stop, but they forgot to take away my free will. They forgot that I might not want to crawl all over a man, using my body to seduce him and then just give him a little love bite straight into his carotid."

He drew in his breath sharply, trying not to groan. The thought of her naked, sliding up any man's body but his was just a little too much. The idea of her biting any other neck but his was just as intolerable. And that said volumes about his present state of mind. "You said no? Even though you've got cat DNA. You must go into heat."

"All the time. Serious heat." She didn't laugh. She sounded sad. Filled with sorrow. Despair.

"Why haven't Ezekiel and Malichai had the same strong reaction to you as I have?" He'd seen the look on their faces, but they had both been able to walk away. He couldn't. Wyatt knew had they not left him to it, he might have turned dangerous—even to his friends.

"I was careful. I tried to keep my guard up and protect them. You shouldn't be feeling it either. I must have slipped up when I got so sick."

Her voice was killing him. He was grateful he couldn't see her. Lying in the dark next to her, he couldn't stop the erotic images from flooding his brain. He gritted his teeth and forced more air through his burning lungs.

"Did you use this particular gift to escape?" He didn't know why he had to ask—or why he sounded so filled with contempt—so jealous. But it was there, swirling inside him, a black cloud of rage that told him he needed a reprieve from her. From the sexual web of her voice.

"You know, Mr. Fontenot, I don't want to talk to you after all. I've gone through this alone before and I'm certain

I will again. I don't need someone around me who believes he's so much better than I am."

He felt her movement before she actually moved. The energy it took wasn't all human. Clearly just sitting was difficult—and painful. Agony twisted through his body. Ripped him in half and sawed at every muscle and joint. He couldn't breathe, and this time it had nothing at all to do with sex. His body nearly convulsed with the pain. His heart pounded, his pulse accelerated and he broke out into a sweat. Thunder roared in his ears.

Recognition came slowly. He should have known all along. He was a damned genius, yet he hadn't figured it out. He'd tied them together when he'd merged his mind to hers. His dreams were her dreams. She'd admitted who-ever had enhanced her had wanted to use her as a sexual weapon and they'd found a way to kick up her drive until it was an outrageous hunger and need.

She had been the one suffering because of their close proximity, even in spite of the venom. Maybe because of it. She wasn't fully in control.

"Lie back down, Pepper." Wyatt used his "doctor" voice. "I'll get you something for the pain."

"I have to use the bathroom—and I don't take painkillers."

He sat up gingerly, waited for his head to explode a cou-ple of times and then pushed himself into a standing posi-tion. "What happens when you take painkillers?"

"Anything that lowers my inhibitions is not acceptable."

His breath slammed out of his lungs at the thought of Pep-per with him and with lowered inhibitions. It was still dark in the room, but he could see her with his night vision. She lay back against the sofa, struggling for every breath. Her skin almost glowed, it was so flawless, even though she was pale beyond imagining. Her hair fell in a cloud around her face, dark and rich, inviting a man to bury his hands in it.

He could see her breasts rising and falling as she fought to draw air in and out of her lungs. Her mouth, a perfect fantasy mouth, drew his attention. Her lips were slightly parted, and once again images filled his mind. He cursed softly under his breath. She lifted her long lashes and her dark eyes met his—only they weren't dark anymore. They were the star-filled sky he'd floated through in his erotic dream, a sultry invitation to another world. He had the feeling if he was ever foolish enough to allow himself to take one step, one kiss, one touch into that world, there would be no going back.

"I'll help you to the bathroom."

"Just point the way," she suggested.

He wished he had earplugs in. Her voice was the perfect weapon against a man, and clearly the pain wasn't allowing her to mask the enhancements at all. He was just grateful his friends were asleep and nowhere near her. Merging with her had been a mistake. He felt possessive of her, so much so, he feared the connection between them could get someone killed.

"You'll fall on your face." He didn't wait for more protests, what was the use? He'd helped to get them into this situation, and she couldn't help what she was any more than he could. He reached for her. She closed her eyes. He knew why the instant he touched her.

The sensation of silk and satin slid over him. Into him. Need crawled through his body in a slow, desperate burn. He picked her up and cradled her against his chest. He'd walked through a hail of gunfire with a friend over his shoulder, he could carry a featherweight a few feet to a bathroom.

He tried not to feel the way her body melted into his or the silk of her hair brushing over nerve endings, setting them on fire. She really was the perfect weapon. She could feel seductive even when she was so ill. He couldn't imagine what she would be like when she was perfectly healthy and *wanted* to seduce a man—but he found himself a little desperate to find out.

He took her into the small, very tidy guest bathroom

closest to the parlor. Nonny had insisted on a bathroom for guests. She had a private bathroom upstairs and a much larger one for all her grandsons to share growing up, but she had been very vocal about needing one just for guests. He couldn't blame her. The downstairs bathroom the boys shared had always been in a state of chaos, although if it got too bad, Nonny would hand them all cheap tooth-brushes and tell them to go to work.

The guest bathroom was charming and always smelled sensational. Nonny used a mixture of flowers and herbs to create the scents she used throughout the house. The moment they both inhaled, some of the terrible need faded, giving them a bit of a respite.

"My *grand-mere* is the real genius in the family," Wyatt said, attempting normal conversation. He set Pepper on her feet. "Can you really do this by yourself? I am a doctor. I'd do my best to be impersonal." He had to admit the truth. Stripping her down would be anything but impersonal, but he'd give it his best shot.

"I'll have to ask her what blend she used. I watched her coming into the wonderful piece of swamp with all the wildflowers and herbs planted together, and she always knew exactly what she wanted. She fascinates me."

"You're goin' to fall on your face if I let go of you, aren't you?" He dropped his hands to her jeans and unzipped them, not looking at her face. "I'll turn away." He hooked his thumbs in the waistband of her jeans and stripped her, forcing himself to keep his gaze to himself. Still, his thumb brushed bare skin along her hips and thighs, and he knew he would carry that sensation for a long time in his body.

"This is humiliating," she said between clenched teeth. "I'm never going to be able to look at you again."

"That's too bad, woman, because I intend to be lookin' a lot in your direction," he said. The declaration slipped out before he could stop it, and he knew he was in trouble.

"Wyatt." Her voice was soft.

He didn't turn around, keeping his back to her like he promised, but the way she said his name, all soft and silky, a husky, sensual whisper of pure seduction, a lure he couldn't get out of his head. No matter how hard he tried to control himself, his body still responded to her voice. He sent up a silent curse that he'd been born so susceptible to sound.

"I'm not a woman you can ever get mixed up with. I don't even know what part of me is real anymore. I don't want to hurt you. The moment I'm back to full strength, I'm taking Ginger and leaving. I have to find a way to get the other two babies out and find a safe home where I can protect them."

"We're goin' to help you get those babies out of there," Wyatt said. "And we'll talk about the rest. How hard are they goin' to come lookin' for all of you?"

She flushed the toilet and he felt her move, staggering to her feet. He whipped around and steadied her, his hands on her slim waist. The moment his hands touched her silky bare skin, his cock reacted, an urgent, wicked demand involving pain as he grew hard and thick, nearly bursting the material of his jeans. He didn't care. He didn't move his hands, just let the heat from all ten fingers sink into her, branding her with him.

She gasped. Even as sick as she was, as weak as she was, she felt it too. He could tell by the shiver that went through her body. He knew women. He knew when one was attracted to him. There was satisfaction in the knowing. He forced air through his lungs.

"Don' fall," he cautioned.

Wyatt waited until she felt steadier and then he tugged up her clothes, fastening them as she leaned into him and washed her hands in the sink, all the while studiously avoiding looking at him.

Pepper swallowed hard. She had to tell him the truth. He had to know what he was up against. She often was desperate for sex, but not like this, not in direct reaction to a man. She knew what she felt for Wyatt Fontenot was dangerous to her. Wyatt wasn't a man to be controlled. He took control. It was in the way he walked. The set of his shoulders. The stamp of his mouth.

Heat flared in his eyes when he looked at her, and something else. Something she'd never seen before but recognized as possession. He wanted her. That wasn't anything new, but the *way* he wanted her was.

"Dr. Thomas Braden, the head of this company, has several scientists working for him in France. That's where the children were created, born and worked on. I was an orphan and brought up in the school there. Braden is the one who decrees when an experiment has to be terminated."

She felt a wave of weakness wash over her, and without thinking she leaned into him, her back to his front. His breath hissed out. She felt the heavy, thick erection pressed against her, but she couldn't have moved if her life depended on it—and maybe it did. There was no sanity, no thinking, only feeling. Her body betrayed her, burning between her legs, her breasts tingling, achy and swollen. It didn't help that her blood ran hot when she needed to slow everything down so the venom didn't have a chance to make things worse.

"Breathe," he ordered softly into her ear.

He knew. She was mortified that he knew. She tried to straighten, to stand on her own two feet, but his fingers turned to steel and he held her close.

"Don'. You know better. Just breathe slow and it will settle a little. Enough that we both can manage."

"I'm sorry. I didn't mean for this to happen."

"It's not your fault, sugar," he said, his breath on her neck.

She closed her eyes, and allowed herself to lean against his chest. His rock hard erection. The man that was stamping his fingerprints into her bones. She slowed her breathing, fighting to stay upright when pain was hammering to get in. The pain wasn't just physical either.

"I—he—I angered Braden," she admitted reluctantly. "I wouldn't cooperate with things he wanted me to do. He threatened to terminate the babies if I didn't do what he wanted, and I lost my temper. It wasn't good. Two months later, he sent us all here. He has four trackers—he calls them his elite—although I think someone else provides them, otherwise he would have sent them after me right away. But they'll come. He also has his own special little army that he created."

She had just attained freedom. Only just. She'd lived her life under the control of others. Orders. Discipline. She barely knew there was another world out there. The taste of freedom was in her mouth. In her heart. She responded to the wildness of the bayou, the primitive, primal swamp. She had been so close and yet now . . .

She looked over her shoulder at Wyatt Fontenot, at the strength in his face, the intensity of his eyes and a mouth a woman might give up a lot for. She was lost. Not because he was sexy and hot. He was a family man and he protected and cared for those he loved. In all of her life she had never thought she might find such a thing. She had secretly longed to find it, especially when she was up all night with the three little ones, wishing she had a partner to help lighten the load for one moment.

Wyatt Fontenot would be a man like that. He could be ruthless and merciless and yet kind and compassionate. He would be a man who would put those he loved first, and he would always stand in front of them. Temptation was a wicked, sinful thing, and yet she knew she wouldn't do what her body and her mind wanted her to do. So easy. It would be so easy. But it wouldn't be real.

"Stop thinkin' so much, honey. It's all goin' to be okay. You'll see."

Wyatt picked her up, cradling her body gently. The pain broke through her mind and bled into his several times, but he was more prepared, now that he knew what was happening to them.

She was killing him with her thoughts. She didn't realize

she was so ill she couldn't compartmentalize, and they already had formed a connection. She was spilling over into him and he wanted to shield her from every ugly thing she'd ever experienced.

"Have you heard of a man called Whitney? Dr. Peter Whitney?"

She bit her lip, calling his attention to it. Worse, the tip of her tongue slipped out to ease the bite mark, drawing his attention to that.

Pepper nodded her head slowly. "Yes. He came in and consulted with Braden a couple of times. He watched through the glass as one of the babies, Thym, bit me. He reminded me of a real reptile; his eyes were dead. Braden, who is very arrogant, was somewhat respectful toward him. Although I could see he didn't like Whitney."

"Are you certain it was Braden, not Whitney, who issued the termination order on the babies and you?"

She frowned. Her long lashes fluttered. His groin tightened. Her body seemed as if it was cooling fast when she'd just had a raging temperature. He needed to get her back to bed.

"I honestly don't know if there's a termination order out on me. There wasn't when I escaped, but there certainly could be now." Her head lolled back against his shoulder, as if the energy it took to converse was too much. "Braden called me into his office and asked me for some special favors. Not asked. Ordered. I refused. He told me if I didn't cooperate, he would consider terminating the children. All three of them. That's what he said. Consider. Like they were garbage. Nothing. Not human. Not children." She lifted her hand and wiped her face as if trying to erase the memory.

Wyatt realized he was just standing there, holding her in his arms, looking down into her face. Her eyes. He felt a bit like a man who'd just been hit over the head and was seeing stars. Very gently he deposited her back on Nonny's sofa and drew the covers over her. She had begun to shiver again.

"This is the worst. I know I'm not going to die, but it feels like every muscle in my body contracts and turns into hard knots that just won't let up. I don't know what DNA cocktail they used for little Ginger, but the pain is incredible."

"I can put you in a much more private room, give you fluids and painkillers through an IV and keep you away from everyone," he offered.

Her gaze jumped to his face. Her eyes looked like a doorway to another galaxy, one he wanted to go through. A paradise of sheer feeling. It was impossible to look directly into her eyes and not feel sexual awareness.

Pepper bit her lip. "Don't tempt me, Wyatt. Not now when I know what's coming. I've done this before and I know I can get through it."

"You didn't make that connection between us, Pepper." Wyatt felt compelled to admit the truth to her. "I did. When I tried to heal you. I merged our minds and somehow we stayed attached. What you feel, I can feel. Maybe the other way around as well. You didn' let your guard down, and you certainly weren' the one to compromise us. I did that all by myself."

Pepper's lashes fluttered. Her long, black lashes, thick and curved, two crescents as sexy as the rest of her. "Thank you for that, Wyatt. I don't know how true it is, maybe we're both a little responsible."

"The point is, I can take away the pain and you don' have to worry that somethin' will happen. You're strong. You'll manage."

A shudder ran through her body, a ripple of pain that had him nearly doubling over. He couldn't fight what he couldn't see. That pain wasn't his. The venom Ginger had injected into her wasn't solely that of a cobra. Pepper's immunity to the cobra bite was fairly strong. This was another strain that compromised her muscles and produced such pain.

"Damn them. Ginger is both, Elapidae and Viperidae, isn't she? The idiots wanted to make certain she could kill no matter what. I looked at her mouth when Grand-mere picked her up and there was no evidence of fangs. She's more viper, isn't she? But her bite is the deadliest because they mixed in cobra."

Pepper turned her face away from him. "You're the genius." Her voice had dropped nearly to a husky whisper. If he hadn't had such acute hearing he wouldn't have heard her.

"Baby, I'm not sayin' anythin' against her. I'm tryin' to help you through this, and I have to know what kind of venom is inside you." He pushed back her hair. He couldn't help himself, he had to touch her. He knew his tone was all wrong, but what he wanted to do was let out a string of curse words his grandmother would frown on and then go kill a few scientists—slowly.

"She's a seventeen-month-old baby who didn't ask for what they did to her. They gave her a high IQ and that scared them to death. She already knows what they did to her and why they want to use her. They think she's a monster, and she knows that too. They forced her to bite me over and over, and when she wouldn't, they hurt her. She killed three of the workers. She didn't mean to, but she strikes out when she's threatened. She's programmed to."

"Did you think you could give her a normal life?" Wyatt asked, sinking down onto the floor beside the sofa. He dropped his face into his hands. Trading his easy life in the bayou for enhancements seemed rather ridiculous to him now. Especially over a woman who had run out on him—a woman he realized if he'd just stepped back and taken a good look at he would have known she wasn't at all right for him. His problems were minuscule in comparison to that of a seventeen-month-old baby with termination orders out on her.

"No. Of course not. But I could give her a loving home. She's like any other human being. She needs love. She needs to know she's all right just the way she is. I can teach her the control she needs."

Her long braid had fallen over the edge of the sofa and

he wrapped it around his fist, wishing he could push back all the strands that had escaped and curled around her face, but he didn't dare touch her so intimately again. Not when his body just wouldn't settle and his mind seemed consumed with her.

"I can see that. What are the other two like?"

"Beautiful and smart, just like Ginger. They used the same cocktail for all of them. Three little identical girls."

"Three?" That surprised him. He would have thought they would stick with two of them. "They used in vitro to develop the child they wanted and produced three with the same DNA. Snake, cat and human?"

"Dashes of snake and cat," she corrected. "They're human."

She made a sound and drew up her knees, writhing on the sofa. Her breath slammed out of her lungs. He pressed her braid to his face. She didn't want a painkiller, but if it got worse, she was going to get one anyway.

He waited until she was able to lie still again. Hoping to distract her, he continued the conversation. "She ran barefoot, just like you. In the swamp. Neither of you should be able to do that. Not to mention it's unsanitary."

"The babies have feet like a cat, with a cushion. The soles of their feet don't look as if they do, but they're tough and actually aid them in running, jumping long distances and climbing."

He looked at her feet. She had washed them when she first entered Nonny's home and they were small, fine-boned, almost delicate. There was no paint on her toenails and no adornments such as toe rings or ankle bracelets. He'd never had a foot fetish but he considered starting one now. He tugged the blanket down around her feet again without running his finger over the sole of her foot. He already knew it would be deceptively smooth.

"Why did he want three the same?"

"He needs one for a control and two for his experiments. He wanted to know what situations would push the girls to become more dangerous." She broke off abruptly, a soft moan escaping. She clamped down hard on it, her breath hissing out between her teeth. She drew her knees up and rocked her body back and forth.

"I can't stand this," Wyatt snapped.

Abruptly he stood, picked her up, blankets and all, and carried her to his boyhood bedroom. She didn't protest, her eyes closed tight. He doubted if she could protest. She could barely breathe.

He laid her on his bed and tucked the blanket around her. His equipment was just down the hall in the little office he'd used to see a few patients there in the bayou. Most, he visited in their homes, the old-fashioned way. Quickly he set up an IV beside the bed, pushing fluids and a heavy painkiller into her system.

Pepper shook her head, her eyes wide with fear, her hand reaching for the needle he'd put into her vein. Wyatt covered her hand with his, sinking down beside her. "Leave it, sugar. I mean it. You're in no condition to fight me and I'm not goin' to let you have this round. Take the damn painkillers and let them do their work."

Dangerous to you. To the others. Out of control. She shook her head again, those dark purple eyes looking so frightened he took a breath and forced his voice to be gentler when he was feeling anything but gentle.

"No one else can get into this room, Pepper. I've locked the door. I'll keep you safe, I promise, and I won' hold you to anythin' you say or do while on this drug. If you want me to, I'll wear earplugs. The truth is, I can' stand to see you suffer. I want you to sleep through this if possible."

Her gaze drifted over his face. His heart jumped. Pounded. His pulse reacted. The physical pull to her was far stronger than he'd imagined it could ever be between a man and a woman. He sure as hell didn't want his friends feeling the same thing for her or having the same erotic fantasies playing through their heads.

Was she feeling the same way? He was certain she was. He told himself the enhancements they'd given her had made her a sexual being. Every move she made, the way she talked, it was all very sensual. His fantasies were most likely hers and she was sharing them with him through the connection he'd forged when he'd merged their minds—at least that was what he wanted to believe.

He saw the moment the drug took her, sweeping her up and away from the pain the snakebite had caused. Her muscles still cramped, but he was pushing fluids that would help. He examined the bullet wound first. His heart contracted for no real reason other than she looked vulnerable. The white knight was rising fast and he didn't like it. He'd already been a fool once; he didn't need to do it twice. Except . . . Sometimes a man just had to take what he wanted and make it work.

Wyatt set his jaw and picked up her arm to examine the site where the bite had been inflicted. Pepper was a good healer. Oftentimes, a bite from a viper could cause tissue damage—a lot of it. The older marks were faint, just small white scars. The new bite was more of a dark bruise where the puncture marks were, and already the arm was very swollen.

Clearly she had built up somewhat of an immunity against the viper bite as well. He supposed that it would be a good idea to start the process for him, and maybe Flame and Gator as well as his other two brothers . . . What the hell was he thinking? He'd lost his mind. He was going to help get those babies free and shut down whatever Braden was doing in that laboratory, but that was all. No way were those babies staying in his family home.

What had she said? They used the laboratory as a disposal site. His bayou. They were killing children in his bayou. The walls around him expanded and contracted and he breathed away the anger.

He could tell by her breathing that Pepper had finally drifted off to sleep. He stretched out on the other side of the bed, exhaustion suddenly hitting him. It wouldn't hurt anything to close his eyes. Just for a minute.

Wyatt didn't remember stripping, although he'd never liked wearing clothes to bed, but he was stark-naked when her hands began to slide over his body. Her hair was free of the intricate braid and sweeping over his chest as she moved over him. Her body was warm and soft and all curves. His hands came up to catch her waist, to slide down over her exquisite hips to her perfect butt.

She slid her leg over him, straddling his thighs, leaning down to lick at him like a cat. Her tongue felt like a velvet rasp, teasing at his body, promising him so much more. She made soft little sounds, purring like a cat, the vibration riding through his cock and spreading through his body. He cupped her breasts in his palms, the sweet weight, his thumbs teasing her nipples into hard peaks.

"I'm not a gentle lover," he warned her softly. "You start this, I'll be finishin' it."

"Be as rough as you like, Wyatt," she replied softly. "I'm all for rough. Anyway you want me."

He caught her hair in both fists and pushed her head toward his aching cock. He needed her mouth around him. Right. Now. Pepper gasped. Moaned. Writhed. He tightened his hold on her hair. Aching. Needing. Desperate.

"Damn it, woman, get your mouth on me right now." The command came out more of a growl. His cat reacted, wanting to hold her down, sink his teeth into her, force her submission once he had the control.

His fists tightened and he felt his blunt nails driving into his palm. His eyes opened and he found his hands holding nothing at all. He had a savage erection—his cock nearly bursting out of the front of his jeans, stretching the material beyond endurance, but there was no woman crawling over him.

Swearing in his native language, beads of sweat running down his body, he forced himself to roll to the side, away from her. He needed to get up. To take a cold shower. To stop the erotic images playing in his head like some crazy porn flick. It was only then that he became aware of her breathing, the rush from her lungs, the gasping pants.

"Oh, hell," he whispered softly, grateful they were surrounded by the dark. Either he'd shared his dream with her or she'd shared hers with him, but the results were the same—both bodies were in a desperate state of arousal. At least she had drugs to get her through. He could only grit his teeth and hang on.

Wyatt sat up slowly, carefully, making certain he didn't break any important parts. Very slowly he turned his head to look at her. He knew, before he did it, that it would be a mistake, but he couldn't resist the compulsion.

He didn't understand how she could look so beautiful to him when she had gone through so much. Her body had to be able to repair itself at a rapid rate. Ezekiel and Malichai as well as every other member of their team were able to heal quickly, but he'd never seen anything quite like the way Pepper's body fought against the venom. It was no wonder she hadn't been on a termination list. Her body would be a gold mine for a pharmaceutical company, or at least a secret weapon for the enhanced soldiers.

He leaned over and brushed back the wild strands of hair that had come out of her braid, just as he'd wanted to do all night. Her skin was warm and soft, her breathing rapid, breasts rising and falling. Beneath the thin material of her shirt, her nipples had peaked, pushing through the lace of her bra in response to her dream.

He'd sworn off women, and here he was, breaking his vow, because this particular woman interested him as no other ever had. He was going to get more than heartbreak if he insisted on pursuing her. Other men would covet her the moment she opened her mouth, or looked sideways at them. Worse, she was more than just that sexual lure—she had to be lethal.

Wyatt didn't care if the man overseeing the project was

someone named Thomas Braden. Pepper was one of Dr. Whitney's experiments, and that meant she was meant to be a soldier. She had killer instincts and the ability to kill silently and swiftly just like any other GhostWalker.

Her breathing calmed. So did her body. And that made him think he was the instigator of the dreams—not Pepper. That didn't make him happy. He'd always been sexual. Hell, every one of his brothers was as well. He was a true son of the bayou. Sultry nights and beautiful Cajun women just plain put such thoughts in a man's head.

"Don't." She said it softly, her tone drowsy from the painkiller. "Don't think about sex anymore. I'm having enough trouble with the bite this time."

"I'm sorry. You're . . . potent. I don' know what it is, woman, but you've got me tied up in knots." And harder than a damned rock. His sense of humor was beginning to kick in and that could be fatal. "Before we go any further in our relationship, you might tell me just what other weapons you have available to you besides sex. Just in case we should argue or somethin'." Deliberately he drawled the question.

Her eyelashes fluttered. Her mouth curved into a smile. "Our relationship? I'm not certain what that means, bayou man."

"That means you and me. Together. You've got that knife, and the men in our family are really fond of women who carry knives. Which reminds me, I forgot to return Nonny's to her. One of the guards at the laboratory stole it from her."

"That's why you were there?" This time her eyes actually opened and she looked at him. "To get your grandmother's knife back?"

He swept back her hair again, using his palm in order to feel her forehead. "That and to beat the livin' daylights outa Larry the guard. He shoved her. She's no spring chicken, although *never* tell her I said that. She'd take a switch to me just to show me she's still spry."

For the first time she actually smiled. "You really went

there to call out one of the guards? It had nothing to do with me or the babies? I knew it. Somehow I just knew that's what you were doing."

"Well, Grand-mere did mention the presence of the Rougarou in the swamp and told me she was keepin' the shotgun handy. I think she did expect me to take care of that as well, but seein' as how you and the little one turned out to be the swamp monsters, she'll be happy enough that I just gave the guard a beatin' and took her knife back."

"It was a serious beating," Pepper said. "You weren't kidding around, and I could tell you were going easy on him."

"So you were watchin' me all along," Wyatt said, giving her a grin that spoke volumes. "Likin' what you saw. You just had to come here and show me that knife, didn' you?" Before she could answer he frowned. "You and Nonny didn' cook this up together, did you? She's been wantin' a woman and babies outa us boys for a while now." He poured suspicion into his voice.

"Now that you say that, she did mention it a time or two that you were hopeless at finding a woman yourself and she was thinking of buying you one of those mail-order brides to help you along your way." Pepper delivered the revelation with a straight face. "We had a lot of time to talk while she was fixing up the bullet wounds."

"I wouldn' put it past her," Wyatt said, sobering instantly. "Don' you enter into any conspiracy with that woman. We'll end up married with ten or fifteen little ones runnin' around the bayou. If she had her way, this house would be filled with children."

"She has a good heart. She put out blankets and food when she could have turned the dogs loose on us like everyone else did."

"Best heart in the bayou," Wyatt agreed. "She called us home because she thought something was wrong at that compound. A few years back there was a mental institution on that land. Whitney owned it. He had one of his experiments housed there. I think the woman he kept there was supposed to be terminated, but she escaped and now is married to one of the GhostWalkers. The place burned down and the land was sold. I'll bet Whitney set up a dummy corporation and bought his own property back."

"I wish I'd known about her. I've never been outside other than on carefully supervised field trials."

"You're fast. Very fast. How could they contain you?"

She touched her throat with shaking fingers. "They have a shock collar—one that can put you down fast and hard. I could never figure a way to counteract it. And then after . . . there were the babies. I was introduced to them when I was labeled uncooperative. They broke my heart. Someone had to care about them and love them."

"Do they love you back?" Wyatt figured if those three little viper babies were going to be in his grandmother's home, or he had to handle them, he wanted to know if they were little serial killers in the making.

She nodded and winced, her breath catching in her throat.

He knew better than to touch her, but he did it anyway. This woman had a sense of humor, and that along with her knife was skating close to his dream woman. He smoothed back her hair, the pads of his fingers gliding over her forehead. He felt the touch all the way into his gut. "Is it bad again? Do you want another dose?" He glanced at his watch. "We slept for a couple of hours."

"No. You got me through the worst part. It's not too bad now. And they aren't serial killers. They're wonderful children who need love and guidance. It isn't their fault that someone cooked them up in a petri dish." There was definitely a defensive note in her voice.

"Don' go all commando on me, sugar," Wyatt cautioned. "You gettin' all bossy just turns me on, and right now there's not a damn thing either one of us can do about it. I'm just askin' questions here, tryin' to get a sense of how much danger Nonny might be in."

Those dark eyes searched his face. He felt the impact in the region of his cock, but that didn't surprise him much. Everything about her was felt in that region.

"The babies don't know anyone but me. Not like that. They've been used for experiments, not nurtured as they should be. There's only been me."

"That's why Ginger tried to bite me, she was tryin' to protect you, wasn't she?"

Pepper closed her eyes again, turning her face from him. "Yes. I'm the only one she has—the only one fighting to save them. She knows that. She's seen death. She knows it's permanent. She won't hurt your grandmother, Wyatt. She won't."

"I hope not. Ezekiel is sleepin' on the floor right outside her door. It would kill him to have to hurt a child. He's a roarin' tiger when it comes to readin' from the good book, but he's a softie for women and children."

"He's scary," Pepper said, her voice back to a thread of sound.

"I'm scary, and you're here with me."

A slow smile curved her mouth. "Is that what you are? I was trying to figure it out."

Damn. Humor and a knife.

CHAPTER 5

$\sim$

Wyatt sensed movement. Danger. He didn't move, but he knew he wasn't alone. The danger was in the room with them—and he'd locked the door. Pepper appeared to be sleeping. He'd given her a second dose of painkillers when her body had cramped up again, every muscle locking up and fighting to shut her down. The fluids and painkiller had helped immediately, but she'd slept through it and that had worried him a little. Clearly her body wasn't used to any kind of drug.

He waited, his body relaxed, his breathing even. Patience was a hunter's weapon, and he had learned that from a very early age. At the end of the bed, the sheet bunched near his feet. He felt a slight weight ease onto the mattress. He knew immediately what had come into the room so quietly.

"Good mornin', Ginger," he said softly, keeping his voice low and using his ability to soothe shamelessly. "Did you come to see Pepper?"

He opened his eyes and slowly sat up, keeping his movements slow and nonthreatening. The child looked as if she'd been crying for hours. She didn't look at all dangerous. She looked like a normal human seventeen-month-old baby who needed comfort. He could see how that would be a problem. Her eyes were large and very dark, but now were ringed with red. His instinct was to gather her up and cuddle her, but he didn't want to startle or frighten her—knowing she could so easily inflict a lethal bite on him. Those little tiny baby teeth were going to be introduced to caps as soon as possible.

"Pepper is fine. Do you see how peacefully she's sleepin'?" He shifted his weight, easing his legs out from under the covers. It was far better to be safe than sorry. He needed to be able to move fast if he had to. He didn't want the baby to get the wrong idea, and she was looking over the fluids going into Pepper's arm.

"She hurt last night. Her muscles cramped hard, so she needed fluids to help that go away." He was counting on the fact that Pepper had said the child was extremely intelligent. Her too-old eyes told him the same thing, although she still looked like a baby to him, a very upset baby.

"Do you understand what I'm tellin' you, Ginger? Pepper is fine. You made a mistake, but it's all right now. She isn' goin' to die."

The little girl's eyes welled with tears and his heart clenched. He could never be the father of girls. They'd break his heart. He needed rough-and-tumble boys. That he could work with.

"Are you hungry? Do you need to be changed?" He felt like a fool asking her questions. She might be the smartest baby in the world and understand every word he said, but she couldn't talk yet. Maybe a few words, but she was still mostly human and that meant even intelligent babies didn't have a huge vocabulary of words they could actually say—understand maybe—but not pronounce.

Ginger lifted her hands and made a couple of gestures, clearly conveying something to him.

He frowned and leaned toward her. "Do you sign? Is that how you communicate with Pepper and the others? With your two sisters?"

The little girl nodded her head several times, her gaze clinging to his. He had time to study her face. She was beautiful, her little face oval with high cheekbones and large, very dark eyes. Her lashes were black along with her wavy dark hair. He thought her hair might be thicker than normal for a baby her age, but her hands and feet were very small.

"I'm not the best at signin'. My brothers and I used to sign when we were kids and didn' want Nonny to know what we were plottin'." He took a breath. "Which of course was *very* bad on our parts and we'd never do such a thing now."

The baby smiled at him. For the first time he allowed himself to relax a little. She didn't look as if she'd go all viper on him and strike out with those tiny little teeth that he already found quite charming in her.

She signed with her fingers. She had to do it three times before he caught what she was saying.

His heart clenched again. He shook his head. "No, baby, why would I want to kill you? I don' want you dead. You're safe here with Nonny and me. And we'll keep Pepper safe too. Ezekiel and Malichai will help me get your sisters free if we can. As long as you're in my home, I'll make certain no one hurts you."

He tried to sign as many words as he could remember, even as he said them aloud to her. He was going to have to build a seriously lethal arsenal and get his home secure.

Don't mislead her.

Pepper lay quite still listening to the sound of Wyatt's soothing voice. She loved his drawl. The slow easy charm. The smile in his voice. His cool confidence. She'd never come across a man like him, not in all the men she'd met in training. She wasn't supposed to feel attraction to the actual man. He was supposed to feel attraction to her. She had a sex drive to end all sex drives, but it was only that—being in heat. She detested her body most of the time, especially around men. She didn't want them to find her attractive. That only made it much more difficult to keep her resolution.

Until Wyatt. She had lain in the bed with him and breathed him into her lungs. She'd touched his soft, wavy black hair and her heart had nearly melted in her chest. Every time he spoke, whether it was in a low soothing voice he was using now, or his sexy, commanding one, she felt slick heat gathering between her legs. His voice also wrapped around her heart and became the thing of all her fantasies.

Still, she couldn't allow him to charm Ginger into thinking he would stick around with his voice and his ability to make a child—or a woman—think they weren't alone in the world. She couldn't allow that to happen.

Don't tell her something that isn't true. She's been lied to her entire life.

Wyatt turned his head to look into Pepper's violet eyes. There was no diamond starburst, only pain. His gut knotted. He didn't like his woman being in pain. He might tell himself different, but he was going to claim her whether or not it made sense.

Pepper's voice slid in his mind, warm honey pouring into every empty, broken crack, filling him with warmth, with the knowledge that he wasn't alone. His body reacted, coming alive, every cell humming, but not necessarily in a sexual way. Pepper was definitely stronger. He could feel the difference in her.

I'm not. Nonny would never allow us to leave two small babies in a place like that. This house is safe for them. We're GhostWalkers. Maybe you haven' heard the term, but we're like you, no matter whether or not you think you're the only flawed one. We're all flawed, Pepper. Clearly you haven' been around any of us.

We have to keep moving. It's the only safe thing to do. These children can't go to a school, or be around other children until they learn discipline.

There was no note of hope in her voice, but still, he felt it through their connection, probably a remnant of hope she didn't even recognize she felt. She'd been utterly alone for a very long time with an overwhelming responsibility. The three children couldn't be let loose on the world, not when they were teething. Not when they truly didn't understand consequences.

First, that's your trainin' talkin', sayin' you got to keep movin'. They'll expect that, he pointed out.

That's the problem with the babies. They do understand, but they don't have the discipline to stop themselves when they feel threatened. Pepper replied to his thoughts, not his words.

It wasn't the first time she had responded to something in his mind—and he had a lot on his mind. Wyatt couldn't help worrying about keeping the babies in his home, not that he was concerned they'd hurt Nonny. Very few creatures in the bayou would harm her. She had the "gift," a miracle she'd passed down to her grandsons. Still, he had brothers and neighbors to think about, yet where else could they go?

In the bayou they could play and learn and have freedom to grow and thrive. They couldn't be in a city or a place where neighbors were too close. They'd been engineered as soldiers with soldier's instincts. Their games were bound to be . . . dangerous. Who better to raise them than Pepper and the GhostWalkers right there in the bayou? It all made perfect sense to him.

Moving them constantly won' give them the security they need to feel, Pepper. You know that. If we clean out the hornet's nest, which we're goin' to do no matter what, then the bayou will be safe for them. That's my job. To make all of you safe.

Pepper's heart fluttered. A small shiver crept down her spine. Such simplicity. Wyatt spoke as if he meant every word, and she was connected to him. In his mind. She could feel his resolution. As much as it terrified her to rely on or trust another human being, she knew this one wasn't lying to her. She was there. In his head.

She was so tired of trying to figure out how to keep the children safe by herself. There were three of them. Most of the time she was just trying to stay alive with them. She didn't know family. She didn't do family. Wyatt was all about family. She couldn't stop looking at his face as he interacted with Ginger.

He was beautiful. Truly beautiful. His bone structure. His dark, beautiful eyes surrounded by long lashes. All that thick, wavy hair. He was the most sensual man she'd ever seen, and she'd seen a lot of men. Her world had been mainly men. Very few women were brought in to work at the school or in the field with them.

She had the urge to sink her fingers into his hair and put her mouth to his—that mouth she couldn't stop thinking about. For once in her life, she wanted to be kissed by someone who saw her. Saw past her looks and all the enhancements Braden had made to make her so alluring. She wanted to be seen. She had a feeling Wyatt Fontenot saw her.

Wyatt turned his attention back to the child. Ginger watched his face intently and then switched her gaze to Pepper, as if she knew they had been communicating telepathically. He knew there was always energy pushed into the air when there was any kind of movement, and psychic movement felt different. Most GhostWalkers knew when another used it.

He hadn't felt energy coming off Pepper or the child. He was uncertain which of them, or maybe it was both of them, could shield their energy from other soldiers like he could. He held out his arms when he realized the baby was nervous.

"Come here, Ginger. Sit right between us. You can touch Pepper gently and give her a kiss if you want to. That will make her feel so much better. Can I look at your arm and make sure it's healing properly?" The sight of her little arm bandaged sickened him.

Wyatt looked down at Pepper's face, wanting to read her expression when the little girl came close. There was no fear at all, only love. Her eyes glowed softly, and her smile was warm. She looked almost transformed. He thought she was beautiful from the moment he'd laid eyes on her, but now, in spite of the harrowing night, her face, as she looked at the child, was more beautiful than ever.

She might as well have given birth to Ginger. She couldn't have loved her any more than a birth mother. He knew the baby had been born to a surrogate, a woman who had carried the mixed cocktail for Whitney or Braden, whichever had ordered the experiment, but when he studied Pepper's face and Ginger's, his mind tricked him into seeing similarities.

This child really was conceived in a test tube?

It was difficult to think that even from birth Ginger had never had a parent who cared. It was even worse to go all the way back to when she was first conceived, realizing she didn't have two people who loved her coming together. That knowledge somehow made him feel as if a monster in a lab from a horror movie had thrown ingredients together to concoct her.

Yes. Pepper reached out with one hand, sliding it along the bed until she caught Ginger's fingers in her own.

Wyatt's heart performed a curious somersault in his chest when he saw the tiny little fingers curling around Pepper's. The hand was so small and perfect lying in Pepper's palm. His heart actually ached. That was the healer side of him, that sentimental idiot who had believed in happy-ever-after endings.

He didn't want to feel that way about these two females.

He wanted to see them as nothing but problems—preferably someone else's. He couldn't get over the resemblance between Ginger and Pepper. Ginger's hair was dark and wavy, a baby's hair. She had a small dimple that appeared occasionally on the right side of her mouth. Pepper didn't, but her mouth was Pepper's mouth. They had the same high cheekbones and oval face. He looked into her dark eyes, so dark, yet he could see the beginnings of a faint amber ring, surrounding the darkness, much like Pepper's eyes.

Wyatt continued to stare down at them, his mind suddenly putting pieces together. Pepper had an immunity to cobra bites. Cobras couldn't kill one another. She'd said the doctors were trying to build her immunity to snakebites and develop an antivenom that could be used for the soldiers. She hadn't specified which snakebite though. She was already immune to the cobra bite. It had been the viper venom that had made her so ill.

"She's your daughter," he said aloud.

Pepper frowned at him. "I consider her my daughter, but I've never given birth, which is required for what I think you're talking about. I'd claim her if she was mine."

He shook his head. "Not if they used your eggs, which, believe me, honey, if Whitney is involved, he collects such things from anythin' or anyone GhostWalker."

Wyatt couldn't keep the note of bitterness out of his voice. He'd been deceived when he'd gone into the program. Whitney was supposed to have been long gone, on the run, a man wanted by the military to answer for the crimes he'd committed. That wasn't exactly the case. Someone high up was protecting him and aiding him in his experiments. Whitney still worked for the government, he was just far more covert.

Pepper studied Ginger's face, the little hands and the mop of hair. There was no horror on her face, if anything, she examined the baby with a hint of eagerness. "Maybe a little. It would be absolutely wonderful, a miracle, if that were the case, because I intend to take care of all three of them, to be their mother. They need one. But you might take another good look at her, Wyatt. She looks more like you than she does me."

Wyatt stared down at the child.

"Not to mention, you're the genius," Pepper pointed out.

His eyebrow shot up. "And you're not? I guess babies all look alike." He shrugged. "Does she need to be changed?"

"She uses the bathroom like a big girl. She'll sign like this." Pepper closed her fist and shook it. "If you give her a little step, she can make it on her own."

"How did she break into the room when it was locked?" Wyatt asked.

"All three acquired the skill of picking locks at a very early age."

He laughed and teased one of the waves on Ginger's hair into a corkscrew curl. "We did that too, when we were little. All of us. Gator was the instigator. He taught us, I think. I don' really remember, but Nonny said we were barely walkin' when we started gettin' into trouble."

He kept his mind as blank as possible, which took a tremendous amount of discipline considering the thoughts running through his head. He could feel Pepper's pain beating at him. She was worried too, probably about the other two babies left behind in the laboratory. He found it strange that they were still so connected that without merging his mind or using telepathic communication, he could feel her emotions—and if he could feel hers, did that mean she could feel his?

He used telepathic communication with the other Ghost-Walkers often, and never once had he been able to feel their emotions—he could guess, maybe, but not actually feel them. His body ached everywhere. His muscles and joints screamed at him and always, in the back of his mind was the pressing worry that they were running out of time. That was all Pepper—not him.

The last thing he wanted at that moment was for her to catch one single thought swirling around in his brain. He kept his expression as pleasant and calm as possible. He was a doctor and a GhostWalker. He could be stone if needed.

"You need more painkillers this mornin', Pepper," he said.

She shook her head. "I have to have a clear mind. I need to get on my feet."

"No, you need to stay right where you are. I'm the doctor, remember? Ginger can look after you while I help Nonny with breakfast, and then you can give us a detailed layout of the laboratory along with how many guards and where they are. You must have studied their routine."

She nodded. "We were sent here about two months ago. I snuck out a lot and studied the bayou and swamp. I knew what that place was the moment I entered it. I knew I didn't have much time to get the children out of there."

"I'll go help Nonny with the food. Ginger, I'm countin' on you to watch her. She needs to rest. I won' be long." He had something important to do. Very important. Because he was a smart man who'd done a very stupid thing, and he had the feeling others were suffering the consequences.

Pepper reached out and caught his hand, moving faster than he would have expected, knowing the pain running through every muscle in her body. The moment her skin touched his, he felt the shiver run through her body. The same electrical current rushed through his veins.

"What is it, Wyatt?"

"Nothin' at all, honey. You just rest." He tugged until she let go of him. He had to check. When he got feelings, strong ones, he was rarely wrong, and the feeling was strong enough to put knots in his belly.

He slipped out of the bedroom and hurried down the hall to the staircase leading up to his grandmother's room. The pictures were there, lining the wall. He took the stairs slowly, studying each photograph of himself. With each stair he climbed, he grew younger, until he found himself face-to-face with a little boy not more than a year and a half. His hair was dark and wavy, a thick pelt that refused to be tamed. Dark eyes stared back at him, and right there on his right cheek was that tiny little dimple he'd noticed on Ginger.

His stomach lurched. The baby picture could have been of Ginger. They looked identical. The child wasn't Pepper's; she was his. Whitney had used him to father a child—not one, but three. Something terrible had gone wrong with his experiment and he'd sent the children to the bayou—straight to Wyatt's backyard. Why? What was the man up to? This was no coincidence.

Nonny knew. She probably had known the moment she laid eyes on the child. She'd been insistent that she was safe with the baby and that she wouldn't allow Wyatt to keep Ginger from her. He should have known right then that something wasn't right. It was unlike Nonny to fight him over something they both knew wasn't safe.

He sank down slowly onto the stair and scrubbed his hand over his face. That baby—that little viper—was his daughter. *His.* He didn't need a paternity test to tell him the truth. Hell. The picture on the wall might as well have been of her.

"Wyatt?" Nonny sat down beside him right there at the top of the stairs. She gestured toward the picture. "You know then."

"You saw it right away, didn' you, Grand-mere?"

She put her hand on his shoulder. "I don' know what's goin' on, how that child came to be like she is, or where she came from, but she's a Fontenot. There's no denyin' it."

"There's two more, Nonny, at that laboratory, and they plan on killin' them because they're dangerous."

She sucked in her breath and gripped his arm. "But you aren' gonna let that happen, right, Wyatt?"

He shook his head. "I wasn' about to let it happen before

I knew they were mine." He straightened his shoulders and made himself look into those old, beloved eyes. "I'm sorry, Nonny, for bein' so damned stupid. Gator told me about the program he'd joined and, of course, we both know what Whitney did to Flame, givin' her cancer an all, so I should have known better than to join too."

"You joined because the three of you boys always followed Gator's lead," Nonny said, her voice matter-of-fact. "If he did somethin', you boys were sure you could do it as well. Never did mind what it was or iffin it was good for you."

Wyatt closed his eyes briefly. It didn't much matter how he'd gotten himself into trouble—it was already done. Three children had been created without his permission or knowledge, but they were still children—and there wasn't a doubt in his mind they were his. Not Pepper's or his other brothers'. *His.*

"The woman, Pepper," Nonny said. "The baby looks like her too, something in her eyes. Do you suppose she's the mother?"

He shrugged, rolling his shoulders as if he could shrug away the entire mess. "I have no idea. She thinks and acts like their mother, but she's like me. If she's the biological mother, she wasn't told. I think the resemblance is there, but maybe I didn't want to see the resemblance to me."

"My breakfast is goin' to burn. Malichai is tendin' to it. He says he knows his way around a kitchen, but I wasn' so certain. The first thin' he did was grab my apron and put it on. Then he sorta stood there in the center of the room and turned in circles." She gave a little Fontenot smirk. "I done asked him if it was some kinda ritual he did before he started his work."

"And he said?" Wyatt prompted.

Nonny laughed softly. "He said, yes ma'am, jist as purty as you please. I snapped the tea towel at him."

Wyatt winced on Malichai's behalf. Nonny was hell on wheels with a tea towel. He'd been a recipient more than once of that snapping bite. She was accurate and deadly with the weapon and could raise a welt if she desired.

"That boy done said he had a gun on him, so I gave him a little taste of what it was like to threaten his helpless *grand-mere*."

There it was. The reason he was the luckiest man on Earth, no matter what was happening. He had Nonny. He'd always had her. He had his family. His brothers. They'd come a running if he called for them. Wyatt began to laugh with her. The idea of his petite grandmother chasing Malichai around the kitchen with her tea towel was just too funny.

"Helpless, Nonny? You're a holy terror."

"Let's eat, son. We'll figure the rest out on a full stomach."

Wyatt stood and reached down to help his grandmother up. He hugged her close, inhaling the scent of fresh food that always signaled home to him. "Let's go rescue breakfast, Nonny. I'm surprised you left Malichai alone with the food. There won't be much left if we don' go rescue it."

She hugged him back hard and then turned and rushed down the stairs, raising her voice. "Malichai Fortunes, don' you be eatin' before we sit down and give thanks to the good Lord."

"I was tasting, not eating," Malichai called back. "Do you have eyes in the back of your head, Grand-mere? Every cook has got to taste his food."

"If you did the cookin' I might believe you, boy, but I did the cookin' and you keep doin' the tastin'."

Ezekiel stood just inside the kitchen laughing as Nonny chased Malichai out of the room with her tea towel. "I'm sorry about my brother's manners, ma'am. He was raised a heathen, and I suppose there's no changing him."

"I'll cut me a switch out of that tree in the backyard," Nonny threatened. "Ezekiel, you did good with the boy. He just loves his food a little too much."

Malichai swept his arm around Nonny, sneaking up on her from behind. "Is there really such a thing as loving food too much, Grand-mere? Especially when you're the one who did the cooking?"

He kissed her on the cheek. "Watching you cook is a thing of beauty."

"I'll admit that's true," Wyatt said. He picked up the food warmers and took them to the table.

"Wyatt, bring down the wooden high chair from the attic. It's right in front covered with an old sheet. Ginger will need it," Nonny instructed.

"I need to check on Pepper. Ezekiel, do you mind getting the chair?" Wyatt cleared his throat. "While you're at it, take a good look at the photograph on the wall at the top of the stairs."

Ezekiel sent him a sharp look. "I looked last night."

Wyatt let out his breath. He hadn't even realized he'd been holding it. His gaze shifted to Malichai. Of course Ezekiel would share information with his brother. He read knowledge in Malichai's eyes.

"Puts a whole different light on things," Malichai said. "We'll get those kids out of there, Wyatt."

"Thanks." He felt humble.

He was more than lucky to have such good friends, who knew they'd be risking their lives, but didn't hesitate. And Nonny; who had a grandmother who wouldn't hesitate to accept children who had lethal bites? He would have to consider how to minimize the risk to her. He couldn't overlook the fact that an accidental bite from one of the babies could kill. He definitely would have to cap their teeth as an interim solution.

And what the hell was Whitney's end game? There had to be one. This was no coincidence. Had the attack on his grandmother been orchestrated in order for her to call one of her sons home? Had Whitney known all his brothers were out of the country? That was a possibility, but how could he know Wyatt and the others were wounded? He couldn't have orchestrated that event. Or could he have? It was odd that his team had been ambushed the way they had. Could Whitney have been behind that?

What had Pepper said? She'd arrived at the laboratory two months earlier with the three children. *Two months.* Why had they waited two full months before issuing termination orders on the babies?

He stalked back to the bedroom. He could hear the baby laughing as she blew strawberries against Pepper's neck. The moment he stepped into the room, he felt the love Pepper surrounded the child with. He also felt pain beating at her. Leaning one hip against the doorjamb, he studied the two of them. He knew they were aware of his presence. How could they not be? They were both GhostWalkers.

"Ginger, I hope you're hungry," he greeted softly. "Nonny has fixed breakfast and it looks wonderful. Go on into the kitchen and eat. I'll be right in. Nonny will help you."

The child looked at Pepper. He couldn't feel the shift in energy, but they definitely communicated with one another. Ginger slipped off the bed and hurried out of the room, running on her little bare feet. He'd wanted to get a good look at her feet and made a mental note to examine them soon.

"When were the orders to terminate the children given?"

"About three weeks ago." Pepper turned her head to look up at him. "Why?"

Wyatt sighed. He didn't know this woman. Could she be part of a conspiracy? She looked innocent enough. Beguiling was more like it. She'd already admitted to him she was made to be a seductress for Whitney.

"Where were you and the children before you came here?"

"In France. At a laboratory in France."

"Yet you speak excellent English. Your accent is flawless."

"I speak several languages." Pepper struggled into a sitting position, clenching her teeth when pain beat at her. "Why? What's wrong?"

He felt the same pain, a blow to his system, and had to breathe deep until he could accept and absorb it as she was doing. He steeled himself to interrogate her. He had to be certain before he put his team and his family in danger.

"What's wrong is this all seems like an enormous coincidence to me. When did you first meet the children?"

She frowned at him and lifted a hand to push back the stray tendrils of hair tumbling around her face. The action lifted her breasts, immediately drawing attention to her body. He detested that his body reacted to her. That made him suspicious as well. He was a doctor, and he had both control and discipline. He'd never had a problem looking at female patients in his life. Not ever. Not once. Until Pepper.

Now, all of a sudden, he couldn't get this woman out of his mind. He wanted to keep her. Make her his own. *Keep* her. Make it permanent. Hell. What was wrong with him? The driving need seemed to be so strong, he felt primitive when he was around her. Caveman primitive. He'd always been dominant, but he had never been jealous, not even of Joy when he stupidly and mistakenly thought he was in love with her. But this one . . . Pepper. He didn't want his own friends coming near her.

"I think they were born in the same laboratory where I was kept. I was put in charge of caring for them when they were about three months old. I didn't mind. I didn't have a family, and I loved spending time with them. I was told when their teeth came in they might be dangerous but that I was immune to the venom." She pressed her lips together and shook her head. "They neglected to tell me all three babies carried both types of venom and I wasn't yet immune to viper venom."

"And that's what they were trying to do with you? Create an antidote to either of the two types of snakebites? A universal donor, so to speak."

She nodded slowly, her strange eyes moving over his face. "Yes. Without causing so many allergic reactions.

But then suddenly, after my fight with Braden, we were told we were being moved."

"*Right* after?"

She wasn't lying to him. He knew the truth when he heard it. Every small nuance of her voice, every tone, every breathy sound, connected to him.

"No. It was a few weeks later. Suddenly. Almost out of the blue. We boarded a private jet. The company, Wilson Plastics, has their own corporate jet. They flew us to a military base and then brought us here. That was just over two months ago."

"And yet they didn't issue termination orders until a couple of weeks ago."

She nodded again, her gaze never leaving his face. "That's correct, although I knew what that place was. I didn't know why suddenly they would want to get rid of us. I actually thought it was me they were going to terminate. I wasn't cooperating with them. They wanted to use me to assassinate someone and I refused."

"Who?"

"A sergeant major in the Marine Corps. He's a good man, at least when I did some research on him, he appeared to be. He's married, and they told me it would be difficult to get him to have an affair with me. They could get me in to work in his office, and I was to take it from there."

"Which sergeant major?"

"His name was Sergeant Major Theodore Griffen."

Wyatt stiffened. Sergeant Major Theodore Griffen ran one of the GhostWalker teams. He sighed and shook his head. "Why would they allow you to research this man if they knew you had scruples? Why not just send you off, spinnin' a story about how he's sellin' out his country?"

"I don't know." At his piercing look she shook her head. "I swear to you, I don't know."

"Did you know those three children are my children?" He watched her face carefully. If she had known, she was a damned good actress. Her face was a total mask of shock. "This mornin', right on that bed, you casually said Ginger looked more like me than you."

"Yes, but that's because you asked if she was mine. You said she looked like me and I just pointed out that she looked like both of us . . ." She trailed off, inhaling deeply. Her face went pale, more than pale; stark white.

Pepper felt her heart go crazy. Hammering. Hard. Her lungs burned, refused to draw in air properly. He stood over her, intimidating when men didn't intimidate her. Tempting when men didn't tempt her. Beautiful when men shouldn't be beautiful, and he was telling her the three little girls she loved so dearly could very well be their children. His. Hers. Theirs. A tidal wave rolled over her stomach and she shook her head.

"I don't understand. Why would they create children in a laboratory and then have me watch them if I'm their biological mother? Why not just tell me? I love them as if they're mine, but when you said Ginger looked like me, I have to admit, I had a few suspicions over the last year, but then I just . . ." She broke off, reaching for the needle in her arm. "I have to get up."

She had to do something. Anything. Not lie here like a lump while the world around her shifted yet again. She was tired of being exhausted and afraid. She needed to find some kind of balance, and nothing was making sense. Nothing at all. She could only blame her sluggish mind on the snake venom and her own raging hormones. Wyatt Fontenot was messing with her mind. He had to be.

He moved fast, pinning her hand, preventing her from removing the needle. At the touch of his hand on her bare skin, little tongues of fire flickered over her. The breath hissed out of her and her gaze jumped to his face.

"Don' be touchin' that, honey."

"Don't tell me what to do," she snapped, and felt childish for lashing out at him when it was only because she was beginning to panic.

"Get used to it. I'm like that. Bossy. I like things my way. Right now, the number one priority is to get those children out of that prison. To do that, I need you to be one hundred percent healthy. I know they're mine. I believe you're their biological mother, but I *know* they're mine and I'm not leavin' them there. You're goin' with me to get them."

She stared into his eyes, her heart beating fast. Even being a dominating jerk he was horribly handsome. She really detested that she was so drawn to him. If she wasn't, she could be in complete control of him in two seconds flat, but she didn't dare go that route with him. She would lose. She knew she could seduce him, that wouldn't be a problem, but she would lose. "You think I'm setting you up for them, don't you?"

"It crossed my mind. If you are, know this: I have three brothers and some powerful friends. They'll hunt you down, and eventually they'll find you and they'll kill you if you're a part of this and something happens to me. It won' matter how fast you are, or how lethal you can be. They'll get the job done."

"A part of what?" Pepper struggled not to cry, forcing back the burning tears. She didn't so much as whimper. Her lips didn't even tremble. She struggled to understand what he was conveying to her. She was intelligent. She was quick. But she just wasn't getting this. "Are you saying those three babies who have been through hell already are being used for some purpose? That they were given termination orders to draw you into this?"

She searched his face, trying to get past the masculine perfection and her attraction to him to see if he really believed what he said.

"Whitney knows our family. He knows we know just about everythin' happenin' in the bayou. The moment those men touched Grand-mere, he knew one of us would be comin' to read those men from the good book. Almost three weeks ago, I was in a firefight and was shot. We were ambushed, called to a location on a rescue mission that wasn't that at all. It was a setup. They attacked us, and our chopper went down. We had to fight our way out of there."

"Where were you?" The thought of him in a firefight, his helicopter going down left her weak. Shocked. Frightened.

"That doesn't matter. The point of this is, I was wounded and had leave comin'. Nonny suddenly contacted me and told me what happened to her."

"So you think because you were wounded and Nonny happened to call you home that this is some scheme, an elaborate setup. Do you have any idea what it would take to orchestrate something this complicated? To make all the pieces come together?" Pepper said. "Now you're just being paranoid."

It would take a brilliant man who loved games. Games like chess where people are being used as pawns.

She heard it. Or she thought it. She didn't know what came first, but his hand was still burning a brand through her skin straight to her bones, and all of a sudden his stupid conspiracy theory was actually beginning to make sense and that scared her all the more.

"Really?" Wyatt straightened up, taking a step back from the bed to lean against the wall. "Not when you think about it. He used my sperm and I suspect your eggs and enhanced them in vitro. They were planted in surrogates there in France where they had you in their little laboratory. He gave the babies to you to ensure a bond. He knew your maternal instincts would kick in and that, because you're highly intelligent, you might even figure it out."

"But I didn't," Pepper denied.

"Yes, you did. You know you did. You suspected they were yours, and you let yourself love them because you couldn' help yourself. You played right into his hands, not that any normal person could have resisted three innocent babies. He waits for the right moment, and believe me, Dr. Peter Whitney is a master at creatin' right moments."

"I told you, he was there only a couple of times. It was Dr. Thomas Braden who was in charge of the laboratory there in France." She didn't want any of it to be true. If it was true . . . she was in far more trouble than she could ever handle alone. How could she possibly keep her daughters safe from such a madman?

"It doesn' matter who was in charge. Whitney can' possibly be in ten places at the same time. He has to have men who run the various laboratories for him. Others have to conduct the experiments. He has a network now, a large one, but it's Whitney at the helm, and this is classic Whitney."

"What is *this*?" Pepper demanded, feeling like her head might explode. She raised both hands and covered her ears as if that could drown him out. "Because I still don't understand."

She didn't want to understand. If she understood the actual scope of the forces against her, she might give up and she had three little girls depending on her. She felt terrified and exposed. Vulnerable. Never ever show that to the enemy. That had been drilled into her.

"Sugar." Wyatt caught both her wrists in a gentle but unbreakable grip and pulled her fists to his chest.

Sugar. That was all he said. It was the way he said it. Soft. Whispery. Into her. *Sugar.* Who would ever want to be called sugar? It was bad enough that her name was Pepper. But Sugar? She couldn't believe she melted inside when he said it, but she did.

"You always forget to breathe, baby. This is just a fact. Nothin' huge goin' on here. Nothin' we can' figure out together and beat. A little over four months ago I received orders to go to Afghanistan. It was my third tour, so I didn't think anythin' about it. We're usually sent into the hottest zones because we're enhanced. We always run the night rescues. The last one resulted in taking heavy fire. No one should have known we were comin'. No one. We knew they had to have been tipped off."

She was horrified. The thing was, she didn't know if she was horrified at the thought of Whitney betraying soldiers that way, or by her reaction to the thought of Wyatt in such danger. Her entire body rebelled at the idea, and what did that mean? If he kept holding her hands against his chest, they were both going to be in trouble. Snakebite, IV and gunshot wound aside.

She licked her lips and forced herself to try to carry on a conversation while subtly pulling at her wrists. "This Whitney would work against the United States for the enemy? Do you really think he has the power to know your orders and to get word to the enemy that you were in the vicinity?"

Wyatt acted like he didn't even notice she was in a small struggle with him for possession of her hands. She sighed and gave up, curling her fingers into his shirt. Into that heated rock wall. She felt the definition of his muscles behind the thin material and it did things to her body she hadn't expected.

Wyatt smiled down at her, a cocky, masculine grin that might have meant he knew he wasn't only curling her fingers but also her toes.

"Absolutely he does. He's still workin' for the government, or some covert branch of it. We can' uncover who has his back. We chop off one head and two more seem to grow. I was wounded. Several of us were, and around that time, probably the moment Whitney heard we were safe and back in the States, he issued a termination order on the babies so you'd grab them and escape. The timin' is just too coincidental for me to stomach. He brought you here, created a reason for you to escape and a reason for me to come home."

She closed her eyes briefly. He was making sense. She

was so screwed. How could she fight alone against a man who could set up an ambush of a rescue helicopter in Afghanistan? The thought was absolutely, utterly, terrifying.

"How could he know your grandmother would go out to harvest plants at the precise time the sirens went off?"

"Why did they go off? Were you spotted?"

She shook her head. "I heard the sirens and rushed to the laboratory hoping the other two babies had made their escape. I wanted to help them."

"So all he did was wait for Grand-mere to go to the swamp to harvest and then he set off the alarms. His idiot guards did the rest for him, and she called me just like she knew he would. The question is, why did he do this? Is there a trap inside that laboratory waitin' for me?"

His thumb slid over the pulse beating rapidly in her wrist. The brush alone sent her pulse rate up and blood rushing through her body. If he thought to check if she was lying that way, he would never get an accurate reading.

CHAPTER 6

Wyatt looked around the table at the two men and his grandmother, the people who would be most affected, other than Pepper, with his decision to try to get the other two babies out of the laboratory. Ginger sat in the hand-carved high chair that had been his, the only thing left of his grandfather's, before the man had passed away leaving his wife to care for the four young boys alone.

"I'm lucky to have all of you," he said. "But we have to be realistic. Ginger, honey, I'm goin' to talk in front of you, and hope you can understand most of what I say."

"Wait." Pepper staggered into the room, her skin covered in tiny beads of sweat. "I'm not going to miss this."

She carried the bag of fluids with her. Clearly she'd been to the bathroom already. She'd tried to tidy herself up, but she looked as if she might fall over any moment. Wyatt had felt her determination, and several bursts of pain, but he hadn't realized she'd gotten out of bed—and he should have. She just didn't seem to give off the GhostWalker energy—or she was very adept at shielding herself.

He was immediately aware of her. Of everything about her. And he knew both Ezekiel and Malichai were as well. It was impossible not to notice how her clothes clung to every curve, how her skin looked petal soft and her beautiful eyes held pain she was desperately trying to cover up. She looked small and fragile, very vulnerable, and his every instinct rose to protect her.

Before either of the other two men could go to her aid, he was on his feet, gliding to her with purposeful steps, his body language not so subtly warning the others off. He swept his arm around her waist possessively, pulling her into his body, taking most of her weight. She trembled. Her eyes met his. The impact hit him with a low, wicked punch.

This isn' a good idea, he whispered softly into her mind. His grin said he didn't give a damn whether it was or not, he was glad to have her there pressed close to him.

I know. I'm sorry, but I need to hear.

He acknowledged to himself that he would have been the same. Whether or not the children were hers biologically, she'd been their only mother and she loved them. She had the right to hear what he had to say.

"Zeke, would you mind gettin' a more comfortable chair from the parlor? Stick it in the corner there where I can hang this bag for her." He didn't take his gaze from hers. He let her see he was devouring her. Savoring. Keeping her.

She blinked rapidly and glanced down to his arm, rubbing her hand over the tattoos there.

If Ginger doesn' understand and wants to, sign for her as best you can. I want her to know I want her here and so does Nonny.

Pepper scowled at him with a quick shake of her head. *You can't take her away from me. That's not right.*

Who said I was? Pipe down for a minute and think logically. You can' handle all three of them alone as they're growin' and you know it, nor can you run with three

babies in tow. Seriously, woman, you're enough to make a
man crazy. I'm keepin' them and I'm keepin' you.

But . . .

You're in my world now, babe. Go with the flow.

He lowered her into the chair, fussed over the bag of
fluids and examined the catheter in her arm. He knew he
was touching her skin because he had to feel it against his
own, not because he was being any kind of healer. He
should have felt guilty, but all he felt were the sensations
pouring into his mind and body. Whatever she was, he felt
as if she had been made for him.

His ridiculous infatuation with Joy had been so childish, a teenager's dream and later, a knight in shining armor
rushing to the rescue. He hadn't seen her for what she was.
Joy had wanted money, a handsome husband and the bright
lights of the city. She wanted a glamorous singing career,
and there was nothing at all wrong with that. Unfortunately she still looked to a man to get her out of the bayou,
even after all that had happened to her. She didn't believe
Wyatt was that man—and she'd been right.

Joy didn't need or want him. She didn't see him for who
he was or love him for it. He had known love growing up
and he wanted a woman who would stand with him through
anything. Anything at all. Even protecting three little vipers
from anything or anyone who would harm them.

That woman was sitting in a chair, snake bit, shot, muscles still cramping painfully and yet determined as hell to
listen in on how they were going to rescue her children.
And she had a knife. He knew because he felt it right there
at her waist when he pulled her close to him.

Reluctantly he went back to his chair, aware Ezekiel
and Malichai both were grinning from ear to ear. He pre-
ferred their knowing grins to their drooling over his
woman.

"I could get her a blanket so you could tuck that around
her," Malichai offered. He hastily bent his head toward his

plate when Nonny fixed him with a stern eye, but he didn't bother to hide his grin.

Wyatt might have risen to the bait, but his grandmother looked as if she'd had enough, and Pepper looked as if she might faint from the pain. He found her pain actually made him feel sick, so he pushed his plate away from him and leaned back in his chair.

"We're goin' to get the children out. I know I'm their father. Nonny knows it too. I can feel it. They took somethin' from me without my consent, and now I've got three little ones to look after. I take bein' a father very seriously."

Ginger's eyes were wide. She looked from him to Pepper and signed frantically. He waited while Pepper did her best to explain to a baby genius just how such a thing could be true.

"There will be some problems and we're goin' to have to prepare for them. We'll need to have things ready for them before they get here. We'll also need better security before we tip our hand and go after them. Pepper thinks they're safe for the moment, but they're babies and they have to be terrified. I want to beef this place up fast."

Ezekiel nodded. "We'll need a few others to get the work done. We'll need weapons and bunkers and a safe room."

"We have to childproof the house," Nonny added practically.

"They're good at escaping," Pepper said.

There was instant silence in the room. Wyatt glanced uneasily at his friends. Ezekiel sat up straighter, his gaze leaping to Pepper's face at the sound of her voice. That soft, silken glide that moved under a man's skin. Malichai looked shell-shocked.

"Darlin'." Wyatt pinned her with his dark gaze. "Don' talk. I'm lettin' you stay because you got the right to hear, but don' waste your energy or you'll find your pretty little butt right back in bed. You hearin' me?"

Her eyelashes fluttered. Her lips parted in protest but no

sound emerged. He was fairly certain it was because she was too outraged to speak so he sent her another, much more charming smile.

I don't understand you.

She sounded so lost he wanted to pull her into his arms and hold her close to him. *I know, sugar, but right now you don' have to. You just have to concentrate on gettin' better. I want to know you understand and you'll just relax right there. You got somethin' to say, say it private to me.*

Pepper moistened her lips with the tip of her tongue, and Malichai groaned. Wyatt set his teeth to keep from swearing.

You're killin' me, baby. Just don' move. Don' speak. You're still not able to block your voice and I don' want to have to kill a friend. So don' open your mouth unless it's askin' me to kiss you. You hearin' me? Say it. To me. You're hearin' me.

Pepper swallowed hard, glanced at Malichai and Ezekiel. Color crept up her pale skin into her cheeks. She nodded.

Say. It. To. Me. He bit the command out, enunciating each word.

Her gaze flicked back to him. *I'm hearing you.*

"If they're good at escapin', we'll have to make certain they understand the danger. Pepper, right now, is the only one they trust. Ginger"—he smiled at his daughter—"you can help us with this. When we bring your sisters home, you have to help us make them understand they'll still be in danger, but not from us. Can you do that?"

Ginger looked to Pepper, who signed to the baby. Wyatt was fascinated by the expression on Pepper's face as she looked at the little girl. Her eyes, a strange, deep almost purple, had gone soft and warm. The diamond burst bled into the purple, giving off a look of radiant love. He'd seen women look at their children with love, but there was something intense and focused, as if the child was everything to her.

He touched her mind very gently, wanting to feel what she felt for the child. All encompassing. Real. He went soft inside. How could he not? Pepper didn't have a family until the babies were given to her. She'd known nothing about children, but like any good soldier on a mission, she had researched as much as she could to be the best she could without practical experience.

And she loved. She knew how to love. Little vipers. Little tiny lethal baby vipers who bit her and made her suffer. She loved them anyway.

Hell, woman. You belong in the bayou. Right here.

Pepper glanced at him again, her dark midnight eyes meeting his. His body stirred, went rock hard. He was grateful the table was large.

Ginger nodded her head vigorously indicating she would help with her sisters, making them understand they would still be in danger and couldn't escape.

"If anyone comes after them, we'll need to be prepared. I think he'll send his elite soldiers Pepper referred to, or try to take us there in the laboratory. This could be a trap. In fact, there's a good chance this is a trap. No one has to go with me. This is my responsibility."

Ezekiel kept eating. So did Malichai.

"Really good breakfast, ma'am," Malichai said eventually into the silence. "I might be worried about gaining weight if I didn't have all these missions to run. Keeping blockheads alive gives me a mighty hunger."

Wyatt had known they'd go with him. They were a team, but more than that, they were family now. "I'll have to call in a couple of the others as well," he added reluctantly.

"Trap," Malichai said immediately. "And Draden."

"Mordichai," Ezekiel added.

"He's babysitting Joe," Malichai reported, chewing and

swallowing so he could shovel more food into his mouth. "But he'll come as soon as Joe's clear."

He needed to lay it out. Pepper was not going to like it, but he had no choice, not if he was being fair to the others. "I know we need them, but Pepper's enhanced."

She made a sound. At once she curled into herself, her eyes jumping to his face. She gave a quick shake of her head. He could see the hurt in her eyes.

Wyatt stood up and caught his chair, dragging it around the table to set it next to hers. He sank into it and wrapped his arm around her. *It has to be done. We have to work as a team in order to get them out. You know that. There's no shame in what or who you are, Pepper, but these men are my friends and they're riskin' their lives for us.*

He took her hand and brought it to his mouth. She was still tense. Shivering. A little shocked, but she nodded.

"She was meant for seduction and assassination. She can' help who she is any more than we can. She's learnin' to tone it down and tryin' to shield everyone from her voice and her . . . uh . . . movements, but it's a process. She's one of us, and she'll need a little help from us. And she's mine. Exclusively. The mother of my children. I won' be happy if anyone else tries makin' a move on her."

"Yeah, Wyatt," Ezekiel said. "I think we got that about you and her."

Pepper frowned, looking puzzled. She opened her mouth to speak.

Don'. Don' say a word right now. I'm protectin' you and them the only way I know how. Just let me do this and we can sort the rest out later.

Her gaze clung to his. Studied him. She nodded. She really had no other choice but to trust him. She needed him.

What happens when I don't need to be rescued anymore, Wyatt?

She struck a target with that question. Just as he was in her mind, she was in his. He didn't give a damn and that was the truth. His dark gaze drifted over her, deliberately possessive. He brought her wrist to his mouth and slid his tongue over her pulse, felt her shiver and watched her eyes go an even darker purple.

Somthin' tells, me, sugar, you're always goin' to be gettin' yourself into trouble and I'll always have to go rushin' to your rescue. You got trouble stamped all over you, woman. Any man can see that a mile out.

He winked at her, and turned his attention back to the table. "So you understand the problem if we bring in more men."

"We'll help her," Ezekiel said. "So will they. If she's yours, she's ours."

Ginger had been watching carefully, and she signed to Ezekiel. Wyatt felt a lump rise in his throat. Ginger signed she belonged to Wyatt too and did that mean she was theirs as well.

Ezekiel nodded his head. "You bet, little lady."

Ginger laughed with delight. Evidently Ezekiel had the right answer.

"We'll need much more security to guard all three children and Pepper." Pepper. He had no idea what he was going to do about her, but she came with the package.

I'm not part of any package, she hissed into his mind.

He winced. He so deserved that. *Sure you are, sugar. You're the hot part of the package, all spicy and exotic. Lookin' forward to tastin' that.*

Her eyes went wide. Shocked. He grinned at her and prevented her from tugging her hand away from him.

"The number one thing we have to do is figure out how to make certain anyone who plans to be around the children is immune to their bites."

Ginger frantically signed again, her gaze jumping from one to the other.

"I know none of you want to bite, baby," Wyatt said gently. "But sometimes accidents happen. Pepper was very sick last night. She's still in pain. Those bites would kill Nonny, or possibly one of us. It's important we prepare for an accident just in case. No one thinks you would ever do something like that deliberately."

Tears welled up in Ginger's eyes. Nonny instantly got up and took the child from the high chair to cuddle her on her lap.

"There, there, little one, everythin' is goin' to be all right now. Your *pere* will take care of those bad men and you'll never have to be around them again."

The child signed. Wyatt tightened his hand around Pepper's. The floor shivered. Ginger's little fingers had said quite clearly, *They hurt me. They hurt my sisters and Pepper.*

"I'm sorry, baby," Wyatt said. "I didn' know about you or I would have come for you sooner. We'll get the others out and we'll protect you."

Ginger signed, *When?*

"You'll have to be patient. We have to know we can protect you and keep them from takin' you back. That means preparation, but it won' be for a few more days." Her face dropped, and he couldn't stand it. "As soon as possible, I promise, Ginger."

"For a temporary measure, we can try caps on their teeth. I'll have to study them to see how the venom is delivered. When we go for the children, I'll hit their computers and take as many files as possible to give us a jump-start. Trap is amazin' in a lab. He'll figure it out even if I can'. The problem is, everythin' we do is invasive to a degree. They've been studied enough."

Pepper hissed out a soft protest.

"It's for their protection. We have to develop an antivenom that will work for anyone in the household." Wyatt looked Pepper straight in the eyes. He had to brace himself. He'd been there before, floating through the night sky with her. "Were they successful when they tried making the antivenom from your blood? Did they test it?"

Is this a test? You said not to talk out loud.

He felt laughter start in his groin first. It traveled up to his belly. The woman knew how to start a fire. She had sass. *I'll let it go this time.*

Her fingernails dug into his palm, but he held on, pressing her hand to his thigh. She ignored him and refused to struggle in front of the others, something he noted for future reference.

Pepper cleared her voice and tried hard. The problem was, even in a conversation like the one they were having, her voice came out slow and husky, a whisper of temptation. It didn't matter what she said, her voice twisted its way into a man's gut.

"They tested the antivenom several times. Those bitten were far sicker than me, and all of them died but one. The idea was to build soldiers up, to give them small doses over time so that they had a natural immunity to both types of venom."

"Different snakes in the same families still require different strains of antivenom, don't they?" Ezekiel asked. He avoided looking at her. Instead, he concentrated hard on the tabletop. "I thought it mattered what type of snake bit you."

"Yes, that's true," Wyatt said.

"But," Pepper explained, "the idea was to make me a universal donor, so that any of the soldiers, no matter what type bit them, would be covered."

Malichai had a mouthful of food and chewed it slowly, his eyes studiously avoiding Pepper's face. "Might want to try to tone it down, Pepper," he muttered. "I'm sitting at Grand-mere's table and wouldn't want to embarrass myself and then have Wyatt stab me through the heart with that knife he's got his fist around."

Pepper's gaze dropped to Wyatt's *other* hand—the hand that wasn't pressing her palm tight into his thigh. Sure enough, his fist really was wrapped around the hilt of a knife. She forgot all about the way her hand felt sandwiched between his thigh and palm. Burning. Hot. Now her cheeks were. Something heavy took hold of her heart and squeezed.

She gasped. "Oh, no. I'm sorry. I shouldn't be here. I can't control . . ." How absolutely utterly humiliating. Even Grand-mere would see what she was. "I told you I was a reject," she admitted in a low voice.

"Stop that," Wyatt ordered. "I mean it, Pepper. Don' you ever call yourself that again, and certainly not in front of one of the children. We all have to fight our natures, guard against natural instincts. Do you think it's easy for any one of us?"

"We're in this together," Ezekiel reminded. "We're a team, and we help one another. You need a reminder, we'll give it to you. Wyatt has to work on pushing down his instinct to shield you. I have to keep from hunting prey. Malichai has to work on . . . well . . . *everything*." He sent her a little grin.

He's right, honey. They're tryin' to help you. You're not flawed. Nothin's wrong with you. All of us have to keep on workin' to overcome some of the instincts and character- istics we don' want to show in polite, civilized company.

She didn't know what to do so she held very still. His voice could mesmerize her. The drawling sound of him could send flames racing through her body. That had never happened and truly, he had to be nearly as lethal as she was when it came to seduction.

Wyatt leaned close. *When we're away from polite, civi- lized company, I have no problem with anythin' you might want to do or practice. I'm a willin' participant in all your exercises.*

He made her want to laugh even at the worst of moments. She didn't know whether to believe that these men would include her in their camaraderie. She'd spent over ten years with several of the same teachers and guards and none of them had ever teased her or made her feel as if she was part of something.

Don' you cry. You'll break my heart, little darlin'. I'm serious here, woman. Blink until they go away. Ezekiel and Malichai want to help. We're a team. We can do this together, just the way we're goin' to raise those three little girls together.

How could she not cry? They didn't know her and yet they seemed so willing to accept her.

Malichai can' be too enamored, either that or you're losin' your touch. He's shovelin' food in faster than Grand-mere can make it.

She knew he was trying to save her, to make her laugh. His hand slid over hers, pressing harder. He leaned toward her, his lips against her ear, although he spoke telepathically, not aloud.

You've got this, Pepper. We're in it together. Just relax and go with the flow. I'll deal with it. They'll deal with it. If you cry, I'm goin' to pick you up and carry you back to bed. That will get us both in trouble eventually.

She'd never had anyone care whether or not she cried. She could feel his distress. It rolled off of him in waves. He detested that she was upset. She knew Wyatt Fontenot was a danger to her in ways she'd never even considered. Her heart could be in jeopardy and that was unacceptable—wasn't it?

Pepper glanced at Nonny. She didn't know anyone else she might be able to talk to about things she didn't understand. She was highly educated, but in this situation, she was educated in all the wrong things.

Wyatt threaded his fingers through hers and brought her hand to his mouth. The warmth of his breath sent a shudder through her body. He actually drove pain back for a moment with that simple movement. She was beginning to think he was the one trained in seduction.

She nodded her head. *I'm all right, but fading fast. Let's keep going.* She needed the distraction. Not from the pain, but from his presence. She'd never been in a setting like this one. She could feel the camaraderie surrounding her—the good will in the room. All three men and Nonny helped with Ginger's food, cutting it into small pieces and feeding her with a small spoon, almost without thinking.

Their kindness to the child was automatic. Several times Ezekiel brought a glass of warm milk to Ginger's lips and held it for her, talking quietly to her, encouraging her in learning to drink from a cup rather than a bottle. Wyatt reached out with a napkin and just as gently wiped her lips free of her milk mustache.

The sight of these men, so big and rough, being so caring and gentle to a baby—one that hadn't known any love or consideration other than from her—melted Pepper's heart. She wanted to draw her knees up and just watch them all. It was better than any movie she'd ever seen, which wasn't difficult. She'd only seen training films, including techniques on sex. None were about family or caring or love. She didn't know a thing about those topics, but she knew she was witnessing it right there.

Wyatt brought Pepper's hand to his mouth again, biting gently on the tips of her fingers to distract her from her thoughts. He could feel her confusion and knew tears were burning close. He had no real idea why it upset him so much that she felt the need to cry, that she didn't understand that all of them were flawed in some way. It wasn't only Pepper. She had to get over the notion that she wasn't as good as they were.

"Pepper, were they givin' you other venom as well?" Wyatt asked, keeping her knuckles against his mouth. "From various other snakes?"

She nodded. "I'm capable of killing just the way the children are, which is why the cobra venom doesn't affect me. The idea was to seduce the male and inject the snake venom and leave. No one would ever suspect I had anything to do with the death."

Wyatt ignored the fact that Ezekiel and Malichai both looked up from their dinner and then exchanged a long glance with each other. Pepper had obviously made an effort to tamp down the seductive quality of her voice, but it was almost physically impossible to do. Her voice was her own. When she spoke aloud, everything she said sounded like an invitation to hot sex.

"That doesn't make sense, Pepper," Wyatt said. "You can't possibly have been in vitro with a cocktail of snake."

"In vitro has been around since the first test tube baby was born in the late 1970s," Pepper pointed out.

"But not genetic altering. That's rather new and advanced. What are you, twenty-two, twenty-three?"

"Twenty-three. I trained with five other girls as a soldier from as far back as I can remember. I didn't have parents. Whether Braden created me or picked me up off the street, I have no idea, it's difficult to believe anything he said, but all of us were flown to various countries to learn how to survive in hostile terrain. We also went to school daily, no matter where we were, to continue our educations. I excelled in languages, but all the girls had to learn the same things."

Wyatt had to set his teeth against the temptation of her voice. He studiously avoided looking at his friends, hoping time might dull the impact. He had one hell of a hard-on and didn't want to know if they were struggling with the same effect.

He'd been right all along about a woman like Pepper. Sexy. Hot. Trouble with a capital "T." He had always known he was a Cajun through and through. He lived hard, loved hard, worked hard and played hard. When he fucked up, he did it royally, such as joining Whitney's GhostWalkers, although truthfully, he was beginning to think maybe he wasn't going to regret his decision so much. Why? Her beautiful ass was parked in his kitchen chair and one of his beautiful little viper daughters was laughing with Nonny at his kitchen table. What more could a man ask for?

His passions were intense, his temper, his love, his protective instincts, his jealousy. The thing was, none of those traits had been engaged until Pepper. He'd never been jealous around Joy and other men and that should have told him something right there. His brother Gator spent a great deal of time with his teeth clenched when his woman was in a bar with him. Wyatt should have known that was just part of their nature. Living and loving hard meant skating the edge of control or just plain losing it sometimes.

I'm sorry, Wyatt. I'm trying.

That voice spread through him like warm honey. *So worth it, sugar. You're doin' fine. Just keep tonin' it down. You'll get there. Everythin' takes practice.*

Malichai cleared his throat. "Did you always have a lethal bite?"

Pepper glanced at Wyatt. He tightened his hand around hers to give her courage. He was grateful he'd connected the two of them somehow when he'd attempted to psychically heal her. He could feel fear and confusion beating at her, although he couldn't see it on her face. She didn't want to do anything to upset the balance in the room and she was feeling her way.

He found the fact that she knew nothing about family or friendship yet had taken on three children and was desperately feeling her way right now, trying to do everything right when she had no road map, absolutely valiant. His heart contracted and he pressed her hand to his chest, right over it.

Pepper took a breath and shook her head. "I don't think so. At least, to my knowledge, I never killed anyone by biting them, not as a child. We were training in India and I was bitten by a snake, a cobra. I was fifteen at the time. I got very, very sick. We were out in the country. They brought in a helicopter, and that's the last time I ever saw the other girls I trained with. I was taken back to France, but held in a different area, away from my unit."

That had been much better. She spoke a little slower, almost drawling, but it helped to alter her natural tone enough to take the sensual edge off a little. He smiled at her and nodded to let her know her technique worked.

"Were you treated for the bite?" he asked gently.

Now they had everyone's undivided attention. Both Malichai and Ezekiel propped their heads on their hands, elbows on the table, staring at her in some shock. Wyatt didn't warn them that they were in danger of Nonny's fork, although she was listening with rapt attention as well.

"I don't know. I don't remember very much. But I was operated on three times after that. All three times I was very ill. For weeks the first time."

"What are you thinkin', Wyatt?" Nonny asked. "Your first thought."

"It's preposterous," Wyatt answered slowly. "Totally impossible. Do you know your country of origin? Is it possible Whitney found you in India?"

Pepper frowned at him. "Yes. But Braden told me I couldn't possibly be a native even though I was supposedly in an orphanage there. He speculated that my parents were living there and either died in an accident or from some sickness."

"Do you have any scars from your childhood? Unexplained scars?" Wyatt persisted.

His mind began to race with the impossible. If Whitney had found her in India, he wouldn't have bothered with her unless she had psychic ability. Ezekiel could control reptiles—a very rare gift. Nonny did to a lesser extent, as did Wyatt. But it was rare to be like them. As far as he knew no other GhostWalker had that gift.

Pepper might have been abandoned, as female children often were, especially if she came from parents not of Indian descent and was an orphan. Most likely she'd been found in the areas where deforestation had taken place, displacing snakes. If she had the ability to control snakes, as a child, would she have tried to play with them? Would she have been bitten? If she had, he doubted if the snake would release much of its venom into her, not with her gift. Was it possible that over time she'd developed an immunity to snakes on her own?

Pepper nodded. "I had several scars, but they were removed when I was a teenager."

It was all coming together in his mind, just like it did when he was on the path to finding answers in his own lab. "Can you control a snake with your mind?"

Ezekiel swung his head toward Wyatt and then back toward Pepper, waiting for an answer. Wyatt knew that Ezekiel had spent the night outside his grandmother's bedroom, and that he'd whispered to Ginger telepathically each time he heard her wake.

It was no wonder Pepper had been put in charge of the three babies. Wyatt already knew the answer to his question. Pepper definitely could control snakes.

"Yes," Pepper admitted, her voice so low it was almost impossible to catch.

"It's all makin' sense now," Wyatt said. "You were the inspiration behind his great plan."

"You keep saying 'him.' You mean Dr. Whitney. I never saw Dr. Whitney when I was young. Only Braden. Whitney came later, after the children were born." Pepper frowned in concentration. "I see where you're going with this, but even if I was bitten repeatedly as a child and built up enough of the venom in my system, wouldn't I have to keep getting bit for the toxins to remain at high enough levels in my system to do any good? And could my liver handle that?"

"Some of the best snake handlers gave themselves venom daily and it worked to keep them alive," Wyatt pointed out. "A few used diluted venom and others used pure venom."

"But they would have had to have daily injections," Pepper pointed out.

"What if your body, as a child, adapted to the venom?" Wyatt said. "We're always adaptin'. If one or both of your parents handled snakes, specifically cobras or kraits, and were bitten repeatedly . . ." He trailed off, his mind moving fast.

"Wait a minute," Malichai interrupted. "Are you saying she could have been born already immune to a cobra bite? That her parents passed that to her?"

"I think it's possible. If she was born with receptors that have one difference from ours, the bulky sugar coatin', she might have been able to survive a bite as a child." He also thought it possible that Whitney had discovered her when her parents were alive and he'd made her an orphan so he could have her. That would have been just like him.

Pepper was intelligent, she understood exactly what they were talking about, and if her parents were prominent in the field of herpetology, they could have come to Whitney's attention. He would have considered Pepper extraordinary. She was intelligent, gifted and possibly an answer to a universal antivenom.

"Why doesn't a viper bite cause necrosis of the skin? Even the most careful and famous of snake handlers have lost fingers," Malichai asked her.

"That's a good question," Ezekiel agreed.

"What do you do when you're bitten by one of the babies, Pepper? We'll all need to know, especially Nonny," Wyatt said.

Pepper frowned, thinking it over. "My response feels automatic so I have to actually go through the steps I take right now in my mind. I know what's coming the moment I've been bitten. I slow my heart, cool my body temperature and flood the bite site with as much oxygen and cold as possible."

Wyatt nodded. "That's how she keeps the site from necrosis. She fills the tissues surroundin' the bite with oxygen while she lowers the body temperature around the site." His eyes met Pepper's. "I'll need a sample of your blood. Maybe I can figure out what's not quite right about the mixture they gave you."

"I'm still pretty sick."

"From the viper venom, not the cobra venom. And when I tried to heal you, I could see how fast your body absorbed the venom to neutralize it. You're healin' fast, faster than I ever expected, but still, a soldier won' have a bed and fluids and painkillers to get him through, out in the field. But, any GhostWalker can control their body to the point of lowering body temperature and . . ."

"Now you're beginnin' to sound like a mad scientist, Wyatt," Nonny reprimanded. "What's all this nonsense anyway? I want you and the boys to go get my great-grandbabies. Now, Wyatt. They're all alone in that horrible place."

CHAPTER 7

———————⟳———————

Wyatt took a breath before he answered his grandmother. When she asked for something—anything at all—his tendency was to get it for her immediately. She was everything to him and his brothers. She was home. She was family. He knew why she felt such an urge to go get the other two little babies out of that hellhole, but he also knew someone would come after them and he had to be prepared. Already, they were at risk because they'd taken in Pepper and Ginger.

"Nonny, we can't rush off and just grab the other two babies without some kind of plan in place to protect them and all of us. Someone is goin' to come lookin' for them," Wyatt objected. "We also need to know anyone around them is safe from accidental bites. I want the children out as fast as you do, but we'll need help."

"Call Flame," Nonny said. "She'll come a runnin' and she loves children. You know how she longs for children."

"No." Wyatt stared his grandmother down. "Absolutely not. Don' even think about callin' her. She'd come in a second, yes, but she's Gator's entire world. He wouldn't survive without her and you know that. He nearly lost her once and I'm not about to take any chances with her, not until I know she'll be safe."

"She would be a huge help even with the rescue," Nonny said. "And her feelin's might be hurt if you didn' call her."

"Maybe," Wyatt conceded, "but I never had a sister until Flame came along. We're *not* chancin' it, Nonny. It's bad enough takin' chances with your life. If somethin' happened to you, I'd never forgive myself."

"Don' you go a thinkin' you're gonna be bossin' me around, Wyatt Fontenot. I'm not leavin' my own house. I can see it in your eyes. You're a thinkin' you'll send me away too, but these are my great-grandchildren and I'm goin' to help them."

He knew his grandmother and how stubborn she was. He also knew that all the years she'd spent in the swamps and bayous, running free as a child and hunting game and flowers and herbs, she'd never once been bitten. Not a single time. Like all of them, she'd encountered her share of venomous snakes, but they'd left her alone. Of all of them, Nonny might actually be the safest.

"So what do you want us to do, Wyatt?" Ezekiel, ever the practical, asked.

"Let's get the house set up for all three babies. We'll need cribs and blankets and high chairs." Wyatt turned to Pepper. "Do they drink milk, or formula?"

"All of them drink milk and they prefer it warm."

"How soon before you're on your feet?" he asked.

"Another day. Two if I need to fight."

"So we'll need at least two days before we can go in, Nonny. At least that. We need to build a fortress here, and I have to set up my lab and get the house prepared. We've got a lot to do." He pressed Pepper's hand closer to his chest. "Are you certain they'll be safe, that no one will decide it's best to terminate them?"

He no longer believed that was the goal. Whitney liked to play games. He liked to experiment, but he would never risk losing Pepper and the three little girls, not when they were clearly so important to him. Wyatt's mind began to fill in the puzzle pieces. Whitney wanted him to know the girls were his daughters. He wanted him to break into the secure facility to remove them from harm. He might even be planning to throw all kinds of things at them to see how far they would go to protect their venomous children.

Pepper stirred, drawing his gaze. Her eyes met his, the brilliant starburst of diamonds showing through the nearly purple, midnight sky. "Has it occurred to you that none of his scientists could figure out how to make the antivenom in my body work for anyone else? And that he expects you'll have to do it. That you'll have to find a way to make the children less lethal? And when you do . . ."

"He'll come after them again."

Pepper was getting tired. He could tell by her voice—the soft, sultry note had crept back in. He didn't reprimand or remind her. He set his teeth and endured it, not looking at Ezekiel or Malichai, hoping they could see how worn out she was.

"The minute you said you needed my blood, I knew you were more than a soldier. You really are a genius, aren't you? Both you and Nonny, and along with that, you're chemists and deal with toxins all the time."

Wyatt nodded slowly. "The swamp has many plants that cure and take away pain, but it also has plants that can kill in minutes."

Pepper made a small sound in the back of her throat, her large eyes on him. Fringed with impossibly long feathery lashes, her eyes pulled at him. They were filled with fear, and this time she didn't try to hide it.

"You're risking your life, Wyatt. Whoever this man is, he's after you."

Wyatt shook his head slowly, once more bringing her

hand to his mouth. He nibbled on her fingers for a brief moment, holding her gaze, enjoying the fact that she was worried about him. "No, he's too cold to make anythin' personal, babe. He's all about science. I'm all about *famille*. He just *thinks* I'm all about science."

He had a full lab in the garage. He'd had one since he was a child, experimenting with the various plant extracts in order to perfect the drugs for the people in the bayou that couldn't afford medical care. Maybe all along he was using the things Joy had said to him as his excuse for joining the GhostWalkers, when it really was the science. Whitney would certainly see it that way.

Dr. Peter Whitney didn't understand families, and he'd never be able to understand a family like Wyatt's. His grandmother had sacrificed everything, including an education, to take care of her parents. She had taken on the four boys when their mother and father had died in an accident. She'd done so instantly and without a thought to what it would cost her. She gave herself selflessly to the people in the bayou, helping the older ones who couldn't hunt or fish by bringing them food and clothing. And her pharmaceutical field was magnificent.

In Whitney's eyes, Nonny was uneducated and backwoods. That's what he saw when he looked at her, not any of the rest of it. Wyatt doubted if the man even knew the boys got their high IQs from their grandmother.

"We've got only a few days to pull the house together, childproof it and put in extra security. I don' want to leave the children there any longer than I have to." He shot a glance at his grandmother, wanting her to understand. "I'm goin' to call in a couple more of my friends. They'll help build up our security and the lab. Once I sort out a way to ensure if someone is accidentally bit that we can minimize the damage to them, I'll call Flame and ask her to help." He made that concession to his grandmother.

The truth was, his brother's wife would be a huge help.

Flame could get in and out of places few others could. But she was his brother's world and he'd nearly lost her to cancer. Whitney had repeatedly given Flame cancer. She was one of his throwaways.

Wyatt loved her as if she'd been born into the family. It broke his heart that she couldn't have children and he knew she would love nothing more than to help them, but he wasn't going to risk her no matter what Grand-mere or Flame said.

"Let's get to work," Ezekiel said. "Ma'am?" At Nonny's sharp glance he cleared his throat and tried again. "Grand-mere, do you mind if I go exploring in your attic? If the high chair was up there, we might find a crib or two. I'm handy with tools and if they need repairing, I can do it."

"I'll go up with you, Ezekiel," Nonny offered. "It would be nice to bring life back to some of the things I've cherished in my lifetime."

Wyatt finally turned his head and looked at Ginger. He'd been avoiding her gaze throughout the conversation. He didn't know the first thing about babies, but something told him this one was very sensitive. "Ginger, I know you're sick of people pokin' and proddin' you, but I'd like to take a look in your mouth and take a few samples of your saliva."

The child turned her head to look at Pepper, her little fingers signing.

Pepper signed back, reassuring her. "Her saliva isn't venomous, as one would think it would be. The doctors in the first lab were shocked by that. If she were made like a snake, she would be secreting the venom in her saliva."

Wyatt frowned. "That's interestin'." He caught Pepper's look. "Don' be thinkin' I'm goin' to turn my daughter into a guinea pig. She isn' a test tube for me. I'll need to study her to see how I can keep others safe and maybe reduce the risks to her as well. However, I will be askin' you to help me out quite a bit. You know what the danger is in havin' three baby vipers around."

"Don't call them that." Pepper glared at him.

He grinned at her, unrepentant. "It was said with affection, woman. Get a sense of humor. You're goin' to need one around my *Cadien famille*."

He didn't take his gaze from hers, feeling her through their connection, the slow, smoldering burn that was more sexual than angry. She was fighting her attraction to him, and he'd already decided they weren't going to fight it, they were going to go with it. She just hadn't caught up yet.

Havin' a hard time keepin' your hands off me, aren' you? Must be the famous Fontenot charm at work.

A faint smile curved her mouth into a woman's secret weapon. She could take his breath away without half trying. Images of her mouth wrapped around his cock rose up fast and hot, her hair spilling around him, brushing his bare skin. The image was so vivid he could actually feel the sensations.

He blew out his breath and stretched his legs out in front of him to give himself some relief from the instant tight agony of urgent need.

Is that what you call it? Fontenot charm? I don't think so, bayou man. I think you're used to getting your way with the women and you don't have to try very hard.

He had to get up, just for a minute, ease away from her just enough to function. She would be addictive. He already knew that and was past caring. He would crave her every day, every minute, but he had all the confidence in the world that he could make her feel *exactly* the same way.

When he'd managed to breathe away most of his hard-on, he winked at her and got up to pour himself a cup of coffee. He was just going to have to get used to the idea of walking around semihard all the time. It wasn't a bad way to live, at least he knew he was alive.

He held up the coffee cup. *Hot. Just the way I like it.*

She rolled her eyes at him.

"If you two are finished making googly eyes at each

other," Malichai said, pushing himself away from the table, "I'll do the dishes and get the kitchen clean while Grand-mere and Ezekiel go up to the attic."

"Pepper, you should lie down for a while," Nonny said with a small, telling glance at Wyatt. "I don' think we have toys for the baby, but maybe she could play on your bed for a bit."

"She wouldn't know what a toy was," Pepper said. "They don't have the babies playing. Not like you mean. Everything they're exposed to is to educate them. They're learning six languages as well as sign language. It's crazy the accelerated program they're on."

Nonny's eyebrows shot up. "Surely they had playtime for them."

Pepper shook her head. "Braden even had a martial arts instructor come in and start working with them. Everything they've been shown on the television has been instructional videos on hand-to-hand combat, weapons, or things like mathematics, of course the beginnings, but they know the alphabet or characters of all the languages and at night, not only are they read to, but the words, as they're being read, are up on a screen."

"That's not right." Wyatt glared at her as if she'd been the one to make the decision to give the babies only educational material. "What's wrong with a little fun while they're learnin'?"

He was asking her questions, but she *had* to stop using that soft, sultry, I'm-so-ready-for-bed voice. It didn't help to think of her in bed—his bed. He stood across the room from her, just looking at her. Beautiful. A work of art. She was as perfect as a woman could get with her face and flawless body, with her brain and her courage. And the knife he knew she had on her right now.

Pepper frowned. "It wasn't my decision. I was raised pretty much the same way. It definitely made me a good soldier, but when I got out into the real world, I had no idea what people were talking about. I didn't know the movies they referred to or the characters in cartoons. I didn't know fairy tales or anything but history and what Braden considered appropriate literature that would further my education. The lack of that made me feel socially awkward. I don't fit in anywhere."

Wyatt went very still. He felt a flash of her pain, of hurt—not physical, but a kind of anguish at the knowledge that she was different and would never be normal. She would never fit in anywhere. She felt absolutely alone, a terrible, almost emptiness that had been filled for a moment when Wyatt had poured himself into her. For that moment, she had felt whole. Content. Even happy.

He had been caught up in the way *he* felt. The sexual tension building between them. Fitting her into his family. Keeping her from tempting his friends so he wouldn't be a fool and do something he'd regret. All about him. He hadn't stopped to consider what she felt, trapped in his home, her child claimed by a man she didn't know or trust. She was biding her time—waiting until she was at full strength before she made her move to leave.

He went to her, ignoring the others, and gently helped her to stand. Handing her the nearly empty bag of fluids, he lifted her into his arms. "I'm not goin' to hurt you, Pepper," he murmured softly, needing to give her reassurance even more than she needed to hear it. He couldn't bear for her to feel afraid, or lonely or a misfit.

She pressed her lips together tightly and gave a little shake of her head. She knew what he meant.

"Look at me, baby. I want to see your eyes. I want you to look into mine." He waited there, cradling her close to his chest. When she finally complied, very reluctantly, he held her gaze captive with his. "I'm not goin' to hurt you, woman."

She blinked back the tears that were suddenly swimming in her eyes, making the color more purple than black. The sight turned him soft inside.

"You can't know that, Wyatt," she whispered. "You don't even trust me."

He carried her through the house back to his bedroom. "I don' know you—yet. But I intend to, after all, you're the mother of my children. I think we owe it to them to get to know one another, don' you? We'll need to know each other so well that we'll be able to read each other's every move. We'll have to be that close. I don' think we have a choice."

She leaned her head back against his shoulder, her eyes searching his. "Why? Why do you say that?"

"We'll be the ones protectin' them from men like Whitney and Braden. Who else is goin' to do it? You know how dangerous and determined the men we're dealing with are. It will take both of us. Maybe others as well, but we'll do it." He injected absolute confidence into his voice.

"Are you really going to help me take care of the children?"

He deposited her gently back on the bed, carefully laying her down on his grandmother's homespun sheets. "Yes. I believe I'm their father and you're their mother. They trust you. If they see you interactin' with me, they'll accept me more readily. The only person I really worry about is Nonny. She's not so young anymore, and even if I were to manage to develop an antivenom, I would be afraid to use it on her."

Pepper frowned. "There's something about Nonny I can't explain. It's a feeling I get when I'm close to her. I know Ginger feels it too. It's the same way we both feel when Ezekiel is close."

Wyatt scowled at her, a dark shadow moving through him. "What the hell does that mean? Exactly how does Ezekiel make you feel?"

"It isn't how he makes *me* feel. It's how *he* feels to both of us. He has this energy of sheer calm. It's very soothing and not a threat or a food source. I can't explain it any better than that." Pepper's gaze searched his face. "You don't have to be jealous, Wyatt. You give off that same soothing energy. Ginger would never have tried to bite you, but she thought you were a threat to me."

"I am jealous, darlin'," he admitted. He wanted her to know how dangerous it would be with her tempting other men. "You need to get it into your head right now, that there isn' goin' to be any other man for you. You aren' goin' to be usin' your charms to seduce my friends or anyone else to get your way. You look to me if you've got an itch. I'll take care of you."

"How lovely. How does that make you different from any of the others?"

He swept back her hair, his hands framing her face. "I am different. I'm offerin' you a family. A man who will work a lifetime to make you happy. To make us work. I'll keep you happy in bed and out of it. But I'm no pushover. You're not goin' to be able to use sex to get your way."

Her lashes fluttered, a sign, he was coming to know, that her temper was rising. "I do not use sex to get my way. Why do you think they threw me away?"

Her voice, if anything, had gone softer. It found its way right under his skin and stroked his cock into a very hard demand.

"I know they created me with the idea of seducing the enemy, getting close to him with seduction, but I didn't cooperate and I've never been remotely interested in a man." *Until I came across you.*

He heard the words distinctly in his mind, only they weren't words, he actually caught her thought. She blinked, veiling her expression with long lashes.

He frowned at her. He didn't know what he wanted from her, but she seemed absolutely guileless in that moment. He usually knew lies when he heard them, and

Pepper sounded honest. Puzzled. Confused. Joy had never been honest with him. He'd left his home and gotten himself into a mess because he'd been wrapped up in thinking he loved a woman. That wasn't going to happen again. She wasn't going to run his life, that much he wasn't confused about.

He stroked a finger down Pepper's face, feeling her soft skin beneath the pads of his finger. Sex with Pepper was bound to be off the charts. He could already taste the passion in his mouth.

Pepper jerked her head away. "I'm sorry you caught that. It wasn't a green light. You did connect us in some way and I can read you just as easily as you do me. I'm not looking for anyone to be my children's father."

Her voice sank into him. All heat. "I *am* their father, little darlin', whether you like it or not."

"I meant you don't have to do this because you think you can seduce me. I don't want that from you. Just because I don't have a last name, and I'm a failure as a soldier, a seductress and an assassin doesn't mean I have such low self-esteem I'd take a man who loves another woman and thinks of me with such contempt. More than contempt. With suspicion. I have no intentions of seducing you. You're perfectly safe and so are your friends."

He winced. He deserved every word she said. He wanted her attention centered on him, not looking at any other man, yet he didn't want to feel anything back for her, not real emotion, but it wasn't for the reasons she thought. He told himself it was her enhancements that drew him, that sexual lure she wove—except she didn't seem to be weaving it for him or anyone else. At least she claimed she wasn't and that meant some—or most—of it could be coming from him. She was the kind of woman a man didn't walk away from—ever. She would always have the upper hand whether or not she knew it—if he loved her. And he would love her if he let himself.

"I'm not in love with her," he denied. "Where did you get that?"

"No, you just feel you threw your entire life away for her and she got you into this mess. The children aren't your 'mess.' They're human beings, no matter what Braden or anyone else did to them. I don't want them anywhere near someone who feels they're a 'mess,' just a responsibility one has to clean up. They're children and they deserve a happy life."

Her hot little temper made him want to smile. That wasn't a good idea when he was so close to her. He knew she could be lethal, and he didn't want to test her until he knew exactly what he was dealing with. He hid the grin. "I didn' mean the children."

She shrugged and turned away from him, subsiding against the pillows. "I'm tired. I need to sleep."

Dismissing him. "No way, sugar. That doesn' happen. We talk thin's out in my world. Pepper, you're not goin' to run off with these kids because you're angry with me. That would be sheer stupidity, and you're not stupid."

"Maybe not, but I'd rather they feel loved than be with someone just hanging around because they feel they have to. That's not the way to raise a child."

"You caught a small glimpse of my thoughts and you're condemin' me. That's not right. When I first came home, that first night, I stood lookin' at this house, Grand-mere's house, my home, and I knew then what a fool I'd been over Joy. And then, long before I knew about the children, I acknowledged I was in a mess. When I joined the program to be enhanced, it was for a psychic enhancement, not a genetic one. I received both. I was goin' to have to go to *ma grand-mere* and let her see what I was—what I'd become— and I was ashamed of myself for doin' such a stupid thing over a woman who didn' want me and worse, and more importantly—*I didn't want her.* I was never in love with her, only the childish illusion of rescuing her."

"You mean like you're rescuing me?"

Her long lashes fluttered. He could see the sweep of them, feathery and full, sending little shock waves through his stomach straight to his groin. Her profile was beautiful, a work of art, and he realized no man could have produced that even with heavy sculpting. She had a small white scar on her neck just below her ear, but her face was flawless, rose petal skin smoothed over perfect bone structure.

Revelations were the very devil, and he didn't like where his mind, his *brilliant* mind, was taking him. All along, from the moment he'd laid eyes on her. Practically from the moment when he'd been aware on some level that the Rougarou in the swamp was really a woman. From the time he'd seen those small fingers curled around the hilt of a knife. The parlor floor had trembled under his feet and it had nothing at all to do with his temper and everything to do with this woman's impact on him.

He wanted to believe Whitney had created her for him. He wanted that excuse. He wanted to blame her for the sexual lure he felt every time he was close to her. He thought about her all the time, and he'd tried to make her less than human so he could believe himself superior to her. He even wanted the excuse she just handed him—that he wanted to rescue her. Even if it were true, there was far more to it than that.

Wyatt sank down onto the side of the bed, pushing one hand through his thick, wavy hair. He wanted to grab it and pull, to feel the shock of reality. "It's interestin' to me how humans manage to delude themselves into believin' the things they want to believe. You aren't tryin' to seduce me, Pepper. But I'm still bein' seduced. And no, I didn't want that. I wanted to believe I was madly in love with a woman who was heartless. But she's not. She just wanted somethin' different, somethin' that wasn't me. I realized I never loved her. I made up a fantasy and never saw who she was or what she needed."

Pepper turned over, her dark eyes moving over his face.

"She wanted out of the bayou, and I love it here. She wanted away from everythin' and everyone I call home. I wanted to blame her for what I'd done, but in the end, I have to face the fact that all along, ever since I saw my brother and the things he could do, I wanted that as well. I'm too much the scientist. My brain likes puzzles and answers. *I* did this. Not Joy. *Me.* Just as *I'm* the one attracted to *you.* Not the sexual enhancements, that's not the lure for me. It's just you."

Her eyes changed, going from the deep purple to warm violet. He watched in amazement as the diamond-colored ring surrounding the dark color began to bleed into it, a strange, beautiful starburst that changed her eyes completely.

"Maybe rescuin' you is part of the attraction, or maybe you're rescuin' me. Did you ever think of that? That you might be *my* savior?"

She reached up with her bare, slender arm, her fingers curving around the nape of his neck one by one, and she slowly pulled him down toward her.

Wyatt's breath rushed out of his lungs, leaving him burning for air. The ground shifted and the bed trembled. He could see every detail of her beautiful, perfect face. The long feathery sweep of her lashes, the strange starburst in her eyes that beckoned a man to fall into paradise. He knew the details of this moment would be branded for all time in his mind.

Her skin, close up, was soft and flawless, a lure of satin, and her thick hair was luxurious silk. He wanted to pull her braid apart and bury his hands and face in the dark cloud. His gaze dropped to her lips. The soft curve, the formation, the fullness. His heart pounded nearly out of control.

She brushed a kiss over his lips. A whisper, no more. There was nothing sexual in the gesture at all, yet it was the most intimate, sensual thing he'd ever experienced. His body reacted with a need and hunger bordering on primal. He felt that small whisper slide inside of him and take hold.

He'd been with women and he'd kissed a lot of them. This was no kiss, yet he felt more than he'd ever felt in his life. A shiver of acute awareness crept down his spine. He wanted to gather her into his arms, strip her naked and spend hours tangled with her, sharing her body, skin to skin.

Her arm slipped from his neck and she subsided on the pillow, as if the energy it took for the one small movement was too much. "Don't be so hard on yourself, Wyatt. Sometimes our brains are just as needy as the rest of us. Yours is just a little more so, but in the end, it's the intelligence the children got from you that's allowed them to stay alive this long. They understand danger and death. They know they can't bite even when they're teething and it hurts. So thank you. I wouldn't have them without you, and I love them. I want to take care of them. So, again, thank you."

He sat back, away from her, away from that potent lure he couldn't seem to resist. He still felt her touch, as if the small gesture had been a stamp that had her name and branded her as his. His body hurt. Ached. Demanded. The blood pumped fast through his veins, a hot turbulent rush of pure need. It took great effort not to touch his mouth with his fingertips—or to get up and lock the door.

"I'm not certain that was the best idea you've ever had," he said.

Her moody gaze moved over his face. "I got that the moment my mouth touched yours."

She had lit a match and he was on fire. Clearly she was too.

"What the hell is going on between us?" Wyatt asked. "Do all men react like me?"

She shook her head slowly. "I wasn't trying to seduce you. I have to try with the others. It isn't natural, I have to create the feelings in them, feed them. I don't feel anything as a rule. With you . . . it's different. Real. I don't know why and it's a little scary."

He didn't trust what he didn't understand and he sure didn't understand the volatile chemistry between them. He would have leapt off the bed and put the distance of the room between them, but it was impossible to move at the moment.

"I just want you to remember that I wanted to take Ginger and leave. From the beginning, I wanted away from here. You insisted I stay. I'm not part of some big conspiracy and neither are the babies."

"Don' kid yourself, Pepper, you're definitely part of a conspiracy and so are the babies. The question is, are you a willin' participant?"

"I'm tired and I hurt. I understand why you might think that way, given the circumstances, but I'm tired of trying to convince you."

"Well, that's too damn bad, because when I go into that laboratory to get the children out, I won't be alone. Ezekiel and Malichai will be with me as well as a couple of others. I don' want to get my friends killed because you're doin' Whitney's biddin'."

Pepper let her gaze drift over his face. He was beautiful. Perfectly beautiful. It was hard not to allow herself to be drawn to him. She'd always wanted to feel something for a man, just to know she could. Her body felt as if it was in a constant state of arousal. She'd been programmed that way and she couldn't seem to do much about it, but it was her body's doing, not some man. Until this one.

She was shot, snake bit and in a terrible situation, but she craved him. If she closed her eyes, she could taste him. Feel him. Why? The question beat at her. She might take the chance if it was just her, but it was the babies as well. She wouldn't risk them. She just couldn't. This man was dangling his family in front of her. He was offering her a home, but he wanted a relationship with her that didn't include anything but a sexual one.

She didn't want to be wanted for sex. She needed to know she was far more than an object, a body Wyatt wanted.

It hurt more than she wanted to admit. Maybe if she wasn't so connected to him, if he hadn't opened some door between them, she could live with just sex for the sake of the children, but she saw into him. She saw what he was capable of giving and she wanted that for herself. If not with him, then with someone else . . .

He paced across the floor, a restless, lethal jungle cat, his eyes smoldering with fire. She could actually see the cat in him, his eyes focused on her, angry, possessive.

"Don'. Don' even think about being with another man. You aren' takin' those children from me. They're mine. I can protect them here. I can raise them here with a family that loves them. You throw another man into this mix, Pepper, and someone is goin' to get seriously hurt. You aren' goin' to win this one, so just accept that this is the best thing for everyone and we'll work out the problems."

He was truly fascinating when he was angry. He looked powerful. Intimidating. Scary. Yet she didn't feel physically threatened. Wyatt wasn't a man who would ever harm a woman. She would have known that even if she hadn't been inside his mind.

"You told me to trust you, Wyatt, but you don't trust me. You still think I'm some kind of bait to lure you into the laboratory for whatever reasons you think this Whitney has to get you there. Why do you even believe the other two girls exist? Why believe me at all?"

His eyes didn't leave her face. She should have known better than to bring his entire attention on her when he was already focused on her. He saw too much. She didn't want charming, sexy Wyatt. She wanted the jerk. The man with an edge so she could keep pushing him away. She didn't dare believe in him. She'd never been able to believe in anyone but herself. She detested that she was so drawn to him that she could put aside life's lessons to believe him. He offered a dream. A fantasy. But it was hollow. Who knew what he really wanted? But it wasn't her.

"Baby," he said softly, and her stomach rolled.

She shook her head and tried to close her eyes against his allure.

"I hurt you, didn' I? You misunderstand me. I'm not afraid of what part you might have in all of this. I've been in your head just like you've been in mine. I do believe Whitney is usin' you as bait, but for what, I have no idea. Of course I have to warn you, just in case you're a far better actress than I believe you are, because if you betray us, you'll end up dead, and that's the last thing I want."

"How did I misunderstand you, Wyatt?" She kept the tears out of her voice with an effort. She wasn't about to show him more weakness than she already had. She could control tears when she wasn't under the influence of painkillers.

There wasn't any misunderstanding. He still considered she might be part of a larger conspiracy theory. And yes that hurt, right after he said he wouldn't hurt her.

Wyatt was silent so long she couldn't help but look at him. He took a breath and let it out. Shook his head. Raked his hands through his hair.

"If we're bein' honest here, Pepper, lovin' you would be too easy. You'd become my world and wrap me around your little finger. You don' know what I'm like, but a woman like you, a man like me lovin' her, that could be paradise or sheer hell. I've got to figure out which before I put us in that position."

The bottom dropped right out of her stomach. The heat between her legs increased tenfold. Her heart contracted. Wyatt forced himself to his feet and left the room. She didn't say anything at all.

CHAPTER 8

What had possessed him to tell her the truth? To confess his fear? And he hadn't even done a thorough job of it. What man wanted a woman who could become his world? To be tied up in knots? She had the potential to really crush him. Shatter him. Walk the hell all over him. Pepper was that kind of woman.

There were some women who were the kind you knew from the moment you set eyes on them that they were going to tear out your heart and keep it in their hot little hands. Wyatt knew he was going to keep her, and the risk to him would be enormous. He might pretend to her that she didn't matter, but she was always going to matter.

He needed to find his grandmother. She was soothing. She was wise. She wouldn't say a word unless he opened his mouth and asked her what the hell he was doing. He already knew it didn't matter whether he knew what he was doing or not—he'd started down the path and the pull toward Pepper was too strong to walk away.

There were the babies. Already he didn't want to let

Ginger out of his sight. She was sweet and easily wrapped them all around her little finger. Everyone wanted to be the one to make her laugh. She was a very sober baby and didn't know about dancing and music or joking. He wanted to be the one to teach her about family.

Instinctively, he headed for the parlor and wasn't surprised to find his grandmother there playing with the baby. They were laughing together, Ginger delighting in the swamp pop music Nonny liked to blare every now and then. The little girl turned in circles in the middle of the worn, faded rug, mimicking Nonny's movements.

He leaned one hip lazily against the doorjamb and watched them, the tension draining out of him. He remembered the music and the joy Nonny brought to the household. There had been plenty of hard work to be done in their home, but there was always more laughter.

He realized, watching the baby as she learned the joys of dancing, that he wanted this for his children—the freedom that came so easily in the bayou. They would learn to survive here and grow up to be loving, giving adults who believed in working hard but playing and loving just as hard.

It suddenly occurred to him that Pepper had never experienced this. She'd grown up a soldier. She didn't know any more about laughter and love than Ginger. His childhood environment couldn't have been more different. Still, she loved the children fiercely. He knew she'd walk through fire for them. She fought for them in her own way, and he had to convince her this was what was needed for them. This home. These people. His three little vipers would be at home here. He suddenly wanted to rush off half cocked, just like Grandmere, and get the other two babies and bring them home.

A tingle of awareness went down his spine. Ezekiel, on the stairs, paused, let out a low warning whistle and instantly Ginger ceased dancing. Wyatt was across the room in one short leap, scooping up the baby.

"No, Nonny, keep the music goin'," he cautioned when

his grandmother reached to turn off her favorite song. "Malichai, get rid of the high chair. Come on, little one, you need to stay quiet and watch over Pepper for me. Can you do that?"

Ginger signed frantically.

"Too fast, baby. Your *pere* isn' so good at signin' yet."

She slowed her little fingers enough that when he entered Pepper's room he knew she sought reassurance. "Yes, they're here, but they won't take you back. Stay in here."

Pepper's eyes were on his face, a mirror of Ginger's. His heart contracted. He didn't have time to gather her into his arms and reassure her like he was doing with the baby, but he never wanted to see that look in her eyes again.

He slipped a gun from his boot and a knife, handing both to Pepper. "Stay quiet. We'll get rid of them. They can get in through the windows, but you'll know they're comin' if they try it. And they won' be happy. Grand-mere planted stingin' nettles under all the windows to keep us from slippin' out at night."

"Take this out of my arm. I have to be able to move," she said.

There was no nonsense in her voice, and he knew if he didn't remove the catheter, she would do so herself. She looked different. He could still feel her pain beating at him, but it didn't show in her eyes or her body. She was all warrior. After one flash of sheer terror, she was all steel— all business. That was the moment he believed in her.

Good girl. We've got this, sugar. Don' you worry. They aren' takin' our baby from us. Not now, not ever.

Pepper didn't answer him, but while he removed the needle and set the rigging out of the way to give her more freedom of movement, her gaze clung to his. At his reassurance, she nodded, just as determined as he was.

"Stay quiet," he repeated. "And know who you're shootin' before you pull the trigger. Nonny's with us and she has a tendency to rush into the middle of the fray."

Pepper nodded. "Just be careful, Wyatt."

Wyatt turned to go, but caught the baby's look. Anxiety was there. Fear. The baby was terrified that they would take her back to the laboratory. He leaned down and brushed a kiss across the baby's forehead, his heart turning over.

"You're about to learn *votre pere* is a badass, Ginger." He kissed her again, avoiding Pepper's gaze and left the room, closing the door softly behind him.

He felt like he had his own family. Stupid really. He'd *always* had a family. Pepper and Ginger were the ones who didn't know what that felt like, but he was the one with the lump in his throat and the fire in his veins and belly to protect them.

"Nonny, the guards are approachin' the house. Get your pipe and your shotgun and sit here in the parlor, right in this chair," he instructed, patting the one in the corner away from the windows. "Keep the music on. Zeke is on the roof and Malichai is goin' to be circlin' around behind them. He'll take out anyone creepin' around the back windows." He kissed the top of his grandmother's head as she settled in the chair without a murmur. "And, Nonny, thank you for plantin' those nettles at the window. They're suddenly mighty handy."

"Don' you worry none about me, boy. I can shoot the wings off a fly if I have to. No one's gonna be takin' your woman or child from this house." There was determination in her voice.

Wyatt's heart contracted painfully. Everything he needed to be happy was in this house. Everything but his two other children. It didn't have to make sense to him that he was already bonded to them. He was a family man and he'd always secretly longed to have a woman like his sister-in-law. She was loyal and courageous and she loved his brother with every fiber of her soul. He had tried hard to get that from Joy and had failed utterly. Now he knew why.

It had taken three little vipers in jeopardy to open his eyes. Three little girls with a mother made of steel and silk.

He went to the door. *Pepper, can you hear me?*

Yes.

I'm sorry for doubtin' you. I didn' want to see what was right under my nose. I don' trust so easily.

Amusement flooded his mind, warming him. *I got that about you. Not that I blame you. I'm struggling a little bit with this setup myself.*

We seem to communicate quite well this way. Maybe talkin' aloud should be banned. They're close, honey. Keep the baby quiet.

She'll stay quiet, but I've been thinking about all of this and what you said. If you're right and someone orchestrated all this, then it's really about you, not us. Not the children or me, but maybe they need you for something.

I think you're right about that. But even if I figure out the answer, and I'm goin' to try, they aren't goin' to get the results. Wyatt stepped out onto the porch. It was easy enough to hear the approach of the guards. They were coming up the canal in an airboat, a nice fancy one. Fast. He recognized the make and model. He'd always wanted one.

You have figured this out already, haven't you? Why we were brought here?

I think so. The problem with Whitney is he can' ever figure out what makes humans tick. He doesn' get relationships or how people bond. How they fall in love or feel the need to protect their children. He can't get what he wants until he knows why we all do what we do.

He could smell them now. They were wary, but they weren't afraid. And that was a mistake. They figured they had him outnumbered.

They brought the dog with them, Ezekiel reported. *They want it to sniff out the baby and Pepper. I can control it, but maybe you ought to take it this time. I practiced enough last night. Right now I'm itching to squeeze this trigger. I can take out maybe three of them for sure, maybe four before they can take cover.*

A little bloodthirsty this mornin'? Wyatt inquired. He tried to include Pepper in the conversation, building a bridge so she would know what was going on at all times. *Don' be shootin' anyone until we know what they want.*

Wyatt had told Pepper that all of them had things to work on, things they had to constantly keep in check. Ezekiel was a hunter, the cat in him stronger than in either Wyatt or Malichai and it was bad enough forcing the two of them to hold back in a fight. For Ezekiel, it went entirely against his nature.

I'll have to move position once they get on land, Ezekiel warned.

Before you move, make certain none of them try to circle around. And be watchful of a land approach as well. They can come at us from the road.

Goes without sayin', Doc. Seriously, this isn't my first firefight. Ezekiel's voice dripped with sarcasm.

Malichai gave a snort of pure derision. *We know you're up there sneaking a smoke of Nonny's tobacco. I saw you inhaling when she was smoking that pipe of hers early this morning.*

Wyatt's churning gut settled nicely with the familiar banter. He might not have the rest of his team around him, but he had two men who would fight with everything in them to protect his family. You couldn't ask for more than that.

Are any of them GhostWalkers, Malichai? You're closest to them.

He watched the airboat slide up to the pier. One of the guards from the previous night, Jim, caught the rope and tied it up. There were five altogether and they were going to need a lot more than that. He was a little disappointed in them. He'd beat the hell out of Larry, so one would have thought they'd be a little more leery—or they had another team approaching from the road.

Stay alert up there, Zeke. Why send only five when they know we can fight?

They probably don't know you can dodge bullets yet, Malichai pointed out with a small laugh. *And no, they all seem normal to me with no enhancements. I think they're ex-military. They carry themselves like it. And they know how to handle guns, but these aren't Whitney's supersoldiers.*

That worried him too. Pepper had alluded to the men she was certain Braden would call in to track her and the babies. "Elite trackers." That sounded to him like Whitney's supersoldiers. He had taken the men applying for the psychic enhancements who had failed psychological testing and enhanced them and used them as his own private army. She'd mentioned that Braden had his own soldiers enhanced in some way. Where were they? Why send civilians into the game?

To Whitney, the supersoldiers he created from the men who had failed the testing were expendable, and he used them as pawns in his private war games ruthlessly. Wyatt knew they were ticking time bombs. The psychic enhancements came with a multitude of problems, although the earlier experiments such as Team One of the GhostWalkers suffered far more than the rest of them did. Whitney continued to perfect his technique. But still, some of them needed an "anchor," another GhostWalker to draw the psychic energy away from them when they became overloaded.

Adding physical enhancements as well added more to the strain. Being so outside normal society was extremely difficult. Eventually being so alone and isolated became wearing. He hadn't even realized how wearing until he returned home and stood on the sturdy pier he'd built himself out of love for his grandmother.

The men spotted him as they came into the yard; he could tell by the way they stiffened and then exchanged long looks with one another. If they were armed—and he was certain they were—they kept their weapons out of sight. He sent word to Nonny's two hunting dogs to stay quiet before reaching for the guard dog. It took a moment to penetrate the dog's barrier and overcome its natural instincts. He dulled its senses, pushing the scents of the bayou as well as that of his cat DNA so that the dog would be more interested in him than his prey.

This is a huntin' party. A recon. They're lookin' for signs of Pepper and Ginger, he warned all of them. *Whitney appears to have no patience. He's a scientist, not a hunter, and he doesn' quite get this end of the game.* That didn't make sense to him, but sending out the guards to their home was a huge mistake.

Pepper stirred in his mind. *You keep dismissing Braden as if he isn't important. He's the one running the show here in the bayou. He directs everything that goes on at the laboratory in France as well as here. They run a legitimate plastics company, or at least a skeleton of one for show, but no move is made without Braden's say-so.*

Wyatt thought that over. Whitney was used to having long-term goals. That meant he was a man of patience. He wouldn't make this kind of mistake. Pepper was right, Braden had sent these men, not Whitney, and that would cause a rift between the two. Wyatt was absolutely certain Whitney gave the orders to Braden, and right now, Whitney would not be happy that Braden was going out on his own.

So Braden took the initiative and sent his men to look for you. You know that can only mean one thing. Whitney doesn't have him in the loop for his end game, Wyatt said. *No one goes against Whitney and lives to tell about it. No one. He's utterly ruthless. I'm not certain the man actually has blood in his veins. More like ice water.*

Like Trap, Ezekiel said. *He's our iceman.*

Not like Trap, Wyatt denied. *Trap feels compassion; Whitney wouldn't know what the word meant.*

The guards made their way toward the porch. Blake,

Jim and Larry led the way. The other two men had dropped behind them, slowing their gait in order to check their surroundings.

Wyatt stepped up to the edge of the porch. "What can I do for you gentlemen?"

All of them stopped instantly. Larry heaved a sigh. "I came to apologize to your grandmother. I wasn't certain you were serious, but even if you weren't, I thought about what you said and I owe her one."

"It takes five of you to come here to apologize to one little old lady?" He hoped Nonny's music was up loud enough that she didn't hear what he'd called her. She'd probably box his ears. He reached up and pulled on his earlobe, thankful he didn't have cauliflower ear.

Larry shrugged. "We actually had some other work to do, and because it took us in this direction, I thought I'd take the opportunity to make my apology."

"How is it you know my grandmother and where she lives?" Wyatt asked.

"Since we've been working at the place, your Ms. Fontenot has been out to that section of the swamp numerous times. It's fairly remote and we get a hunter or two occasionally, but she's been there regularly. Our company has to guard against industrial espionage, so we had to check her out."

"You thought a little old lady plantin' and harvestin' was committin' industrial espionage?" He grinned at them. "Seriously? Because she's gonna love that."

"All right," Larry said, looking slightly annoyed and embarrassed, "we had no choice. When the boss says to investigate someone, you do it, no matter how ridiculous."

Wyatt nodded. "I can understand that. After you shoved her, she thought maybe you were making dirty bombs in that place and the lot of you were treasonous terrorists." He watched their faces closely.

The men looked at one another. Jim hid a smile. Blake

raised his eyebrows, and the two in the back coughed behind their hands.

"She said that about us?" Larry asked.

"About you in particular, Larry. You do realize that Grand-mere is an icon here in the bayou. If you really investigated her you would have found out her *famille* dates back to the first settlers and that she creates the medicine here. Had she gone to the other families here and told them, they would have strung you up by your balls."

Larry winced. "Would you mind if I just said my apologies and we let it go at that? I'm still sore from your little lesson. I don't think I need another one."

He moved a few steps closer with the dog. The dog didn't cast around looking for any other scent, his total concentration was on Wyatt.

The others spread out behind Larry, an easy maneuver, as if they were just hanging out while Larry approached the porch. The dog came with Larry. Wyatt didn't want his grandmother exposed to possible trouble, so the best scenario was to allow Larry into the house. The parlor was a distance from the bedrooms, but if the baby started to cry or Pepper made a sound, the dog might alert before he could control it.

I would prefer to bring Larry and dog into the house. It would go a long way to makin' them believe we aren' harborin' any fugitives such as the Rougarou. Pepper, you'll have to make certain Ginger doesn' make a sound.

She won't, Pepper assured. *She's a soldier.*

He winced at that explanation. He didn't want his daughters to be soldiers or experiments. He wanted them to be happy children, with no worries of evil men who used them as experiments.

Your grand-mere *might inadvertently give them away,* Malichai cautioned.

Ezekiel grunted, his amusement more felt than heard. Grand-mere *won't give anything away, Malichai, and shame on you for even thinking it. I never could teach you to see past the obvious. She's a wily woman and nothing gets by her.*

Wyatt was pleased Ezekiel had noticed. *And she'd better not hear you even thought that she'd give them away, because if she does, you won't be eating at the table for a long time to come.*

Blackmail material. Oh, yeah. Ezekiel was elated.

"Just you. You and the dog," Wyatt said. "You can come into the parlor and have a word with Nonny."

Larry glanced back at the others. Jim couldn't keep the triumphant look off his face. Yeah. They had been military, but they weren't cloak and dagger.

I'm bringin' him in. Stay quiet, Wyatt reiterated.

Ginger doesn't cry, Pepper reassured. *Not when danger is close. They were already in training, remember? The first thing they were ever taught was to maintain silence.*

There was the merest hint of indignation, not in her voice, but in the way she felt. He knew neither of the others could tell and it made him feel closer to her.

I know, babe. I just needed to touch base and know she's okay in this situation. But caution her about bitin' just in case.

She has the right to defend herself if they come through the window and try to take her, Pepper objected.

She might have the right, but I don' want her livin' with the consequences, knowin' she killed another person, he said firmly. *We're her parents. We'll do the killin' if it needs to be done, not her.*

There was a short silence. He could feel the hurt in her. His words stung. He hadn't meant them that way, but he didn't want his children to have to ever look back and know they'd killed someone when they didn't have to. In the laboratory, they'd had no choice, and he could explain that to them, but in their home, the adults did the protecting.

You're right, Wyatt. I'm sorry. I should have thought of that.

She hadn't because she'd never had a childhood, parents or a family. She thought first like a soldier, not a mother. She didn't have experience to draw from. She had no parents of her own to give her a road map to follow. There would always be gaps in her parenting because of that, gaps he could fill in. She needed him whether or not she wanted to admit it.

Why should you have? You don' have that kind of experience. I was lucky to have Nonny. She taught me a few things that might come in handy. He's on the steps.

Wyatt stepped back to allow Larry to come onto the porch. *Malichai, they're restless out here and I can guarantee they'll be on the move the moment we're inside.*

No worries, Ezekiel assured, suddenly all business. *I've got him covered. I've got a good vantage point.*

"I don't know if you've heard of strange happenings in the swamp lately," Larry said, suddenly wanting a conversation. He even managed to pitch his voice friendly.

"There's always somethin' strange happenin' in the swamp," Wyatt confirmed.

Now he knew the reason the guards went to the Huracan Club. They wanted to hear the news, the gossip going around.

"Just go to one of the local bars and you'll hear every kind of story you'll ever want to hear about what goes on in the bayous and swamps," Wyatt said with a small, almost friendly grin. Unlike the guards, he *was* cloak and dagger.

"We can tell some stories. Funny thin' is, most of them are true." He could be just as chatty as the next man. "We've got the Rougarou. That's a beast, a shapeshifter. Our own neighbors can be accused of bein' the Rougarou. We've got moans and screams and all sorts of strange noises. I've been huntin' the swamps my entire life and I've seen some strange thin's."

He stared into the dog's eyes, keeping command of the animal. "My *grand-mere* may be tough, but I don' want that animal to bite her. I'd have to kill it, and it's a good-lookin' dog. I know you care for the dog, so you're gettin' that one warnin'."

"He won't bite without provocation or command," Larry assured.

"Then come on in," Wyatt said. "Nonny's in the parlor with her pipe and music. Most nights she smokes on the porch, but once in a while she takes to smokin' in the parlor and then we know to mind our business. She's missin' Grand-pere."

The smell of Nonny's pipe tobacco would also mess with the dog's ability to locate Pepper and Ginger. The aroma of the big pot of jambalaya on the stove and the bread rising beneath the tea towels also helped.

"Nonny." Wyatt raised his voice above the music. "We have company. The gentleman from Wilson Plastics has come to have a word with you."

Nonny took the pipe from her mouth and looked at them. Straight. Her eyes steady. Her mouth firm. She reached over casually and turned the music down, but she didn't turn it off. Nonny would never have a conversation with a neighbor with music playing in the parlor. She would consider that rude. Larry didn't know it, but he'd just been insulted.

She looked pointedly at the shotgun and then back at Larry. "Mights' well take a seat, boy," she said and gestured toward the one closest to her. "Mighty fine dog you have there. I like critters a whole lot better than I do varmints."

That was another veiled insult Larry didn't get. There was nothing wrong with Nonny's mind. She was sharp. Wyatt had to hide a grin and keep himself from kissing his grandmother right there on the spot. She was special, a woman to walk beside a man. He should have known all along that anyone who didn't see that in his grandmother didn't belong anywhere near his family. Joy had not been overly fond of Nonny. He'd been such an idiot over Joy, and he owed his grandmother an apology, possibly a much bigger one than Larry did.

Larry's eyes darted around the room, looking at every detail. This was the parlor Nonny entertained guests in. There was nothing out of place. She'd opened the window behind her as if she blew her tobacco smoke in that direction, but the slight breeze just circulated the spicy scent throughout the room. The dog, instead of alerting, dropped down to Larry's feet and put his head on his paws. Larry relaxed visibly.

They're spreading out and moving around the house, Ezekiel said. *Looking for tracks.*

I went out this morning, Malichai reminded. *There were a couple of small baby prints and smears of blood. They're gone.*

Thanks, Malichai, Wyatt said.

He leaned against the wall and crossed his arms over his chest, striving for casual, his fingers inches from his throwing knives—and he was very accurate with a knife.

Wyatt, when I brought Ginger here, we were both injured. I hadn't thought about leading them straight to your house. We were going to be in and out in an hour or less. I'm sorry, Pepper said. *I know better than that.*

She hadn't been thinking like a soldier. The baby was bleeding and so was she. She wanted medical attention for the child, and she knew, as did anyone staying more than a day or two in the bayou, that Nonny Fontenot was the woman to see. If she couldn't fix you up, she called in the local *traiteur.*

Malichai took care of it, Pepper.

But I led them here. What's wrong with me?

Wyatt felt guilt and even humiliation beating at her. Tears. She was fighting tears. He couldn't have her crying right then, not when he couldn't comfort her. He had to stay focused on the guards surrounding the house.

Honey, don' be gettin' upset over this. We have com-

pany and you have to keep Ginger quiet. They'll be movin'
around to your windows in a couple of minutes. They won'
be able to see in, but they may try to open them. Like I
said, those stingin' nettles are there and their boots won'
be much protection.

It's the painkillers. I told you not to give them to me.

"Ms. Fontenot," Larry began, glancing up at Wyatt.

"I'm over here," Nonny stated.

She had let the pipe go out. There was never smoking in
the house. It was forbidden, *especially* in the front parlor.
She had sacrificed her rigid rule in order to cover the scent
of the two fugitives from the dog. The tobacco, combined
with the cat scent and Wyatt's firm hold on it, prevented
the dog from doing its job.

Wyatt waggled his finger at Larry and the guard
whipped his head back around to face Nonny.

Someone's at the window, Pepper said. *They're trying*
to open it. I can hear them cursing.

It was difficult not to laugh. The stinging nettles were
carefully cultivated by a woman who had a gift for the
land. The plants were tall, thick and spread out, climbing
up the side of the house and looking innocent. By now they
had wrapped themselves around whoever had stepped up
to that window.

I'll bet they're cursing. He allowed laughter to show in
his voice.

Wyatt wanted Pepper to relax and realize they could do
this. They hadn't even been prepared, but they'd send the
guards home empty-handed with no more knowledge of
Pepper and Ginger's whereabouts than they had before
they came.

"I'm sorry for what I did back there in the swamp,
ma'am," Larry said in a little rush. "I've regretted it ever
since, and when your grandson came to let me know just
how he felt about it, I have to admit, I thought I deserved
what I got."

To Wyatt's utter astonishment, Larry's voice rang with honesty. He might be embarrassed to come and apologize to Nonny, but he was more embarrassed that he'd treated her the way he had.

"I don't know what came over me that day. There was a leak in one of the labs and the dog went crazy and I took him out to settle him down. He isn't vicious. He does his job, but he doesn't just attack without provocation. The alarms went off and I don't half remember what happened, other than when I shoved you. It felt like I was moving through heavy fog—that someone else had done it, not me."

Wyatt stiffened. What kind of chemicals were they testing in that laboratory? Whatever they were, they had affected both the dog and the guard. Had it been on purpose? More than ever he wanted to get into that lab.

"I mostly wanted my knife back," Nonny said. "It's been in *ma famille* for over a hundred years."

A faint smile appeared. "I really liked that knife." His smile faded. "I never saw anything like it, but every time I looked at it, I remembered what I'd done to you." Larry shook his head. "That's no excuse, but I was raised better than that." He glanced out the window as if he didn't want the other guards to hear him. "I really am sorry, ma'am, and I hope I didn't cause you any real harm."

"I accept your apology," Nonny said. "You're a good boy."

Larry started to rise and then subsided, once again glancing outside, before turning back and leaning toward her, lowering his voice even more. "Ma'am, I've heard you're kind and people around here trust you. There are things, dangerous things around right now. Be careful."

"I've been in the swamp my entire life," Nonny said. "I'm always careful, but thanks for the warnin'."

Larry looked as if he wanted to say something else, but he stopped himself and stood. Instantly the dog came to its feet as well.

"I'm glad I came, ma'am. If you come back out to the

swamp to harvest, you won't get the same reception from me," Larry assured. "I'll look out for you."

Nonny smiled at him for the first time. "I'll bring you some beignets and *café*."

Larry nodded and followed Wyatt back outside. On the porch he stopped. "There really is something dangerous loose in the swamp. She shouldn't be out there."

Wyatt studied the man's face. "Did somethin' get out of that lab that could hurt her or anyone else?" he prompted.

Larry shrugged. "Just watch her. I can't say more."

Wyatt nodded toward the two men trying to get into the locked garage. "I understand. Is that why the others are lookin' around my property?"

"Yes." Larry's voice went clipped. Tight. "What's in the garage?"

"I'm a doctor. My equipment and lab are in there. And no one's goin' to go through my things. It's a sterile environment." Wyatt put a little hard-ass into his voice.

Larry and the dog stepped off the porch. He whistled. The two men by the garage turned and noticed Wyatt watching them from the porch. They didn't move.

"You might want to warn them, there's a high-powered rifle trained on them right this moment and the man behind the trigger doesn' miss. Not ever. They break that lock and he'll kill them." Wyatt's tone was back to mild.

Larry visibly paled. He hurried over to the two men. They argued for a moment, and then one of them, Blake, took a careful look around, still shaking his head, clearly not believing.

Put one right in front of his boot. In front, Wyatt emphasized, *not in his boot.*

The bullet hit dead center, less than an inch from Blake's boot. The sound of the single shot echoed through the bayou. The three men froze, raising their hands slowly. Two more men rushed around the corner of the house and skidded to a halt. One was limping and his clothes were torn up. Wyatt would have bet any amount of money that he would be pulling nettles out of his legs for some days to come. He was going to be one uncomfortable man for a while—and that was if he wasn't allergic.

"Gentlemen," Wyatt said, beckoning them toward him. He waited until they walked slowly up to the porch. "I believe I've been more than patient with you. This is my home and *ma famille*. I will defend them with everythin' in me. By now, you can tell this isn' my first party. Next time you come round my property without bein' asked, I'll be feedin' you to the alligators."

"Don't think this is over," Blake snarled.

"Shut up, Blake," Larry said. "It's over. These people have nothing to do with our business. We're going," he added.

Wyatt nodded, feeling a little sorry for the man. Larry had a job to do, and he had no real idea of what he'd gotten himself into. Probably most of the other guards were like him. They'd been hired to guard a plastics company that they'd probably been told was a front for a military laboratory. They were convinced someone was trying to break in and get their secrets. The guards had no idea what else was in that laboratory.

Not that he excused them. They knew something else was going on and, although they were leery, they didn't bother to check because they didn't want to lose their jobs. There had to be one part of the building none of them were allowed into. They were told to keep whatever was in there inside, and everything else out. He didn't think ignorance was an excuse, not when you knew your place of business was lying their ass off to the outside world—and to you.

He watched them all get onto the airboat, knowing both Ezekiel and Malichai watched their every move as well. He would definitely need a couple of more members of his team and soon. These men were not part of Whitney's crew.

They were civilians, and the GhostWalker teams could get in and out without detection.

The moment Whitney heard that Braden had sent his guards to the Fontenot residence, he would send for his own supersoldiers, and that would make things a whole lot more difficult.

CHAPTER 9

"Wyatt, I can't do this," Pepper said. He was crazy. There was no other explanation. She hadn't seen insanity in him until this very moment.

Wyatt grinned at her. "We're just goin' into town, little darlin', nothin' all that difficult. Here's how you do it all nice and easy."

She glared at him while he pulled open the door to the passenger side of the Jeep and gestured.

"Just hop up there on the seat and put your seat belt on. If you don' know how to do that, I'll be more than happy to show you."

She backed away. "I'm not getting in that vehicle, and I'm certainly not going to any town with you."

"Yes, you are. We need supplies. Clothes for the girls. I have to order some things to be delivered. Too many days are gettin' away from us."

"You can go by yourself."

His eyes didn't leave her face and she found herself shivering. *She* was supposed to be the seductress, not him, yet standing there, draped against the Jeep, his dark eyes moving over her face with faint laughter and way too much intensity, he looked so sexy she was afraid to move an inch, afraid she might fling herself at him.

The terrible hunger that was never sated, that crawled through her night and day without reprieve, had settled on this man. That was a bad thing. A very bad thing. She had to fight herself, her nature, not to deliberately entice him. Not with her voice, her body, her movements.

She moistened her lips with the tip of her tongue and instantly his gaze dropped to her mouth. The impact on her was frightening. She took in a deep breath, struggling for strength. His gaze dropped lower, to the fullness of her breasts, caressing her, stroking her soft skin until her nipples peaked. *He hadn't even touched her.*

"Stop." She whispered it. Implored him. "You have to stop."

"Pepper, get in the Jeep."

His voice was low and firm. Commanding. Affectionate. She'd never known affection. He was getting to her in spite of all her resolve. She took two more steps back, wanting to save him. Going with him would be a disaster. He just didn't understand.

Swift impatience crossed his face. His jaw set. A small muscle ticked there, warning her, and then he was on her fast, so fast, she hadn't even seen him move. His arms swept around her and he lifted her easily off her feet, swinging her up to his chest.

She caught him around the neck, undecided whether or not it was worth it to struggle. He was enhanced. A Ghost-Walker. There was no winning in a battle of strength. The heat of his body seeped into hers. She was always that little bit cold. He was always so very hot. She felt as if her skin melted into his. He set her body on fire. *Fire.*

Fear spread through her on the heels of the flames consuming her. There would be no going back if she gave herself to him. She would be lost. Maybe she was already lost, seduced as much by the idea of family as the man himself. Confusion and fear reigned. Like an idiot, she struggled, even knowing it was futile.

"Babe."

Wyatt's voice slipped under her skin, pierced her heart. Did things to her bloodstream. Her gaze jumped to his. His face was inches from hers. A scant two inches. Her fingers curled hard into his shoulders. She was drowning, and there was no way to save either of them.

His mouth found hers and the world shifted away from her, spun out of control. She could spend a lifetime kissing him and never come up for air. He did things with his mouth she hadn't known were possible. He took complete control of the kiss and just devoured her, his tongue and teeth and all the hot masculine macho *sexy* energy poured into her, inflaming every cell in her body.

She felt the seat against her back as Wyatt pressed her into the passenger seat, and, still kissing her, snapped her seat belt around her. Only then did he lift his head. She felt dazed. A little drunk even. Her bones had turned to liquid and every brain cell she had was seriously fried.

Wyatt closed her door firmly and she watched him move around the hood of the car to the driver's side. Even the way he moved, all fluid and easy, was sexy. She had sex on the brain. Maybe that was the trouble and once she gave in, she'd be over him.

Wyatt slid in beside her, smoothly clicked his seat belt in and started the Jeep before looking down at her. "Honey, you're broadcastin' loud and clear. You're not goin' to be over me. We're goin' to have sex, lots of it, often, and you're still not goin' to get over me. Just put that right out of your head."

She closed her eyes against his cocky, *sexy* grin. "You do it on purpose, Wyatt, and you're playing with fire. What happens when I can't resist you anymore and I stop trying to protect you from me?"

"Paradise, sugar, that's what's goin' to happen for both of us."

He set the Jeep in motion, gave a little wave to Ezekiel and Malichai, who were busy with a new security system—cameras, motion sensors, alarms. The Fontenot property was large and they had a lot of work to do to make it into a fortress.

"I can't shield everyone for too long, Wyatt. It takes a toll on me. I don't know why it's so difficult, but after an hour or two I need a respite. My head feels like it's going to explode. What do you think is going to happen when we're in town and I just can't do it anymore?"

He reached out and covered her hand. She hadn't realized she'd been rubbing her palm up and down her thigh. At his touch the burning between her legs grew hotter and she snatched her hand away. The Jeep's interior didn't allow her to shrink away from Wyatt's warmth. He was everywhere, surrounding her with his scent, his masculine hunger beating at her every bit as strong as her own.

"I think you should drop those shields right now, Pepper. It's just the two of us. You and me. You know where this is goin'. So do I. I want to be inside you. I dream of bein' inside you and I know you dream of havin' me there. I want to feel your body wrapped around mine. I want to taste every inch of you. It's goin' to happen and both of us know it. There's no need to hide from me. Be as sexy as you like. Seduce me. I'm a grown-up, babe, and I can handle a woman. I can give you whatever you need."

He was killing her. He didn't understand what they'd done to her. The heat and fire inside that burned and burned until she thought she'd go insane. If she dropped her guard, as connected as they were, and he saw the erotic images in her head, saw her cravings and her terrible need for him—for *him*—she would be lost. He would always be able to control and manipulate her. She wouldn't be the weapon, he would be.

Desperate, she actually touched the door handle, thinking she might try to escape. There was no escape from her body's demands. None. She couldn't quiet the terrible hunger crawling through her veins, centering between her legs like a torch. Her mouth craved to wrap itself around his heavy erection every single time she saw it—which was hourly. He always seemed to be as hard as a rock.

She couldn't think with wanting him. She couldn't sleep. Her skin was hot and her breasts ached. She needed him . . . She just plain needed.

Wyatt swore in Cajun French, a bastardized version of the French she knew. "That's it, Pepper. That's all the time you've got. I was goin' to do this the right way, courtin' you like you deserve, showin' you we could be a normal couple, but I underestimated what they did to you. The hell they gave to you. Needin' sex is damned uncomfortable, and no woman of mine is goin' to suffer when I can do somethin' about it."

Pepper just looked at him, feeling despair. She was fairly certain other men didn't contend with the mother of their children needing sex the way she needed it. She was suffering. It was agony. She'd had a handle on it until she met Wyatt; now she couldn't think of anything else.

Wyatt turned off the main road onto an adjacent road, much narrower, one that ran along the river for a distance and then veered away from it for a while.

"Pepper, take it down. The shield. Let it go. Give yourself to me."

Her gaze dropped to the front of his jeans. His fierce, thick bulge. She licked her lips. Her mouth watered. The fire grew between her legs. It hurt to have her clothes on. Did she dare do what he asked? Reveal the dark side of herself to him? What would he think of her then?

"Damn it, babe. Open your blouse for me. Unbutton all those cute buttons. The moment you put the damn thing on, all I wanted to do was unwrap you."

His eyes cut sideways toward her, his gaze so hot she

felt her stomach somersault. Hot liquid spilled between her legs. Fine. There was no saving either of them and right then she didn't care. The Jeep was hurtling through the swamp now on some old dirt road. He knew where he was going and he wanted to get them there fast. She hoped it would be fast enough.

Very slowly her hands went to the top button of the blouse Nonny had found for her. She might never get this chance again. She'd never been with a man who mattered, one she wanted, one who wasn't training her. Aside from whatever made her outwardly tempting to men when she walked into a place, she was skilled and knew how to please a man, how to bind him to her. Never once had she ever wanted to use her craft. She hated it. Despised it. Until that moment. Her one chance.

There was Wyatt. A man who knew how to love. A man of family. A man who could take command of a situation, lethal one moment and gentle and loving toward a child the next. That man. Her man. She knew him better than he knew himself. He wanted her giving herself to him, but he was holding a part of himself in reserve. That was okay too. She recognized that this one time might be the only time, but she was going to let herself enjoy every single second with him. And she was going to make certain he was going to enjoy it too, that he'd never regret being with her.

She wanted to touch him. To feel his skin beneath her fingers. She was very tactile, and needed touch. Craved it. But only from him. Wyatt. She had no idea if the nightly erotic dreams had fed her hunger for him, and she didn't know if they were her dreams or his, only that she couldn't stop thinking about him.

"There's no one else on this road, Pepper. We're headin' to the camp. Got a huntin' cabin there." His dark eyes moved over her, hooded, sensual, desire intense. "Keep opening the buttons, sugar. You're makin' me crazy goin' so slow like that."

Wyatt was lean, all compact, very defined muscle with just enough bulk to him to look as if he could handle himself with ease. He was all man and she wanted him so badly it actually terrified her. Her hands trembled as she slid the last button out of its closure. His voice was nearly a growl, but a sultry, sexy one. She found herself shivering in anticipation.

Wyatt pulled the Jeep onto a narrow bumpy trail. He couldn't exactly call it a road, but he knew it like the back of his hand. Since he'd been a child, once he'd been somewhere, the twists and turns could never throw him off. He remembered everything.

Plants grew over the faint tire treads left behind in the mud. Great sweeping fans of moss fluttered around the Jeep as he drove through the cypress grove toward the hunting cabin. He glanced at Pepper again. Her blouse was open, but she hadn't parted the edges—and her hands trembled. She twisted her fingers together in agitation. His little seductress was actually nervous.

"Baby," he said gently. There was no way to keep the growl from his voice. He wasn't going to lie to her. He wanted her with a vengeance, and he damned well was going to have her. They'd programmed her to need sex on purpose, mostly, he was certain, to gain her cooperation, but they hadn't counted on her strength to defy them. She was still shielding him, still afraid to allow him to see the real her.

"Look at me, Pepper." He reached over and pried her fingers loose so he could curl her palm around the broad width of his cock. "You put that there and you weren't even tryin'. You did that. Not an enhancement. Not some fleeting physical attraction. I'm hard as a rock and I need you. *You*. Not some other woman."

She shook her head, a low moan slipping out of her throat. He had the urge to stop the Jeep and lick her throat, to take her moan in his mouth.

"This could ruin everything. You don't understand what my life is like," she whispered, refusing to give him her eyes.

"Why? Because you want me too? You may wake up every morning needin' sex, babe, but here's a newsflash: so do I."

"It isn't the same. You have no idea."

She sounded a little desperate. He didn't care anymore. He'd had enough of seeing her suffer. He'd had enough of suffering himself. She was his woman whether she knew it or not. Her fear was that she would tie him to her with sex and that's what they'd have and only that. He knew better. Their bond was complicated, and intensely sexual, but it wasn't all about sex.

He pulled the Jeep into the small overgrown pad for parking on the right side of the cabin and yanked on the brake. He was ending this right now. She was afraid to move, one way or the other. She was holding herself very still because she didn't know what to do.

Wyatt leapt out of the Jeep, went around to her door and jerked it open, reaching over her lap, his shoulder brushing soft skin, over her soft breasts as he unsnapped her seat belt. The small little touch sent electrical shocks through his body, straight to his groin.

"I can' bring two more men into the house until we're settled, Pepper. Until you belong to me all the way. Until you know for certain that you do." His fingers curled around her arm and he pulled her out of the Jeep, up tight against his body. "I'm not killin' a friend because you can' make up your mind."

"I don't want this. I don't want to be like this." Pepper shook her head again, desperation filling her. He was too close. Too hot. His body so tight against hers she felt like she was melting into him. But if she let go, if they had sex together, for the rest of her life, that's all she'd ever be to him.

Despair mixed with her rising temper. He didn't know

the first thing about what he was getting himself into. "I don't want you killing a friend or anyone else over me. That's what I'm trying to protect you from. You're so arrogant, Wyatt. You don't think I know what's going to happen? Having sex with me isn't going to make it better. It's going to make it worse. That craving will never stop. Never. You'll wake up with it. You'll go to bed with it. You'll be at work with it. You'll make yourself crazy wondering who I'm with, what I'm doing. Worse, you'll be suspicious of your friends and the males in your family. The women won't accept me around their husbands."

"You can tone it down."

"I can't," she burst out, hating the tears filling her eyes. She didn't even have the painkillers to blame this time. She tried again to step away from him, but his strength defeated her. She looked up at him, desperate to save him, willing him to understand. "I can't." That came out in a whisper, and God help them both, her control was already slipping away.

Wyatt stared down into her eyes. More purple than blue or black, with tears shimmering, with the strange starburst moving through the dark color, he saw far more than she would ever want him to. She needed him. She wanted him. There was paradise waiting. There was also hell. She was showing that to him. Both.

He was no kid. He knew prices had to be paid. It would be steep for both of them. He was willing to risk it and he wasn't going to let her back out. His palm curled around the nape of her neck.

In that moment, he recognized just how dangerous he could be and it didn't matter to him. And that was what she'd tried so hard to warn him about. It wouldn't matter. Nothing else would matter but having her. He was willing to burn in hell as long as he could have this. She shook her head, again, her body struggling against his, and he felt his temper rise to meet that challenge.

"You want this," he hissed. "You fuckin' want this, Pepper, just as much as me."

"Not with you. Not *to* you," she denied.

But she did. It was there in her eyes. In the way her body moved against his. The heat. The fire.

"With *me*, yes," he decreed in the face of her denial. "Only me, absolutely yes."

Hunger starkly raw, fully aroused, he brought his mouth down hard on hers. There was nothing gentle about his kiss, not one single thing, but it didn't matter. The moment his mouth touched hers, she went up in flames. There was no holding back no matter how hard she tried. She'd waited her entire lifetime for him.

A growl rumbled deep in his throat. His arm was an iron band, dragging her closer, fitting her body into his as his mouth sought to devour her. He drove her back until she hit the side of the Jeep, never once lifting his mouth. Pepper stroked her tongue along his, along the edge of his teeth, feeding the fire, tasting desire. His. Hers. She was familiar with hunger and need crawling through her and clawing at her relentlessly. This was entirely different.

His arousal was a fever pitch matching the terrible heat of hers as he cupped the back of her head in his palm, holding her still, not allowing her to move while his mouth turned her body into pure liquid fire. He'd lit a match and thrown it right into a pile of dynamite without thinking it through, but it didn't matter to her now.

Pepper heard her own soft little growl and her arms circled his neck as she fiercely kissed him back. The wildness in her unfurled. Stretched. Spread through her like a firestorm that raged out of control. Her body moved against his, rubbing like a cat in heat, desperate to get closer to his skin.

Her body was sensitive, too sensitive for clothes. She needed them gone. Her mouth moved under his. Mindless. Insatiable. Hot. She was so hot she was burning from the inside out. He had gone from charming to pure primitive savage, sweeping her up, still kissing her, still devouring her mouth, taking long strides to take them inside the hunting cabin.

She barely recognized the change from outdoors to indoors. She didn't know how she got there. She did know that she was more out of control than Wyatt, and it wasn't supposed to be that way. That didn't matter either. Only the taste of him, bursting on her tongue, sliding through her body, feeding her terrible need, the ache that would never go away. Now it was Wyatt she craved. She was addicted to. Wyatt's taste and the heat of his body, the press of his hard muscles against her softer body.

Her growls of demands had changed to moans and soft little pleas. His growling had deepened, a primal sound of a male claiming his woman. She couldn't think, not surrounded by him. She could only feel, needy, hungry, so breathless her lungs burned.

Wyatt swept her away, commanding her in a storm of fire, ruthless, decisive, yet he was every bit as wild and out of control as she was. He pinned her to the wall, lifting his head to look down into her eyes. For a moment she couldn't breathe. The fire there, the possession, it was stamped, no, carved deep, into his face.

His eyes glittered down into hers, and a shudder of desire rippled through her. Still, there was a ripple of fear. He would own her. This man holding her so tight against the wall was taking her over and she was letting him, already craving him. He matched her heat and fire. She hadn't thought that possible. His face could have been etched in stone in that moment, and it would have been caught for all time, the look of a conquering male predator, sensual and implacable.

She made a single sound of protest, and that was her undoing. Sheer male dominance crossed his face and he dropped his mouth to her throat. He wasn't gentle about his claiming, suckling and biting with sharp stings followed by the heat of his tongue as he left dozens of marks of his possession. He stripped the blouse from her shoulders, snarling as if the material offended him, sending it flying across the room.

"If you want to save that skirt, get it the hell off," he snapped, his mouth already finding her breast beneath the bra she wore. His hands were busy, and the bra followed the blouse, sailing across the room.

His mouth was on her, hot and demanding, and she cried out, a keening wail she couldn't stop. It felt so good. His teeth scraped over her soft skin while his tongue became a wicked insistent instrument of torturous pleasure, pressing over the hard tight bud of her nipple again and again. His arms locked her closer, while his mouth devoured her with an urgent hunger that only fed her own.

He sounded feral, hot growls that rumbled from deep in his chest. "Lose the damn skirt, Pepper," he snarled, and closed his mouth once more around her breast.

She arced into him, a small mewling sound escaping as she desperately tried to do as he commanded. Nonny had given her the skirt and she didn't want it torn, but that thought was fleeting. She couldn't hold anything in her head. There was too much sensation pouring over and into her.

With fierce impatience, Wyatt hooked both thumbs in her skirt and dropped it to the floor. Pepper kicked it out of the way. His fist bunched her hair in his hand and he yanked her head back.

"You're mine. Do you understand me? *Mine*."

The ferocious declaration should have scared her, not thrilled her, but hot liquid seeped between her legs onto her inner thighs at the glittering look in his eyes. No one had ever matched her fierce passion, the deadly need that stalked her day and night. Wyatt with his burning hunger more than matched her, he took her with him to another place that was both frightening and thrilling.

She waited too long to answer him, and his hand

tightened warningly. She could see the fierce cat in his eyes, the driving need for domination, his mate submitting to his will. The prickles in her scalp sent another flood of liquid heat. His other hand went to her nipple, fingers tugging hard, rolling and stroking until she gasped, panting with need.

"Fuckin' answer me, Pepper. You're *mine*. Say it. And know when you do, there's no takin' it back. We stand together no matter what. Say it, damn you."

He drew her breast into the inferno that was his mouth, using the edge of his teeth until she cried out. His tongue soothed her even as his fingers tugged at her other nipple roughly.

Her body was no longer her own, burning up, a fiery storm of flames she couldn't control. She needed to feel his skin against hers, but he was still fully clothed. He kept at her body, using teeth and tongue, suckling, tugging and nipping until pleasure and pain mixed into one snarling ball of need that had her crying out, pleading incoherently with him.

He ran his hands over her rib cage, her flat belly and the flare of her hips, possession in the strong fingers everywhere they touched her, as if he was branding her with his own name. It felt like that, his touch a brand, sinking deep beneath her skin to her very bones. The world faded, the room, even the floor beneath her feet. There was only Wyatt with his demanding hands and his mouth and tongue and teeth and the ravenous hunger that only grew between them.

Fingers of desire danced down her thighs, teased the insides of them until every nerve ending she had seemed raw and exposed, throbbing between her legs. She felt the bite of his teeth, of his nails, another mark of possession on her body, his cat DNA feeding his fierce voracious hunger. A sob escaped.

With a low, rough growl, wholly sensual, Wyatt grasped her panties and yanked, ripping them away from her body. His palm pushed hard against her moist heat at the junction of her legs, that fierce furnace, the liquid spilling into his hand.

She gasped, cried out, thrown into an orgasm with just his touch alone. Her body rippled, quaked, tumbled hard into the wild ride as he clamped his hand over her, his thumb pressing deep against her hottest button.

Again. Give it to me again. He snarled the command, giving her no choice.

His fingers pushed deep inside her, thumb stroking, manipulating, while his mouth pulled strongly at her breast and ran up her throat, kissing and biting, until she was nearly mad with desire. He drove her up fast, his hands implacable, fiercely demanding she give him what he wanted. Her body careened over the edge a second time, this orgasm much stronger, ripping through her hard, rushing up toward her breasts and down toward her thighs, leaving her gasping and panting and crying out his name.

Look at me, damn it. See who I am. See all of me.

It took a moment to pry her eyes open, with the tremors rocking her body, but she did. His sensual features were stamped with violence, with predatory hunger, and sheer unadulterated possession.

I can handle you, all of it. I can give you every damn thing you need. You're mine. Now fuckin' say it. I want the words. Give yourself to me.

She hadn't realized the scope of his need for domination, the wildness or passion that raged in him just as it raged in her. But there was no mistaking that look. She found herself drowning in that look.

"I'm yours," she murmured out loud. "Yours."

"*Only* mine. You make certain you know that, Pepper. Because I would kill another man who put his cock inside your body. Any man who dared touch you. Do you get that? Make me know that you understand. I want this over and done with so we never have to revisit it. You're givin' me your word, your vow and I'm doin' the same with you. Say you understand that."

All the while his fingers pushed inside of her and his dangerous, talented thumb never stopped stroking, so that the tension once again began to coil tighter and tighter.

"I understand," she gasped, closing her eyes, because she did. She gave herself to him. Gave herself to an uncertain future. Wrapped them both in a sexual heat that could be a nightmare they could never escape.

She didn't care. She wanted him. Wanted this. His hands and mouth on her, his hard body claiming hers. She needed this as she had never needed anything else in her life—and that was the very horror of the moment. Still, she couldn't stop herself, or him, and she didn't want to. Hunger lived and breathed in her, clawing for supremacy.

Wyatt fought to hold the raging instincts of the cat under some semblance of control, but the feral nature was totally dominant now, the heat and fire sweeping through coupled with the need to make her know no one could ever touch her. She belonged to him. *Belonged.* They fit. She was probably the only woman in the world who could match—and take—the fierce domination of the cat that raged so strong in him.

His cock was desperate to feel the hot glide of her wet, silken sheath closing around him like a tight fist. He pushed his fingers deeper just to feel the muscles tightening around him, clamping like a vise. She was perfect. Perfection. A jackhammer beat at his head. Thunder roared in his ears. His tongue fought with hers while his fingers pushed deep over and over, forcing a third orgasm. *His.* She was his alone. He could do this to her. Bring her to this. Give this to her.

The sounds she made when she came with such wild abandon fed his own wild cravings and he dropped his hands to his jeans, tearing them open, pushing them off his hips so that his erection sprang free. The relief was tremendous, but the cool air didn't relieve the fierce heat or the terrible hunger.

He caught her wrist and dragged her hand to him, wrapping her palm around his thick throbbing erection. Pepper knew exactly what to do. Her fingers stroked and glided. She cupped his sac and rolled his balls. Her fist closed around him and he was instantly in paradise, but it wasn't enough.

"Give me your mouth, babe. Put your mouth on me right fuckin' now." He bit out the command through clenched teeth. Her fingers kept his cock jerking and throbbing with desperate need as she slid her thumb over the leaking drops, smoothing them over the head and shaft.

His voice was ruthless, his eyes hooded and demanding, his hand on her shoulder, pressing her down, the other fisted in her hair, pulling her head back as she was forced to kneel at his feet. His cock was alive, inflamed, desperate for the feel of her. Every movement she made was sensual, her skin, her eyes, her hair, her pouting mouth.

He was hot, but she fanned the flames with the way she knelt, her knees wide, feet tucked under her, her eyes on his as she allowed him to guide her head to his cock. He could see droplets of moisture, glittering like diamonds caught in the whorls of tiny curls at the junction of her legs. She looked impossibly sexy, her large eyes drenched in purple, the diamond burst beckoning toward heaven.

"Your mouth," he demanded, harshly, a warning growl rumbling in his throat and chest. "Give me your damn mouth." He knew what she was doing, making him wait for it, driving him toward the edge of his control, but he was already there.

Damn it, Pepper, don' be stupid. You can see how I am. Don' push me any further. You already have marks all over your body. He was rough with her and he knew the violence swirling in him would only make him rougher. "Get your fuckin' mouth on me right now." He gripped her long, thick hair harder, pushing her face toward his inflamed cock. He had to have her mouth wrapped around him right then or he might not make it through the next few minutes.

There was something truly sensual in seeing her kneeling at his feet, stripped of all clothing, naked, her skin gleaming, breasts high and firm, nipples tight and inviting, her legs open for him while he was fully clothed. His harsh language didn't make her wince or in any way deter her. She was his match in every way. If she was a little afraid of their union, it only seemed to add to the hunger raging between them.

The head of his cock bumped impressively against her mouth and she slid her small, pink tongue out to lick at him delicately. He groaned as fire shot through his body, a lightning strike that shook him. She lapped at him like a cat might with a bowl of cream, licking up and down his shaft and swirling over the sensitive, flared head. She was killing him.

He jerked her hair, forcing her eyes to meet his. She had the audacity to smile at him. Her tongue teased along her own lips, licking up every pearly drop. His gut twisted and his cock, so long, so thick and so aroused, hurt like a son of a bitch.

"Fils de putain," he ground out in Cajun French.

He forced his finger to the side of her mouth, parting her lips and shoving himself deep. His cock was instantly in paradise, her hot, wet mouth wrapped tightly around him. She suckled strongly, pulling him deep, her tongue dancing up and down his shaft, teasing the sweet spot under the flared head and then swiping over it as she drew him out and took him deep again. Her purr vibrated through his cock.

Her mouth grew hotter until he was in a tube of fire, her need to please him consuming him. Burning. Scorching. So tight like the tightest fist. Pulling strongly and then letting him go to give her talented tongue a chance to dance once more down his shaft to his sac and then back up. So greedy. She was greedy as she suckled, clamping tight to milk him.

His cock swelled more, impossibly so, but it didn't matter. Nothing mattered beyond that hot mouth robbing him of his mind, of all control. He brought both hands to her hair, on either side, guiding her, feeling the swell of his cock in the torturous glide of her mouth. He held her head still and pushed lightly with his hips, testing, making certain she could handle him.

He held her absolutely still and thrust, his cock bumping the back of her throat. Her eyes widened in a kind of shock. Vicious pleasure burst through him, just like the starburst in those purple eyes of hers.

He withdrew and thrust a second time, allowing the brutal burst of sensation to engulf him, to take him out of his own body and push him careening toward the edge of all control. He didn't give her much choice, but then she didn't ask for it either. She relaxed her throat and suddenly he felt the tight hot, convulsing grip and lost all control. His body jerked. His hips surged. His cock exploded, pouring his seed down her throat.

Still, even that wasn't enough to sate his body. He had known it wouldn't be. He had known taking her any way would never be enough. He pulled out of her mouth, his eyes on her face. Her lips were swollen and there was evidence of him there. Satisfaction poured into him. *His.* She was his.

Her breasts were rose colored, her nipples tight, hard buds. Her breathing came in gasps and pants and there were more diamond droplets in the curls between her legs. She leaned forward and stroked him with her tongue, lapping gently, careful of his sensitivity. She licked up his shaft and around the head, soothing this time, as if she really were a cat caring for him. Up and down his shaft, along his sac and over the flared head.

He was growing harder with every stroke, just as if he hadn't already expended seed, energy and passion.

CHAPTER 10

With one hand, Wyatt ripped his shirt off and flung it to one side. His skin felt as scorching hot as his cock. She had some kind of biochemical in her mouth, something that fed his arousal. With every lap of her tongue, she inflamed him more. The same biochemical had to be emitted through the pads of her fingers because each stroke of her hands, the touch of her fingers, made his head roar with hunger.

He gripped her shoulders and forcefully pushed her backward to the floor. There was no give there, nothing to cushion her when he pounded into her. He stood over her as she sprawled out, her dark hair cascading around her, dark as a raven's wing, pools of it spilling in whorls, masses of silk against the old, discolored wood. Her knees were open and she started to move, to close them.

"Don'," he instructed harshly. "Stay just like that."

She swallowed and nodded, subsiding, allowing her knees to stay wide open to his view. He shed his boots fast and then his jeans, all the time watching the rise and fall of her breasts, pleased with the marks covering her, showing she belonged to him, especially pleased with the need spilling out between her legs, calling to him. Her scent enveloped him and he knew the same biochemical was there, wafting up to him, driving him insane with hunger, with lust.

His mouth watered. His cock jerked, just as hard and edgy as before, the need edging on brutal. She was flushed, her breath coming in ragged gasps. In need. Just as hungry and inflamed as he was. Waiting for him. Desperate for him. He wanted her that way. She was the thing of fantasies. She could control men easily through sex but she would never be satisfied. He knew if he was going to keep her, she couldn't be in control of him. He needed to show her he could satisfy her always.

He could take away the desperate hunger that built and built in her until she thought she'd lose her mind. Only him. He could match her passion for passion. Fire for fire. He could tie her to him this way and she'd never escape. She'd been so afraid of tying him to her through sex, that she had never stopped to consider it might go the other way. He'd been careful to keep that information to himself.

He was a fucking genius, and she should have known he'd approach his claiming of her with advanced knowledge, already certain of every move. He'd studied her over the last few days, watched her, had been inside her mind. He knew exactly what to do to get her—to keep her. They could teach her every trick there was when it came to sex. They had found a woman with exceptional beauty, someone naturally sensual and appealing to men. Still, there had to be something else they'd done to her, something to make her need sex, and appeal to every man. The only real answer had to be biochemical.

He had watched to see the cycle, knowing there had to be one. He could match the sex she needed with her cycle to leech the biochemical from her body, to maximize the output so she would have more control. He wasn't ever going to be stupid enough to tell her—or anyone else—he'd found the secret. For the first time he was grateful for the cat DNA slipped into him. His cat was fierce, feral and dominating. He could match her passion for passion.

Without a word, he dropped to the floor, yanking her knees farther apart. She let out a gasping cry. He stared into her wide, shocked eyes, his hand cupping her sex, feeling the scorching heat. "Mine," he claimed, making it another demand. "You are mine. This is mine and I don' share well with others." He wanted to make that point over and over so if she ever went into heat without him close she would know better than to act on it.

She swallowed hard. That wasn't enough for him. Not nearly enough. He dragged her body to his, using her legs, keeping her wide open.

"I want the words. When I tell you somethin', you answer me."

"I didn't realize it was a question, Wyatt," she soothed, evidently realizing he was bordering on violence. "I want to be yours. Only yours."

"No one else *ever* puts their hands, their mouth or their fuckin' cock here, you got that? There's only me for you. *My* hands, my mouth, my cock, you got that?" He snarled it at her, allowing his feral side to slip further out. Just the thought of her with another man made him dangerous. She needed to see that and to see that he would never, under any circumstances, allow her to manipulate him using sex.

He had hoped the wildness he'd been born and bred with combined with the enhancement of big predatory cat would make him the perfect partner for the biochemical rushing through her body. He'd been right. He could match her passion, take her all the way, drain her of the biochemical and leave her sated, even if for a small amount of time. For a woman who couldn't be sated, who always was in need, it would be everything.

She swallowed hard, her gaze clinging to his and nodded silently. When he stared at her, his eyes beginning the change, she bit her lip and mumbled her reply. "Yes. I understand, Wyatt. Please. Please. I'm burning up."

He didn't wait. Didn't give her any time. Her soft little plea affected him more than he ever wanted her to know. The heady scent of her, the beauty of her, sent him tumbling right over the cliff into such a heightened lust he'd never ever achieved before. He went willingly.

He lifted her sheath to his mouth, his tongue stabbing deep right into the hot vortex of sweet, honeyed cream the cat in him needed. She screamed and nearly bucked out of his hands. He held her tight, refusing to allow her to squirm away, his hold on her rigid. The moment he put his mouth on her, tasted the exotic, hot mixture of spice and honey designed to trap a man, he knew he was lost.

Her taste was addicting. He'd crave it for the rest of his life. Never get her out of his mouth or his mind. It didn't matter either. He devoured her, blood rushing to his groin, filling his cock to a painful, needy very relentless ache. He feasted while she dug her heels into the old wood floor and tried to writhe away, gasping for air.

Again she bucked her hips, desperate, the sensations too much, but he refused to stop. In truth, he was already out of control, desperate to lap at the cream spilling out of her like molten gold. He gave her a warning growl, a hot, feral sound that rumbled through the small cabin, almost more beast than man as he greedily took what belonged to him.

When she didn't—couldn't stop, his palm smacked her buttocks, a second warning. That sent more liquid gold spilling into his mouth. Her little chant, please-oh-please-oh-please, rang in his ears, a kind of music to cut through the thunder already roaring in his ears. She was ready for him, wet, hot, her body clenching and spasming, so desperate for his, but he refused to take her over the edge.

"Wyatt." She called his name. Pleading. Her hands curled in his hair, pulled as if trying to bring his head up.

He gave her another warning swat, caught the hot liquid

reaction on his tongue even as he growled again, sending vibrations rocketing through her hot little channel. He lapped at her, plunged his tongue deep and then added his teeth, scraping against her tight, hard bud.

She screamed, and he pulled her thighs wider apart, refusing to back off, finding the little trigger with his mouth and sucking hard as he used the flat of his tongue and the edge of his teeth. She sobbed out a plea. Bucked. He could actually feel the burst of pleasure ripping through her as he threw her into another vicious orgasm. This one was even stronger than the last, a tidal wave taking her so that she sobbed with pleasure.

He didn't stop. As sensitive as she was, he still refused to stop. "Another," he demanded. "Give me another."

His mouth was back on her, his fingers in her, his thumb playing her body again, driving her up fast and hard. The more he devoured, the more he craved.

Pepper thought she might be going insane. She hadn't even known it was possible to have such intense orgasms. One right after the other. He was going to kill her if he didn't stop, and he didn't show signs of slowing down. His face was a hard mask of sensuality, harsh with passion and the need to dominate.

"No," she gasped when he swiped his tongue through her folds and her body shuddered with pleasure, the aftershocks nearly as strong as the original quake.

His head came up, a tiger scenting prey, eyes focused and fierce. "Did you just tell me no? Because your body is sayin' yes. It's screamin' yes. Don' lie to me, Pepper. You want this. You even need it, the same as me."

"It's too much . . ." She trailed off, gasped and then screamed when his mouth descended again, throwing her into another vortex of sheer pleasure.

His tongue laved and flicked her clit relentlessly, sending the flames leaping until she was so scorching hot she was certain she would spontaneously combust. She could feel the orgasm building, every bit as relentless as his wicked tongue. She thrashed, her head tossing back and forth, her hands at his shoulders, nails alternately digging into him to inflame him and then pushing at him to try to release her thighs from his merciless, iron grip.

His mouth never stopped, until that sensitive bundle of nerve endings caught fire, a storm of flames devouring her along with his tongue and teeth. His tongue stabbed deep over and over, refusing to relent, to give her a moment to catch her breath, to stop the building of the next orgasm.

The more she thrashed and bucked, the more his body hardened, his eyes more cat than human, his enormous strength pinning her down while he fed on her. He lifted his head slightly, licking at the droplets tangled in the curls at the junction of her legs and then followed a trail of slick heat down her inner thigh.

Her body was damp with tiny beads of perspiration. Her silken hair was a mass of tangled curls. Her breath came in ragged little gasps and moans. He bit down, a stinging nip that drove her over the edge again, the pain/pleasure sweeping her right off the cliff before she knew she was at the precipice.

Wyatt rose to his knees, watching her face as she rode out the wild orgasm. She looked . . . taken. Thoroughly taken. Her body flushed, her hair everywhere, her beautiful mouth open and her eyes wide with shock. He grasped her hips and lodged the head of his erection into that fierce inferno. She was slick—on fire—scorching hot.

He inhaled and threw back his head, holding still for just a moment, struggling for some semblance of control. She tried to move, but he held her still, pushing another inch inside of her and again stopping, feeling her surround his sensitive head with fiery heat and a tightness that nearly strangled him. Still, he held on, clenching his teeth, waiting for her eyes to meet his.

She thrashed for a moment, desperate to draw him into

her, but it was necessary to keep her thinking he was in total control while she was burning out of it. Pepper had to know he could take her heat.

Her lashes lifted and her gaze moved over his face. He held her legs draped over his shoulders, shifting just a little, lodging a bit deeper. Pleasure flared, warred with intense desire in her dark, purple eyes. The strange, beautiful starburst had gone through her eyes so that they glittered like diamonds back at him.

"Who are you goin' to trust with you, Pepper?"

She didn't hesitate this time. "Wyatt. You. I trust you with me. Please, Wyatt, make it go away. Just take it away."

He knew what she meant. The terrible driving hunger that never left her alone, that grew and grew until she thought she would lose her mind, until she had no choice but to go out and find a man to seduce. They'd done that to her in the laboratory, given her a curse beyond all others, and he damned well was going to beat them at their own game. Pepper was his, not theirs. She would know he would take care of her, protect her and when she needed this, crazy, violent sex, he would be more than happy to give it to her as well.

He ran his finger from the valley between her breasts down the center of her body to her belly button, watching her shiver in anticipation. All the while her tight channel surrounded the scant inches he'd allowed himself inside her, closing around him like the tightest of fists.

She bucked her hips, trying to force him deeper, but he held her there, knowing she needed this brutal, almost violent possession. He read it in her mind, although she'd tried to hide from him, ashamed of what they'd made her. Terrified he'd despise her for what she was. A tinge of fear skated into the deep purple of her eyes, as she tried to hold still for him, tried to give him what he silently demanded.

He rewarded her, sliding in another inch, forcing his way through those tight folds. She was more than ready for him, but so tight he could see the burn of discomfort in her eyes, on her face, before the pleasure took hold once more.

"I need you now," she gasped out, pleading.

He surged into her. Hard. Fast. Deep. The floor didn't give an inch and the thrust was brutal, taking him all the way. Her sheath was tighter than a skintight glove. Wet. Slick. A raging fire surrounding him with silken flames. He began to piston his hips, a fury of deep thrusts, each bumping her cervix, piercing her to go even deeper.

He felt her muscles reluctantly stretching to accommodate him, but still, she was tighter than any fist and the friction sent fire streaking through his cock to his belly and thighs. Her inner muscles gripped him, clamping down hard like a vise, trying to strangle him. He let go of every thought, spinning out into space, letting the pleasure take him.

He was rough, taking her in a violent storm of powerful, hammering strokes, giving himself up to the fantasy, the perfect lover, the woman he could do it all with. Every erotic thought or dream, slow and lazy, or rough and brutal, her body accepted and craved his.

He watched them come together, his cock slamming into her, disappearing while fire streaked through him and the breath left his lungs in a heated rush. The view was erotic, her breasts moving with every hard thrust. He loved the look on her face, the stark need and the wild passion to match his own.

He rode her hard, driving in and out of her until the agonizing fire consuming them both was nearly intolerable. His cock expanded, pushing back at the tight muscles, increasing the terrible friction. She cried out, clamping down around him in a vise-like grip, her body trying to strangle his. He thrust harder, using powerful strokes, feeling the throb in her body.

He rode the wave of madness, pleasure drenching him until his body was covered in a fine sheen of sweat, and still he pounded into her. Her body clamped down a second time. Throbbed again.

"Now, baby." It came out a command and he meant it that way, but he gentled his voice, praising her. "That's my woman." Letting her know he wanted this for her. That she was pleasing him. "Come for me. Give it to me. Give me you, Pepper. Wild. Hot. Give yourself to me."

She cried out and her body tightened around his, clamping hard. Hot, delicious cream enveloped him, scorching him, but he welcomed the fluid, the biochemically treated honey that he'd be forever addicted to. He wanted her to have multiple orgasms, produce as much as possible of her liquid gold. It was the only way for her to ever get a respite from the terrible drive that refused to allow her peace. He was giving her that gift.

She cried out again and again, as her body rippled with another powerful orgasm. He waited for the aftershocks, breathing through his mouth to stay in control when his own body wanted to rocket with her. He didn't allow her to catch her breath. He timed it perfectly, moving again, slamming deep, driving home to take her back up just as her body was settling.

"Again, baby, give it to me again," he demanded, moving inside her, feeling the pleasure pouring over him.

"I can't. I can't, Wyatt." Her head tossed back and forth, but her eyes clung to his and he could see the need still there.

"Yes, you can. Because I want you to. You'll do it for me. Just let go for me. I'm here. I'll always be here for you." He dropped his voice an octave, but he had to say it behind clenched teeth.

The silken glove was scorching hot, holding him in its fist as he slammed into her ferociously with his cock, over and over, driving deep and hard. He found her left nipple with one hand, tugging and rolling until she was crying out again, and he felt her muscles gripping even tighter.

He could feel her fighting to stave off the impending

orgasm. There was fear in her eyes, but so much hunger, so much desire, he didn't hesitate to pound into her, letting the flames take him higher.

Pepper stared up at his face, undecided if he was the very devil or not. There was no way to stop him, no way to catch her breath. She didn't want to stop but feared he was going to kill her if her body went over the edge another time. She'd lost count and was terrified that she was the one out of control—not him.

Tension coiled deep inside her and mindlessly she shook her head, trying to deny the flood of pleasure pouring into her, melting even her bones. She was somewhere between darkness and subspace, teetering right there, unable to distinguish between pleasure and pain but wanting him never to stop.

For one moment, everything in her stilled. She could hear her sobbing breathing, so ragged, her lungs desperate for air. She could hear the slap of their bodies coming together as with each stroke, fire arced through her. His hand at her nipple was relentless, pulling, tugging, and as if her nipple had a direct line to her center, she felt the spasm start there first.

Wyatt felt her body clamp down hard on his. It was exquisite. He'd never felt anything like it in his life. Her silken sheath, so hot he was burning up, dragging over his sensitive cock, making him feel more alive than he ever had in his life. He wanted her to feel exhausted, limp with sex, fully satisfied and too tired to lure other men, the biochemical drained from her body so that she had a long reprieve.

He felt the gathering in her body, starting around his cock, building to hurricane force. He tightened his grip on her hips, tilting her body to fit even more tightly with his, so he could go deeper. Around him her body rippled and gripped, while her head tossed and her body writhed, fighting off the inevitable storm as he slammed into her again and again in a kind of wild fury.

She stiffened under him, her body clamping down on his, a vicious vise. It seemed impossible to breathe, to get air into his burning lungs, but that didn't matter. Nothing mattered to him but the ferocious joining of their bodies. He drove through the fury of the storm once more, burying himself with the flames stroking over him. He thought he might have gone a little insane, the inferno so hot and tight it bordered on pain, but there was no stopping the driving force that had him hammering into her over and over like a machine totally out of control.

Agonizing pleasure radiated from his groin to every part of his body as her body shuddered, clamped down on him even tighter, milking and strangling, a fiery massage that sent him careening off the edge of a cliff. His body of its own accord went still. He felt the pulse throb in his cock. A single heartbeat of pure anticipation.

Pepper screamed, nails digging into his back and shoulders, a wild, heart-wrenching cry as the orgasm took her with hurricane force. It ripped through both of them, every cell in their bodies, muscles, bones, radiating down their thighs to the soles of their feet and up through their bellies to chest and finally the roar in their heads.

His body shuddered, the release so violent, his seed jetting deep into her over and over again. The sheath surrounding him seemed to be made of living, breathing hot velvet, as it kept squeezing and milking long after the thunder in his ears subsided.

He allowed himself to collapse over her, pinning her to the floor with his weight, his body blanketing hers. He needed to feel her soft body imprinted on his. He kept his arms around her, refusing to allow her to withdraw from him.

"Put your arms around my neck, sugar," he whispered softly, keeping his voice gentle. She was fighting for breath, but he could feel her sudden confusion, the wariness in her, as if suddenly, he might have become the enemy.

Slowly, almost reluctantly, her arms crept around his

neck. He kissed her throat and blazed a trail up to her chin, all the while enjoying the aftershocks. He held her to him, nuzzling her ear, nipping at her earlobe.

"What are you doing?"

"Did you think we would just get up and put on our clothes?"

Wyatt lifted his head to look into her eyes. Definitely confused.

"I don't know. I've never done this. Training involved me doing things to others, not them doing anything to me. I've never felt like this and I don't know what I'm supposed to do now." She sounded lost. Afraid. Vulnerable. "Aren't we finished?"

Because any man she seduced was supposed to die. That was her job. Seduction and assassination. There was no aftermath, no loving arms to be held in.

"No, baby, we're not through yet. We got what we both needed. What we had to have, but I still want to love on you. I need to do that, sugar. It's important to me."

He kissed her eyelids, her temple and smoothed back her hair. "I get to love on you, honey. Just like this. Hold you close to me and let you know how amazin' you are. How much you matter to me. That what we did together wasn' just about sex. It will never be just about sex with you. I don' know what's growin' in me for you, but it's there, Pepper."

She lay beneath him, looking up at him with questions in her eyes. His hand stroked her long hair from her face, his fingers gentle, soothing even.

"I don't understand."

"You deserve tender. Gentle. I can do that now that we've been through the storm of the century." He grinned at her as he leaned down to brush a kiss along her throat. His hand stroked her breast and then he leaned down and flicked her nipple with his tongue before rolling off her to lie on the floor close, his body pressed to hers. "You are incredible, Pepper. My woman. Incredible. How do you feel, sugar? Are you all right?"

Was she? Pepper wasn't certain of anything. She lay very still beside him, wanting to touch each place on her body where he'd kissed her. Where he'd touched her with such gentle fingers. He'd gone from fierce to tender in minutes and the change threw her. Wyatt was . . . She didn't know.

And then it dawned on her. Her body wasn't hurting. There was no burning. No tension. For the first time she could recall in years, her body was her own. Completely sated. Satisfied. There was no terrible drive for sex. No unwanted hunger she couldn't assuage or stop.

"Oh, my God, Wyatt." She turned to him, her eyes wide with shock. "It's gone." She felt the burn of tears, her only warning and then she was sobbing, breaking down completely, another first for her.

Wyatt immediately gathered her to him, holding her close, cradling her in strong arms, sitting, his back to the wall with her in his lap. He actually rocked her as if she were a child in need of soothing, and at that moment, Pepper had to admit she was. No one had ever been kind to her like Wyatt. Never. She couldn't remember anyone ever holding her or brushing kisses over her temples or down to the corner of her mouth.

"I'm sorry," she managed to blurt out in the middle of the storm of tears.

"Don' be. I'm here. I've got you. I told you to trust me, honey. I'm not goin' anywhere. When it happens again, we know what to do."

He touched her mouth with his finger, and then slid his finger between her lips so that she sucked on it. Extracting it, he put his own finger in his mouth, tasting her. Tasting that addicting spiced honey. His cock twitched. He couldn't lie to her, as much as he wanted this moment for her. She had to know.

"It will come back, Pepper. That need. But I'll be here

to take it away for you. Whenever it gets too much, long before it begins to drive you insane, do you understand, babe? Me. I'll do that for you."

Pepper's heart clenched hard. He was right. Sadly. For the moment the terrible need was gone, wiped away by Wyatt, but if he wasn't around . . . "You can't really tie yourself to me, Wyatt. We both know that. Living with me would be hell. You'd lose all your friends, even family members. You won't always be around. You're a Ghost-Walker and you have to leave to go on missions. What happens then? What if I have a meltdown and can't take it?"

He ruffled her hair and dropped a kiss on top of her head. "Silly woman. Your man is a fuckin' genius. One of my best friends is even smarter than me. Do you think we can' beat them at their own game? Once I have the children squared away, we're devotin' our time to helpin' you out. We'll find a way to overcome it or at least tone it down so you're not sufferin' every minute of the day without me."

"It's so horrible, Wyatt. Once it starts the hunger builds every day and I can't think. I can barely eat anything. How can you keep up with that?"

He laughed softly. "Seriously, babe? I'm a GhostWalker. I guess I'll just have to do my duty."

"It's not funny." But there was a faint smile in her voice.

"It's occurred to me that if I get you pregnant, the cycle will stop for the duration. If that's so, every time I have to leave, you'd better be prepared to have a baby. We might end up with a dozen little ones runnin' around, but I'll know you're not steppin' out on me." He was half serious. He'd given it a lot of thought and it would make sense that if she got pregnant the biochemical might not be able to move through her so quickly.

"A dozen? *Children?* Are you crazy?"

"I'm Cajun, babe. Of course I'm crazy." He looked down at her face. "Are you okay now? I didn't hurt you, did I?"

She moistened her lips. "I'll be a little sore, but in a nice way. Thank you, Wyatt. For understanding and trying to help me. No one's ever done anything like this for me."

He didn't like a certain note in her voice. A hesitation. A kind of embarrassment. "What we did together is a good thing, Pepper," he said, trying to understand what was going through her head.

She took a deep breath and let it out, shaking her head and then subsiding against his chest, her head tucked down so her hair fell around her face.

"No, honey. You're not hidin' from me. From us. We talk things out. That's how we're goin' to make this work. I know you're not used to a partner, but that's what we're formin' here. A partnership. You tell me when somethin's not right. Or when you're upset. I'll do the same. We have to be honest with one another."

Pepper kept her head down, her mind racing. Wyatt made her want the life he was tempting her with so much she couldn't breathe. He didn't know how truly bad it would get with other men wanting her when her guard came down, or the women despising her for being around their men. But she wanted him to be *her* man. The moment he'd used those words, a thrill had gone through her.

"Put your eyes on mine, sugar. Right now."

She even loved the way he could go from an easygoing Cajun charm to a commanding arrogance that sent shivers of need through her body. She had never wanted to please a man before, but she wanted to please him. She wanted to belong to him. She wanted his body and his mind and his protection. Most of all, she wanted him to love her. She had never considered being loved by anyone until she met him. But to confess that to him . . .

She shook her head before she could stop herself, a metallic taste of defeat in her mouth.

Wyatt caught her chin in a firm grip and lifted it, forcing her head up. "Say it." His voice was rough, but his eyes were gentle. Tender even.

"I don't want you to want me for sex." She blurted it out in a little rush. "I don't understand how all of my training failed. I didn't realize how truly flawed I really am. The one thing I'm supposed to be good at, controlling a man through sex, just went straight out the window. You were in control, not me. And still, I don't want you to stay with me because of . . ." She broke off and waved one hand down their naked bodies.

"Because the sex was better than either of us ever imagined or thought possible?" he finished for her. He bent his head to hers and brushed a gentle kiss across her mouth. "You're really fucked up, aren't you, babe? They did a real number on you. The sex is off the charts and I'd be a fool not to want that every day of my life. That's all you, sugar. Not their damn enhancements. I have three little girls who desperately need a mother who will fight for them alongside of me and protect and love them. That's you. I need a woman who can put up with my jealous, arrogant, demandin' nature and love me anyway. That's you too. I like holdin' you in my arms and feelin' you in my bed. I like listenin' to you laughin' and touchin' your skin. I like knowin' you're goin' to be wet for me and that anytime I want you, that you're goin' to want me right then, at that moment."

She swallowed hard, his words penetrating through her brain and finding their way to her heart. It hurt, an actual physical pain in her heart to hear him talk like that—to her—about her. Did she dare take a chance? She'd be risking so much more than he realized. She'd be risking him. Wyatt.

As if he knew she was still struggling, he tipped her face up farther, holding her captive with his eyes.

"Do you have any idea how strong I am? Let yourself go, Pepper. Trust me enough to put you back together if you break apart. I'll do the same. I'll trust you. If I'm fallin', I'll expect you to shore me up. That's what partners do for one another. Give us this chance. Give the girls this chance. I'll be a good father to them and their home will be filled with laughter and love. We'll surround them with that."

"Be very sure you want me, Wyatt, not a fantasy," she whispered, her heart pounding hard. "I don't know the first thing about families or parenting."

"That won't be hard. We have Nonny and she'll be there for you one hundred percent. She already has made up her mind to keep you. Fontenots are that way. I made up my mind when I saw you with that big knife."

"Do you know that you rarely swear until you have sex, Wyatt?" Pepper asked, slowly pushing back, her hands on his forearms.

At the word "sex" his cock jerked. She felt it rubbing against her bottom, an exquisite feel of silk and sword. She bent forward to kiss his chest, right over his heart. Her hair swept around her face, tumbling down to brush his thighs. It was the first time she'd ever dared to really touch him. She was still a little afraid of herself, but she liked the freedom and he didn't stop her.

"It's the only time I know for certain Nonny won' hear and wash my mouth out with soap," he explained, laughter in his voice.

But there was a hitch too. He liked her touch. She kept touching, running her fingers down his body to his flat belly. She scooted back to give herself room.

"We still have to go into town," she murmured. She glanced up at him to see his eyes watching her. His beautiful eyes. She could drown there.

"That's true." His voice was noncommittal.

Pepper kissed her way down to his belly button. "The answer is yes, Wyatt. I want to be your partner in every way." Her tongue swirled in his belly button.

She watched his eyes the entire time, needing to see his reaction. His eyes went dark and then filled with a kind of heat that drove her crazy in a good way. She liked seeing the look on his face, that stamp of desire, the possession and the growing affection. It was there as well.

His breath caught in his throat and he slid his fingers into her hair, massaging her scalp gently. "You know I can be bossy. Especially durin' sex."

She laughed softly, deliberately allowing her warm breath to envelope the growing shaft. She liked the look of him, how masculine and perfectly built he was. He was unashamed of his body, if anything, a little arrogant and totally confident, which she admitted to herself he had reason to be.

"I'll admit, I caught that," she teased, and lazily swiped her tongue over him.

His body gave an answering shudder. His cock grew and thickened. With just one swipe and she was thrilled. *Thrilled*. This was her. Pepper. The woman, not the seductress. She was going to make certain her man was thoroughly sated. More, her body would be more than satisfied and when they went into town to shop for the children and supplies, there would be no mistakes.

"You goin' to tease me or put your mouth on me, woman?"

The demand in his voice made her laugh. She realized she had fun with Wyatt. She hadn't known fun or laughter.

"I believe I'll put my mouth on you," she replied, and allowed him to feel her laughter, her happiness right through the most sensitive part of his anatomy.

CHAPTER 11

Pepper stayed very close to Wyatt as they walked around town together. He seemed to know everyone. His hand held hers tightly, and she felt his occasional glance. She liked that it mattered to him that she was all right. She was acutely aware of her lack of underwear. Wyatt had torn her panties to shreds and there had been no salvaging them. He didn't mind, but it was one more thing she was embarrassed about. She had no idea how to act or what he expected of her, so she stayed very quiet and tucked herself in close to his side.

"Babe, you're trembling," Wyatt said softly, pulling her to a halt in front of a store.

She couldn't help it. She looked up at him. Hadn't he noticed the looks the men were sneaking at her?

"I'm okay. I've never walked around like this before. I feel exposed. Out in the open. When I went on training missions, it was dinner parties. Small. Intimate. Or rugged terrain if I was training to be a soldier. I've never done anything like this in my life."

Wyatt smiled down at her. "You're doin' great. Let's go in here and find you some clothes."

"Underwear," she said firmly.

"I like you without it."

She couldn't help but laugh softly at the humor in his voice that told her he was part teasing and part telling the truth. He had the cocky smile she liked. The one that told her he liked being with her as well.

"Of course now that I'm givin' it a little thought, we'd better buy you a lot. I like rippin' it offa you too. Choices are always good."

His grin felt good in spite of her nerves. His hand was tight around hers, giving her some comfort. She tried not to notice how some of the men on the street turned their heads to watch her walk. She wasn't feeling as if she had to shield them from her raw sexual hunger but maybe . . .

"No, babe, don' do that to yourself. You're naturally a beautiful woman, and men like to look at beautiful women. It's that simple. I'd be starin' at you too, if you weren' tucked up tight against me. I like havin' you at my side."

"You're not jealous?" She didn't want him to feel uncomfortable with her.

"Why should I be jealous?"

His hand swept down her back, over the curve of her butt. His touch was light, but it was possessive. She could feel the caress of his hot palm right through the thin material of the skirt, and deep inside a small tingle of awareness answered the gesture.

"You're with me and I have your full attention. Now you start smilin' and flirtin', that might be somethin' else altogether." He reached around her to pull open the door to the little boutique. "Flame likes this shop. I hope you find a few things you love."

In spite of herself, she felt excitement. She'd never been shopping for clothes. Wyatt continued to give her firsts.

She found herself clutching his wrist with her other hand, her heart pounding as she walked into the store.

I've never done this. I don't have any money and I don't know how much things cost.

Wyatt looked down into Pepper's upturned face. She was glowing. He'd put that look there. Her eyes held trepidation, but they sparkled with anticipation.

I want you to have every possible experience, sugar. Shopping for you, for the kids, even for me, will come natural to you once you do it a few times. Let me worry about the cost. I've got it covered, no problem.

She bit her lower lip with her small, pearly white teeth he often found himself fascinated with. He'd never particularly cared for shopping, especially with a woman, but her obvious enjoyment superseded his discomfort. He glanced at the clerk. Of course he knew her.

Mrs. Marsh. She's the biggest gossip in town. Loves to get in everyone's business. She'll especially like me holdin' up sexy little lingerie for you. She'll probably take pictures on that cell phone of hers and send them far and wide.

He meant to tease her, to make her laugh, but the color leeched from Pepper's face. She shook her head and took a step back, her body behind his.

They can't send that picture around. Braden has eyes everywhere. He'll know I'm with you and that Ginger is too. He'll send his soldiers after us.

Mrs. Marsh had spotted them the moment they'd walked through the door, her bright, curious eyes finding Pepper right away. She frowned, not liking that she didn't recognize a local woman with Wyatt. Her gaze immediately dropped to their linked hands.

I was teasin', baby. Don' panic on me. Trust me to take care of you.

Pepper took a deep breath and managed a smile as Mrs. Marsh hurried toward them, her high heels clicking sharply on the floor.

"Wyatt! How lovely to see you."

Except she wasn't looking at him at all. Her interested gaze stayed on Pepper the entire time, almost as if she couldn't believe what she was seeing.

"Mrs. Marsh. Nonny sends her regards. Flame told me you were workin' here and that you were a tremendous help the last time she was in the shop. I've brought my fiancée to pick up a few things from here because Flame *loves* this boutique." Flame *had* said the woman knew her business, so he wasn't exactly lying.

Mrs. Marsh looked pleased. "Your fiancée? I didn't know you were engaged, Wyatt. Nonny didn't say a word."

Because her gaze had already dropped to Pepper's naked finger, he held up her hand. "She didn' want to say anythin' until we got the ring, and I wanted to get it from Lew at the jewelry shop. This is my home and I buy local. Pepper will be livin' here with me, so we want to start out right, isn't that true, baby?"

Deliberately he softened his voice, going tender, raising Pepper's hand to his mouth and kissing her knuckles before tucking her hand against his chest. "Mrs. March, my fiancée, Pepper. Honey, this is Mrs. Marsh. I've known her since I was a boy. She's the best at this kind of thing, accordin' to Flame." He switched his gaze to Mrs. Marsh, all charm. "That's high praise. You know Flame. She loves her clothes."

Mrs. Marsh looked pleased, even flushing a little. "I'll certainly do my best to help you, Pepper. What is it you're looking for?"

Not only could he see the panic on Pepper's face, but he felt it. She had no idea what she was looking for.

"She's not from around here and the weather is different, so we thought a few everyday outfits as well as a couple of dresses. She'll need some really pretty underwear as well."

Mrs. Marsh was all business now that she knew she'd have a big sale. She was in her element, finding the right clothes to suit anyone. "You're quite beautiful, dear," she commented, briskly leading the way through the racks of clothing. "I know just the thing for you. Wyatt will love this on you."

Within a matter of half an hour, the clothes in front of Pepper were piled high and Wyatt was seated on a chair just outside of the dressing room. He stretched his legs out in front of him. Pepper had protested several times as Wyatt had found more and more to add to the clothing Mrs. Marsh had chosen. He got his way of course, shooing her into the changing room by walking his fingers in the air.

"I want to see them all," he decreed.

Pepper made a little sound of protest, but she disappeared behind the white double swing doors. Wyatt found himself grinning for no reason other than his woman looked more flustered than he did in the boutique. He was the one that should have been protesting the number of outfits she should try on, but instead, he'd added to it, genuinely wanting to see her face when she came out in each of them. Well, her face and the way she looked in the clothes they'd chosen.

The door to the boutique opened and closed and he scented perfume and a man's cologne. He glanced up and instantly recognized the male. He'd gone to school with him. Harley Jetter had been born and raised in the bayou, just like Wyatt. They'd been fast friends, fought on and off and gone their separate ways. Harley had chosen a life on the river while Wyatt had gone to college and then med school. It had been years, but those years had been good to Harley.

He stood up as the man approached, his gaze sweeping over Harley's woman. She clearly wasn't from around there, her pencil thin skirt and flared jacket screaming city. Her blonde hair was cut in a soft swing that framed her face. She spotted Wyatt before Harley did and instantly pulled off her sunglasses to make eye contact. If Pepper did that to another man, he'd have quite a lot to say to her. Harley didn't notice. Wyatt would have.

"Wyatt!" Harley greeted him with a smile and an out-stretched hand long before he actually made it to Wyatt. The woman hurried after him in her platform heels.

Wyatt gripped his hand, taking care not to use too much strength. "Long time, Jetter. Good to see you."

"What are you doin' in here?" Harley asked, looking around as if he were on an alien planet. He grimaced. "Lucia likes to shop."

"Harley," Lucia hissed in an aside. "Introduce us."

"I dragged my woman here," Wyatt admitted, looking confident and casual as if he hung out in the boutiques all the time. "I like to see her all dressed up." He glanced at Lucia, barely nodding his head to acknowledge her. He'd met dozens of women like her, always looking to trade up.

Babe. Come out here lookin' good and save me.

Lucia was used to being the good-looking woman in the room and she didn't mind embarrassing her man at all. She flirted openly and she showed off her assets right in front of Harley. She clearly had the man wrapped around her finger.

"Wyatt?" Lucia said, her voice saccharine-sweet. "I'm so pleased to meet you." She held out her hand as if she were a princess and he should kiss her fingertips.

Pepper had perfect timing. She swept out of the dressing room in a summer dress, one that clung to her high breasts and emphasized her small waist. The cool lavender color suited her eyes, as did the dress. It was simple, but elegant, the skirt swinging around her shapely legs. She'd clipped her long hair out of the way when she'd gone into the little room, but it flowed down her back like so much silk.

"Baby, can you help me with this zipper . . ." She trailed off when she saw the couple standing beside Wyatt.

The look on her face would have won her an Oscar. She had known they were there before he'd even said anything to her. She was a GhostWalker. Enhanced. She had to have caught their scents, just as he had. She smiled directly at Harley and then transferred that exact same smile to Lucia even as she came right up to Wyatt, right into her space to stand close to him. Claiming him without a single word.

The couple had exactly opposite reactions. Harley's head jerked up and his breath slammed out of his lungs. Lucia scowled, looking pinched around her mouth.

"This is my fiancée, Pepper." Wyatt circled her shoulders with his arm and drew her even closer, bending to brush a kiss along her temple. He turned her gently. "Lift your hair for me, babe," he instructed.

She did, and Harley's mouth fell open as her breasts lifted with her arms, drawing his attention. Every move Pepper made was sexy. Her walk, the turn of her head, the sway of her hips, the lift of her arms. Those things had been drilled into her from the time she was quite young and she knew no other way to move. That had little to do with enhancements.

Wyatt knew she was naturally sensual. Any man who wasn't blind could see that. Harley wasn't blind. He drew the zipper up the rest of the way and dropped his hands on her shoulders. "I love this one. Is it comfortable?"

She nodded, smoothing her hands down the skirt. "The material is soft, barely there. I like it too."

"Definitely in the yes pile," Wyatt decided. He glanced at his watch. "Change for me, honey, we're on the clock. Can you get the zipper back down?" His voice changed deliberately, dropping an octave so that the sound was caressing.

She flashed him a siren's smile. "Definitely, Cajun man. You stay right there."

Her voice implied all kinds of things. She lifted her hand and waved her fingers before disappearing back inside. There was a stunned silence. Pepper looked elegant, classy and as if she were worth a million dollars. She carried herself like a princess, but seemed approachable and friendly at the same time. But her attention was all on Wyatt. Every move she made, every look she gave him had been that of a woman who saw no one else. He was her center. He almost believed it himself.

"Your fiancée?" Harley's voice came out strangled.

Lucia sent him a dark look that promised retaliation. Shoving her glasses on her nose, she caught Harley's arm. "Let's get out of here."

"I thought you wanted to shop."

"I forgot I have some errands to run. Right *now*, Harley." Her voice was demanding. High-pitched. Angry. She lowered her voice. "And what kind of stupid name is *Pepper*, anyway?" She hissed the last out. "That's a comic book character."

Wyatt, pretending not to hear and hiding a smirk, lifted a hand when Harley shrugged his shoulders and muttered good-bye. He also didn't fail to catch Harley's glance toward the dressing room. Even without the biochemical spilling from her body, Pepper was potent. She was sexy as hell and that couldn't be toned down any further than she'd already done. He was okay with that, as long as he was around. He couldn't imagine her going into a bar by herself. Every unattached male would make a beeline for her.

Are you upset with me? Did I do something wrong? I thought you wanted me to rescue you from the woman.

You did exactly what I wanted, sugar. You drove her right out of the shop. She couldn't take the competition.

He'd better learn to be comfortable around the competition, comfortable and confident.

She came out in outfit after outfit, and he realized it didn't much matter what she put on, he liked it all. Slim vintage jeans or a dress for dancing, every bit of clothing she tried on clung lovingly to her curves. He made certain she walked up to his chair and turned around for him, just because he enjoyed watching her walk, the smile on her face telling him this new experience mattered to her. He decided he wanted to get her some killer heels, not necessarily to wear for anyone else, but he wouldn't mind in the bedroom, which necessitated a trip to another store.

Wyatt had a lot of time to contemplate what it was about his woman that made him feel so great when he was with her. He realized her entire focus was on him. Unless Ginger was close, she was there, in his mind, or watching him, even if she appeared otherwise occupied. She focused completely on him.

With his legs stretched out in front of him, his cock stirred, thinking about how she was concentrated on his pleasure when she took him into her mouth. When his body moved in hers. It was all about him. He was the one who made the experience about her for himself. Otherwise, she would have given him anything he wanted—or needed.

They left Mrs. Marsh extremely happy and Pepper even happier. She had quite a bit of new, lacy, Wyatt-approved underwear. He wasn't certain how he was going to get all the way home thinking about all that lace and what it covered, although he wasn't delighted she had already put a pair of lacy panties on. Still, it was probably a good idea since the shoe store was their next stop.

They walked in and his happiness went down another notch. He knew the clerk. He'd been the most popular boy in the school, a handsome, charming man who loved the ladies—and the ladies loved him.

Pepper tucked her hand into the crook of his elbow, moving closer, looking up at his face, her dark purple eyes drifting over his harsh features.

I'm okay with not coming here, Wyatt. What's wrong?

There it was. Complete focus on him. She saw every mood swing when everyone else thought his face was stone. Her hand slid down his arm, her fingers threading through his and she leaned into him, her face upturned to his. He couldn't help himself, he bent his head and took her mouth. Right there. In public. His arm swept around her back to drag her close, so close her body melted into his.

There was fire in her mouth. An addicting taste that drove a man right out of his mind. He didn't care. The earth moved when she kissed him. There was gold in her mouth, paradise, and he couldn't get enough. Yeah, and it gave him a hell of a hard-on as well, but that was becoming fairly standard.

Are you all right? she asked again when she lifted her head, her beautiful eyes searching his face. She lifted a hand to his mouth. *Tell me what's wrong?*

He didn't want her to know because this was the perfect opportunity to see how things went when she was in the company of a man who thought every woman wanted him and he had a right to her.

I'm okay, babe. I know that man.

She barely glanced at the clerk, but Wyatt was beginning to realize she saw everything. *You know everyone.*

He'd grown up there and certainly just about everyone he met on the street had greeted him warmly.

Alain Daughtry glanced up and his entire being stilled. Wyatt watched his face change the moment he spotted Pepper. His eyes moved over her openly as if inspecting her. Wyatt stiffened, slid his hand down once again to hers and tugged until they were all the way inside the shop and walking toward Alain.

He couldn't help himself, he made certain to give Alain a warning that Pepper was already taken—by him. He curved his arm around her waist after sliding his hand across her hip and bottom, a purely male proprietary gesture.

Alain's gaze jumped to him for a moment and then was back, feasting on Pepper. Wyatt smiled at the man. "Hey, Alain. How's it goin'? I didn' know you were in the shoe business."

Alain barely glanced at him. "Best way to meet ladies, Wyatt, they all love shoes."

Pepper frowned and looked to Wyatt. *We do? Am I supposed to love shoes? They're heavy on my feet.*

You don' wear shoes, sugar, the girls won' either. We can' have them runnin' barefoot in the bayou.

He brought her knuckles to his mouth even as he looked at Alain. "We're lookin' for some boots and maybe some kick-ass heels. Or boots with kick-ass heels." He flashed Pepper a cocky grin, the kind that said she'd be wearing those boots in the bedroom.

Pepper laughed softly, and Alain's head nearly jerked right off his shoulders. The sound filled the small store, melodious and sexy, a low invitation to a night of sin. Wyatt gripped her hand tighter and worked his way over to the women's shoes where several pairs of boots and heels were displayed.

He picked up a pair of wine red boots with ropes circling the bottom, a zipper up the back. They looked chic, without the high stiletto heel. Comfortable even. "You could wear this pair with that little summer dress you love and a couple of the other outfits. What do you think?"

Her eyes were on him, not the boots. "I think I'll try them on for you, but you're really looking at those heels."

He'd decided against the heels when she'd revealed her disdain of shoes. They'd be uncomfortable for her. *Just because I was thinkin' of fuckin' you in those heels and nothin' else doesn't mean we need 'em.*

Her eyes went darker, drenched. The starbursts spread through the midnight color. *We definitely need the heels then, Wyatt.*

Her tone was low and sexy, vibrating through his body and spreading like warm molasses through him. The sound, as well as her answer, only served to make his erection grow.

Babe, you're killin' me. He made it a groan. He loved that they had telepathic communication. It was intimate and kept them locked together. It didn't matter to him how many men leered at her or lusted after her, as long as she looked only at him.

Although, truthfully, the smell of Alain's musky testosterone made him want to smash his fist into something, preferably Alain's face, but that was his problem, not Pepper's. He couldn't fault her and other than the addicting biochemical in her mouth, she wasn't putting off the vibes that she was hunting for a man to bed her. In fact, she was clearly stating, without a word, that she was taken.

"Alain, we've found a couple of pairs Pepper would like to try on."

Alain moved in close, reaching around Pepper to take the boots and heels from Wyatt's hand. His shoulder grazed Pepper's breast. She didn't glance at him, but moved into Wyatt, wrapping her arm around his waist and settling her breasts into his back.

"You're going to love those heels on me, baby," she said, nuzzling him with her chin. "I promise. It will be worth it."

Her voice was so sexy he had to close his eyes and just absorb it into his skin and bones and other particular more sensitive parts. Alain's mouth watered. His breathing changed. Wyatt almost made the mistake of telling her to tone it down when he realized she wasn't trying to affect anyone but him.

His hand swept down the fall of her hair, fingers tangling in the silk. "I love everythin' on you, honey. I have fun takin' it off."

Alain cleared his throat several times. "Size. I need a shoe size."

It was Wyatt who answered. "She's a six and a half."

Pepper sank into the chair Wyatt indicated. "How could you possibly know that, Wyatt? I don't know."

"I know every measurement on your body, sugar," he admitted with a small grin. "I've committed every inch of you to memory and that's the plain truth."

Her eyes moved over his face for a long time. Finally, she sighed and shook her head. "You take my breath away. Sometimes I can't believe you're real."

Pepper felt lost again. She had no trouble with Wyatt

when he was being bossy or arrogant. She had no trouble with his demands in bed. She had trouble with his tender. His gentle. His taking care of her. That mystified her. Threw her into confusion. Sent her stomach somersaulting and her body naturally growing damp for him. He could be so sweet she wanted to cry. Like now. Did other men say such things to women?

He swept his hand through her hair, tucked it behind her ear, his fingers lingering against the pulse in her neck. "I'm real, baby. You're mine, I take care of you."

Wyatt made her feel special. Cared for. Protected even. She knew she was relying on his strengths, so she didn't mind at all when he directed her. She had enormous gaps in her education. And his directions so far had always been rewarding. She'd gone hours without the terrible, clawing need rising to swallow her whole. Wyatt had given her that. Wyatt, who wanted her to be the mother of his children — who trusted her enough to bring her into his home with his wonderful grandmother.

She might not understand family, but the moment she'd entered that house, when Nonny still thought there was a possibility of a Rougarou loose in the neighborhood, she'd known she was somewhere special. The house had smelled different from anywhere she'd ever been. It had *felt* different to her. She wanted that for herself, for her three little girls. The laughter and music and flowing conversations in Wyatt's home both warmed and intrigued her. Wyatt. It all came back to him.

Alain returned and drew up a short little bench, positioning himself between her legs. Pepper pressed her lips together and glanced sideways at Wyatt, hoping to get a cue from him. Was it normal for a salesman to do that? He reached out and took her ankle in his hands. A shiver of alarm went down her spine. Every cell in her body recoiled, shrunk back. Every muscle tightened. She could feel something lethal beginning to coil in her belly.

To her horror, Pepper felt the sudden leak of venom in her mouth. That hadn't happened since she'd been in Braden's office. Quickly she turned her face away from Wyatt.

I can't do this, Wyatt. I'm sorry. I want to please you, but his hands on me . . .

Wyatt reached out instantly and clamped his hand over Alain's, forcibly removing his fingers from Pepper's bare skin. "Step back away from her."

Wyatt's voice was quiet, low even, but commanding. She felt the faint trembling of the floor beneath their feet. The warning was too clear for anyone, even Alain to miss. He dropped his hands immediately and leapt up. Wyatt shifted position to the small stool, bending to reach for her ankle.

You want him? You want to fuck him?

His tone made her tremble. His hands were gentle, belying the fierce temper rising. She felt it like a gathering hurricane, a volcano set to blow any moment. The relief of feeling Wyatt's fingers against her bare skin was tremendous. She gave a little shudder, shocked at how repulsed she'd been. More shocked that she hadn't felt the least little tingle of hunger.

You misunderstand, she said softly, her fingers twisting in the material of her skirt, bunching the fabric into her fist nervously. *He triggered aggression in me. Venom. I was so repulsed I wanted—even needed—to protect myself. I didn't know if I was supposed to allow him to touch me like that, but it felt wrong. I didn't like it at all.*

She felt the change in him instantly. His hands stroked up her leg and back over her calf. He gently removed her shoe, his head down as his hands glided over her foot. He lifted her foot just a little, his palm sliding over the heel, the arch and finally to the ball and toes, a caress. She felt his touch as if it was an arrow piercing her heart.

The venom receded. The tight coil in her belly unfurled.

Her muscles relaxed and the tingles were not only in her feminine core, but her breasts as well. With just his small touch, Wyatt erased the memory of the other man's hands on her skin.

Are you angry with me, Wyatt? She felt anxious, as if she'd let him down.

No, baby, I'm angry with myself. I should have protected you better. Not misunderstood or allowed my jealousy free rein. It won't happen again. I'll do better. This is a learning process for both of us.

Wyatt slipped the high heel on her foot. It was black with black leather lacy cutout all the way up from the middle of the shoe to her ankle. It was the sexiest shoe she'd ever seen. It felt sexy on, or maybe it was the way his hands kept stroking her skin.

Wyatt? She waited until his eyes met hers. *I didn't feel anything sexual at all. Whatever you did took it away. His touch repulsed me.* She took a deep breath before she made her confession. *But when you touched me, I went damp. My breasts ached all over again.*

His gaze turned hot. Intense. He reached up, curled his hand around the nape of her neck and brought her head down to his. His mouth claimed her. Hot. On fire hot. She was fairly certain no other man on Earth could kiss like him. He was a brilliant kisser. She never wanted him to stop. She forgot where they were. Forgot her own name. There was only Wyatt pouring himself down her throat and into her heart.

He was the one who broke the kiss, murmuring softly to her, his forehead against hers while he stared into her eyes. She had to struggle to find air.

"You make me forget to breathe," she whispered aloud.

His smile was slow and sexy, lighting his eyes. His gaze, so focused on her, kept her struggling for breath. "That's a good thin', sugar. Let's get this other shoe on you. I've got plans. I also spotted some very sexy black boots with a nice stiletto heel. We need those too."

His voice had a sexy rasp to it. Suddenly she wanted to know all about his plans. Her gaze dropped to his lap. He was hard. He seemed to always be hard. Pepper knew what it was like to be in a constant state of arousal and it wasn't comfortable. She frowned as he slid the other high heel onto her foot and slipped the tiny buckle into place.

Did you somehow trade my state of being sexually aroused to you?

Nope. Just lookin' at you makes me hard. Don' worry about me, sugar, I figure you can always take care of me with that super-talented mouth of yours on our way back to the huntin' cabin. And then I can take care of you. See how that works?

She laughed softly and stood up, one hand on his shoulder for balance. He slipped his hand around her ankle and moved it up her calf and then past her knee while she stood there. Possession. It felt good to be his. To have him claim her in little ways, with his hand, with his eyes, with the way his body stayed so close to hers.

She was well aware of his enhancements. His nose was quite close to her center. He couldn't fail to scent her eager compliance. *I see you have this all worked out.*

He nodded solemnly, sliding his hand up her thigh, his fingers caressing and stroking. *I've been givin' it some thought and I definitely want your mouth on me. Doesn' help me thinkin' about it. Just makes me harder. But that's okay because when I slide down your throat and you're suckin' I'll be in fuckin' paradise.*

Pepper laughed and strutted across the room, knowing his eyes were on her every step of the way. She ignored Alain, who stared at them with his mouth open. He didn't matter. She could care less what he thought. There was only Wyatt. Sweet, wonderful Wyatt. Her wild, sexy Cajun man.

"We have to have those, babe," Wyatt declared. He crooked his little finger at her. "Now the boots. We still have to put in the order for the supplies and go shopping for the girls. I don' know if I can wait that long."

Deliberately she took her time walking back to him, her smile for him only. *You don't have to wait for the ride home, Wyatt. Find us a secluded place and I can take care of you right now.*

She saw his breath catch in his throat as he slipped the heels off and replaced them with the boots.

Now? In town?

I'm getting hungry for you. The taste of you is in my mouth.

He groaned aloud as she once more walked across the room. *Woman, you're goin' to kill me.*

I know you were looking forward to that ride home, but we can conduct a little experiment and see, after taking care of you here, whether or not I can make you hard all over again on the way home. It's important to know, right?

She felt totally exhilarated, teasing him. She felt part of him, intimate, as if she truly did belong to him.

Wyatt held out his hand to her as she came back across the room. His fingers enveloped hers and he brought her hand to his mouth, lightly biting down on the pads of her fingers before letting her go so he could pull off her boots.

I have always enjoyed experiments, babe, but you're not blowin' me in any fuckin' bathroom. No woman of mine is goin' to go into a germ-riddin' place like that. I'll have to give this some thought.

On the pretext of reaching for her own shoes, Pepper brushed her palm over his lap, over his fantastic bulge, feeling the heat right through the denim he wore. His cock jumped beneath her stroke, reaching for her, as eager as she felt. The best part was, the way she was feeling was entirely natural.

You make me happy, Wyatt. Thank you. She hadn't known

what happiness could feel like. There was no way to explain that to him.

Pepper stayed very close to him while he paid for the boots and heels. In fact, she made certain to stand in front of him, leaning into his body just to feel the hard length of him pressed into her skin. His arms reached around her as he handed Alain money for the purchases, his chin finding the top of her hair.

Pepper reached behind her and stroked a caress over that thick bulge. *I'm getting impatient. I really, really want you in my mouth.*

She made certain her palm was cupping the thick berth of his shaft when she whispered her confession to him into his mind, letting him see her eagerness. The hunger for the taste and feel of him. Her need to give him pleasure in return for all the pleasure he gave her.

I know just the place, honey. There's a Christmas tree farm adjacent to the river. It isn't far to walk and we can find a secluded place. He bent his head and licked behind her ear, and then his teeth nipped her earlobe.

We're definitely visiting the cabin on the way home, she decreed. *I'm already getting hot and wet for you. After this and then shopping more and then the car ride, I'm going to need you.*

Laughing softly, he locked his arms right under her breasts, dropping his mouth to the side of her neck to kiss her there. *I'm plannin' on ridin' you long and hard, babe. Let's get movin' before I burst.*

Pepper moved.

CHAPTER 12

Trap Dawkins was a billionaire. He hadn't inherited the money—he'd made it, starting up his own company at the age of thirteen. He was a certified genius as well as a gifted healer. What made him join the GhostWalkers no one knew for certain because he rarely explained himself. Sometimes Wyatt allowed himself to think Trap had followed him there. It wasn't a good feeling, and Trap always went his own way without explanation, so Wyatt reminded himself of that whenever that niggling guilt showed its ugly face.

Trap had ice water running in his veins, and Wyatt was never quite certain whether he actually had the fear gene either. He doubted if Trap's heart rate ever rose. The man was cool under fire, and every member of their team knew they could count on him to walk through hell for them.

Wyatt had liked the man from the moment they met that first year of college when they were on the same path. Trap was in his early thirties but seemed much older. He rarely smiled and he had an amazing singing voice. He didn't use it often, but in their worst moments, with the sky raining bullets and the bloodied bodies of fellow soldiers in their hands, he would suddenly break into a church hymn. Nine times out of ten, no one sang with him because they were too awed at the power and beauty of his voice.

Trap was also a straight-up assassin. No one could get in and out of buildings or encampments undetected like he could. He was a total enigma. Wyatt was eternally grateful that the man was on his side. He'd agreed to come the moment Wyatt called. His agreement had been a short grunt and the conversation was ended because he was already on the way. He'd known Trap would come if he asked for help. Trap considered him a friend—more a brother—even more, he was part of their GhostWalker unit, which sealed them as family.

Trap was a little taller than Wyatt, with blond hair and piercing blue eyes. Not just any blue, but a cold glacier blue that chilled a man to the bone when Trap stared at him. His nickname had come not only from the ice water running in his veins, but the glaciers he had for eyes.

Draden Freeman, aka the "Sandman," had been a model. He had the kind of body no one believed could be real. He'd been in demand by the largest high-end companies and made bank, enough to put him through college, grad school and his master's program. When he had his degrees he joined the GhostWalkers. Like Trap, there didn't seem to be a reasonable explanation for it. He was a man seemingly with everything and yet, like each of them, he was driven to do something all of them knew was a little insane.

Draden was fast with his hands when working with the injured, able to find collapsing veins and salvage the situation when everyone else might think the patient was lost. Wyatt wanted him in his corner if he was wounded. Draden would never stop fighting for a wounded soldier, breathing for them if he had to.

He seemed easygoing enough, much like Wyatt, but

like Wyatt, he wasn't at all. He was moody and ran long distances. Wyatt suspected he ran to distance himself from his demons—whatever they were—but they always came back to haunt him. Draden was a hard worker and never shirked. He often pulled double shifts because he didn't sleep much. In fact, Wyatt wasn't certain he actually slept. Certainly he'd never seen the man do so.

Still, Draden had the same loyalty to his team they all had. They were a tight bunch, protecting one another and watching each other for signs of overload. Draden was one of the rare anchors who could pull psychic energy away from any team member who needed it. Like the rest of Team Four, Draden was a natural healer.

The two team members got out of the taxi just at the gates of the Fontenot property. Both looked fit in spite of the fact that they'd been nearly crushed when the helicopter had gone down. Wyatt still wasn't certain how Draden had survived, buried under the wreckage the way he'd been, or how Trap had gotten to him, moving heavy metal with his arm broken in three places.

They greeted him with their usual half smiles, carrying their duffel bags effortlessly, although both bags weighed a considerable amount. Wyatt gave them a one-handed hug, looking them over for the effects of the firefight they'd been in. Touching both helped him to "see" their injuries. Ghost-Walkers healed rapidly. That was part of their DNA now, and Trap and Draden, like Malichai and Ezekiel, were nearly 100 percent.

"Thanks for comin'," he greeted.

Trap shrugged. Draden grinned at him. "Wouldn't miss it for the world. Our Wyatt, already a daddy. And three little ones. Triplets, no less. You always said you wanted a big family."

Malichai and Ezekiel joined in the laughter. Wyatt had sworn off women and declared he was going to his grave an old lonely man rather than deal with one again.

"Bayou man got himself a woman with a knife," Malichai reported. "Once he saw that, it was over. The love bug bit deep."

"Bug?" Ezekiel teased. "More like the viper sank her teeth deep."

Trap raised his eyebrow. "Are you calling his woman a viper?"

"Maybe not his woman, but his little girl has some nice fangs on her," Ezekiel clarified. "And the apple doesn't fall far from the tree."

"Oh, you boys are a laugh a minute," Wyatt said. "Until one of them accidentally does their teethin' on you. Ginger's been eyein' Malichai lately."

"Does she really release snake venom?" Trap asked, his eyes serious.

Wyatt turned to lead the way back to the house. "Yes, but I don' honestly know yet whether or not she has to *always* release venom when she bites. Most snakes don' have to and they can control the amount. Pepper told me they were all failed experiments. The three little ones are scheduled for termination."

Trap's breath hissed out of his lungs. "That's bullshit, killing a child you created because you screwed up."

"They would be difficult to raise," Draden pointed out. "Not that I advocate killing them, but taking them on is a huge responsibility. They could accidentally kill a family member."

"Which is why I called both of you to help," Wyatt said. "Not only do I want to get the other two out of that lab, I want to try to figure out a way to keep us all safe. We can cap their teeth as a temporary solution. Pepper has natural immunity to the cobra venom. I think her body is beginning to develop an immunity to the viper venom as well. If we can find a way to do that, not only for *ma famille*, but for the GhostWalkers, we could save a few lives."

"Do you have a lab?" Trap asked. "Because I've got one at my house that would be helpful."

"Unfortunately, Trap," Wyatt said, "we have to stay here. The children need this place for now, and I have to keep *ma grand-mere* safe as well."

Trap shrugged. "No big deal, we can build one here."

"I've got a small one started."

Trap stood on the porch, duffel bag in hand, looking around the bayou and the Fontenot home. "You build this?"

Wyatt nodded. "We started with a traditional frame home and my brothers and I built this one for Nonny."

"It's nice, Wyatt. Really nice," Trap said. "It feels like a home, not a mausoleum."

"I can't wait to meet your grandmother," Draden said. "You talk so much about her, I feel as if I already know her."

"She's the best cook," Malichai said. "I'm not even hungry. Well . . ." he hedged. "Okay, an hour or so after I eat, I go back for more. And there's always more."

"Which reminds me, you need to go out and check the traps," Wyatt said. "You're depletin' the supplies."

Laughter rang out again. Wyatt started to pull open the door just as the laughter faded to be replaced by the sounds of the bayou. The rhythm was broken. Off.

Someone's out there watchin' us, Wyatt said.

I feel them, Ezekiel said. *I can slip around back and go hunting.*

Take Malichai. I want to see if Whitney's soldiers have been called in to guard the compound or to track Pepper and the baby. If they have, it will make things much harder and more dangerous for everyone when we go in to get the other two babies out. Supersoldiers are unpredictable and volatile as a rule.

He made them into throwaways, just like he did those babies, Trap said, an edge to his voice.

He did, Wyatt agreed, *but they were willin' participants for whatever reasons, just as we were. We knew goin' into this that the outcome might not be all we wanted it to be. Those babies—and the women—had no choice.*

He yanked open the door, just a little bit harder than necessary. He detested reminding himself just how ridiculous he'd been allowing enhancements, although honestly, he knew he wouldn't give them up now.

"We can't help being who we are, Wyatt," Trap said quietly, placing one hand briefly on his shoulder. "You have a mind like mine. We ask too many questions and we need answers. You know me. I can't sleep for days on end sometimes when I'm working on something interesting. And when I'm bored . . . That's the most dangerous time of all."

Nonny greeted the two newcomers with a big smile. Both men towered over her diminutive figure. "Trap, it's good to finally meet you. Wyatt told me so much about you over these las' years. He tells me you boys serve with him."

"Yes, ma'am," Draden acknowledged with a slight nod of his head. "We're in the PJs with your grandson." The Pararescue Jumpers were the Air Force Special Forces team.

"Thank you for comin'," she said with great dignity. "The house is sturdy and warm and the fixin's are good, although nothin' fancy."

"We're not used to fancy, ma'am," Draden said, and then glanced over his shoulder at Trap. "None of us."

Her smile widened. "Wyatt tells me you boys know your way around a weapon or two. We may need that ifn' those men come lookin' for Pepper and Ginger again."

Pepper sat at the kitchen table and rose slowly to her feet as the two men came in. Her gaze jumped to Wyatt's face and then came back to rest on the newcomers. She'd argued about bringing in more men. Wyatt knew she still didn't trust the situation, not any more than he did. They were still learning how to cope with her enhancements and his reactions to other men around her.

He saw Draden stop dead, his mouth forming a silent "O." Trap's reaction was a hesitation and a frown before he ran his hand through his hair.

"My fiancée, Pepper. She's the mother of my children." He wanted to stake his claim immediately and also indicate he expected them to protect her and give her respect. "Honey, this is Draden and Trap."

Draden nodded his head. Trap just stared at her. Wyatt knew he had to get used to men's reactions when they first saw Pepper, but still, it got under his skin.

"You can stow your gear in one of the bedrooms," Wyatt said to distract them.

"I expect you're hungry," Nonny said. "You can talk about your break-in over food. Night's still a couple of hours away and you'll need your strength." She looked around, frowning. "Where are Malichai and Ezekiel?"

"They're off scoutin' a bit, Nonny, nothin' to worry about. They'll be back soon," Wyatt assured.

What's wrong? Pepper asked, glancing out the window anxiously. *Have the elite trackers come after us? I told you we couldn't wait very long before we went after the children.*

Trap glanced sharply at the two of them. His eyebrows shot up. "Is there something you two want to say to the rest of us?"

Wyatt shrugged. "She's upset thinkin' we waited too long and the supersoldiers have come to make our lives more difficult." He turned to Pepper. "We had to beef up security, and you needed time to get on your feet. I told you that you had to come with us and you were too sick."

"Wait," Trap held up his hand. "You didn't say anything about the woman coming with us to rescue those kids. Now isn't the time to bring an unknown into the mix, Wyatt. It's too dangerous and you know that."

"The children know her. *I* know her."

"Well, I don't," Trap disagreed, always the hard-ass. "You don't either, Wyatt, whether you think you do or not. She could be part of a conspiracy. You said yourself Whitney might be setting you up."

"I don' think Whitney's settin' me up, Trap. I know. I feel it in my gut and all of you know, that hasn't been wrong yet."

"All the more reason to keep her out of it. What the hell do you plan on doing if she betrays us and leads us into a trap?" Draden demanded.

There was a small silence. Pepper stirred. "He's going to kill me." When they all turned toward her, the men shivering a little at the sound of her voice, she indicated Wyatt with her chin. "If I betrayed all of you, Wyatt would kill me." There was complete acceptance in her voice.

Nonny glanced over her shoulder from where she was stirring the large pot of stew, but she didn't say anything.

"You may think Wyatt's too gentle or too smitten to get the job done," Trap said. "But the rest of us won't be. We're going to be watching out for him, so if you have betrayal in mind, opt out while you can."

"Yeah. Okay, thanks for sayin' that right in front of *ma grand-mere*. She doesn' need to hear that crap," Wyatt said.

"The woman deserves a warning, bayou man," Trap said. "If she isn't part of Whitney's attacks on us, then she won't mind. If she is, well, she has the choice to bail."

For God's sake, Wyatt. Any woman who looks and sounds like she does and gives off the kind of pheromones she's broadcasting, enough to even affect me, is a very dangerous weapon. And she's your fiancée? Do you know what you're doing?

I do. I wouldn't have called you in if I wasn't certain. Wyatt hoped Trap would leave it alone.

Nonny glanced over her shoulder again. "What conspiracy, Wyatt? Is that the same man who gave Flame the cancer? Is he after you now?"

Wyatt closed his eyes briefly. Nonny was intelligent, and she knew most of what her grandsons did was classified, but they all respected her enough to tell the truth when they could. Whitney wasn't part of Wyatt's enhancements—at least he shouldn't have been—and she already knew that name.

Nonny had gone to the hospital with Flame when the cancer had come back. Gator had tricked the woman he loved into getting help from Whitney's daughter, Lily. At the time, Flame believed Lily was helping her father. Nonny had to know everything in order to help. While she was there, Whitney's supersoldiers had tried to reacquire Flame. There'd been a brief but fierce battle, and Nonny had actually participated to help save both Gator and Flame.

"We don' mean to worry you, Grand-mere. I don' believe Pepper has anythin' to do with Whitney. She's an innocent, just like Flame was. I'll look after her."

"That's not what I asked you, Wyatt, and you know it." Nonny glanced at Trap. "I already know Pepper is with us." She glared at her grandson as she pulled plates from the cupboards. "I asked, was that man after you now?"

Pepper took the plates from Nonny and set them carefully on the table. "We don't know, Grand-mere," she answered. "There just seems to be too much of a coincidence in all this. I was in France until a little while ago. Suddenly around the time Wyatt deployed, we were moved here to the bayou. The timing just seems off for us to believe some of this wasn't already planned meticulously. We both know we could be walking into a trap when we go after the babies. You can't blame Wyatt for being worried about his friends or them for being worried about him."

She set the table awkwardly, as if she wasn't certain how, but remembered from watching Nonny. "I'm an unknown to everyone. Of course I'm a question mark."

You're not an unknown, Pepper. Let them get to know you, Wyatt whispered into her mind, not liking the hurt he felt radiating off of her.

"Not to me, girl," Nonny said. "You're no part of Whitney and his *aliene complots*. I don' need proof. I jist know.

Put your gear away, boys, and wash up. Don' wake the baby. She startles easily. Should I call Ezekiel and Malichai?"

Malichai poked his head in through the back kitchen door. "Grand-mere, have I ever missed one of your magnificent meals?" He breezed in and dropped a kiss on her neat little bun. "Not once. I'm moving right in you know."

"Glad to have you, Malichai. Where's that brother of yours?"

"Every now and then, ma'am, he likes to go into the bayou and track some game. Just to keep his hand in, you know. He'll be along shortly, I expect."

Nonny snapped her tea towel at him, but deliberately missed. He leapt back, howling anyway. "I expect that means we have company out there again tonight."

"Yes, ma'am. But it was no one to worry about. Just the Three Stooges."

Pepper lifted her chin, her dark eyes suddenly mischievous as she looked directly at Trap. "Don't forget to wash up. While you're gone, Nonny can watch me and make certain I don't spit venom in your hot *café*."

There was a sudden silence. Malichai turned his head away from the newcomers to look out the window, his lips twitching. Trap and Draden exchanged a long look.

"Can she really do that?" Draden asked.

Wyatt nodded. "I believe she could."

"It's never a good idea to get on the bad side of a snake," Pepper said, her tone purely conversational. She smiled innocently and even batted her eyelashes. "Especially a viper."

Wyatt winked at her as he led the other two out of the room. Behind him he heard Malichai laugh.

"Woman, I could kiss you for that."

He turned back, sticking his head through the doorway to pin Malichai with a glare. "I wouldn't do anythin' stupid, my friend, I own several carvin' knives."

Malichai held up both hands in surrender and backed

away from Pepper. Wyatt sent Pepper a stern look. *Don' even tempt that man. I would hate to have to carve up one of my best friends.*

Pepper raised her eyebrow, but he could tell she didn't know if he was being serious or not. Strangely, he didn't know either. He'd had sex with her dozens of times and each time felt like the first, a crazy, out-of-control ride he would never give up. He'd gotten used to her sense of humor he found downright sexy when she was around Malichai and Ezekiel. Wyatt kept the biochemical in her system from building too much with their marathon sex sessions each night, but with two more men in the house, he found he was having a difficult time. Not Pepper. Him.

Exasperated with himself, Wyatt followed his friends.

"Have you kissed that woman?" Draden asked. "Because she could have venom in her saliva."

Trap frowned as he placed his duffel bag on the bed in one of the spare rooms. "She couldn't have snake venom in her saliva. It couldn't work like that, otherwise she'd be killing everything and everyone she came into contact with."

"Actually, Draden, I've kissed her a thousand times and I've done far more than that. They enhanced her with a biochemical to force her to stay in a kind of heat. She's lived in hell, and she's not goin' to ever again."

Draden and Trap exchanged a long look. Trap shrugged and raked his fingers through his hair. The mop of thick hair was already untidy and he just messed it up all the more. "Maybe I should skip dinner and go right to the laboratory. I'll need to see what equipment you have and what we'll need. I can fly it in tonight and we can get started figuring out what is needed to finish the antivenom and make it safe for everyone to be around those little girls."

"Trap, that all sounds great, but here, in this house, you never skip a meal. Nonny would be insulted," Wyatt explained. "We keep *ma grand-mere* happy at all times."

Trap scowled at him. "Eating is a waste of time, Wyatt.

This needs to be done as soon as possible. It's why you brought me here. Let me do my job."

Draden nudged him. "Remember when you told me to let you know when you're exhibiting OCD behavior? You're back to being obsessive-compulsive."

Trap shook his head. "You're a moron. I never told you to tell me that."

"You didn't?" Draden scratched his head, looking puzzled. "I could have sworn . . . Oh, wait! It was all the others. *They* wanted me to point it out to you so you could get that brain of yours under control. I'm just doing my duty as a team member."

Trap shook his head. "Your sense of humor is getting worse by the minute. Fine. I'll eat. And then I need to see the laboratory. Is it possible to examine the child's mouth without getting bit? Maybe we should try the antivenom on me first so I can do a close examination of both of their mouths."

Wyatt scowled at him. "First of all, you don' want to put your hands on my woman. That would make me crazy. And secondly, you have no idea how fast both of them can move. You know how fast I am and there's no way in hell I could catch Pepper if she's runnin'. You try examinin' her mouth and she'll bite you. And if she doesn', I'll shoot you. Either way, you're a dead man." He was very matter-of-fact about it.

"I see. Is that the way it is?" Trap said. "What happened to swearing off women?"

"She's the mother of those three babies and I'm the father. They need us both."

Trap groaned. "Listen to yourself, Wyatt. Why do you always have to be the knight in shining armor rushing to the rescue? You don't owe that woman anything. You didn't experiment on her . . ." he trailed off.

"You mean like the two of us plan on doin'?" Wyatt asked.

"We're experimenting for a good reason. We need the antivenom."

"Which, I believe, is what Whitney and Braden were lookin' for," Wyatt pointed out. "How are we any different?"

"We're the good guys," Draden said.

"Whitney believes he's the man wearin' the white hat," Wyatt said. "He thinks he's a great patriot and that he's workin' to better the soldiers so there are fewer casualities and wars aren't worth startin'."

"The things he does are against the law. You don't experiment on children. You don't keep women prisoners and force them to have babies," Draden snapped.

Trap put his hand on Draden's shoulder. "Don't get defensive. Wyatt isn't saying Whitney is the man with the white hat, he's pointing out that to Pepper and the baby, we're not going to appear any different, and he's got a point."

Wyatt nodded. "We've got to finesse this one. We can' be the bull in the china shop. They've been through enough. On top of that, I feel extremely protective toward the children. They're my children and they've never been out of a damn lab."

He sighed, shaking his head. "I feel possessive toward Pepper. More than that. Far more. I connected us when I went to heal her and I've been in her head. There's no conspiracy she's a part of. Whatever I feel for her is growin' stronger every day and I can be . . . dangerous. I can feel what she's feelin' and that doesn't make things any easier. If she's upset, I have to take care of that. She's my woman and under my protection."

"And you're certain, Wyatt?" Trap asked quietly.

Wyatt nodded slowly. "She's addicting in ways I can't even begin to tell you, but she's tied to me. Her loyalty is to me. I made damned sure of that."

Draden whistled. "Malichai and Ezekiel know?"

Wyatt nodded. "I'm in a mess here. It's a volatile situation anyway you look at it. You know I'm not exactly the easiest man to get along with."

Trap's eyebrow shot up. "Are you referring to your foul temper?"

Wyatt managed a slight grin. "I've always had to work on my temper, but I've never been a jealous or possessive man. Not once in any relationship I've ever had. Not as a kid and not when I believed I was truly in love. But I have to tell you, this is different. Not easy. And it's me, not her."

He knew he was trying to articulate something he didn't understand or trust—and he was attempting to warn them he could be dangerous around Pepper. He reached for her, a little ashamed that he hadn't protected her from Draden and Trap. She hadn't deliberately enticed them, but they'd still felt her pull.

Are you okay? Did they hurt you? I know there's nothin' to what they're sayin'. They're only tryin' to protect me, sugar. You're very potent.

I wasn't trying to, Wyatt. Honest.

He knew the difference between her keeping her shield up and letting it down. *I know that, Pepper.*

The thing is, Wyatt, I don't care whether they like me or not. I don't even care if they trust me. I care if you do. You matter to me. When you met me, you were just like them, suspicious. I didn't blame you. Ezekiel and Malichai were as well. I didn't blame them either. Trap and Draden come in here and they meet me and I'm ... well ... me. Of course they want to protect you. They wouldn't be your friends if they didn't.

He couldn't argue with that. She had a point. He also didn't mind so much that his opinion was the only one that mattered to her.

Trap shrugged. "Why are you surprised that you would be dangerous around a woman you care for? She's under your skin, under your protection. You're enhanced, Wyatt.

You have physical changes, of course you're going to have emotional changes as well. Along with all the good things there's always a balance of bad."

Wyatt wasn't going to admit that the intensity of his emotions—especially jealousy when he was around Pepper—could be off the charts. That was his problem, not hers, and he didn't want Trap or Draden blaming her for his own weaknesses.

He glanced at Trap's face. The man was sheer stone. He always had been. He ignored all social cues. He just didn't care about fitting in or making friends. Even in college, he'd ignored everyone. As far as Wyatt knew, there were only the team members who accepted Trap's brutally honest personality. He couldn't imagine a woman putting up with him for very long.

He was also the most dangerous man Wyatt knew, and all members of the team were hell on wheels. Trap was just . . . lethal. He didn't hesitate to go into an encampment of the enemy utterly alone, move like a ghost through the guards and take out the primary target.

There was no doubt that he was brilliant and everything he touched seemed to turn to gold—although Trap could care less about money. He didn't have any family, and Wyatt felt a little sorry for him at times. Trap wouldn't understand that. He didn't long for things he didn't have. He had a strict code he lived by. He knew he wasn't good at any kind of relationship, and when he'd joined their team, he'd been brutally honest about himself to the team members. They'd all liked him better for it.

Wyatt had found that if Trap gave out a piece of information, it was always correct. Always. One didn't question Trap's abilities or knowledge, because he was a walking library of facts, which made him an unbelievable asset both on and off the battlefield. It was easy enough, once you accepted his personality, to like him.

Wyatt shrugged. Trap was right. He should have realized that when his DNA had changed, so had his emotions.

"Let's go eat before Nonny disowns me. And Trap, Nonny's important to me. Very important. Her protection and happiness. I know it's hard for you to bother with the little niceties, but I would greatly appreciate you tryin'."

Trap frowned and looked to Draden for an explanation. Draden clapped him on the shoulder. "Play nice with his grandmother, Trap."

"And Pepper," Wyatt warned softly. "She's important to me as well."

Draden nudged Trap. "Remember that book of manners I gave you and you read in three minutes flat? Use those little tips and be courteous."

"You gave him a book on manners?" Wyatt asked.

"Actually he gave me three different ones and I found a couple of others," Trap said, serious as usual. "They didn't make a whole lot of sense. I can see why society would want to implement some of the rules, but others are just a waste of time."

"Use them anyway," Draden suggested as they approached the kitchen.

"If we're going to actually waste time eating, shouldn't we at least discuss our entry point into the compound? When you called, I found someone to help us out with the blueprints, specifically the water system. That might be a point of entry."

Draden groaned. "Just because you're a fish in the water doesn't mean the rest of us are." He pulled back a chair and plopped in it, giving Nonny a big smile. "Ma'am, this looks like a feast. Thank you for going to the trouble of fixing us all food." He kicked Trap hard under the table.

Trap looked up, blinking as if coming out of a fog. Wyatt wanted to laugh. Trap's mind was far from their dinner, already trying to solve the puzzle of how to get them safely in and out of the laboratory without bloodshed or raising an alarm.

"Yes," he murmured, clearly unsure of what he was supposed to say or do. He actually looked a little helpless.

Wyatt covered his mouth and coughed. "Ginger isn' eatin' with us?"

"We've been trying to get her into a routine," Pepper said. "Children do much better when they have a routine."

"She's right," Trap said, "Statistically, routines actually provide children with the feeling of security as well as teaching them self-discipline." He looked across the table at Pepper. "You've been with these children since they were born?"

She shook her head. "I was brought in when they were around three months old."

"Were they already exhibiting signs of superior intelligence?" Trap asked eagerly.

Pepper nodded slowly. "I think that's one of the reasons they brought me in to help. They were already communicating with each other. That was very clear."

"But not verbally. They wouldn't have been developed enough to create actual words," Trap continued.

Draden sighed. "At least put food on your plate, Trap," he encouraged. "You need to keep the fuel up, remember? We had a long talk about why a person needs to eat nutritiously. You took my bag of chips away and gave me a twenty-minute lecture."

"I can assure you, Trap," Nonny said. "That fish stew is very nutritious."

Trap ladled a large helping into his bowl, frowning a little. "That would entirely depend on the fish and whether or not it was exposed to any kind of pollution. Since the hurricane . . ."

"Trap." Draden shoved a piece of fresh warm bread into the man's mouth. "Don't talk anymore. Just eat."

Trap chewed thoughtfully for a few minutes and then

looked up at Nonny. "Ma'am. Apparently I'm not good at conversation, so I apologize ahead of time for any mistakes I make."

Wyatt was proud of his sincerity. As a rule, Trap could care less if he hurt someone's feelings. He didn't notice.

Trap started to pick up his coffee mug. Pepper made a single sound, a low, long hiss escaping between her small white teeth. Her dark eyes radiated a diamond-colored starburst as she looked at the man. Trap cautiously removed his hand from the mug, and looked across the table at Pepper.

Malichai grinned at Ezekiel. "Better think twice, Trap. She might of really done it." He winked at Pepper.

Instead of laughing with the others, Trap leaned toward Pepper, his face carved so only his eyes were alive with curiosity. "Do you really have the ability to spit venom? Can the babies? I can't wait to get them in the lab and examine their teeth and mouths. I'll have to look at you too. Do you know if you're their biological mother?"

There was a silence. Pepper continued to stare at Trap. Wyatt felt her instant fury, although she looked sweet and innocent, her smile alluring. He felt the sudden electrical charge building between the two. He stood up so fast his chair fell over, breaking that swelling charge.

Judging by the shocked faces and stares, he knew no one else had seen or felt anything out of the ordinary. Only him. He knew Trap was in trouble immediately. He barely registered anything but the current tying a thread between Pepper and Trap. He reached out and shackled Pepper's wrist, uncaring of the consequences. He yanked her out of her chair and dragged her out of the room, away from the others.

"What the hell do you think you're doin'?" he demanded, his voice low and more than a little threatening as he took her down the hall and into his bedroom. He retained possession of her wrist as he kicked the door closed and shoved her hard against it. Stepping close, he trapped her body between the hard wood and his body.

"What are you talking about?"

"Don' play innocent with me, Pepper. Do you think I'm not aware of every single thin' you're doin'? Where you are in this house? Who you're talkin' to? Every single thin' you do? Every breath you take in and exhale. Don' lie and tell me you aren' aware of the same thin' with me."

He pinned both her arms above her head. "Admit it, Pepper. Admit to me you know where I am at all times."

"Maybe I do, but that doesn't have anything to do with your behavior."

He heard the desperation in her voice. The ache. He knew the exact feeling. It was always there for both of them when they got together, especially if emotions were running high. "What the hell are you doin' throwin' out a lure to Trap? Do you want to get one of us killed? He came here to help me and he's my friend. Are you angry with him because he threatened you?"

"I don't care that he threatened me. Of course I want him to be loyal to you and to make certain you come back alive, but he doesn't care anything at all about the children. He's like the men in that laboratory and the ones in France."

"It shouldn't matter a damn what he's like. You don' use that lure on any other man, do you understand me? You belong to me, not someone else. We'll sort it out between us. You're not goin' to bring anyone else into the mix. It's too dangerous."

"What other weapon do I have to protect myself or the children? Unless you want me to kill him, because that's always a possibility."

"You trust me. *Me*, Pepper. To look after you and the children. I wouldn't have brought Trap here if I thought he'd be a danger to the kids. He's my friend. He's different, yes, and he's analytical and a little obsessive, but he's loyal to me and my team, which means . . ." He put his hand over her mouth when she would have protested. "Which means he's loyal to my family."

"You're not being fair, Wyatt. I might know you, but I don't know him. I trust you with me and the girls—but not him. He wants to put them right back into another lab and dissect them. I don't know who you'll choose, us or your friends if it comes down to that."

Anger ripped through him like a tidal wave. "You know me." He bit the words out between his teeth. "You're bein' a coward and you know it."

Before she could protest, he took her mouth. He wasn't the least bit gentle. He didn't feel gentle, not with adrenaline pouring through his body like a fiery, hot stream. He leaned into her, deliberately imprinting her body on his, all her soft skin and lush curves. In that moment he could care less whether or not her kiss was lethal. His hunger for her was brutal. Coupled with his volcanic anger, there was no way to stop the rising passion, the terrible need that was so primal he almost couldn't control it.

He poured himself into her, his mouth hot and demanding, forcing her response. The taste of her burst through him like an addicting drug he would never be able to find anywhere else. Never be able to get enough of. Her arms slid around his neck and she melted into him with a small gasping sob.

Her mouth moved under his and he was lost in her sexual web. Drowning. Going under for the last time. The thing was, he didn't want to come up for air. Not ever. He could kiss her forever and it would never be enough. The ground shifted, and he didn't know if it was his reaction or hers. Only that the world dropped away until there was only the woman in his arms and her incredible mouth breathing for him.

He dragged her closer, desperate to be skin to skin. She was made for him. She fit. Perfectly. The chemistry just got hotter the more they kissed, inflaming his every sense until he couldn't think straight. Until there was no way to do without her. She was inside of him, living and breathing, and without her body to sustain his, there was no Wyatt. He knew part of that was the biochemical spilling from her mouth to his, but more, he already knew the taste of her, what it felt like to be inside of her. Once he started kissing her, it was difficult to pull back without having her.

This isn't going to work, Wyatt. It's not.

She didn't take her mouth from his, but she protested, and that made him all the more crazy. Thunder roared in his ears. He slammed his palm against the wall beside her head. He had never wanted a woman so much in his life. Not just wanted her—needed her. No one else was ever going to satisfy the craving inside of him, a terrible empty hole that only she could fill.

You damn well aren't goin' to change your fuckin' mind because I'm angry with you. You had no business throwin' out a lure to him and you know it.

She startled when he hit the wall, trying to draw back, but there was nowhere for her to go. Wyatt had her there, captured between the wall and his body. His prisoner. He held her there, his brooding gaze drifting over her face.

"You belong to me and no one else."

"You don't own me," she denied.

He could see the panic in her eyes, feeling it rising like the tidal wave of sheer lust had risen in him. "I do," he said softly. "You're mine and I'll be damned if I'm ever goin' to give you up, so just know that, Pepper. Know as much as you belong to me, I belong to you. We're in this together. We had this conversation. We talked it all out. I've been inside you dozens of times. You knew when we first started this that there was no goin' back."

"What is *this*?" She sounded as scared as she looked. "Doesn't *this* scare you, even a little bit?"

Her body trembled, shivering against his. He leaned down and brushed a much gentler kiss over her mouth. Her eyes were huge, her breath coming too fast. She was very close to panic and seemed more vulnerable than ever. Wyatt realized her fear was very genuine. Pepper hadn't been made to feel passion and attraction—only to make men feel it. She had no idea what to do with the intense chemistry sizzling between them. She had no idea what to do with him, especially when he was angry.

"You're safe with me. You are. I'm a loyal man, a family man. You don' have to be afraid of what you're feelin'. I'll take care of us."

She shook her head. "How do you know what you're feeling is genuine, that I didn't cast a lure for you too?" She touched her mouth with shaking fingers. "Because a week from now, I don't want to hear you say that."

He captured her hand and brought it to his mouth, his teeth scraping gently at the pads of her nervous fingers. "I can not only feel the lure when you test the waters, but I can see it as well, a thin line of energy going from you to your victim. No one else in that room spotted it and they're all GhostWalkers. What does that tell you?"

She winced visibly and lowered her lashes. They were wet. Spiky. His heart contracted hard in his chest. He pushed back the stray tendrils of cloudy waves that just refused to stay tamed in her braid.

"Don't say 'victim,' Wyatt. Don't use that word."

"I know you didn't deliberately seduce me, Pepper, because you're scared to death of me—of what you feel when you're with me. I connected us when I attempted to heal you, but you connected us long before that, when you jumped between Ginger and me and took that bite. I knew in that moment that you were the one for me. There was no sex involved right then. None. Just a woman showin' tremendous courage, the kind of courage a man livin' in the bayou needs when he wants to raise his family here."

He tugged at one of the strands of silk. "Now, when I look at you, I want you with every cell in my body. Again, that isn' you comin' on to me, because you don' ever do that with me. You feel what I'm feelin' and that terrifies you. I know because there's no denyin' that connection between us. I can feel the intensity of your emotions. You want me just as much. I just scare you a little when I get angry, but I'd never hurt you. No matter how angry I get, I'd never hurt you."

CHAPTER 13

———⌒———

Pepper stared up into Wyatt's face a long time, her body at war with her mind. Could she trust him? Did she dare? If it was only her, but there were three little children who had been locked in laboratories all their lives. She was making a decision for them. When Wyatt was close to her, when his mouth was on hers, she couldn't think reasonably.

Right now, his body was hard and aggressive. She could see the warrior in him, a predator who hunted the swamps and bayous, went out on his missions and came back with more scars, but triumphant. He was a throwback to the Vikings she'd read about in the history books. He appealed to her on that level.

Who was she kidding? He appealed to her on *every* level. She'd grown up in a world where everyone was deceptive and wanted something from her. Not just her, the babies. She hadn't been able to give them any kind of life. She hadn't even known what she wanted for them until she'd entered Nonny's house. Until she'd seen the love Wyatt had for his grandmother.

Wyatt's face changed from that of a challenging conqueror to sweet, and she knew instantly she was in trouble. She tried to move, but he'd pinned her against the wall and he hadn't so much as rocked back when she pressed her hands against his chest.

"Baby, listen to me," he said, his voice so gentle she closed her eyes against it, needing to shut him out. "You're just scared. We've added two more men into the mix, one of them a natural-born scientist. I understand that, but it isn't something we can't take care of together."

Reluctantly, Pepper opened her eyes and let herself drink him in. Her obsession. Her addiction. Her savior. But was he real? She'd never been so scared in her life. She'd faced guns and knives and even one of Braden's supersoldiers, but Wyatt . . . Wyatt disarmed her with kindness and his voice, and sex.

"I'm scared for the children and I'm scared for you as well. This can't be a coincidence, you know that, Wyatt. It's too much. Too intense. How can I go all this time, being around so many men and never feel anything at all? Not even a ripple of excitement. Not even when they were training me. I didn't want any of them to even look at me let alone touch me."

"That doesn' upset me in the least, knowin' you aren' lookin' at other men."

She took a breath and confessed in a rush. "And then I saw you. Out there in the swamp, beatin' that man for what he did to your *grand-mere*. I was alone, afraid and I'd been shot. So had Ginger. I knew I had to get both of us help, but I couldn't look away from you. I couldn't. And that terrifies me because I don't put anyone before the children. I shouldn't have stopped to look. My heart shouldn't have beat faster. I shouldn't have gotten damp and my breasts shouldn't have felt swollen and achy when you were exhibiting such a penchant for violence, but it happened."

He groaned at her description. "You're killin' me, honey.

Don' use words like 'damp' and 'achin' breasts,' not when I can' do anythin' about it."

"Don't you see? That's how I feel, and then you offer me everything. The entire world. Just like that. When you kiss me, I can't think. I want you and nothing else. Why is that, Wyatt? I'm supposed to be the one that can use sex as a weapon, but I'm the one caught, not you."

His hand drifted over her face, his touch so gentle she ached inside. "God, baby, they really did fuck you up, didn't they? You don' know who to trust. I'm standin' in front of you and you've been inside my head, and you're still so scared you can' see me."

Tears burned. "The babies, Wyatt. I have to consider them first. Who else is watching out for them? If I can't think when I'm kissing you, when I'm standing this close to you, I have to question that."

He dipped his head and pressed kisses along her jaw, blazing a trail to the corner of her mouth. "You are questioning it, Pepper. I'm standin' right here with a hard-on the size of Texas pressed into your hot body and you're still askin' questions. Your brain is workin' just fine. It's gone in the wrong direction, but you're still thinkin'."

He tipped her chin up. "Look inside me, sugar. I like it when you're inside my head. I don' mind. I want you to feel safe with me."

His grin sent a slow roll through her stomach.

"Of course, not safe in the sense that I'm not goin' to jump you every chance I have. But Pepper, you need to know I'd protect you and the girls. They're my daughters. I'm all about family. If you don' know anythin' else, you have to know that about me. We made a decision together to keep them safe . . ."

Her head went up, her eyes flashing at him. "Even from him? Your scientist friend? You'll keep them safe from him?"

Wyatt didn't look away from her steady, accusing stare. He didn't even flinch. "I brought Trap here deliberately because he's a man who can help me figure things out. He's brilliant. Those girls can't grow up segregated completely from society. We don' want that for them. That means, Pepper, we figure out how to keep them from killin' someone accidentally. Trap can do that for us. He'd never turn them into lab animals. Give him a chance. Trust me enough to know who is goin' to have our backs."

His body was so hard and hot, not giving an inch. Her own body had long ago betrayed her. "Wyatt, are you like me?" She watched his eyes, terrified of the answer, but she had to know. "Can you do what I do? Is that why I can't resist you?"

His smile was slow in coming and it melted her heart and wreaked havoc with every cell in her body. "I didn' realize you couldn' resist me, honey. You just handed me the world. I can' seem to resist you either. The real you, not the one who goes huntin'. Are you goin' to trust me on this, babe? You got to come to me all the way. With both feet in. If we're doin' this, both of us have to be all the way in."

"I'll kill him. You don't want to see that I'm capable of being every bit as lethal as you and your friends, Wyatt," she said steadily, wanting him to see the real her. "If you want me, you have to know that's part of who I am. If he hurts one of them, if he makes them feel as if they aren't human, I'll kill him and never look back."

He pressed closer to her, his grin going wider, his eyes dark and sensual. "You think that's goin' to put me off you? Is that your way of tryin' to push me away? Because it only makes me hotter for you. I like attitude, babe, and I like a woman who knows her way around a knife and a gun. You're not sayin' anythin' I don' want to hear."

She shook her head. "I hope you believe me, Wyatt. I won't hesitate to protect my children."

"*Our* children, Pepper," he corrected. "Never forget that. They're *ours*. Ours to protect. I'll do that with the last breath in my body. And just so you know, you're *exactly* my kind of woman, honey. I'm countin' on you to protect *all* of our children with your last breath as well. I want a partner, babe. But you got to trust my lead."

His hand came up to bunch the hem of her shirt, drawing the material up. "We good, honey? Because I've got this wicked hard-on that you just made harder. It's a hell of an ache."

She swallowed hard. "You plan to do something about it?"

"You have no idea," he answered, and lowered his mouth to hers once more.

Fire raced from his mouth to hers. Flames poured down her throat and spread like a wildfire through her body. She heard the soft little sound of despair escape before she could stop it. Already her hands had run up his chest and curled around his neck, dragging him closer. She was lost in him. She'd always be lost in him. Tears burned behind her eyes, but as if he knew, he lifted his mouth from hers and kissed both of her eyes.

"Don' do that, sugar, you're breakin' my heart. I'll take care of you and the girls. I want you just as much as you want me. It isn' just you in this. You aren' alone."

She lifted her head to look at him. She'd already memorized his face. Every line. Every edge. "I don't know what love is, Wyatt. But whatever we have between us is strong and won't let up."

"I'm going to teach you all about love, honey. My kind of love. It's fierce, burns hot and has stayin' power. Enough for a lifetime." He drew her shirt over her head and tossed it aside.

She reached for his. She *had* to believe him. She'd been in his mind. He was tough and hard, but he wasn't a deceptive man. She could keep her eye on Trap, but she'd warned Wyatt. He was intelligent enough to believe her. He saw her with all of her flaws and even her terrible need and weakness for him—and he still wanted her. Like this. A firestorm of passion that burned so hot they both were in danger of going up in the flames.

"I'd burn in hell for you," Wyatt whispered against her throat.

"*With* me," she corrected. "Burn *with* me."

Wyatt couldn't move fast enough, his hands dropping to his jeans. He just pushed them down, off of his hips and thighs so his cock sprang free. He jerked her jeans and lacy panties down to her ankles.

"Kick off the shoes, babe," he instructed. "Hurry it up."

Already her addicting spice called to him, the scent drifting up to tease his cock and make his mouth water. "Damn it, woman, hurry the hell up."

"You're always in such a frenzy."

Her laughter curled inside of him, around his heart and lungs. He pushed two fingers deep inside her slick, hot channel, and found her sensitive button. She gasped, and he took her mouth ruthlessly, hot blood surging through his veins.

She damn well had to stop questioning their relationship. He wasn't going to allow her to walk out on him before they even got started. Aggression mixed with lust was tempered and colored by the curious melting around his heart. He kissed her over and over, making certain she knew exactly who was kissing her. *It's my fingers inside you, Pepper. And it's my cock you're goin' to be ridin'. Don' think about leavin' me again. We have a problem, you talk to me about it. You don' just decide we're over. You're scared about somethin', you come to me to fix it. Do you understand?*

He knew he sounded harsh and dominant, but he didn't give a damn anymore. She had to know they were supposed to be together. Hell or heaven, it didn't matter. They had to be together.

He stroked and tugged on her clit, brushing his thumb over the bundle of nerves again and again as he pushed his fingers deep into her. Her breathing came in ragged little pants and gasps, music countering the roaring thunder in his ears. Finally, *finally*, he heard the shoes drop to the floor.

Instantly Wyatt swept her up to his waist, drawing her leg around his back. "Like that, sugar. That's good."

She got the idea, wrapping her legs around him, her hands at his neck.

"The bra, hon, that's got to go." He lowered her just enough to lodge the throbbing, burning head of his cock in her scorching entrance. His voice had gone low, growly, almost hoarse.

"Put your hands under your breasts and bring them up to my mouth," he instructed.

He watched her eyes darken. Fill with lust. The starburst through the midnight purple. So sexy. She licked her lips, her sweet mouth he went to bed with and woke up with wrapped around his cock. He felt the electric current racing through his body straight to his groin at the sight of her tongue on the curve of her lower lip.

She moved then, a slow undulation, her channel grasping him with greedy fingers, closing around him tightly in pure silken heat. Even as she moved, her eyes still on his, she brought her palms under her firm, high breasts and offered them to him. Already her nipples were peaked. He could see the marks of his possession from the night before on the round, soft globes. He liked seeing her skin branded with him.

He dipped his head and sucked her left breast into his mouth. Simultaneously he lowered her hard as he surged upward with his hips. She threw her head back, colliding with the wall, her mouth open in a silent scream.

He loved how much she enjoyed sex with him. She never tried to hide what she was feeling. He gave her pleasure and she returned it tenfold. It was never enough for either of them.

She picked up the rhythm he wanted immediately, taking her guidance from his hands. That left him free to feast on her breasts and nip and bite and kiss all along her throat and neck and chin.

It didn't last as long as he would have liked because he was burning from the inside out. The slow, easy ride went hard and fast and then harder still. There was no way to prolong the pleasure, not when her muscles were milking him insistently and she was so close.

"Don'," he commanded. "You wait for me. Hold on."

"I can't."

"You can. You will." He poured command into his voice. He was so close, but he needed this, hammering in and out of her, her tight, hot, wet, silken fist wrapped around him, driving him out of his mind.

She leaned forward and bit down on his shoulder. The sharp sting only added to the pleasure building and coiling inside of him.

"Please, Wyatt, I can't hold back."

He knew she could and would. She always did when he told her to. For him. She did it for him. He liked knowing she would. Just like he always anticipated what came after. Just the thought drove him over the edge.

"Now, babe. For me. Give me yourself."

Her body clamped down on his, a strangling vise that felt like heaven and burned like hell. Her muscles tightened impossibly, rippling with life, a tidal wave overtaking her, overtaking him. It started somewhere in his toes, boiled in his balls and rocketed free, jetting into her, filling her with his essence. He loved that. Loved that he was deep inside her. He didn't want to leak out of her. He wanted to stay there, his scent all over her.

He held her while her legs slowly dropped to the floor, leaning into her, the wall holding them both upright. Her arms circled his neck, her fingers in his hair. He found her mouth and kissed her over and over. Gently. Rough. Mixing in tenderness because he always felt tender toward her at this moment.

When he finally slipped out of her, he turned them so his back was to the wall and he could rest there, catching his breath. He was still in his shoes, his jeans around his ankles while she was wholly naked. He waited, his eyes on her, a silent command, and she smiled her sweet, loving smile she didn't even know she had.

His. She was his. She knew it. Her body and heart knew it. Her brain hadn't quite come to the same conclusion, but she was working it out. Pepper caught up his shirt while he stood there, draped against the wall. He loved watching her every move. He could watch her forever and never get enough.

Silently she handed him the shirt. He just held it in his hand. Waiting. Anticipating. Loving her. Damn it all. *Loving* her. He could admit he was long gone now. He didn't want to be, but she'd managed to find her way in. That part scared him. He hadn't expected it to happen.

Pepper leaned forward and kissed his throat. Her mouth ran down his chest to his belly, her hands gliding over him like silken gloves. He felt the spicy biochemical doing its job, sliding into his pores with her addicting flavor. He accepted that whenever she touched him she would still have traces of the biochemical on her hands and he would crave her touch just like this.

But it was her mouth he'd come to need. The way she knelt down, lovingly took his sac in her talented hands, the biochemical giving him a rush through his balls and groin when she held him. The first swipe of her tongue always sent his head spinning. She lapped at him gently, every inch of him, curling her tongue around him, sucking gently and then . . .

He closed his eyes and let himself savor the rush when her mouth settled around him and drew him deep. His body was the magnet for the biochemical and it rushed to invade, to pour into him through his skin. He hadn't realized at first that that was what helped to leech it from her system, that his own body somehow worked in conjunction with hers to pull the biochemical from her into him.

He loved her mouth on him. She had done this to him their first night together and since, it had become a ritual. Once he realized what happened, that his body drew the biochemical from her system, he initiated it a second time. He'd come to love this ritual. To even need it. But she needed it more than he did. To him, it felt as if his woman worshipped him, cared for him. Her mouth was always gentle. Loving even. It was the sexiest thing he'd ever seen.

His hands smoothed her soft hair. "God, babe, that feels so fuckin' good I don' even have words to tell you."

Sometimes, he found, with her mouth working him, he got hard again and she took care of that as well. Other times, like now, it felt so loving and tender he actually felt a lump in his throat and a burn behind his eyes.

She sat back on her heels and inspected him carefully, making certain he was totally clean before she leaned forward again and brushed a kiss across the head of his cock. "I'm glad."

"You make me feel like you enjoy takin' care of me," he said.

"I do or I wouldn't do it." She sent him a small smile and then rose gracefully to make her way to the connecting bathroom.

He heard the water running. She didn't know. She didn't yet understand that his body could remove the biochemical for a time, giving her a respite. She thought it was the sex. He didn't want her thinking that. He wasn't taking chances she might turn to someone else.

He walked to the doorway and leaned his hip against the wood. "Babe." He waited until her eyes met his. She had a warm washcloth in her hand and was slowly washing his seed from her thighs and between her legs. She didn't have a stitch on and her small waist emphasized her full breasts. As she bent to use the washcloth, her breasts moved invitingly. Everything she did was invitation.

"Somethin' else I haven' told you. I've been figurin' thin's out. How it works with your body and the heat cycle."

Her hand paused and she swallowed. "Can you fix me?"

"Sugar." He said it like a reprimand. "You don' need fixin'. No, not like you mean. You secrete a biochemical that goes into your system slow and begins to build. If you don' have sex, your body overloads on it. You have to release it. When we have sex, that helps, but more than that, it's in your mouth, on your fingers and palms. That's why when you touch a man, he can't get you out of his head. It's addicting."

She took a deep breath and looked as if she might cry. "You? Have I done that to you, Wyatt?"

"No. Not through the biochemical anyway. My body seems to be a magnet for the biochemical. When you touch me, or put your mouth on me, my body draws it away from yours. I seem to absorb it. I'm addicted to how you transfer it to me, but not the biochemical itself. That's why I can stay in control."

He kept his gaze on her face, watching her process the information. "Babe? Look at me. I want to see your eyes when I tell you this. I want you to hear in my voice and see it on my face that I'm being brutally honest."

She nodded, her eyes meeting his.

"No other man can do that for you. There's me for you. That's it. That's your option. You can't get that anywhere else. Do you hear what I'm sayin'?"

"Yes, Wyatt. I don't know why you would think I'd want another man. I'm not attracted to anyone else."

"Maybe if you'd get off the fuckin' fence, Pepper, and give me your word you'll stay, I can get a handle on my own shit. I despise bein' jealous of my friends when you're close to them. If I knew for certain you weren't goin' to walk out at the first fight we have, first disagreement, I could relax around the boys a little easier."

She stood up, tossing the washcloth into the sink and coming straight over to him. When she moved, it was sheer poetry. His heart tripped and gave a little stammer. His greedy cock stirred. She put her arms around his neck, curling her fingers into his hair, leaning in close to him, rubbing like a cat.

"I'm sorry, Wyatt. I don't want another man, only you."

She hesitated just for a moment. He could feel her brace herself, but she continued to look up at him. He knew whatever she said to him would really matter.

"I don't want you to be with me for my body. For sex. I want my man to love me the way men love their wives. I don't even know what it is, or how to do it myself, but I want it. Not for the children and not for sex."

He tucked her hair gently behind her ear and smiled down at her, his heart turning over. "I want you for myself, Pepper, for all the reasons I gave you. I thought I loved one woman some time ago and I realized what a mistake she was. She was all wrong for me. The thing is, what I feel for you is a million times more than I ever felt for her and we haven't even begun yet."

He felt her relax into him. Her gaze didn't waver. "I'll commit to you fully. I'll be your wife and live in your home and burn with you as often as you want me. Because that's what I want. I'll take care of our children and have a dozen more if you really want them. I can't promise I won't be scared and do silly things, but I'll do my best to come to you first before I panic. It has nothing whatsoever to do with your ability to take away that horrible clawing need and everything to do with the man you are."

He found himself grinning, pulling her close again, his hands sliding down the slope of her back to her rounded buttocks. "You just put your scent all over me on purpose, didn't you?"

He massaged his fingers into her firm muscles, deliberately pushing her mound against his thigh. "There are goin' to be days, babe, when I make certain you're wantin' me and I'm goin' to make you wait so you'll come screamin' for me five or six times. I may even go for a record."

She laughed and pushed at his chest. "We have to plan how we're going to break our children out of that horrible place. So don't get me going until we know they're safe."

"I'll do my best," he promised and dropped his arms, allowing her to escape.

She dressed with efficiency, but it didn't matter. Every movement was sensual. She was a living monument to the female body. He waited for her and inspected her carefully, making certain there were no marks showing on her skin where others could see. Making certain he kissed her several times. He even smoothed the tangles from her hair with a brush and handed her the clip she wore to pull it back.

"You ready?" He held out his hand.

She threaded her fingers through his, smiling up at him. He liked how relaxed she looked after having sex with him. They walked back to the kitchen together. Nonny was already outside, sitting in the rocking chair, holding Ginger. Clearly the boys had been a little too loud and had woken her up. Nonny glanced at their joined hands through the window and nodded her head, sending Wyatt a pleased smile.

"You two good?" Trap greeted, glancing at Wyatt and then turning his cool gaze onto Pepper as they entered the room. He was standing at the kitchen table looking down at several large blueprints.

"We're good," Wyatt said.

"I'm sorry about before," Pepper said. "You talked about the babies the same way Braden talked about them. As if they aren't human."

She kept her gaze steady on his, no remorse, even a challenge. Wyatt reached out and caught her hand in a warning hold. She didn't relent, didn't stop focusing on Trap.

Trap blinked. "I did?"

"Yep." It was Malichai who answered. "Like they were little rats in a lab just waiting for you to come along and study them." There was the smallest bite to his tone, as if, like Pepper, he hadn't liked what Trap had said earlier about studying the babies.

Trap shoved his hand through his hair. "Pepper, I don't think like that. Wyatt's family to me. That means those kids are family. If you're his choice, you are. That's the way it works with me. I can't help the way I am. My mind solves problems, and I don't think how to word something when my brain is running a hundred miles an hour."

"That's true," Malichai agreed. "He's like a processor running at top speed."

"And he's clueless when it comes to social skills," Draden added.

Trap scowled at them. "The point I'm trying to make is, I would never experiment on babies or children. I just wouldn't do it. But I'll find a way for the girls to live as normal a life as possible. When I'm being insensitive, kick me in the shins or something. Eventually I'll figure it out, but know I'd never use those babies."

There was no way to miss the sincerity in Trap's tone.

Pepper nodded. "Thanks for explaining, Trap. I know you didn't have to. Unfortunately you triggered the mama tiger in me."

"Um, no, darlin'," Wyatt corrected with a small grin. "That would be the mama snake."

Pepper laughed softly with the others, just as he'd wanted her to do. She turned her attention to the blueprints, the smile fading as she bent closer to look them over. Immediately the team surrounded the table.

"These blueprints are all wrong, Trap," Pepper said. "The first floor is probably the closest to what this looks like, but the rest of it . . ." She trailed off, shaking her head.

"The outside follows the blueprints, but the inside, not so much," she continued.

"Can you fix them, babe?" Wyatt asked.

Pepper nodded. "I studied the place, I can give you pretty good details. Why don't you go put Ginger back to bed? She's getting used to you doing that, and I'll sketch the floor plans and put in all the changes. I should be done by the time you get back."

Wyatt had been putting Ginger down at night, hoping she would get used to him. He liked holding her in his arms and rocking her while he gave her a bottle of warm milk and looked down at her little face. Love had taken hold sometime around the first or second time he'd done it.

Nonny handed him the baby as soon as he stepped outside with the bottle and a blanket to wrap her in. He was grateful the bayou was rarely cold. Ginger had trouble holding on to her body heat. She lifted her face for his kiss and snuggled right into him when he dropped into the chair beside his grandmother.

"That's my girl," he whispered to the baby. "She's so beautiful, isn't she, Nonny, just like her mama."

Ginger didn't like to hold the bottle. She liked him to hold it for her as she cuddled against his warmth, the blanket snug around her.

"She's beautiful," Nonny agreed. "Looks just like you when you were a babe. Glad you finally figured out what you needed in a woman, boy. Joy didn' belong here. She would never have made you happy. That one in there"—she indicated the kitchen—"she's the kind that will stand by you."

"Yeah, I kind of figured that out." He watched in awe as Ginger's little fingers wrapped around his index finger.

"Pepper is a woman of great courage. She fought for them even when she knew if she did those people in that lab would probably kill her. She braved the swamp with a child in tow. Tha's a woman who will stand with you through anythin'. She'll walk through fire to get to those she loves. She'll sacrifice anythin', even her own happiness, to protect them."

"There might be a reason for our attraction to one another . . ."

She leaned over and shook her head. "I spent a lot of time with Flame when she was so sick with the cancer. She talked, some in her sleep, and some when she thought she was goin' to die. I know all about Whitney and how he pairs his soldiers."

"Nonny, you can' talk about that."

She laughed. "I don' expect he's got him a listenin' device planted somewhere in my home and if I talk to you about this he'll send someone blastin' at me with a gun. I'm old, Wyatt, and I'm not afraid of very much. Life is to be lived. It doesn't really matter the how and why of things. It matters how you choose to live. I taught you to live life large. Tha's all, Wyatt. Love when you can. Laugh. Sing. And take care of your family and friends and then your community. It's not always easy, but it's good and at the end of it all, you'll be satisfied."

"You know I'm a rescuer." He sighed. He hadn't ever voiced the one concern nagging at him. He was certain of Pepper. He wasn't going to give her up, even if what he was doing was playing the knight in shining armor. "This feeling I have for her, it could be wrapped up in my need to rescue someone."

Nonny smiled at him. "Or you have it all wrong, boy, and she's the one rescuin' you. It's possible you need her every bit as much as she needs you. Let things be, Wyatt. Don' question them so much and just let things happen."

He smiled down at the baby's face and lifted her little fingers to his mouth. "Actually, Nonny, it's important to me that you like Pepper. I've never felt more alive, or more content and passionate in my life. I know what's comin', the battle to get the children back, but I know we're goin' to succeed. I'm lookin' forward to every morning the moment I open my eyes. I look forward to nighttime. She's the one. I know she is. If I find somethin' different when we get to the laboratory . . ."

Nonny held up her hand. "Don', Wyatt, don' even say it. She's loyal to those she cares about. She isn' about to betray you, no matter what your friends think."

"Trap's a good man, Nonny. He's different, but he's a good man."

"I'm a good judge of character, Wyatt. I see him. He's a driven man and his mind won' let him rest. It's good he has such good friends."

"He's goin' to help me work on an antivenom so that anyone around the children will be safe. I don' want anythin' to happen to you or anyone else. Flame isn' goin' to stay away once she knows we've got them here, and I have to know I can keep her safe."

"I have no doubts you'll both do what it takes to keep everyone safe, Wyatt. I don' worry about such things because I know you do."

Her gaze dropped to the baby in his arms. Her face softened and for a moment he thought he caught the sheen of tears. He didn't blame her. Sometimes when he looked at his little girl, he felt a little like crying himself. She was a beautiful, intelligent child and far too sober. All of them were working hard to make her relax and laugh. To be a child.

"I'm grateful we have them, Wyatt. I need them."

His heart clenched. Nonny didn't say things like that. She seemed invincible. Ageless. He was aware of her hair, white now with age, and the laugh lines around her eyes. She moved slower, but she still felt powerful. He couldn't imagine losing her.

He swallowed down emotion. Nonny wouldn't appreciate him plying her with questions on her health. "Then I'm glad we have them." He glanced down at Ginger's little face, the sweep of her lashes. He smiled at the baby. "I need them too. All of them."

Ginger reacted by pushing the bottle away. It was mostly empty anyway. She nodded her head vigorously. She was eager to see her sisters again.

"We'll bring them home, sweetheart," he whispered to his daughter. "I'll need your help once they're here. You can show them everythin' and help us teach them they're safe."

Ginger wrapped her arms around his neck and hugged him close. He looked over her head to his grandmother.

"I don' know if I ever told you how grateful I am to you. My childhood was happy, Nonny, thanks to you. I loved growin' up here. I always knew I could count on you. I always felt safe and loved. I want that for my children. And for Pepper. She never had that either. My daughters don' know what havin' someone like you in their lives is like. My heart aches for them." He wouldn't have said that to anyone but his grandmother.

"Mine too, Wyatt, but you'll sort it out, and we'll make it right," Nonny assured.

CHAPTER 14

Standing in the doorway of the kitchen, Wyatt closed his eyes and simply savored the sound of Pepper's voice as she explained things quietly to the team. Soft. Sultry. Ultra-feminine. She had a way of speaking that got inside a man and just refused to leave him alone. He loved the sound of her voice and her perfect little ass that her jeans clung so lovingly to as she bent over the kitchen table to point to various things on the blueprints.

The team surrounded the table and they were good-sized men. Pepper looked tiny beside them. Small and feminine. The thing in him he despised, the mindless black jealousy, stretched and clawed in the pit of his belly. For the first time he realized the unworthy trait was fed by his cat DNA. His woman was always close to the heat cycle and he naturally wanted to protect what was his.

Realizing what was riding him helped, but didn't completely alleviate the problem. Still, he could see Trap and Draden were a little more accepting of his claim on her, but Wyatt wanted to make certain they knew he was serious.

Ezekiel and Malichai knew, and they respected a certain distance from her that the others hadn't quite gotten yet. Trap, especially. Trap didn't pay the least attention to any kind of cues.

Wyatt stepped up behind Pepper, his body close to hers and leaned over her back, his head at her shoulder, arms on either side of her body so his hands could rest on the table. He caged her there between the table and his body. Taking up that position enabled him to box out the other men so they couldn't get close to her, which kept his crazy temper under control.

Just as she had to learn to keep her shield up—and he could see she was getting stronger every day—he had to learn to handle his own shit.

"Fill me in," he ordered, and moved the sweep of clipped hair off her neck so he could breathe against her much more intimately as he leaned down to look at the blueprints.

She turned her head to look at him over her shoulder. His heart stuttered and his cock jerked hard. There it was. The smile that was for him alone. "Did Ginger go down without a fight?"

He brushed a kiss on her mouth. "I told her we were bringin' her sisters home tomorrow night. She was very happy."

"I missed putting her to bed." There was regret in her voice.

"She knew you were plannin' out the rescue, sugar. She was okay with that." He brushed another kiss on her mouth, ignoring Trap's sigh. "I told her you'd be in later to kiss her good night."

She nodded and turned back to the blueprints. "The first level was built twelve feet from the ground, using very thick concrete," she said. "Apparently, that's where they built the crematorium and the holding cells for anyone they plan on killing. There are six cells on either side with four feet of cement in between the two sides. There is no way out once you're down in the cells, other than elevators. Each side has its own elevator."

"So basically, if the cells are flooded, no one gives a damn," Wyatt said. He felt his gut start a slow smolder. "Are you tellin' me the babies—our babies—are down in those cells alone? Is anyone else down there?"

The table trembled and for a moment the walls of the room contracted. Pepper glanced uneasily over her shoulder at him, nodding slowly. Her eyes held sorrow.

"I'm sorry, Wyatt, I tried to get them all out, but they were in separate cells and it took time to get them open."

"It's not your fault," he said tersely. She flinched. He felt the flinch right through skin and bones. Deliberately he stroked his hand down her back, and pressed closer to her, trying to surround her with comfort. "I'm not upset with you, babe. This isn't your fault. Whitney just makes me so damned mad. How could he do this to children and live with himself?"

"It isn't Whitney," she denied. "I'm telling you, Braden authorized our transfer to this place, brought us in by a private jet and then he issued the termination order a couple of weeks ago. *Braden.* Not Whitney."

"Braden works for Whitney," Wyatt said. "There's not a doubt in my mind."

Trap nodded. "Seriously, Pepper, we've known for a while that Whitney could never pull all these experiments off by himself. Even I have an assistant. He's got too many facilities. He has to have someone he trusts overlooking each laboratory, but Whitney definitely calls the shots."

"So is anyone else down in those cells right now?" Wyatt asked.

Pepper nodded. "A woman. They brought her in recently. They may have already terminated her. She was on the other side, not with the babies. Braden was definitely afraid of her. I don't think they were even feeding her. They wanted her weak before they tried to move her to the crematorium. At least, I kind of got that from bits and pieces I overheard. I never saw her. She was brought in right before the order was issued to terminate the children."

"How'd they bring her in?" Ezekiel asked.

"There's a large cargo elevator on the first floor. It's located right here." Pepper circled a spot toward the middle of the western wall. "It's huge. They drive trucks right in so the other guards don't ever see one of their throwaways."

"What other guards?" Draden interrupted.

"They have guards who protect the plastics plant. It's a working plant. They know it's a cover for a research facility with military contracts, but they never enter any part of the building other than where the plastic molds are manufactured," Pepper explained.

"So there is an actual product being produced on the second floor?" Ezekiel asked. "They'll have vents and air conduits as well as things like conveyor belts and plenty of equipment."

Pepper nodded. "On the second floor, yes, meaning if you count the actual first floor where they hold and terminate their prisoners."

Wyatt moved his leg very casually closer to the table, wedging it between Pepper and Trap, his thigh pressing tight against her body as he leaned down to study the drawing of the large building she'd superimposed over the blueprints.

"The cargo elevator is here." He drew a line with his finger. "So this has to be the recreation room for the guards who don' have any real knowledge of what's takin' place in their own backyard. The kitchen and cafeteria. You've got bathrooms and the plastic plant itself. So those workin' the plant itself are kept away from anythin' they might be able to talk about."

Pepper nodded. "They bring in prisoners through the cargo elevator enclosed in a truck. Everyone's used to the trucks bringing supplies for the plant. When a prisoner is brought in, they're completely enclosed in a type of crate and sometimes unconscious. The woman they're terminating was definitely unconscious. I was hiding in the vent just opposite the second elevator and I saw them take her in the crate down to the cells on the other side."

Wyatt scowled. "Where were they holdin' you?"

"Down in the cells with the children. They keep it cold down there, so it makes it harder for us to move around or fight them."

Wyatt closed his eyes for a moment, trying not to think what would have happened to her and the children had the cells flooded. The water table in the swamp was particularly high, which was the reason most houses were built fairly high off the ground.

"I think I'd like to break Whitney's neck," he said softly, his Cajun accent deepening in direct proportion to his temper.

"Get in line," Trap said. "Can you imagine if he happened to employ a sadistic guard to look after his prisoners? No one would be around to know what was done down there, and if the prisoner was going to be terminated, anything could happen and be gotten away with."

All the men looked at Pepper. She took a deep breath and let it out. Wyatt noted that her hand trembled.

"Those guards and lab workers come in only when they have prisoners there." She changed the subject hastily. "When we came, no one else was there. The laboratory is on the third floor along with sleeping and recreation quarters for those personnel."

I'm here, baby. Don' think about it. We'll sort that out later.

I'm good. I'm here. I've got you and we're getting the children out.

Still, she was shaken. He had the feeling those guards hadn't been easy to manage. He didn't want to think what they might have done to her.

"And the elevators go all the way up from the cells below to the third floor, is that correct?" Malichai asked. "Are they guarded, Pepper?"

"No, they aren't guarded, but both are locked down by codes and palm print scans. You have to have both to get into the elevators. And yes, all elevators run to all floors, but those two can't be accessed by everyone."

Wyatt was proud of her voice, smooth and steady. Whatever memory Trap had brought up with his mention of the guards she had tucked away and then kept strictly professional.

"I take it on the third floor they have all kinds of chemicals," Trap said.

Pepper nodded. "I've gone up there numerous times with the children. I'm more familiar with the third floor than the plant floor."

"How were you able to move around in the plant without detection?" Ezekiel asked.

"I can fit in very small places," she explained. "I'm very flexible."

Wyatt nearly groaned aloud. *Don' be sayin' thin's like that out loud,* he cautioned. *I'm standin' right behind you, remember?* Deliberately he smoothed his hand down the curve of her butt. He wanted her to laugh. To feel his presence and know she was safe with them. *That means I can feel your skin against mine and I'm breathin' you in with every damn breath I take. I'm as hard as a rock and I can' exactly move right now. Usin' a word like "flexible" is just bound to conjure up images neither of us wants to think about.*

Pepper leaned back, pushing her bottom tight against him. It was a subtle move, but the contact with his heavy erection sent flames dancing through him. *You're a little insane, aren't you? Does your* grand-mere *know she raised an oversexed crazy man?*

I'm Cajun, honey, we know what the good thin's in life

are. Food. Fightin' and lovin'. He nudged her with his thigh. *Not necessarily in that order.*

Pepper coughed and covered her mouth as she looked back at him over her shoulder, but it was impossible to cover the flash of laughter in her eyes or the answering spark of desire. Wyatt found the laughter was every bit as important to him as the desire was. She wasn't a woman who ever had much to laugh about.

"Pepper?" Ezekiel prompted. "If Wyatt can quit trying to charm your panties off, we might actually come up with a plan."

"I have no idea why you're accusin' me of misconduct," Wyatt said. "And don' be thinkin' about her panties or I'll have to pound you into the ground. Don' even say the word 'panties.'"

He groaned inside his head deliberately, centering Pepper's attention on him. *Now he's got me thinkin' about your panties. You are wearin' some, aren' you? Wait. Don' be answerin' that. If you're not, we're goin' to have words about it, and if you are, I'll be deeply disappointed.*

You really are obsessed with sex.

Ma'am, I do thank you for the compliment. It's true. Absolutely true. Know I'll take good care of you and anytime we have an argument, I will find the perfect way to make things up to you.

Wyatt poured sincerity into his voice.

Pepper burst out laughing. "You really are insane, and if you keep it up, I'm telling Grand-mere on you."

He placed his hand over his heart. "I'm just reassurin' you, darlin', that I can take very good care of you, that's all."

"Miss Pepper," Ezekiel said. "Would you like me to take him outside behind the barn and teach him a few manners? I'd be happy to do that for you."

"I wouldn't mind getting in on that," Malichai added. "Having been on the receiving end of his lessons on manners quite a few times, I can testify that my brother has excellent skills in this particular area."

"Don' even think the two of you city boys could take on a Cajun born and bred in the bayou and win," Wyatt cautioned. "'Specially when a lady is watchin'."

Pepper tapped the blueprints. "Maybe we should just forego the lesson in manners altogether. My guess is, Grand-mere tried her best, and if she couldn't get anything through that thick skull of his, no one could."

"So how did you get out?" Trap asked, bringing them all back to the important matters at hand.

"The ventilation system, which, by the way, is very narrow. I actually was afraid I'd get stuck a couple of times. Every eight feet they have high-speed fans. I believe it was more to ensure against escape than to ventilate, but I could be wrong."

"So thick concrete, elevators requiring both palm prints and a code," Wyatt said. "Whose palm print?"

"A specific guard. There're only two of them. They always are the ones to accompany the prisoners. They escorted me and the children, and they left and came back with the other woman."

"You had no communication with the woman?" Draden asked.

"I didn't say that," Pepper said. "I just don't know anything about her. We used a kind of Morse code. Every soldier is taught it at school and I knew she was one of us—the flawed rejects, not worthy of being called a soldier."

"Don' say that." The table trembled and Wyatt pulled his fists from the top of it and put his hands on her narrow waist. "That just pisses me off. You're one of us—a GhostWalker—and so is that woman. If she's still alive, we'll go in and get her out. We don' leave anyone behind."

"Her name is Cayenne. That means she was developed at the school in France. Everyone there was given the name of a spice. She wasn't with my group, so she's probably a little younger than me."

The men looked at one another. "That means she can't be more than eighteen or nineteen. Twenty at the oldest," Wyatt said. "What the hell did she do to get herself on a termination list?"

"Unfortunately, if you don't follow orders and you try to escape or you refuse to do something they think is important, with Braden, that's pretty much all it takes, especially if they already think you're dangerous."

"Every GhostWalker is dangerous," Trap pointed out. "We're supposed to be. I think the original idea of enhancing our psychic abilities was lost a bit when Whitney switched that over to genetics."

"Whitney uses women and children to experiment on," Draden said, "to perfect his ideas before he tries them on his male soldiers."

"Damn him," Ezekiel said. "Why can't one of us get to him?"

"The intel on him is that he moves every couple of days. He can be anyone," Wyatt said. "He's become that good."

Malichai nodded. "He was actually at the White House for an event with Violet Freeman a couple of months back. Violet is now officially a widow. Senator Freeman died. Whitney used an alias, but Lily Miller, Whitney's daughter, has facial recognition software constantly searching for him and it identified him positively. While he was there, he met with several top members of the president's staff. We don't know why, of course, but we think he's moving Violet into position to run for president next election year."

"Violet's a GhostWalker," Wyatt added to Pepper. "But for some reason, she betrayed the other women in her unit and has aligned herself with Whitney. Our sources say she's actually in a relationship with him."

"I'm not certain I believe it," Trap said. "Unfortunately, I'm just a little too close to his personality, and I would find it very difficult to maintain a relationship with anyone—or at least they wouldn't be comfortable for very long with me."

Draden nudged Malichai. "I'm comfortable with him. Aren't you?"

"Well, since he read those books on manners and social behaviors, he's gotten a little more tolerable," Malichai replied. "But I think you still have work to do on him, bro. Miss Manners? Maybe she gives a course he can take. We can hire someone to teach him."

In one smooth motion Trap drew a knife from the sheath between his shoulder blades and threw it at Malichai. The knife took off the material of Malichai's shirt along his right shoulder and lodged in the wall behind him, the material pinned there.

"You're in such trouble now," Malichai said. "Grand-mere said no playing with knives in the house. *Especially* her kitchen."

"I didn't know the rules before, so she can't really get angry with me," Trap justified. "In any case, if I take you out back and skin you alive, she'll probably thank me."

"She's got a soft spot for me," Malichai declared. "I appreciate good cooking, unlike certain cretins who don't even know what they're chewing on."

Nonny wandered in, glancing at the blueprints spread out over her kitchen table. "When you boys are through playin' with your knives and guns, I've got me an idea, now that we'll have three babies and Pepper to protect."

Trap rolled up the blueprints, clearly trying to be discreet. Wyatt straightened and stepped back to allow Pepper to stand straight. He wrapped his arm around her waist and drew her into him, covering his body against Nonny's sharp eyes.

"What's your idea, Grand-mere?" Ezekiel asked.

"I watched this movie where some rich folks got invaded

and they had them a little room they could hole up in. I liked the look of that little room. I've been sittin' outside, smokin' my pipe and thinkin' a little room like that with beds for the girls and some supplies, where no one could get in, might be jist the thin' when those bad boys of Whitney's come callin'. You all could make me that room."

Trap frowned, his mind working fast. "That might not be such a bad idea. We've got building supplies. We've brought in top-of-the-line security and every kind of weapon and enough ammo to take out a small country to defend ourselves. We need to focus on personal protection for the women and children."

Pepper stirred in his arms as if she might protest. She was a soldier after all, but Wyatt wasn't going to let her get into semantics.

Let it go. He pushed the command into her mind.

She turned her head back to look at him, her eyes dark with censure. *I'm not part of your team.*

Meanin' I don' get to tell you what to do? He pushed male amusement into her mind. *Got news for you, baby, I'm always goin' to be tellin' you what to do. You bought that life when you gave me the go-ahead.*

"I think so as well," Ezekiel said. "I've been thinking of ways to shore up the house. Bulletproof glass, even thin armor between the walls, certainly something on the roof, but a room where the children would be safe would be good."

See, even Ezekiel realizes I do not have to be hidden away when there's trouble. I can fight as well as any of you.

Wyatt deliberately nuzzled her neck, his arms locking her in place when she would have stepped away. *I like it when you want to fight me. My blood gets all hot and yours does too and then we both burn in paradise.*

Do you ever think about anything besides sex? I'm the one whose supposed to be sex hungry, not you.

You're supposed to be Wyatt hungry.

He felt her laughter. There in his mind. It was the most intimate thing, having her there, filling him up with . . . her. Pepper.

How had he ever even conceived of loving someone else? Every other woman paled in comparison to her. She made him feel so alive. Anger, passion, humor, all of it was wrapped up in her.

It's a good thing you're charming, Wyatt. Otherwise your bossy ways would get you in a lot of trouble.

I'm the boss, not bossy, there's a difference.

She burst out laughing and then hastily covered her mouth with her hand when the other team members turned to look at her.

"Grand-mere, I'm expecting a large truck with equipment for the lab," Trap said, saving her. Clearly trying to make up for his remarks about studying the babies. "As well as a few more items we need for security. Had I known about the safe room, I would have sent for those supplies as well. They'll be pulling in probably during the time we're gone. My assistant's name is Daryl Monroe. I would take it as a favor if you gave him the same welcome you gave to me. He's been up for over twenty-four hours pulling things together for us."

"Of course," Nonny said. "No need to even ask."

"If we're going to make this a base," Trap added, turning toward Wyatt, "we'll need a topnotch laboratory to work in. I can give Daryl the list of supplies we'll need to secure the house itself as well as a safe room. He'll get it all done."

"Trap, that's too much money," Wyatt protested. "I'm coverin' it, but you're lookin' at top-of-the-line materials and they don' come cheap."

"We're family. I'll be building my own place close. When this is over, they might be selling that tract of land the plastics company is on. I can buy that for my place and try to secure as much land around and between the two compounds for the others on our team. That way, the children and women will have plenty of protection all the time, even when we have to go out on missions."

This time Pepper didn't protest. Wyatt felt the change in her toward Trap immediately. He couldn't say he wasn't happy about it. Trap was family, but still, that dark ugly male, very ferocious and possessive cat inside of him unsheathed claws and raked hard in his belly.

Pepper leaned back into him, her hand sliding down his hip. Her touch was barely there. Gentle. But he felt it right to his bones.

You're a good man, Wyatt. You have good friends, and that says a lot about you. They're willing to relocate at a great expense to keep your children safe. I didn't know there were people like you in the world.

Her voice whispering so intimately in his head soothed the beast inside of him. She really was wholly focused on him. She heard the conversation swirling around her, admired his friends and his grandmother, but he was her center. There was no doubt in his mind and the terrible beast closed its mouth with a snap and went back to sleep.

I am lucky, Pepper. My friends are the kind that always have my back. In this case, that will extend to you and the girls.

I'm so anxious to get them back. They have to be so scared without me. Braden will have told them lies. That I abandoned them. That no one will ever come for them. I just hope they're asleep and that for once, Braden put them in the same cell.

"Who is changing their diapers or helping them onto the potty chair? Who's givin' them bottles at night?" Wyatt asked aloud, a lump in his throat.

"Don't think about it, Wyatt," Ezekiel said. "That will only make you crazy. We can't get them out until we know their prison inside and out. We've got the rest of tonight and all day tomorrow to strengthen our plan. We're going to get them out."

Pepper turned in his arms and buried her face against his chest. Wyatt felt a tremor run through her body and knew instantly she'd been holding herself together by a thread. She knew those babies. She'd been with them from the time they were three months old. She loved them. She might not think she knew what love was, but the children were hers, biologically or not, and she loved them.

As much as it was hell for the team—and him—to think of the babies locked away in cells, it had to be sheer torture for her. He felt the hot tears on his shirt and wrapped his arms around her, holding her close to him.

"I'm callin' it a night, boys," Wyatt said. "Trap, I don' know what to say but thank you. You know I've got your back."

He turned his body to prevent them from seeing Pepper's face. They knew. They all knew. They were Ghost-Walkers. They wouldn't like her tears any more than he did. She would be embarrassed that she cried in front of them, but she would never know that someone would be paying for those tears. She was one of them whether a part of their actual team or not, and none of them liked anyone messing with a GhostWalker.

He caught the grim exchanges the men had over her head. If Nonny caught them, she didn't say a word. She leaned over and kissed Pepper's cheek.

"She needs care tonight, Wyatt," Grand-mere said.

He nodded his understanding and, sweeping his arm around Pepper, walked her out of the kitchen and down the hall. Only then did he dare to look down at her. Tears streamed down her face. She cried in utter silence. Ginger had done that. His baby. His heart stuttered in his chest. He opened the door to the baby's room and let her look in on Ginger. There was a baby monitor, with a camera inside so they could see her while she slept and hear her when she woke. Still, both liked to peek in on her before they went to bed.

He closed the door and took his woman down the hall to his room. Once inside she moved away from him to stand in the center of the room, wiping at her eyes. He locked the door and leaned against it.

"You should never have to cry, Pepper," he said softly. "That's wrong."

She tried to smile. "I'm sorry. I can't stop thinking about them locked away. I've tried to put it out of my head. I know we couldn't just get them without the house prepared for an assault, but still, to just leave them. They really must think I've abandoned them. They're so little, and I know they're scared."

She burst into tears all over again and threw herself on the bed, pulling her knees to her chest in a little ball that broke his heart almost as much as her tears did.

Wyatt sank down on the end of the bed and reached for her left foot. He dragged her shoe off and tossed it across the room with a little more force than he meant. His hands massaged her foot for a moment before he removed the other shoe. Both legs curled back to her chest.

"Babe, we're goin' to get them. Tomorrow night we'll have them with us." He took off his boots and set them aside before he rubbed her hip and bottom. "One more night. They'll be home."

"But still, Wyatt, it's one more night in that horrible place. They give them one blanket. They'll be so cold and frightened. Without me there, I don't know if anyone is even making certain they have food. I shouldn't have left them. I couldn't get them through the fans. There wasn't enough time."

She sobbed, took a breath and continued. "I tried to go back, but they had security beefed up and I was afraid Ginger would follow me inside. If I was caught and she was on the outside, who would look after her?"

It had been a heartbreaking decision to leave the others behind. The only thing she could do was warn Braden she would expose them and what they did there if he terminated the other two babies.

Wyatt tossed his clothing aside and crawled over her to reach the other side of the bed. Sitting with his back to the headboard, he reached down and pulled her into his arms, uncaring that he was naked and she was fully clothed. He only wanted to comfort her. To hold her.

She snuggled into him just like Ginger did, curling up small and fitting into him without hesitation. His arms closed around her, caging her in, holding her tight. His chin dropped down on top of her head and he just let her cry.

The storm lasted longer than he anticipated but he was patient, dropping kisses into the center of her thick, silky hair and nuzzling the nape of her neck.

"I'm sorry," she repeated, her voice muffled by his chest.

"Sometimes cryin' is necessary, sugar, everyone does it. You need it, you cry. I'm right here and I'm not goin' anywhere," he reassured her.

"I don't cry in front of people."

"Fortunately, Pepper, I'm not people. I'm your man. You cry in front of your man. You tell him what's wrong and he fixes it. That's how it works. And if it doesn't need fixin' or I can' do anythin' about it right at that moment, I just listen."

She lifted her head to look at him. "Is that what you're doing right now? Listening?"

"I'm lovin' you, babe. Lovin' the hell out of you. And when you're all tired out I'm goin' to lay you down and love on you some more." He pushed back her hair. "You need that. And then I'm runnin' a hot bath and brushin' your hair for you and puttin' you to bed."

She smiled against his bare chest. He felt her lips move over his skin. "You have a plan."

"I do."

Wyatt pulled her shirt over her head and made short work of her bra. Her full breasts spilled out, temptation itself, and his cock grew, pressing deep against her bottom. Wyatt rolled her off of him, laying her out on the bed, his hands at her jeans. He stripped the clothes from her and threw one thigh over her, shifted and then straddled her.

Pepper held her breath. Wyatt didn't say anything to her. Didn't give her any explanation or cue as to what he wanted her to do. When she raised one hand toward his chest, he caught her hand and put it firmly on the bed beside her. She could barely breathe with the way he looked at her. She'd never seen that particular expression on his face before. Soft. Gentle. Tender even. More than that.

He leaned down and pressed a kiss into her throat. Butterflies took off in her stomach. His tongue was there, she could feel it just for a moment and then he kissed his way to the valley between her breasts. He pressed his lips there. Lingered. Stroked with his tongue, kissed either side of her breasts and then under them. Gently. Reverently. As if he worshipped her body. His mouth moved lower, his tongue and lips finding her rib cage and then moving to her belly button. He swirled his tongue and kissed her repeatedly.

He shifted to move back, picking up her leg by her ankle, so he could kiss behind her knee and then the soles of each foot. Very gently he pushed her knees up and wedged himself between her thighs. His mouth found the inside of her thighs and he kissed her gently, his tongue tasting her skin.

Pepper went completely still. He was doing exactly what he said he would. He was showing her love. It was beautiful. The most beautiful thing in the world. His face, carved so sensually, his eyes glowing with a soft look, his dark wavy hair and sexy mouth, muscles rippling. It was too much and yet not enough.

Already she could feel her body spilling out a welcome. She went slick and hot, yet at the same time, she wanted this slow, leisurely love he was showing her. His mouth was on her, driving her up, and then it was all Wyatt. His cock glided in and out of her while his hands framed her face and he whispered softly to her in French.

"Je t'aime, bébé, et je vais vous aimer éternellement."

She couldn't breathe as he moved in and out of her with exquisite tenderness. He kissed her over and over, pouring fire down her throat. Pouring love. She nearly choked on it, the lump in her throat so enormous.

No one had ever treated her with such gentleness, or said words of love to her. She wrapped her arms around him, lifting her hips to meet his, trying to show him that she felt the same way.

"Wyatt," she breathed his name. It was all she could do. She was too filled with him. Too overcome by him. Wyatt. Just his name, but then, to her, that was everything. Her world now. This man and the family they were choosing to make together.

She showed him she loved him the only way she knew how, when they were finished and he'd kissed her eyes to take away the last of the tears and then kissed her mouth a million times.

She crawled over him down to his cock and gently and carefully made absolutely certain he was clean, all the while her eyes on his. He stretched out, his hands behind his head, his eyes glowing at her, much like a cat in the dark. She loved watching his face when she attended him, loved how he enjoyed every lap of her tongue and her mouth on him.

When she was finished, he drew her back up to the pillow, pulled a single sheet over her and left her to go into the bathroom and run her bath. Lying on the bed, she watched him through the doorway as he moved around, pouring something into the bathwater and even testing it before he came back for her.

She didn't protest when he cradled her in his arms and carried her to the bath. She didn't tell him how much it meant to her when he brushed out her long hair while she relaxed in the water. She didn't say anything until they were both back in bed and he was curled protectively around her, holding her close, his body tight against hers.

Pepper closed her eyes and whispered to the night. To him. *"Je t'aime, Wyatt, avec chaque souffle dans mon corps."*

"With every breath in your body forever, Pepper. For always," he prompted, his voice sleepy, his warm breath on the nape of her neck.

Pepper found herself smiling in the dark. She felt loved, cared for her, relaxed and safe. Wyatt had done that. If he needed the words, she could give them to him.

"Pour toujours, Wyatt, pour toujours."

Forever. For always. And she meant it.

CHAPTER 15

Wyatt maneuvered the airboat through the dark, swampy waters slowly, suppressing the sound so it couldn't travel through the night to the guards patrolling the fence line of the Wilson Plastics compound. No one spoke aloud, using hand signals or telepathy to communicate as Wyatt took the boat as close as he dared to their destination. He needed the boat close in case they had to make a run for it with the children.

Wyatt was grateful he'd come to this part of the swamp so many times throughout his childhood. It made it much easier to avoid the cypress stumps and trees looming up along the shore as they made their way to shallower waters.

They each knew the layout of the building and each had their own enhancements. The five men were used to working together, already a cohesive team, but Pepper was an outsider, one they weren't familiar with, yet they needed her. Ordinarily, they would never have gone into the field with someone they didn't know. Wyatt saw the others exchanging uneasy glances and he couldn't blame them.

Bringing someone untried, someone new, into a cohesive team was a recipe for disaster.

He was certain none of them believed she would betray them, they'd gotten to know her and they all trusted Wyatt. He was connected to her and he hadn't found one hint of conspiracy or an alternate agenda. He'd made that abundantly clear to them. She wanted those children free just as they did. Just the same, she was an unknown. All of them knew they could count on each other, but Pepper . . . He sighed. They would just have to do the best they could.

Draden leapt from the boat when he stopped it and almost instantly disappeared into the terrain. He blended wherever he was, a ghost, moving through any background, impossible to find unless it was far too late and he was already on top of you. He would be their man to take out the guards while Wyatt controlled the dogs. Draden tied off the boat to keep it in place, using a tree stump.

Watch yourself. Snakes and alligators love this particular spot, Wyatt warned. *Zeke, we're countin' on you to keep them away from us.*

Roger that.

In the field, Ezekiel was all business. The cat in him was strong, the drive to hunt sometimes coming close to overpowering him. He was enormously strong and could leap high as well as long distances. He would clear most fences with no problem. Ezekiel was an extremely dangerous man, but he never left a friend, and he would fight to the death to get to a team member in trouble. Wyatt was grateful he was there.

Out of curiosity, Pepper, Ezekiel asked. *Can you control snakes?*

Wyatt felt the instant alertness in the team members. He glanced down at her face. Did she feel it too? Did she feel the sudden change in energy directed at her? She already felt like an outsider, a flawed GhostWalker, destined for termination. Wyatt wasn't as certain that Whitney wanted her dead, but still, he knew she felt very alone.

Her eyes met his as she took his hand to step from the boat. He pulled her in close to his body, wanting her to feel protected. *Not in the way you mean, Ezekiel. I can't make them move away from me, but I can soothe them sometimes if they're agitated. I usually am aware of a snake close to me, but I can't always count on that. Here in the swamp, I had a lucky escape or two. It's possible Ginger can though,* she added, sounding matter-of-fact.

Wyatt knew she didn't feel matter-of-fact. He tightened his fingers around hers and pulled her hand to his chest, pouring his mind into hers, filling her with him—with his belief in her. She wasn't alone and he didn't want her to ever think she was.

I meant the things I said to you earlier, Pepper. We're together in this. We'll get them out. The boys are used to workin' with each other. They trust you, but you're an unknown in the middle of a team that's worked together through many battles. We know how one another thinks.

She nodded her head in understanding. *I'll stay open to you at all times. You can build a bridge between us, Wyatt, so I'm included in your loop.*

And you're under my command. He wanted to make that very clear. *It's important we work together as a team, Pepper. I can' have a wild card runnin' loose when all of our lives are on the line. Our first priority is the children, but if we have to cut and fade, you will come with us.*

She bit down hard on her lower lip. Her guilt and sorrow at leaving the other two girls behind still beat at her. She was afraid for them, afraid they would think she'd abandoned them, and he didn't blame her, but they had to be prepared for a fight with Whitney's soldiers once they took the girls back, and that meant preparation time.

I'll never forgive myself if anything happened to them. I know Braden would have ordered the guards and the lab techs to tell them I left them and I wasn't coming back.

She'd told him that last night, but he let her say it again.

In the midst of a team of GhostWalkers, she had to feel isolated. She wouldn't be there at all if they didn't need her to get the children out. They could kill the guards and use their keys and prints to open the elevators, but that would open an entire new can of worms. The goal was to get in and get out without anyone knowing they were there until after they were gone. The last thing any of them wanted to do was fight their way out with two babies on their hands.

Wyatt took the lead, moving through the swamp, feeling carefully with not only his experience, but also with his enhanced cat senses. Oftentimes, one could take a step and just sink right through to the murky, muddy waters below. The ground could be very thin in places. One had to know where to step, and even then, erosion was always taking place in the ever-changing swamp.

The babies will know better. The guards and lab people aren't goin' to persuade them differently. They'll be able to sense lies. Ginger can, and no doubt the others can as well. I think Whitney wants us to have those babies. I think he studied my personality and yours and knew we'd fight for those children regardless of whether or not we believed they were biologically ours.

Then we really could be walking into a trap. What's to say he doesn't want us all living in the horrible compound, guinea pigs for his experiments?

Wyatt shrugged. *It doesn't really matter much, does it? We're not leavin' them there, so we don' really have a choice. Whitney doesn' like things easy for us. He sets up his hideous little experiments to see how his soldiers work together. That's part of his fun.*

He held up his fist as they approached the end of the tree-line. His team sank low and scanned the tall fence just ahead of them. Pepper followed their example. She'd gone out many times as a child and teenager, into the field to practice and learn maneuvers so she wasn't unfamiliar with their silent signals.

Malichai leapt for the branches of the nearest tree, drawing himself up easily, careful to keep the leaves from rustling or the branches from swaying. He was light and nimble when he needed, a strange phenomenon for such a big man. The others all called him the "rubber man" because his spine was so flexible, much like a large cat's, that he could turn in midair and switch direction. His flexible spine came in handy when moving fast through trees.

Two guards on this side. Our friend Larry and his pal, Jim. They've got the dog, Wyatt. You'll have to reach out and keep that dog moving. He's already scenting the cat in all of us.

I don' think so. He didn' really react when he was near the house and I had my scent everywhere. I think he's lookin' for a particular scent. Snake. He's reactin' to Pepper bein' close. I've almost got him. Give me another minute. Draden, hold your position.

Draden stilled at the very edge of the grass leading to the fence. The dog whined, swinging his head toward them, and then just as quickly, turned away, walking casually close to the chain-link fence with his handler.

Wyatt waited until the two guards moved around the corner of the building. *You're on, Draden, be careful. They've got a guard up on the roof. Don' forget the cameras. We don' want Whitney to see any feed of us workin' together. We give that man nothing at all if we can help it.*

A lazy one on the roof, Malichai said. *That's no soldier. He's lighting a cigarette. He's got a comfy chair up there and a he's settling down to read.*

A literate guard. Wyatt couldn't keep the laughter out of his voice.

The guards at the plastic plant had no idea what was going in or out of their compound and they'd grown a little complacent. Larry, he knew, was suspicious. He'd even tried to warn Wyatt, which signaled he wasn't privy to Whitney's plans. The civilian guards were considered disposable by

Whitney and Braden. Wyatt didn't consider them disposable, and he'd cautioned his team, especially Ezekiel and Trap, to use as little force as possible.

You're absolutely certain of the thickness of those walls? he asked Pepper, building a bridge so his team could hear. *We can't be off at all.*

There was no way to measure, Wyatt. I went off the original blueprints and added what I thought looked right, but if you're planning on setting a charge . . . She trailed off, obviously worried.

Charges make noise. We're goin' in absolutely silent. I would prefer no one knew we've been here, at least not tonight. Trap, we don' have exact measurements. If you can' feel how thick that concrete wall is, don' attempt to get in. We'll think of somethin' else.

Tell me what you're doing, Pepper demanded.

We're goin' to take the buildin'. You'll go in through the air vents just like you did before. In case they're lyin' in wait for you, Trap will go in first to protect you and children.

That's your plan? Are you insane? It's impossible. He's too big. He'd never be able to fit into the vents.

Wyatt curled his fingers around the nape of her neck, his thumb pushing up her chin so she was forced to look at him. He could feel her pulse beating hard into his hands. *He'll be there. If he can', I'll let you know and you abort until we all get inside to take them back. If we have to, we'll kill everyone inside. We don' want to do that, but we won' leave the children in those cells, Pepper. That's a promise.*

She swallowed hard and put her hand on his forearm. *You know someone will be waiting down in the cells.*

Maybe. Maybe not. They've never had a real break-in before, and I would guess they don' believe it's possible.

Pepper took a deep breath and let it out. *How is Trap going to get into the cells where the children are being held without being seen? You never told me.*

That's what he does, honey. Just do your part and get

into position. Wait until I give the go-ahead and then get to the children. And don' let them bite Trap.

Please, don't let them bite Trap, Trap added, faint laughter in his voice. *I'm the one who's going to figure out the antivenom with Wyatt, so really, I'm one of the good guys.*

Wyatt recognized the attempt at humor for what it was, Trap reaching out to Pepper to reassure her. Trap appeared cold-blooded, that was true, but he had a moral compass that often prevented him from going in the wrong direction. He'd been trying from the beginning to make up to her what he'd callously said about the children.

Of all the team members there, Ezekiel and Trap were the most dangerous. Malichai appeared easygoing and even charming, but he was a very close second to his brother. Neither brother would hesitate to kill even the civilians should they pose a threat to the mission. Wyatt wanted to make certain that didn't happen.

I'll tell them, Trap, she reassured.

Send Draden in, Malichai gave the go-ahead. *Our guard on the roof is totally immersed in his book. He has a beer bottle up there with him. Seriously, Wyatt, he's drinking beer on the job.*

Draden took off as if he'd been fired from a gun, streaking across the open ground to the fence.

Drop. Drop. The guard on the roof has company.

Draden dropped to the ground close to the fence in the short grass, right out in the open, and he simply disappeared.

What the hell, Malichai? Wyatt snapped. *How many guards are up there?*

I'm trying to see, Wyatt, but it's not like I have a good view of the entire roof. If they're on the other side, I have no way of knowing.

Pepper, how many damn guards do they have on the roof as a rule? Wyatt asked. *That would have been helpful information.*

I have no idea. I didn't think any. I've only seen the patrols around the building.

I'm moving into position, Ezekiel reported. *I can protect him from the roof as well as the guards patrolling the fence line.*

Don' fire unless someone has a gun on him, Wyatt cautioned. This was exactly what he'd wanted to avoid. They'd reconned multiple times and there had never been more than one guard on the roof. Most of the time, as Pepper had said, there was no guard up there at all.

Stay still, Draden, Malichai advised. *Larry and the dog are coming around again, and Jim is not far behind.*

Wyatt sucked in his breath. Draden was very good at camouflaging himself. His skin, his body, everything became whatever he touched. Several GhostWalkers were able to change their skin color, but Draden was clearly an improvement on the older models. They often gave him a hard time about it. Still, there was the dog and two men who seemed to be nervous, unlike the guards on the roof.

The team members remained absolutely still as the dog pulled toward the fence line and Larry allowed him a little more room. Wyatt clamped down hard on the animal, taking control, not taking any chances. As a rule, when he connected with an animal, he was careful, but Draden's life was at risk as well as their entire mission. He forced the dog to keep moving and not to alert, although clearly the animal smelled Draden lying so close.

We've got a third guard on the roof. I think they're having a party. Seriously, Wyatt, they've got food up there now. Food and beer. Our man with the book has put it away and appears to be entertaining.

You have got to be kiddin', Wyatt said, exasperated.

Nope. They're all popping the tops off beer bottles. I just may go join them. They seem to be having a better time than we are.

Wyatt swore under his breath. They would choose the

night when the guards decided to have a party up on the roof no less. They must have chosen the location in order for whomever it was who had pulled guard duty that night to join them.

Keep your eye on Larry. We're still a go this evening. It complicates things, but at least we know where most of them are. And they aren't in the building.

These were all civilian guards, those responsible for the plastic side of the laboratory. No soldier would party when they were on alert, and there was no doubt in his mind that Braden had put the compound on alert. Larry was far too tense. He had to know about the party and that made him all the more worried. Wyatt was beginning to like Larry in spite of everything. The man took his job seriously and he'd tried to warn Wyatt there could be trouble, indicating the locals should stay away from the plant.

Wyatt willed Larry and his dog to keep moving. Jim seemed every bit as nervous as Larry, cradling his rifle as if it was a woman. He even stroked the barrel occasionally. An alligator bellowed and he nearly jumped out of his skin. Quickening his steps, Jim caught up with Larry.

Strange noises always accompanied nightfall in the swamp. Snakes could be heard plopping into the water from the tree branches overhead. Birds flitted from tree to tree in an effort to find safe harbor. Owls screeched their displeasure when they missed prey. All kinds of insects lent their song to the night. Lights flashed deep in the trees and in the dark waters, eyes shone as predators swam and looked for prey.

Clearly the guards didn't like the night's symphony. Wyatt had grown up there and to him it was a familiar lullaby, but clearly every new noise and howl only made the two guards more nervous. The dog caught both men's tension and began to resist Wyatt's firm hold on it. He couldn't afford to lose the dog and allow it to warn them of Draden's presence, but the harder his grip on the animal, the more he ran the risk of injuring it.

He kept his grip tight on the dog, trying to soothe it at the same time, forcing calm into his mind, in the hope the animal would stay relaxed. The men walked together, Larry eyeing the dog for any signs that something dangerous lurked on the other side of the fence. It took precious minutes for them to make it to the far side of the building and round the corner.

Now, Malichai said. *Go. Go.*

I've got eyes on them, Draden, Ezekiel assured.

Wyatt bit back the need to remind Ezekiel not to take a shot unless absolutely necessary. There was a zone for cats, he'd found, and sometimes they all had to fight to stay out of it, but once there, the need to hunt and kill was nearly overwhelming—a byproduct of their enhancements.

Draden didn't hesitate, taking both men at their word. He was up and over the fence as if the obstacle wasn't there. His job was to take out the patrolling guards so the rest of the team could enter without incident. The guard change didn't take place for another two hours. That, Wyatt was certain, would give them plenty of time to get in and out of the compound without incident.

Draden disappeared around the side of the building. Instantly, Wyatt felt the dog's resistance.

Both men are down. I darted them. They should sleep for a few hours.

Wyatt knew the moment Draden darted the dog. Like the two men, the dog went down quietly.

I'm getting the bodies out of sight. Give me another couple of minutes. Malichai, what's happening on the roof?

I've counted five guards up there. They're drinking beer and eating cake. I think it's someone's birthday.

We're goin' in, Wyatt said. *Trap and Pepper, you stay back until we've cleared the guards on the roof.*

The patrol is cleared, Draden reported. *I'm starting up the wall.*

You wait, Ezekiel demanded. *I've moved around, but need a couple of minutes to get into position to cover your ass. Stay put until I give the okay.*

And give me a minute to come up from the other side, Wyatt cautioned.

He sprinted across the open land, not slowing down when the fence loomed up in front of him. He leapt, using his enhancement to clear the high chain link and razor wire. He dropped to the other side and continued running to the side of the building.

It's a go, Ezekiel said. *I've got you covered.*

I'm in position, Wyatt said. *Let's do this.*

Three stories up was a climb, even for a cat, but he scaled the building, using finger- and toeholds when he could and sheer strength at other times. He went up fast, knowing if another guard happened to appear below him or on the other side, he or Draden would be spotted. Ezekiel had shifted position to cover Draden. Malichai was covering Wyatt.

I'm at the top, Draden. I count five guards. Their weapons are lyin' up against the wall on your side. I see three handguns, but they're probably all packin' more. Two of the three carryin' are close to you, the other is nearly on top of me. I'll dart them first because their hands are close to their guns.

I see them, Draden confirmed. *I'll take the other two. You ready?*

Wyatt took a breath and let it out. *Go.* He calmly darted each man, one right after the other and then switched back to the first one to ensure he'd gone down. The men toppled to the floor, one dropping his beer bottle from nerveless fingers. Wyatt caught the sound, muffling it, as it would have carried in the quiet of the night.

All five down, Wyatt said, pulling himself onto the roof with Draden.

Draden was already collecting weapons as quickly as possible while Wyatt checked the guards to make certain they were all the way out.

Trap, you're up. You go in first. Pepper, if he makes it, you're next.

Get into the lab, Wyatt, we need anything you can find on the antivenom, how far they've gotten in their research, Trap said. *Hell, just get everything they've got. We might find it useful.*

Why are you going into the labs? Pepper asked, suddenly anxious. *I thought this was just about the children. And maybe rescuing the woman they're holding prisoner. Why are you going inside? That floor is heavily guarded and you need palm scans on the third floor for everything. The guards there are different. You didn't say a word about going inside there. It's dangerous. Soundproof. We don't need anything from there.*

There was no mistaking the anxiety in her voice, or her worry for him and he couldn't help but feel a little satisfaction that she didn't want him in danger. He had known all along she wouldn't want them going anywhere near the lab. He'd not told her what he would be doing on purpose. She wouldn't understand their need to get the files on the girls.

We need to find out why they created the children, what they did and how we can counteract it, he admitted to her. *I'll be fine.*

Really, Wyatt, don't go in there. This is crazy. We don't need the information enough to risk your life. She was pleading with him, more afraid of the lab than the cells.

He tried to soothe her, pushing a confident calm into her mind, even as he used his tone of command. *You just get the kids and get out of there. Malichai and Ezekiel will cover us outside. I'll be inside with Draden. Trap will be on the lower floor watching your back and then he'll try to free the woman.*

I just don't see how it's possible for him to get inside, she reiterated.

We're GhostWalkers, ma'am, Ezekiel said, as if that explained everything, and to them it did. *Same as you. You got in and out your way. We'll do the same.*

As Whitney had refined his experiments and learned from his mistakes, he got better and better at enhancing his soldiers without too many repercussions. Trap's specialty was the most dangerous, as far as Wyatt was concerned. Trap had a good mind and was brilliant with numbers, but if his measurements weren't exact or they were off on their intel, he could be in trouble.

Wyatt took a deep breath and let it out, watching from the roof as Trap sprinted across the open space and easily cleared the fence in one jump. He landed softer than any big man had the right to do, making his way to the side of the building where the children were being held.

They know sign language, Trap, Wyatt reminded just in case Trap ended up in a cell with one of the babies. *They bite out of fear, just the way a snake might.*

Okay, mama, are you ever going to let me get to this, or are you going to yammer at me all night? I committed a few books on sign language to memory, and your woman promised to let those babies know I'm on their side.

Wyatt knew he had to allow Trap to do his work, but he couldn't help feeling reluctant. He never quite could shake the fear when Trap was about to pass through something solid. One missed calculation and he was toast.

Trap ran his hands over the concrete wall, ignoring the mold and green slime clinging to the surface. He closed his eyes, tuning himself to the materials used to create the wall. Limestone. Ash. Slag. Aggregate. He let himself find every component, blocking everything else out of his world. He could no longer hear the heartbeat of the swamp, only the faint energy hum coming from the concrete wall itself.

He was a scientist and he still had a difficult time understanding why his body seemed to absorb the past of whatever object he touched. He "saw" the building being made. Felt the thickness. The grade of concrete. He found every piece of reinforced rebar or steel running through the building, feeling as if the same steel ran through his own body.

Once he was tuned to the molecular structure of the wall, he felt his own body stretching toward it. The effect was wrenching and uncomfortable, almost as if he was being pulled apart. He still stood in the exact same spot, but his skin and insides felt as if they were being lifted from his own body and being dragged *inside* the cement.

He took a breath. There was always that moment where he wasn't certain he would actually go through with such an unnatural act. His bones ached. His head felt as if it might explode. He never brought weapons with him or he stashed them outside the wall of whatever building he was entering. They wouldn't go through with him.

Clothing had been a major problem at first, but he'd spent a great deal of time in his lab, coming up with a material that could cling to his skin and break apart in the same way as his body and then reassemble on the other side.

He stepped close and pressed into the green slime, embracing the rock and allowing it to consume him. That was exactly how it felt, as if a giant had wrenched him apart and taken him into its very mouth. There was no light, no sense of being for one terrible moment and he could hear the familiar screaming in his head. Even his intellect couldn't overcome that human response of being ripped apart and absorbed.

There was no way to breathe, to get air. He was never certain if he actually had lungs in that moment, or if they'd been ripped from his body. He counted in his head. He knew exactly how long each pass through various materials took, depending on the denseness of what he was going through, but he'd never attempted a wall so solid or so thick.

He found himself on the other side, shuddering, gasping for breath, his heart pounding, his skull too tight for his brain, and the metallic taste of blood in his mouth. At the same time, he was aware of the two soldiers, whose backs were to him. He was close enough to reach out and touch them. They both were absorbed with tormenting the babies, who were in separate cells.

Both girls, looking identical to Ginger, cringed in the back of their cells. Clearly the three girls were triplets, not from individual eggs but a single egg split. One had tears running down her face but there was no sound. The men had a long metal prod they were using to poke through the bars. On the end of one was a curved open hook they were using to try to snag the neck of the crying child, clearly to drag the baby in close to them. The other had a glass with a cloth stretched over it.

There was no doubt in Trap's mind they were attempting to "milk" the venom from the child. Trap wasn't like Wyatt. He didn't feel anger often. In fact, he rarely felt emotion, he was always far too occupied with finding answers to the problems running around in his head. Seeing two grown men, grinning like apes, poking at babies set his blood to a slow boil.

Both children saw him instantly, but neither indicated his presence to the soldiers. He reached out and caught the nearest man's head, snapping the neck forcibly, using both enhanced speed and enhanced strength. He was on the second man before the soldier could pick up his weapon, a semiautomatic he'd propped near the door. Instead, the soldier went for his knife.

Trap clamped his hand down hard around the soldier's,

trapping the man's fingers around the weapon. "Don't be scared," he said aloud to the babies. "Pepper's coming. Your mother's coming. She sent me to help you."

He didn't know how much they understood, but Ginger understood a lot. Clearly she was a brilliant child. Whitney had deliberately used the egg and sperm of two geniuses with the hope of producing intelligent children. If Ginger was any indication, the man had succeeded in that regard.

Trap drove the soldier back away from the children toward the opposite side of the enclosed space. There wasn't a lot of room. The man's back hit the elevator doors, the sound loud. Pepper had told him the prison was soundproof, and he hoped she was right. The soldier punched him with his free hand, three rapid shots to the face. Trap stepped close, crowding the man, slamming his head into the soldier's head and then bringing up his fist to punch through the Adam's apple.

He let the body drop to the floor. *I'm in. I'm armed. Both children are here in separate cells. If I can get them to trust me, I'll open the cells. Pepper, get moving. It's definitely a trap, Wyatt. They had two soldiers waiting. Soldiers, not civilian guards.*

You're on, Pepper, Wyatt said. *Trap, don' take any chances. Pepper will get there fast. She already knows the way. Wait for her.*

One is crying, Wyatt, and the other is about to.

Damn it, Trap, you follow orders. Don' you go near them until Pepper's there. Wyatt rarely displayed emotion during a mission, but his alarm definitely came through.

Trap turned his attention to the children, keeping a distance from the cell doors. He signed to them that Pepper had sent him and she was on her way. He wanted to open the cell doors but didn't want them to be afraid.

Neither moved for a moment, but he was certain they were communicating. One of them signed fast. He frowned, trying to read the tiny moving hands. He'd learned signing,

of course, from the books he'd read. It hadn't been that difficult, and his mind instantly remembered, but seeing the
movements made with such little fingers was an altogether
different thing.

"You'll have to slow down," he said aloud. "I'm not the
best at reading sign."

He added the words, using his sign language as well.
One of the girls came close to the bars of her cell and
raised her arms in the air, repeating the signs she'd made
before, this time much slower.

He nodded his head. "Ginger is fine. So is Pepper. We're
going to get you out of here. Do either of you know if the
other prisoner held on the other side is still alive?"

The two girls looked at one another. The one who had
signed to him turned back, her fingers moving again.

"My name is Trap. I'm a friend of your father's. We're
like you. Enhanced. I don't know if you know what that
means, but we've had experiments done on us." He bent to
examine the bodies of the two soldiers, looking for keys.
He could open the cells, but it would be easier with the
actual keys.

Adrenaline had kept him going, but now that the two
guards had been dispatched, he felt the effects of the
wrenching of his body through the cement. He felt sick and
dizzy. He couldn't think too much on it because he had to
get out of the cell and into the next one if he was going to
try to save that prisoner as well.

"Give me a minute," he said, and sank down to the floor
beside one of the fallen soldiers.

The children were a little unnerving with their wide,
unblinking eyes staring at him, trying to make up their
minds whether or not he was friend or foe. Still, they
looked just like Wyatt. Wyatt was one of the few people he
could call his friend and he was intensely loyal to his
friends. There was no doubt in his mind that these were
Wyatt's children.

The little girl signed again.

He smiled at her. "Yes, I'm all right. Going through that thick of a barrier, like the outside of your cell, is hard on my body."

She frowned, and he found himself smiling. She was so tiny, her hands and feet like a doll's, but her intellect showed in her facial expressions and she looked so much like Wyatt when she frowned that Trap wanted to laugh. Her little hands moved even faster.

"How did I go through the wall?" Trap asked the question aloud. He put his head down and drew several deep breaths, trying to recover. The idea of repeating the experience was becoming harder to think about. "It's complicated, and no, you can't do it. Your bodies won't allow you to do it."

For the first time, the other child signed.

Trap's heart jumped when he saw her question. "What's a father? That's a good question, baby. I didn't have much of one, but your father is the best. The absolute rock solid best. You know how Pepper takes care of you? Looks after you? That's a mother. A father is the male version of a mother."

He didn't know how better to explain it to them. He felt a little silly sitting on the floor of a prison beside two dead bodies attempting to explain parents to two seventeen-month-old babies. How could they possibly comprehend the things he was telling them?

He opened the jacket of the soldier closest to him, for the first time realizing how cold the cell was. "Do they always keep it cold down here?"

The two babies were both shivering. He had barely registered that fact; now he could see that they were very cold. The more adventurous one signed again.

"They keep it cold so you can't move around very fast, is that right? Is that what you're saying?" Trap asked, feeling a slow burn of anger all over again.

The little heads nodded, the dark caps of wavy hair bobbing around their faces. He felt his heart melting a little. He didn't even like kids. Well . . . that wasn't exactly the truth. He didn't know if he liked them or not. Most of the time they seemed annoying. He ignored their existence, but these children seemed bright. He connected with intelligence, no matter the age.

The idea that these children, who clearly had a difficult time functioning in the cold, were kept in such conditions kept his anger growing. *Pepper, it's freezing down here. Hurry up. I found the keys to their cells.*

I'm on my way, Pepper responded. *It's very narrow in here. I'll be there in a few minutes.*

Don' open the cells, Trap, Wyatt advised.

They're cold and afraid, Trap explained, feeling a little ridiculous. He wasn't the kind of man to even notice such things other than in a purely scientific way, but for some reason, he wanted to hold both little babies close to him and warm them up. He figured it had to be because of his relationship with Wyatt. *They deliberately keep these cells freezing.*

They have somethin' in them other than snake, possibly cheetah, Wyatt said. *So they're extremely fast. I saw Ginger runnin' in the swamp and I couldn' believe how fast she was. Faster than we are, Trap. They must keep it cold down there to keep them from movin' around too much.*

Trap held up the keys to the two children. "Your mom's on her way. She's coming in through the air vent, just like she did when she managed to get your sister out. I can open your cells if you'd like and you can snuggle up in the soldier's coat to stay warm while you wait for her. Once you're warm you'll be able to move faster. But I don't want you to be afraid of me. If you'd rather, you can stay where you are until she gets here. You make the choice."

He figured the children weren't given many choices. The two babies looked at one another again, clearly talking it out in some telepathic language only they spoke. Eventually the more outgoing one nodded her head.

"What's your name?" Trap asked.

"Cannelle." For the first time the child spoke aloud.

"Thym." The other one added.

Pepper, I'm opening the cells. I can't stand them being so cold. If they bite me, at least it saves me from having to go through the wall again to get to our other prisoner.

Trap. Stop. If they bite you . . . Wyatt broke off.

Sorry, man, they're just too little to leave all alone in the cold. I already feel like a monster for killing the soldiers in front of them.

CHAPTER 16

Wyatt rubbed his hands together, generating heat. His palms grew hot and began to glow. He knelt down, cocking his head to one side, listening to the sounds emitting below him, coming from the laboratory. In spite of the "sound-proofing," his acute hearing and cat sonar picked up more movement than there should have been. He knew the soldiers assigned to the lab had a recreation area right next to their workstation, but the rustles were in the lab below him, where the techs worked, not where they slept or relaxed.

He sighed. Nothing was ever easy and few missions ever came off without a hitch. For the sake of his family and his children, he needed to get into the laboratory, soldiers or no soldiers. He had known all along why Pepper and the children had been put in his path. He was too intelligent not to know, but that didn't mean he'd back down. He just had to be faster and outwit Whitney at his own game.

The soldiers in the third-story laboratory were lying in wait for anyone who would come to rescue the two children.

Trap had run into two soldiers in the holding cells. Without a doubt, Whitney had used the babies as bait for Wyatt.

Wyatt listened carefully, noting every position. The soldiers had grown restless, and who could blame them? It was difficult to stay on high alert for days. The civilian guards had dismissed the danger all too readily—other than Larry and Jim, who had maintained their job as best they could by themselves.

The men in the laboratory had to be trained soldiers from Whitney's personal army. He'd smuggled them inside and kept them on alert waiting for Wyatt to make his move. Whitney clearly had expected him to wait for reinforcements or to secure his grandmother's home before coming after the two children.

Wyatt was hot-tempered and sometimes impulsive—such as when he'd joined the GhostWalker program after losing Joy. Whitney underestimated him, plain and simple. And he'd underestimated the loyalty of his team members as well.

Wyatt chose a corner where there was no sound at all. There had to be storage closets, and according to the original blueprints, one was built into that corner. Whether or not it had been changed was anyone's guess, but it was his best bet for point of entry.

I'm goin' in first, Draden. Stay back until I call you in. We've got company.

He felt Pepper's gasp. *Soldiers? How many? You can't go in alone. Wyatt, please, no.*

She'd never said "please" to him. She'd never sounded so anxious over him.

This is what I do, babe. Get our girls out of there.

Wyatt laid his palms on the concrete, pressing hard. At the same time, he uttered a low hum, a sound that couldn't be heard by humans. He waited while the energy built around him. The pressure built until he wanted to scream. His head felt as if it might explode. He slammed his palms down again, pushing the pulse through the cement. As a large chunk disintegrated, he "felt" for the large chunks of debris and stilled them in midair, even as he muffled the sound.

It took a great deal of concentration to accomplish all three tasks nearly simultaneously and his brain actually hurt. He breathed away the pain and slowly floated the debris to the floor. He kept track of the movement of the soldiers in the laboratory. He'd counted five of them scattered around the room. Each moved differently, some more restless than others, but all of them shifted positions often.

No one came to investigate the hole in the roof. He peered down. Below him, he saw several brooms and a mop bucket on wheels. He'd caught a break—the original blueprints hadn't been altered there on the third floor. He dropped down fast, landing lightly on the balls of his feet, as silent as a stalking cat.

Light spilled under the crack of the door. The laboratory was lit up, but the windows had been blacked out so from the outside, the room appeared dark, as if no one was in it. Wyatt knew better. He stayed very still, his cat sonar stretching to find every source of light in the room and mark where the soldiers were waiting.

There were five of them, but they had no idea he was inside the building, or that his team was making their attempt to rescue the children. To the soldiers it was like every other day they'd stayed in the laboratory, under orders to wait for an attack, and that meant they were bored, tired and not paying much attention.

Even now he heard the constant rustling as they shifted position and occasionally whispered to one another. They had no idea the civilian guards had left their posts to attend a birthday party or that down below, in the cells, two of their small army were already dead.

He went over every detail in his mind, planning out every move until his body knew what it was supposed to do. Wyatt exploded out of the closet, moving with blurring speed, going for each of the overhead lights, running up the walls to smash the bulbs, landing on a table and springing to the next light.

He knew the precise location of each heat source and he went after each of the lights first until the room was plunged into darkness. With the windows blacked out, he could see clearly with his cat's vision, but the soldiers would have a much more difficult time, especially those first few seconds. He utilized those precious seconds while the bored and stiff soldiers were shocked and confused. He hit the first one directly in the face, coming off a table with both boots, smashing hard.

He heard the terrible crunch of bones breaking and the man went down. Wyatt kept moving, landing on the floor and springing toward the location of the next nearest soldier. He ran up the wall and launched himself, dropping behind the man who had crouched down and was coherent enough to bring up his rifle. He couldn't fire because he couldn't see, but he was ready.

Wyatt felt energy wash over him and knew immediately this soldier was enhanced. Just as he caught the soldier's head, the man jerked away from him, throwing himself forward and rolling, bringing up the gun. He let loose a short burst just as Wyatt sprang into the air above the man. The bullets streaked toward the wall where he'd been, leaving behind flashes from the muzzle.

Wyatt landed on the table above the soldier's head. He crouched low and waited while the man rolled to his left.

"Put on your gas masks. Put on your gas masks," someone shouted.

He heard the hiss of a gas canister. Immediately he attacked, dropping flat to slam his knife in the chest of the enhanced soldier. He rolled away off the table, landing lightly on the other side.

The other three soldiers were a distance away. The nearest one was in the very center of the room. He could see the man pulling on his mask. He moved with blurring speed, reaching the soldier even before he could fit the mask to his face. Catching the head in both hands, he whirled around, snapping the man's neck over his left shoulder and dropping the body all in one motion.

The fourth soldier, the one who had given the orders, was also enhanced. Wyatt felt the dark, dense energy pouring over him. He'd been lucky to discover one of the enhanced men immediately. This one was ready for him. It was even possible he could see as well in the dark as Wyatt could.

Wyatt used his speed to go up the walls and run along them back toward the last soldier guarding the other side of the room. His energy was every bit as potent as their leader's had been. Whitney had sent three enhanced soldiers along with two normal ones.

The soldier met him halfway, knife in hand, streaking every bit as fast as Wyatt across the room. Wyatt caught his wrist at the last moment, deflecting the blade away from his belly. He continued his forward momentum, holding on to the wrist as he did so, driving the man's arm back toward his own left shoulder. The soldier's feet went out from under him as his body flipped over backward.

He landed hard on his back, driving the air from his lungs, but as Wyatt slammed the wrist down to take the knife, the soldier rolled and took out Wyatt's leg, breaking his own wrist in the process. He didn't so much as grunt in pain. Rather he stood up and tore off his mask, his eyes blazing at Wyatt.

Wyatt shook his head. Clearly he'd picked the wrong soldier, thinking the other would be the most difficult. This soldier was more robot than human. The thought registered as his opponent turned his weapon on him. Wyatt dove forward, under the gun, coming up hard between the soldier's legs, hitting him in the crotch with his head so hard he actually launched the man into the air. This time the grunt was very satisfactory. There were some body parts that were still human for certain.

As the soldier came down hard onto one of the tables, splintering it, sending bottles and computers flying in all directions, the glass shattering as it hit the floor, Wyatt snagged the gas mask and put it on. Only seconds had gone by, but he could feel the first effects.

The soldier rolled, trying to orient himself, trying to get away from Wyatt as he did so. Wyatt shot him twice, a one-two tap to the head. The soldier grunted again.

"What the hell are you?" Wyatt asked aloud, projecting his voice away from his position.

The leader shot toward the sound of Wyatt's voice, firing rapidly in a long sweeping spray.

So much for a quiet entry and exit, bayou man, Draden said. *What happened to Zen and the knife?*

Wyatt returned fire, hitting the leader squarely between the eyes. *That should have been five down, but I've got one who seems to be the walkin' dead. I can' kill the son of a bitch. Bullets don' seem to faze him.*

We've got to get moving, Draden said. *Stop playing down there. With all the noise you're making, the neighbors will be showing up as well, although if we're lucky the soundproofing will hold. Need a hand?*

You'll need a gas mask. They dumped somethin' foul in here.

I'm coming in, don't shoot me. Take care of your little zombie pal while I search this place for the files we need.

I left you a nice big door, Wyatt said.

The soldier he'd tapped in the head suddenly exploded into action, coming off the floor like a jumping spider, arms and legs out as he hurled himself at Wyatt. Wyatt shot him twice more, this time in the chest, aiming for the heart. Wyatt rarely missed. All he heard was two more grunts, as if the soldier felt the bullets, but dismissed them.

The man landed on him, driving him to the floor, his

blade slipping into Wyatt's skin, pushing through tissue and muscle, so sharp at first, Wyatt didn't even know the knife was in him. The breath hissed out of him.

"I've had it with you," he snapped and rammed his thumbs into the man's eye sockets.

At once he felt the exoskeleton, a hard shell beneath the skin and eyes of the man's head. Surely Whitney wasn't producing cyborgs? That was far too science fiction for Wyatt. It was bad enough the mad doctor had turned three little babies into vipers, now he had to contend with a crazy, and very angry robot.

The soldier howled, and twisted the knife. Wyatt caught his wrist and plunged his own knife into the man's leg, cutting the artery. At least he was certain he'd done so. The head and at least part of the chest were covered with what appeared to be thickened bone, almost like armor, but the blade of his knife had gone into human flesh.

Wyatt kicked the man's gun away from him and dragged himself a relatively safe distance away. His hands shook as he tried to get to his field kit. It took a moment to calm his mind, to allow his healing energy to pour into his own body and cut off the steady flow of blood.

Wyatt! Mon Dieu, Wyatt! How bad are you hurt? Do you need help? I'm close to the children, but I can get to you in a few minutes if I have to.

The sheer fear and concern pouring into him lightened his mood considerably. The knife wound had gone from numb to blazingly painful fast. And the miserable refusing-to-die-no-matter-what cyborg-man was making hideous noises and thrashing around.

I swear I'm in the twilight zone, he said to his team.

Privately he responded to Pepper. *Honey, I'm just fine. Sittin' here on the floor makin' Draden do all the work for me.*

He included Trap in his next response. *Get to the chil-*

dren before Trap plays the hero and opens the cells. The babies will bite him just because he's so mean lookin'.

I can feel your pain, Pepper said. *You're really hurt and you're lying to me.*

He couldn't help grinning a little at the edge to her voice. He did love sassy women. *Now, babe, don' go gettin' all feminine on me. You're just worried about my good looks. I'm still as purdy as I ever was.*

How big is the hole in you? she demanded.

Pepper felt sick with his pain. She could taste blood in her mouth and her side throbbed and burned. If he didn't do something about the pain, she might not be able to make it through the vent to the children.

As it was, her body was squeezed so tight in the air duct that she literally was pushing with fingers and toes and wiggling her shoulders and hips to propel herself forward, just as a snake would have to do. Feeling sick to her stomach definitely wasn't helping. Wyatt getting stabbed made her feel not only sick physically, but every single cell in her body demanded she turn around and get to him.

The thought of Wyatt actually dying was more than she could bear. *Wyatt, you can't joke about this. I need to know exactly how bad it is.*

His touch inside her was warm and soothing, like the stroke of his fingertips down her skin. She shivered and pushed forward another few inches.

Don' worry, Pepper, I've survived a lot worse. It hurts like a son of a bitch, but the blade didn' hit anythin' I can' live without.

The burning is making me feel sick. Really sick.

She felt him take a breath. Felt knowledge pour into his mind, but before she could grasp what happened, he slipped away from her.

Wyatt. She waited. The silence was deafening. *Wyatt, answer me.*

She couldn't vomit there in the air duct. She just couldn't. She'd been very lucky that she wasn't claustrophobic or she never would have tried to get into the cells that way. Another fan was looming up in front of her, the blades spinning wildly. She was tired from pushing herself forward in such a cramped space. Every bone in her body ached and her skin felt as if it had been flayed right off in several areas, scraped from the tight fit.

Get to our children for me. Get them out of there. Make certain Trap is safe because he doesn' seem to have the fear gene and tha's necessary to keep him alive.

Everything in her stilled. Something was very wrong with Wyatt. She'd have to trust his team members. He was counting on her to get to the children and Trap.

I'll get them, Wyatt, but you be alive when I get out of here.

She took a breath and studied the blades of the fan as they spun around. It was a matter of speed and timing. Speed was extremely difficult when she was so cramped.

She hadn't explained what it was like to Wyatt or the others. She couldn't crawl like they all imagined she was able to do. She actually pictured herself in the belly of an anaconda, being squeezed from all sides as it tried to devour her as she moved through the narrow air duct.

She had to let go of Wyatt completely if she was going to get through the last fan to get to the children. She lay very still, gathering her strength, counting her own heartbeats and focusing on the spinning blades. She needed to know the exact revolutions per second in order to pause them just enough to get her through.

She wasn't as adept at using her mind to control inanimate objects. She could do it only for seconds and it always gave her a tremendous headache. Right now, after making her way through several of the fans, her head felt as if it might explode. It was no wonder Braden thought she was such a reject. Her mind and heart wouldn't allow her to seduce men and then assassinate them and she couldn't control objects without bringing on a migraine. Great soldier she turned out to be.

Within a few moments, her body was tuned to the rhythm of the blades. She gathered herself, pulling every muscle back, coiling like the snake she was supposed to be. Her mind reached out and took command of the cold steel. At once, she ruthlessly put the brakes on, even as she propelled herself forward, using the blurring speed of the cheetah and the slithering motion of the snake in combination.

She didn't hesitate or think about the possibility of being slashed to pieces by the sharp blades. That way was disaster. She shot forward, zipping between the blades, dragging her legs out of the way just as her mind refused to retain command of the fan. She lay still, her air coming in ragged gasps, like it did each time she stopped the fan. The way back with two babies was going to be even harder.

Wyatt had wanted to open the cells from the outside, using vibration, but it was too dangerous, the entire team had agreed on that. If he shook the building too hard, it could come down on them. And the concrete was so thick he would have had to use a fairly hard blast. Still . . . She closed her eyes for a moment, refusing to think about the journey back.

No one had really told her how Trap intended to get into the cells. Maybe she'd be lucky and they could go out the way he'd come in. Pepper wiggled close to the vent and peered down into the holding area. There were three cells and a small space for the guards to stand. The doors to two of the cells were open and a body lay in each of the cells. The babies lay curled up in Trap's arms where he sat with his back against the wall. It was the last thing she expected.

He smiled at her as she pushed open the small vent. "It's about time you got here. We were all just about to take a nap, weren't we?" He nuzzled the tops of the babies' heads. "Getting nice and warm so they could move faster when they go through the vent with you."

The two little girls both lifted their heads, eyes lighting up, huge smiles showing their tiny little teeth. She dropped into the room, somersaulting headfirst, to land on her feet just to one side of Trap. He seemed to be taking up most of the room, all sprawled out. She held out her arms and both babies leapt into them.

She kissed them both repeatedly and they kissed her back over and over. Little Thym blew bubbles against her neck and then laughed with delight. Cannelle attached herself like a clinging monkey, not wanting a separation again.

"Thanks, Trap. It was thoughtful of you to warm them up." She looked around her. "Did you come in through the elevator?"

He shook his head. "Most likely there are guards in place at the elevator doors. I'll go if I have to, but I'm hoping this woman can get through the vent like you did."

"You're really going to try to get her out?" Pepper frowned. "How are you going to get to her?"

"I'll make it. You just get these babies out of here." He stood up, taking up even more space. "You look pale."

"Stopping the fans is hard for me. I don't usually manipulate nonhuman objects." She glanced at the children and then up to his face. "Wyatt was stabbed. I don't know how bad, he won't say, but it felt bad."

"Draden's with him, right?" Trap asked calmly.

Pepper nodded. "Yes. At least I think so."

"Then he'll be fine. If Wyatt was really hurt, Draden would have raised the alarm and Malichai and Ezekiel would go running. Just stick to the plan, Pepper. Get the babies to safety."

He rubbed Thym's back. "Stay close to your mama and do whatever she tells you. That's important. Stay very quiet. You can do that to get out of here, right? There are men out there who might try to stop you if they hear you."

Thym signed with her hands to Pepper. Pepper nodded. "Yes, baby, I thought the same thing, but we were wrong.

There's several men who are good and want to help because . . ." She broke off, her gaze jumping to Trap's face again. She took a breath. "You have a father. Most babies have two parents, a mother and father. He didn't know where you were and as soon as he found out, he and his friends helped me to rescue you."

"Did she say she thought all men were bad?"

Pepper nodded. "The techs and guards are mostly men. We don't see many women. I did, of course, because I was a soldier going through school with some, but the babies have always been isolated from everyone." She was beginning to get her nerve back. She'd gotten through the vent with Ginger. She could do the same with the other two.

Cannelle signed. Pepper interpreted. "Where will we go? We're going to take you out of here to your new home."

Cannelle signed again, her hand gestures hesitant. Pepper frowned. The baby had asked what a home was. Pepper didn't know how to explain something she'd never experienced.

"We'll discuss that when we have you safe and away from this place," she said. "I have to go first. You follow me. I'll go through the fan, but you have to wait for me to call you through. Each of us has to go through by ourselves. You'll have to move very fast. I'll show you how. Elle, you bring up the rear. Thym, you stay right behind me. Just remember you can't go until the fan is stopped completely and then you have to be very fast." She planned on reminding them over and over so there were no mistakes.

Trap frowned. "Just how dangerous is this?"

"There are fans every twenty feet or so, large industrial ones. The vent itself is very small. I can barely fit in it." Pepper showed him her arms where the skin was shaved off in spots. The tight-fitting sleeves, although thin, had still been shredded in several places, leaving her skin exposed. "The babies will fit through, but each section is blocked by a fan. I have to stop the blades from rotating long enough to get through and I'm not the best at controlling them." She rubbed her temples. "I can do it, but it's not easy."

"And it comes with a price," Trap said. "If you think it's too dangerous, Pepper, we can get the others to take the second elevators. It won't be pretty, but it can be done."

"I got Ginger through. I'll get both of the babies through," Pepper said, infusing confidence into her voice. She jumped up and caught the edge of the vent, drawing herself up. "Put them in after me and good luck."

Trap picked up the two babies and held them close. They were still shivering. The cell was too cold for their systems. He tried to warm them as he waited for Pepper to slowly be swallowed up inside the duct. Cannelle put her arms around his neck and held on while he lifted Thym into the narrow opening. When she had crawled all the way inside, he put little Cannelle in after her.

"Stay close, but don't get near that fan until Pepper tells you," he cautioned.

Cannelle turned her head and looked back at him over her shoulder. He saw a mop of wavy dark hair and large expressive eyes and then she was gone, crawling after her sister and mother.

Trap took a deep breath and made his way to the wall in the center of the small room. This wall was the only wall shared by the cells on the other side of it. The only way to get into that side was through the second elevator. He hoped the cells on the other side were a mirror image of the one he was standing in. He didn't want to come out inside the cell with an unknown woman already condemned to death, especially one declared too dangerous to live.

He put his hands on the concrete and absorbed the feel and structure of it. This time it was a little easier, as he already was connected to the properties in the mixture. He waited, breathing deep, forcing his rebelling mind under control. No GhostWalker left another behind, and he wouldn't leave this woman, no matter what she was.

If she tried to kill him, well, that was another thing altogether, but he'd do his best to convince her he'd come to help her. He let the wrenching sick feeling overtake him as his body was torn apart, pulled in every direction. His skin felt as if it was removed, leaving his insides spilling out everywhere.

Cold set in. Darkness. He was utterly alone. There was no human sound, no human feeling, only the bitter cold and the endless darkness. He came out on the other side, staggering, going to his knees and then rolling onto his butt, his back against the wall, pressing both hands to his gut to keep his insides from spilling out.

For a moment he was so disoriented, he couldn't see his hand in front of his face. Had he arrived that way in the babies' cell, the soldiers would have easily killed him. He tried desperately to drag air into his lungs and calm his quivering gut. When he lifted his head, his neck felt as if it had been wrenched around two or three times.

"Êtes-vous tous droit? Se rapprocher un peu plus, je pourrais peut-être vous aider." The question was asked in a voice that was as sultry as any Louisiana night. Silk and satin. Candlelight.

He looked up, blinking to bring her into focus. His breath left his lungs all over again. She was small, the way Pepper was small. They easily could have been related. She had a cloud of dark hair, as black as a raven's wing, but for the brilliant red streak straight down the middle. On anyone else it might have looked terrible, but on her, it seemed as natural as her huge green eyes.

"Are you all right? Come a little closer, perhaps I can aid you," she repeated in English.

Said the spider to the fly, he reminded himself. How the hell could a woman look every bit the seductive temptress and as innocent as all get-out at the same time? Especially one so young.

He stayed where he was. "Pepper told us about you. She got the babies out and we've come to get you out as well."

Long dark lashes drifted down, veiling the expression in her eyes for a brief moment. "Why would you want to help me?"

"We're like you. Enhanced. We stick together," he added lamely. He couldn't think with his brain still rattling around in his skull, banging away at the sides until he was afraid his head would explode.

"How did you get in here?"

Her voice alone gave him the sensation of fingers trailing down his skin. "I told you, we're like you. We all have different skills. I can get through walls, although this concrete was thicker than I realized and I already went through a wall once. It's hard on the body." And clearly just as hard on his brain.

He couldn't stop staring at her. She was shapely, an hourglass figure, perfectly proportioned for one so petite. Her small fingers stroked the bars of the cell with a mesmerizing slide. There was a pull about her, a lure, and he was afraid most men would succumb. He was a little worried that he knew just what she was.

"I'm Trap Dawkins. I came here to help Wyatt, a friend of mine, get his kids out of this place. Pepper said there was another woman here, so we figured we might as well break you out as well while we were at it."

"I appreciate that. I'm Cayenne, and I don't have a last name. At least I was never called anything but Cayenne."

She had an accent—a French one, but he knew her training would have included proper accents for every language taught to her. She used her looks and her voice as a temptation. Still . . . There was more, something else. He just couldn't put his finger on what it was, but it was potent.

He didn't move, but continued to look at her. "I haven't

made up my mind yet whether or not I take the chance and get close enough to that cell to open the locks. You're a black widow, aren't you?"

She smiled at him. Her teeth were small and very white. Her smile was beautiful. Inviting. "Some call me that," she admitted, as if amused by the accusation.

The smile in her voice only added to the sensation of dainty fingers sliding over his body. Her lips parted in invitation. "Come here. A little closer." She beckoned to him with her finger, a seductive dare in her tone.

He stared her down while his brain tried to work out the puzzle of who and what she was. How she worked. What danger she represented. He was a soldier, but more, he was analytical. He didn't ever think with his emotions. Her voice, her enticement played to a man's instincts and emotions. He felt it, the dangerous, magnetic draw, but his brain shielded him from her temptation.

When he didn't respond, her lashes swept down and then up. Her full, curved lips pursed in an alluring pout. "Can you open the cell? Do you have keys?"

"I can't bring anything metal through the wall." He stuck as close to the truth as possible. He was getting his strength back, his insides settling slowly.

Trap couldn't blame her for using her wiles on him, she was probably terrified. She had to know those in charge were going to kill her, and then he came along and as far as she was concerned, he was probably another experiment she was being subjected to. She was fighting for her life, trying to figure him out the same way he was trying to figure her.

"How did Whitney find you?" he asked, needing a few more minutes to decide to chance opening her cell.

"So you do know Peter Whitney." She couldn't disguise the malevolence in her voice or the sudden flash of hatred and defiance in her eyes.

"Actually, I've never met Whitney while I was awake," Trap said. "I believe when I was put under on an operating table, he came in and did the surgery, a bit more than I ever expected. But I wouldn't know him if I met him on the street."

"I can hear your admiration for him in your voice." She gripped the bars on the cell so hard her knuckles turned white.

"If I have admiration for him, and I don't believe I do, it would be for a great mind," Trap explained, shrugging. "A mind that has clearly gone insane. No one is stopping him. No one is putting the brakes on him. He's got too many friends in high places and too much money. We've tried tracking him, but he moves all the time and there's no way to pinpoint a location where we can get there before him and then kill him." He said it matter-of-factly—the hope of all GhostWalkers. He hoped she could hear the sincerity in his voice.

Her green gaze moved over his face as if trying to see behind his skin to his bare bones. "I don't know whether or not to trust you."

Her eyes were blazing green. An astonishing green. Two glittering emeralds as cool as a forest and as bright as a sun. He wasn't going to allow those eyes or those long black lashes to influence him.

"We're both in the same boat," he admitted. "I'm wondering the same thing. I don't want to let a serial killer loose on the world. Are you like him? Like Whitney?"

Cayenne's breath hissed out in a long slow admission of anger. Her green eyes went vibrant and more beautiful than ever. "I can kill, yes, but so can you. I was made into what I am, but I never let that man program me to be his assassin. Why do you think I'm in this cell on death row? He's afraid of me. Why isn't he afraid of you?"

He found himself wanting to smile. He was in a rather desperate situation, trapped in a small holding area, with a woman condemned to death who easily could be a true serial killer, and he wasn't certain he could even get himself out of the cell, let alone her. He was too weak to fight more soldiers—especially ones enhanced—at least not without sustaining injuries. He calculated his odds and they weren't especially good.

"Well, woman, we have to make a decision here. I'm going to open that cell. Do you have any idea how you'll get out of this holding area once you're out of the cell? Because you're small enough to fit inside the air duct. That's how Pepper is getting the children out, but she said every so many feet there's a fan with spinning blades. She stops the blades just long enough to get through, using mind control. Are you able to do that? Can you control an object?"

She shrugged, her gaze never leaving his, and her shrug was no answer.

"You can't go through the wall. We might go in the elevator, but I can guarantee there are soldiers waiting there. Up on the third floor, where the laboratory is, shots were fired, so that may have alerted the soldiers there's trouble if those shots were heard. Even if they didn't hear them, there are soldiers stationed on every floor with orders not to abandon their posts under any circumstances and that means trouble. They'll be waiting for you, Pepper, the babies or one of us."

"Get me out of here. I can take care of my own escape."

He stepped close to the cell, to the very narrow bars, so narrow his own fingers wouldn't fit through them. She didn't step back and he could smell the fragrance of her, an alluring blend of night fantasies and silken sheets. The tip of her tongue touched her lower lip, moisturizing it further, so that the seductive curve drew the eye.

Trap bent his head to the lock. It was a triple lock. One that required a code and two that required sheer strength. The babies had been in a cell exactly the same, but the locks were different, only requiring two keys. That told him Cayenne was feared far more than Pepper or the little viper babies.

"Can you do it?" Anxiety tinged her voice.

"Yes." He still wasn't certain he wanted to open the locks. There was something about her still eluding him. How responsible was he, thinking of opening the cell when he didn't know the first thing about the woman behind the bars. Just because Whitney had discarded her didn't mean he should rescue her.

He was jaded and cynical. He knew that. He thought with his brain, analyzed everything, probably far too much, but still. The need to open the cell was strong. He feared it was that part of him that needed a challenge both physically and intellectually. He was as driven as Whitney in his own way. The need to know.

He placed his hand on the plate of numbers and let his body absorb them all. Numbers melted into his skin, entered his bloodstream and found their way into his bones. He felt them there, knew them intimately. Numbers made sense to him. They were logical. Always progressive. Infinite. On the plate, the keys moved, following the long sequence of numbers his body recognized. The first lock slid open.

Cayenne's eyes widened. Clearly she was shocked that he was actually going to free her. She watched intently as he wrapped his fingers around the second lock. It was a combination of numbers as well, but the slider was a double bolt and along with the code, one needed a key. That, he didn't have.

Trap moved closer to the cell bars, leaning against them, letting the numbers take him, so that his mind worked just like a processor, seeing the numbers tumble into place, one after another until the lock clicked and all they needed was the key. He used brute strength to rip the bolts back.

Cayenne gasped. Hope leapt into her eyes. "You weren't kidding. You really can get the cell unlocked."

Trap didn't bother to state the obvious. His hand closed over the third lock. It was more complicated in that along with the combination, one steel bolt slid right while two slid left. The key that unlocked the round, solid bolts would have made it much easier. He wasn't feeling his best and the way she smelled was just a little bit too heady. She was disturbing his senses and playing tricks with his mind.

Every breath she took was like a breath of air drawn into his own lungs. He didn't want this woman around anyone he knew. She was well aware she couldn't play him, and that left her frustrated. She didn't know that the closer he was to her, the harder it was to get her out of his mind.

He took refuge in the familiar logic of numbers, pushing her away, grateful he could. His world was one of reason and rationality. This woman was so far outside that realm, he didn't know exactly where to place her—and that disturbed him—but he knew she was dangerous. Lethal even.

A part of him wanted to stop before he could open the third lock, but there was the male in him, the alpha that drove him to accept challenges and not back away from a fight. There was the GhostWalker that didn't allow for one of their own to be left behind. This woman had been created, enhanced and then tossed aside. She'd had no life but that of a soldier. She knew little of the outside world, and he could tell she felt nothing but contempt for men. Who could blame her?

The worst of it was, he very well could have been like Whitney, pushing the envelope to see what he could do without asking whether or not he should, because some things were simply morally wrong. He always had to consciously remind himself of that. He kept emotion out of it, but still, he surrounded himself with others he admired, such as Wyatt, who knew right from wrong.

Wyatt, from the moment they met, had become somewhat of a moral compass for him. He'd cultivated the friendship deliberately, both because Wyatt had an amazing mind and a rivaling intelligence, but also because Trap knew he lacked the things Wyatt had. Trap was too controlled and needed to control everything and everyone around him. His world had to make sense. He didn't fear much and he could be extremely violent when a situation called for it. Wyatt had always provided a way to judge his own morality and he'd been wise enough to allow himself to let the man fully into his world.

He wasn't certain Cayenne knew the difference between right and wrong, but he wasn't going to leave her there. The lock clicked free and he wrenched, first left and then right, destroying the bolts. He stood there a moment and lifted his gaze to hers. Her eyes went wide.

CHAPTER 17

The door to the cell swung open and Cayenne simply stood there, staring at Trap with her amazing green eyes, almost as if she couldn't believe he had actually done what he said he would. He stepped back to give her room. She inhaled, drawing the first taste of freedom into her lungs. Still, she didn't step out of the cell.

They stared at one another. Trap realized she was waiting for something. Long lashes veiled the expression in her eyes, but she appeared wary. He took another step back. There wasn't a lot of room in the holding area, just enough for each of the three cell doors to swing open. He backed all the way against the elevator doors and held his hands away from his sides to show her he wasn't armed.

The moment he moved, she thrust her palms outward and rushed toward him. Long thin strings of spun silk rained down on him, nearly smothering him. Within seconds he was wrapped up like a mummy from head to toe. She jumped back, flattening herself against the wall.

"If you really are who you say you are, then I'm sorry,

but I can't take a chance. I've been experimented on enough for twenty lifetimes. I made certain the wrappings were loose enough that you should be able to get out of them."

Trap glared at her. Beneath the silken filaments, he splayed his fingers wide. He was a man who rarely felt strong emotion, but now, it ran through him like an erupting volcano. Hot blood surged through his veins. His gut churned with absolute fury. He'd risked his life to help this woman and she was leaving him tied up like a chicken for the soldiers to find?

She gasped, and he knew she saw the killer in him for the first time. His cat sprang forward, all roped muscle and sinew, sharp claws, ripping through the silken cords as if they weren't even there. In a fury the beast in him shredded the strings into tiny pieces. She turned and sprang for the wall. He sprang after her.

Trap was on her before she could get up to the ceiling, not that it would have done her any good. He was cat, and he could jump and leap long distances. He dragged her to him and she turned her head, her small white teeth heading straight for his arm.

"Don't." A single word. A command. He bit it out between his own teeth, his fingers tightening around her throat. She stilled, her incredible green eyes moving over his face. "I'll fucking kill you if you bite me. It will take me one second to snap your neck and whatever venom you have in you won't be that fast acting. Don't think for a minute I won't."

They stared at each other, both in a fury. "Do it then," she challenged him. "They're going to kill me anyway."

"I'm trying to help you, but you're not quite bright, are you?" Trap didn't like the fact that her body registered with his. He was suddenly too aware of her shape. Of her soft skin. Of the fact that she was every bit as lethal as he was.

"Insult me all you want, cat man. You don't scare me."

He leaned in close to her. "I terrify you," he clarified. "You can't manipulate me. You can't do a damn thing but wait to see if I'm telling you the truth or not."

She didn't flinch or back down. "I still have choices."

"And what would they be?"

"I could kill us both, you ass. Right now. Sink my teeth into you, inject you with a lethal dose of venom and let you break my neck."

As a rule, he knew black widows rarely caused fatalities with their bites, although they were reputed to have fifteen times the venom strength of a rattlesnake, but without a doubt, Whitney had seen to it that she could kill. Trap believed her. He just didn't care.

He dragged her closer to him, his mouth inches from hers. "Then do it. Fucking kill us both. Die without ever walking free. Be that stupid."

Cayenne's resistance only added to his awareness of her. Her breath. The rise and fall of her breasts as she inhaled and exhaled. The length of her lashes and the way her skin was so soft it seemed to melt into his. He refused to acknowledge his awareness of her. He glared down at her, waiting for her to submit.

"Now who's being stupid?" she asked, and relaxed into him. "You would have died just to prove you're all manly."

"I'm going to let you go, but you hear what I'm saying to you. If I find out that you're hurting innocents for any reason, I'll hunt you down and kill you without a qualm. Do you understand me?"

She didn't look away. She didn't flinch. She stared him straight in the eye, her small white teeth inches from his face. All the while she smiled at him as she nodded her head slowly. He wanted to slap her. Or kiss her. He wasn't certain which.

He flung her away from him, using a little more force than he meant to. "Get out of here, then."

She turned at the last moment in midair. Her hands and feet met the wall and she clung there for a moment before racing up toward the vent. Her small fingers slid into the screen and she wrenched it loose, screws and all. Clearly she had a spider's strength. Her hair fell in clouds of black silk down her back, the streak of red very prominent, reminding him of the hourglass on a spider's belly. Cayenne disappeared into the duct.

Trap swore under his breath and dusted off the last bits of silk. She was ridiculous. Seriously flawed. She had really considered killing them both. He'd seen it in her eyes. She hadn't wanted to submit, not for a moment, to his will. He couldn't imagine the havoc she would have created in Whitney's labs. He still wasn't certain whether or not he'd just let a serial killer loose on the world, but he meant what he said. If he learned she harmed an innocent, he would find her and kill her.

The woman is making her way out through the air ducts, Wyatt. I'm giving myself a couple of minutes and then I'll be out of here. Is Pepper out yet with the babies?

It's slow goin', Wyatt reported. *She's tryin'. We're pullin' everythin' off these computers as fast as we can.*

He sounded as weary as Trap felt. Trap slid down the wall to sit on the floor. He needed just a few minutes to collect himself before he went through the concrete again.

I'll need help once I'm out. He despised admitting it. *Despised* having to tell the others he would be too weak and sick to make it back to the airboat on his own.

I'll meet you outside the wall, Malichai said. *Ezekiel can cover the others as they retreat. Pepper and the children will be coming out on his side. Is the woman coming back with us? Where is she meeting us?*

Hell no. She's gone in the wind and good riddance, Trap said. *That one is more trouble than she's worth.*

Wyatt laughed softly. *You really liked her then?*

Trap swore at him. *No one could like that woman. Not even a saint.* He took another deep breath as he stared at the wall. He didn't like the wall any more than he liked the woman. He swore again just for the hell of it.

How much longer, Wyatt, Ezekiel asked. *Draden says you need medical attention immediately.*

I gave myself medical attention, Wyatt snapped back.

Wyatt, Trap cautioned. *It's not like we can do without you. Any of us.* It was an admission of his weakness. One he rarely admitted to.

I can do this, Wyatt said. *Just get out of there, Trap, and everyone stop worryin' about me.*

Oh, yeah, Malichai said. *He's hurt or he wouldn't be so grumpy. Bayou Bear has joined us and he's never any picnic.*

Shut the hell up.

Now Wyatt really sounded like Trap felt. Before Trap could think much more about it, he pressed both hands into the wall and gave himself up to the properties, the mixture of components that made up concrete. His entire body shuddered. He felt the terrible pull on his skin and his stomach lurched. He nearly pulled away, but knew if he did he wouldn't be able to force himself to face going through the wall again.

He cursed the woman all over again. She wasn't worth this torture. So much for being the white knight. Darkness descended. Bitter cold. He felt lost and alone, afraid he wouldn't make it through. He tried to project a forward motion, tried to stop the mind-numbing terror from taking him over completely, but there was no way out and no one to save him.

Something moved in his mind. Just for a moment. Something or someone. He felt the connection as if a hand reached for him, fingers brushing across his face, and then he was through the wall and out into the night. He collapsed onto the ground, going down hard, unable to catch himself. His hands dug into the soil for an anchor. Anything real. He needed to feel the heat of the night and the dirt and vegetation in his hands.

I'm here, Malichai said, and pressed his hand hard into Trap's shoulder as he crouched down beside him.

Trap nodded and managed to let loose of the soil with one hand in order to cover Malichai's with the other. Tremors wracked his body. It was impossible to move. He had no idea how he was going to make it back to the airboat.

I've got you, Malichai said as if reading Trap's mind. *I'm taking Trap back to the boat. Wyatt, tell Pepper to move it.*

Wyatt sighed. He knew what it cost Trap to go through a wall, and going through one that thick had been dangerous. There was no way he could have shaken a hole in the wall without bringing down the building, but he still felt guilty when he realized just how bad Trap's condition was. All of them felt it.

He touched the pressure bandage and his palm came away smeared with blood. *Pepper, we're all waitin' on you, now. How close?*

You can get out of there if you have everything you need. I'm pushing my way through to the outside right now.

Relief was tremendous. He had gotten as much information off the computers as he believed he was going to get.

Let's shut this thing down. They may have heard the shots fired on the floor below us. No one's come to investigate yet. Likely they were ordered to stand, but someone will come eventually.

Wyatt turned. The motion caused pain so severe he doubled over. The action saved his life. The blade of a knife missed his neck, swishing through empty air where his head had been. Wyatt dove forward instinctively, somersaulting and coming up to his feet. He groaned aloud when he saw his adversary.

"Not you. What the hell are you?"

One eye was gone and part of the skull, and he could see the abnormally thick skeletal structure beneath. Aside from the bony armor, the man still seemed human, so why hadn't he bled out?

His opponent didn't waste time answering. He rushed Wyatt, racing toward him, going up over one of the desks and leaping on a table, scattering bottles and glass in every direction with a kind of clumsy speed. He hit Wyatt with a solid left to the chest, right over the stab wound, even as the two bodies crashed to the floor. Wyatt's chest seemed to disintegrate under that blow.

The only answer was, like Wyatt, he could somehow repair himself. Or . . . Whitney had found a way for the body to repair itself. He knew that some of the soldiers, before going out on a mission, were given a drug to speed up the healing process. The drug also could kill them. That was the more likely explanation.

Even with the super soldier raining blows on him, Wyatt's brain refused to shut off. He was in survival mode, knowing this soldier could easily kill him. Each punch felt like a crushing blow. The man's fists were battering rams, slamming into his ribs and the wound on his chest. Wyatt blocked as best he could, with pain ripping through his chest.

Fire burst through him, a dark, ugly place Wyatt rarely allowed himself to go. The surge of adrenaline through pure rage allowed him to heave the soldier off of him with enough strength to send him flying. Wyatt leapt to his feet and raced up the wall, launching himself at the soldier. He caught him in a flying scissors hold around the neck, taking him down hard, punching low, trying to find a way to disable him.

He hit the soldier twice, two hard punches to the groin and then leapt away, using his speed to keep the man from getting his hands on him. He knew he had to end it fast. Once the rage-driven adrenaline drained from his system, he was going to be in bad shape. He had to find a way to end the maniac once and for all.

Supersoldier turned to face Wyatt, as Wyatt moved back,

his body coiled and ready for action. The soldier spit blood and grinned at Wyatt as he drew another knife from his belt. He ran straight at the Cajun, the knife low, going for the soft parts of the body.

Even injured, Wyatt was faster, his body a powerful machine, with the roped muscles and speed of a cat. He eluded the attack by side-stepping, spinning out of the soldier's path to come in behind him and grip his neck. He wrenched hard, using his enhanced strength. The thick bone protecting flesh and muscle held.

The soldier stabbed down at Wyatt's leg. The blade sank into his thigh as he wrenched at the soldier's neck a second time, this time putting every bit of strength he had into the motion. The crack was loud in the room as the thick plate broke along with the neck. The man slumped in his arms, the dead weight nearly carrying him to the floor.

Pain washed over and through him. He swore softly and sank down to the floor beside the dead soldier. Whitney's experiments were getting out of hand. Or perhaps this was one of his earlier projects he had nearly rejected and then kept for himself. Clearly the doctor wasn't acting alone. He had set up several laboratories in various parts of the world, not just the United States, and he had others running them—others like him.

Draden's hand pressed into his shoulder, holding him down. "Is it safe to pull out the knife? Did it hit anything vital?"

Wyatt felt a little light-headed. He was already leaking blood from the first wound. He forced the fuzziness out of his head and placed his hands around the blade, feeling for the wound. He shook his head. "He missed. Too busy worryin' about me breakin' his neck to see where he was stabbin'."

"Malichai is packing Trap out, I guess I'll do the same with you. Get out a pressure bandage. I'm pulling that knife out of you."

Wyatt drew another pressure bandage from his field kit and took a deep breath before nodding. He let it out as Draden pulled the blade from his thigh. The air rushed from his lungs. His stomach lurched. His breath exploded out of his lungs and he gasped, trying to find more air.

He forced a grin. "Guess I'm not one of those tough guys that can pound on my wounds and say I haven't been shot or stabbed. I'm feelin' it, Draden. Really feelin' it this time."

"Must be getting old," Draden observed. "Either that or now that you've got a woman, you just plain want sympathy."

"I wish I knew I had that woman all sewed up for certain," Wyatt said, "but she's like tryin' to figure out the wind. It just blows any old way it wants to."

Draden raised his eyebrow, watching as Wyatt applied the bandage over the wound. "I thought all women were like that. I duck and run for cover when women like Pepper are around. They're the kind that get you in trouble every time."

"You got that right. I don' know whether I'm comin' or goin'. And hell, Draden, look at me. I've got three daughters and never did get the night of fun. That woman owes me a mighty good time for the rest of her life. Seems like a lifetime might work that debt off." He had to keep talking, it was that or fall on his face.

"You're slurring your words a little, Wyatt," Draden observed. "Let's get you up before someone comes up the stairs and we have to fight our way out of here."

Pepper, are you out? Do you have our children?

Wyatt forced himself onto his feet. The room shifted out from under him and spun in crazy circles. More than anything he needed the sound of her voice. He needed to know that his children were free of a cold, dank cell.

Draden slipped his arm around him. "Lean on me and let's get the hell out of here, Wyatt."

I'm out. Both babies are with me and fine. We're making

our way to the airboat. Ezekiel is dropping back to cover you and Draden.

I want him to go with you. Zeke, stick with Pepper and the kids. He tried to project a tone of command into his voice, but even this telepathic communication bordered on weak and slurring.

Ezekiel didn't bother to answer him, which meant the man was going to do whatever the hell he wanted to do.

Exasperated, Wyatt scowled as he limped his way to the storage closet, Draden taking a good deal of his weight. *That's always been your trouble, Zeke. You're a wild card. Anarchy reigns when you're in the mix.*

I have trouble with authority figures. My profile says so. There was laughter rumbling in Ezekiel's comment. No remorse or guilt.

You had that in your profile? Trap chimed in. *So did I. You should see the things that psychiatrist said about me and authority.*

Mine says I am the authority, Wyatt reminded.

He stared up at the hole in the ceiling. It looked a million miles away. Pepper had to have felt his second stab wound. They were too connected for her not to have had a sudden burst of agonizing pain, yet she hadn't said anything at all.

"Women are a mystery, Draden," he said. "Fickle as hell and a total mystery."

"Tell me something I don't know, Wyatt," Draden said, and stepped back to give him room.

Wyatt crouched low and sprang, using enhanced muscles as springs to propel him up onto the roof. He landed soft but it didn't matter. The air was driven from his lungs in a violent rush and pain engulfed him completely. His body rebelled, and blood soaked both bandages.

Draden leapt through the hole to land beside him. "You've gone gray, Wyatt. Can you make it down to the ground without falling?"

Wyatt didn't want to think about the climb. He might

try jumping halfway, but just the landing on the roof had nearly made him pass out. He'd lost more blood than he thought, which meant his internal repairs weren't holding up as well as they should have.

"Let's just get out of here." Fast. They needed to get home where Trap could take a look at him. *What kind of shape are you in, Trap?*

He dragged himself, with Draden's help, to the edge of the roof. The distance stretched on endlessly.

I'm recovering, Trap answered. *Shaken up. Cold. But my hands are steady and my brain is working.*

Trap was quick. No one ever had to figure it out for him.

I've got two wounds. One in the thigh, and I took one in the chest. As soon as we're clear, you'll have to do some repairs. I thought I had things shored up but I'm losin' too much blood. Might have a broken rib or two.

How much blood do you have on hand?

You'll have to do a transfusion usin' . . . Wyatt trailed off. He couldn't remember who was his blood type. That shook him. He never forgot details, especially details that could save lives. He felt cold all over and that was bad too. He was in the swamp, and even late at night, the swamp could be warm, even hot.

Wyatt, get off that roof right now. That was Ezekiel. *Climb down. If you can't climb, Draden will haul you out on his back, but get moving now.*

The command in Ezekiel's voice spurred him to action. Something wasn't right, and his team needed him *now*. Wyatt forced pain out of his mind and swung over the side, the action jarring him far more than he was prepared for. Even his laser focus couldn't stop the agony rushing through him. His stomach lurched. Hell of a good soldier he was going to be for his men in his condition.

But he climbed down. Sweat beaded on his body and he shivered and trembled with every movement, but he kept going. He wasn't about to let the others down. Somewhere, far off, he heard Ezekiel talking to him, encouraging him, giving him the distance in small increments. He didn't know if he could have made it without that. He just concentrated on Zeke's numbers and went from one point to the next until his feet touched down.

Ezekiel was there. Solid. A rock. His face grimmer than Wyatt had ever seen it. He slipped his arm around Wyatt on one side. Draden took the other and they ran for the fence. Wyatt's movements were mechanical and automatic rather than deliberate. He barely registered his surroundings. Only Ezekiel's voice giving him commands.

"You can do this, Wyatt. You have to jump that fence. We're going to be trapped here, all three of us, if you don't make it over that fence."

The fence looked insurmountable, but Wyatt crouched low, took a breath and sprang. He cleared the roll of razor wire and came down on the other side, landing on the balls of his feet. The landing jarred him, wrenching every bone in his body. The ground shifted and then rose up to meet his face. He felt helpless, unable to do anything to break his fall. He just watched as the thick vegetation came at him in slow motion.

Ezekiel came up in front of him, blocking his fall. Wyatt grinned at him as he hit Ezekiel squarely in the chest with his solid weight. Ezekiel didn't so much as rock backward. He dipped his shoulder and caught Wyatt up, and then turned and sprinted through the swamp, back toward the airboat. Behind him, Draden brought up the rear, his weapon out and ready.

We'll need to stop the blood and get a vein fast, Malichai, Ezekiel said. *Be ready with the equipment. Trap, whatever you have to do to get in shape, do it fast. We need blood. Probably lots of it. I'm his type, so is Malichai.*

What is it? I'll give him blood.

That was Pepper, Wyatt recognized through a fog. It would be interesting to get her blood. Would her immunity to snakebites be passed on to him? He tried to rouse himself enough to ask Trap to let her donate if possible, but then his mind was too fuzzy and garbled to get through to his team.

He wants my blood if possible, Trap, Pepper interpreted. *He thinks it would be an interesting experiment.*

He could feel her, all feminine, pouring into the lonely places, the parts of him always held away from the rest of the world. Those places of doubt and fear he never showed to others.

He reached out to her. She wasn't as far as the others. She was in him. Feeling what he was feeling. He felt her fingers run down his arm to thread to his.

"He's very cold. He's never cold like this."

There was fear in her voice. In her. He didn't want her to ever be afraid again. She'd had enough of that in Whitney's laboratories.

"Open your eyes, Wyatt." That was Trap. He sounded tough and mean, just like Trap usually sounded.

"Damn it, Wyatt, open your eyes." That was Ezekiel. You didn't ignore Ezekiel. Wyatt made the effort. He was a little shocked to be lying flat on his back on the airboat. Draden and Malichai were crouched low and armed with semiautomatics, facing out toward the swamp. That confused him more than ever. He clearly was in a combat situation, but he couldn't remember.

"Am I hit, Trap?" he asked.

Trap was working on him, his face grim, his movements steady, but very fast. "I'm putting a line in your arm, Wyatt. We need to give you blood and we don't want your veins collapsing on us before I get this line in. As soon as we're home I'll do the repairs, but you don't pass out on me, you hear? We need you alert."

Wyatt tried to keep his eyes open. He drifted in a sea of pain and guilt. The last thing he wanted to do was be a burden to his team. He was aware of them all around him, kneeling beside him, their faces grim, their voices low as they worked on him. Ezekiel was on one side of him while they tried to push blood into him.

"We've got to go now," Trap determined. "Get us back home fast, Malichai."

Wyatt watched the night spinning fast above his head. Every bumping jar of the boat on the water sent a ripple of agony shredding through his muscles and bones. The strange spinning made him sick and he closed his eyes.

Wyatt. Pepper's voice was demanding. *Don't you dare die on us. We've got three children who need you desperately.*

I don' plan on dyin', honey. Just goin' to sleep for a little while. I'm tired out.

Well, you can't. We're all tired out. All of us. You're still needed.

He didn't like letting her down, but truthfully, he wasn't certain he could stay awake. He'd never been so tired in his life. And cold. *Is there a blanket around, I'm freezin'.*

"He needs a blanket. Didn't we bring one?" Pepper asked, anxiety turning her voice soft and teary.

Wyatt hated that. He tried to rouse himself but he couldn't move. He turned his head toward her, prying open his eyes just enough to make her out. She knelt beside him, the two babies cuddled on either side. She looked as if she was crying. Worse, the two babies, looking exactly like Ginger, looked as if they were crying as well. All three stared at him with big eyes.

Don' cry, Pepper. You're upsettin' the children. I'm goin' to be fine. Trap's a good doctor. He'll fix me up.

"This damn swamp is a maze," Malichai shouted. "How the hell does he know which way to go?"

"Turn into that canal just ahead," Trap said.

Malichai scowled at him. "Trap, you've never been through the swamp except when we were heading to the plant. How could you possibly know?"

Trap knows, Wyatt told Pepper. *He never forgets anything.*

"He's right," Pepper called, trying to be heard above the

sound of the airboat. "That's the way we came in, Wyatt confirmed it."

Malichai took the airboat into the canal, hoping for the best. All of them felt a sense of urgency. They'd have to prepare a makeshift operating room and Trap would have to do what he did. He wasn't a surgeon, not like Wyatt, but he was a good doctor and he read more books and attended more seminars and classes, watched more operations, than anyone else. He retained everything he read or saw. They'd have to trust that he could find out just where Wyatt was bleeding and repair the damage.

Are you hanging in there, Wyatt?

Trap's voice roused Wyatt out of his comfortable stupor. He didn't want to think, it was too difficult, but something in Trap's voice made him answer.

I'm here. Pepper's hangin' on to me. She won' stop givin' orders. Who could sleep with her bossy mouth? He loved her mouth. Her sweet, sweet instrument that made him feel so good. *I love her mouth. Even when she's bein' bossy.*

I'm not going to put you all the way under. I'll need your help.

Wyatt's heart jerked hard in his chest. Trap had to be worried to tell him that.

I'm tellin' you, Trap, it's just a little repair. The leg's good. It's just bleedin' a lot, but the one in my chest, I thought I'd taken care of it, but it didn' hold.

I can do it, Trap assured. *But diggin' inside you is not my favorite thing. Not under these conditions and in your grand-mere's house. If I make a mistake, that woman owns a shotgun and the one staring at you with moony eyes can bite with venom. Then there're the three little vipers . . .*

Wyatt laughed. Coughed. Hurt like hell. *Shut up before you kill me. Unless that's the plan, to do me in before we get to the house.*

It might be a better option. You've got Ezekiel's blood going into you.

If I need more, use Pepper. I want to see if her blood will give me any immunity against snakebites.

After I give you her blood, do you plan on letting one of the little ones bite you? Trap asked curiously.

Wyatt took a breath to steady himself. He needed to just drift away, go to sleep, but something just wouldn't let him do that. It took a few minutes for his brain to figure out Pepper was locked on to him like a missile. She was firmly in his mind, whispering silly nonsense to him. Talking about the children. Telling him the differences between their personalities, so he could identify them more easily.

Every time he started down the road to sleep, she would whisper again, so low he had to really listen to hear her voice. He loved the sound of her voice. He loved the way it filled his mind and made him feel as if he were a part of her. Sometimes she talked about her dreams. Things he knew she would never tell him if she wasn't so worried about him. Intimate, personal things she would be embarrassed if he remembered once Trap operated on him.

Keep talkin', Pepper, he encouraged when she choked back a sob. *I can feel the boat slowin'. We must be close to the house. Talk to me. I don' feel the pain when you're talkin'.* And he didn't so much that he'd just let go. He couldn't do that to her.

I've been afraid for so long, Wyatt, she confided. *Once I fell in love with the children, I didn't know how I was going to get them out of there or care for them. I'm still scared. How can I be a mother when I never had one? I'm trained to kill, not to nurture. You're so different. So is Nonny. You both know how to love. I didn't even know what a family was supposed to feel like until I met you. Don't leave me.*

Wyatt concentrated on the tremor in her voice. Her tone told him she really was terrified that she would make mistakes with their children.

I don't know how to be a girlfriend or a wife. I don't even like most men. The ones I met weren't very nice. How can I be someone special to you when I won't know how to treat you? What to do or say? I've honestly never been so terrified.

He wanted to reassure her that they would do just fine. They'd find a way to make it all work. That's what he was best at—making things work. He couldn't find the energy to talk anymore, not even when he knew she needed him to. It was all he could do to concentrate on the sound of her voice and keep himself awake.

I thought it would be so much better outside of the laboratories and schools I spent my life in, but at least there I knew what was expected of me. I knew what the rules were. I feel as if I've been thrown onto an alien planet and there's no guidebook to tell me what's venomous and what isn't.

He found that an interesting choice of words. Pepper dealt in venom. She'd been bitten several times and knew what it was like to suffer the effects. She had to be really afraid to compare freedom to a snakebite.

I love that you want me for myself. I never thought that could happen. I don't even know who I am on the outside, but I love that you do.

He made an attempt to squeeze her hand. He was very aware of her fingers in his, but he couldn't tell if he'd succeeded.

I didn't know I could feel such love for anyone. It happened so fast, before I had a chance to think or know what I was doing. I'm afraid, Wyatt, all the time, worried you'll discover I'm not nearly the person you think I am. That doesn't matter, because you have to stay with me. I need you. The children need you even more than they need me. Stay with me, Wyatt.

She needed reassurance. *Babe, I'm not goin' anywhere.* He forced his brain to work, to let her know she wouldn't be alone.

She went very still. In his mind. Her fingers moved ever

so gently in his. *I'm pouring my heart out to you, Wyatt, but I didn't think you could really hear me. I'm sorry. I wanted to keep talking to you. I thought if I did that I could hold you to me.*

You thought right. Keep talkin'. I'm strugglin' to stay conscious.

He didn't want them to bring him unconscious to his grandmother, or to Ginger. The child had become attached to all of them in a very short time. She would be overjoyed to see her sisters, but she was far too intelligent and she would comprehend that he'd been wounded rescuing them.

Wyatt forced his mind to accept the possibility of death. He reached for Ezekiel. *If somethin' happens to me, send for Gator and Flame. Nonny will need them and they can help Pepper with the girls. My girls. I have three daughters, Zeke. I'd like to see them grow up.*

Stop bein' a morbid son of a bitch, Wyatt. You can't die and you know it. You've got too many responsibilities. So just make up your mind to get through this and do it.

Yeah, that was Ezekiel. All soft edges and sympathy. Wyatt would have laughed but it hurt too damned bad.

CHAPTER 18

⟶

Wyatt stood leaning in the doorway, his entire body shimmering with rage. Pure, black rage. The red welled up to join the black and the cat DNA added to the already lethal mixture. He could taste the terrible mixture in his mouth, a terrible concoction of temper, jealousy, desire and possessiveness. The combination was ugly and it was dangerous.

Pepper's soft laughter ripped through his body. There was happiness there. Joy even. His three little girls danced in the parlor, turning in circles while Pepper danced too—with Ezekiel and Mordichai. *Mordichai.*

The man had joined them while Wyatt was unconscious, and he'd certainly wormed his way into the household. Right now, his gaze was on Pepper, drinking her in. Ezekiel at least had the decency to try to keep his eyes averted. With his enhanced senses, the elevation of male testosterone wasn't that difficult to smell. Or Pepper. The biochemical spilled out of her, leaving traces behind.

Mordichai reached a hand under Pepper's elbow when she nearly tripped. She was wearing the boots he bought her. *He* bought her. Wyatt. Not Mordichai. His gaze found Mordichai's hand wrapped around Pepper's bare skin. His stomach knotted and every muscle in his body tensed. He clenched his teeth, the ugly beast clawing at his gut, urging him to claim what was his and destroy his enemies.

The floor trembled. The walls breathed. In and out. Ezekiel stopped moving and spun to face him, his alert gaze noting the direct, focused stare. Very casually, he reached out to his brother and drew him away from Pepper and behind his own body. The smile faded from Pepper's eyes.

"Wyatt. You're up. Good to see you on your feet," Ezekiel greeted.

"Just in time to witness the cozy little domestic scene," Wyatt spat back, his fury rising in direct proportion to the tension in the room.

The three babies stopped twirling and looked at him, puzzled. There was no way they couldn't feel that mounting tension.

"Mordichai capped the babies' teeth earlier this morning," Ezekiel said. "We were entertaining them in the hopes that if it was too painful, we could distract them."

Wyatt's eyes dropped to his children. Every morning, for the last two weeks, they'd played on his bed, Pepper making certain they didn't get too lively and hurt him. He'd gotten up often, this certainly wasn't his first time, but this time he was much steadier and knew he was well on the way to mending.

He noted all three girls had wet circles around the clothing at their necks. A wide wet circle. On their pale skin was a growing rash, rings of red dots. Instantly he was frowning, his alarm kicking in. They were all still cutting teeth and they drooled, but not like that. Not so severely. There was a faint hint of color in the saliva.

He dropped down on one knee, wincing as his thigh pulled and throbbed. Instantly all three girls ran to him. It had taken a lot of work to get Thym to trust him, but she finally had capitulated, mostly, he figured, because he didn't push himself on her. She still kept aloof from most of the others. He was gratified when she wound her arm around his leg.

"Does your mouth hurt?" he asked, infusing gentleness in his tone, breathing away the dark, angry jealousy that was growing inside of him like a fierce beast.

The three little girls looked at one another. He felt the energy swirling around them as they communicated telepathically. He wanted to groan aloud and glanced up at Pepper to see if she understood what kind of trouble they were in with three girls who could talk silently to one another behind their parents' backs.

The moment his eyes met Pepper's he knew she was aware of the monster growing inside of him. He'd tried to warn her he wasn't the sweet guy she believed him to be. All along he'd told her, but she persisted in looking at him through rose-colored glasses. He had to live with her heat cycle and men throwing themselves at her, she could see what was inside of him, snarling and clawing to rip apart anyone who got near her. Then he took in her clothes.

"What the fuck are you wearin'?" he demanded, angry all over. Fury took over, absolute fury. His gaze dropped over her body, and need slammed low and wicked, a powerful punch to his groin. He nearly saw stars.

She looked like a million bucks, sexy as hell. Her skirt clung to her hips and flared out to swing around her calves and clung to her bottom lovingly. There was a slit up the side exposing far too much leg. And the camisole top was bordering on indecency. Worse, she was wearing the boots. The ones with the stiletto heels, the ones that clearly shouted "fuck me" to any male within a five-mile radius.

"Where in the sweet *hell* did you get that outfit?"

The tops of her breasts were barely there, but they were there, the swell creamy and pale and just asking for a man to touch. His breath left his lungs in a rush. He could only guess at how long Malichai and the others had been ogling her and what state their bodies were in.

"Go change. Right now. Get the hell into the bedroom and change your clothes." He bit out every word, enunciating each between his teeth.

She looked hurt. "Nonny went to town, Wyatt," she said, her voice barely above a whisper. "She picked up more clothing for us." Her hand smoothed down the skirt, color creeping up her neck and into her face. She looked uncertain, her gaze shifting toward Ezekiel and Mordichai. "I thought . . ." she trailed off.

His gaze dropped to the boots. "Why the hell would you even think to wear them?"

"You said the girls shouldn't go barefoot in the swamp and if I did, they would, so I'm trying to get used to something covering my feet."

"That's what you're doin', is it?" he sneered, wanting to slam his fist in Mordichai's face because the man wouldn't stop looking at her.

"There's nothing wrong with the way you look, Pepper," Ezekiel said. "Wyatt's just being a pinhead. What's wrong with the girls, Wyatt?"

The warning note in his voice triggered more aggression in Wyatt, but Thym's little hand brushed his arm, bringing his attention back to his daughter. She signed.

Pepper gasped. "She's says it stings and burns around her neck where it's wet. All of them say that. I didn't realize . . ."

"Because you were too busy havin' fun bein' the center of attention," Wyatt snapped. "Zeke, they need those caps off now. Right now. That venom is lyin' against their skin." He turned Thym toward him. "Damn it. She's gettin' a rash. They all are."

He raised his furious gaze to Pepper. She looked as if he'd slapped her.

"We'll take care of it right now," Ezekiel said. "Come on girls. Let's get those caps off your teeth."

"I'll bathe them as soon as you do," Pepper said.

"Nonny can help you," Wyatt snapped before either man could volunteer.

Wyatt, Ezekiel said, choosing to only include him in their private communication. *Just so you know, you're being a bastard.*

Ezekiel reached down and lifted Ginger and then Elle into his arms. "Pepper, you'll have to bring Thym. She only goes to you, Nonny, or Wyatt." He stalked out, followed by Mordichai.

Wyatt could hear the quiet censure in his friend's voice, but it didn't stop the monster in him. She was going with the two men. They were both affected by the biochemical spilling from her body, the enhancement that made a sensual, sexy woman all the more potent. Ezekiel tried hard to ignore it. He knew the cost on her, but Mordichai had only arrived the week before.

Swearing in his native language, Wyatt turned away from them, disgusted with himself and his lack of discipline, angry with Pepper because she couldn't avoid the men, frustrated that she'd been avoiding him, sleeping in the nursery with the babies because of his injuries. He wanted to put his fist through the wall.

Pepper waited, her eyes on him, not moving to take Thym from him. He stayed where he was, afraid if he moved, important parts of his anatomy might shatter. He was being a bastard. Ezekiel knew it. Mordichai knew it. Hell. Even he knew it. The only person in the room who didn't seem to know it was Pepper. She just stood there, entirely focused on him. Hurt and guilt in her eyes. She looked . . . shattered. More shattered than his damned cock would be if he moved. So he moved.

He stood up, the pain in his thigh helping to take some of the action out of his cock, and went straight to her. She didn't move, holding herself still, her gaze clinging to his. He could almost see the thoughts running through her head. She wanted to run. Get away from him. Not because he was a fucking bastard, but because she thought she was too flawed to be around his family and friends.

"You're not leavin' me, Pepper. This isn't about you. This is about me. There's nothin' wrong with the way you look. You're beautiful and sexy and I love that. Don' listen to me when I'm bein' a bastard. Kick my shins or somethin'. You do when I'm bossy. Kick 'em when I'm not nice."

She shook her head and looked down at her hands. "It's happening again, Wyatt, and I can't stop it," she whispered, her voice low. "I told you it would happen. It's always going to happen. It will never stop and eventually, you won't be able to control whatever's in you and you'll hurt or kill one of your friends. You'd never be able to live with that, and neither would I."

"I'll learn." He made it a promise. Not just to her. To himself.

She swallowed hard and reached down to pick up Thym. "You know you'd be better off with me gone. It's going to be hard enough to raise the girls without that kind of threat hanging over their heads. Their father in jail or dead because of their mother."

His heart seized and for a moment he couldn't breathe. The fact that she even indicated he could raise the girls alone meant she had been thinking of leaving for a few days, had actually made up her mind to try to separate herself from the children. He knew how much she loved them, so he knew how serious she was.

"If you dared to leave me, Pepper, I'd find you. There's no place on this earth that you could go that I wouldn't track you down. We'll work it out. That's what couples do. They work shit out."

She shook her head, her mouth curving into a humorless smile. "We aren't a normal couple and this isn't normal shit. This is dangerous and you know it. I can't stop what's happening to me and you . . ."

He stepped into her space, so close he breathed her into his lungs. So close the heat of his body radiated to her cooler one. He knew that was part of the reason the girls accepted him so readily. He was hot and they were always cold. Before his injuries, Pepper always burrowed close, now she wasn't coming near him.

"We would have taken care of this problem a long time ago if you'd stopped hidin' in the nursery," he pointed out.

That rocked her, another body blow. "You almost died. Right in front of me, you almost *died*. It was terrifying. I tried to be so careful and follow orders, when all I wanted to do was lie next to you and hold you."

"What the hell? Whose orders?" he demanded.

Nonny came in and took little Thym. She glared at Wyatt. "Not too old to wash out your mouth with soap, boy," she cautioned. "*Especially* when you talk like that in front of the young'uns."

"Sorry, Nonny," he muttered because it was automatic, but his mind and his gaze didn't leave Pepper. "Whose orders?" he repeated. His voice had dropped another octave. Low. Threatening.

She swallowed, frowning a little. He liked her frown. On her it was sexy. Especially the way she bit her lower lip. "Wyatt . . ."

"No one gives you orders but me. No one, Pepper. You're not a member of the team, and you're not Nonny's child. You belong to me. No one else has the right to give you orders. No one tells you what to do. You have free will, Pepper. Even to tell me to go to hell if that's what you want to do." He was furious all over again, but *for* her not *at* her. "Now tell me who gave you the order to steer clear of me."

A faint smile touched her mouth. "You just said no one can order me around, not even you, but you've got your bossy . . ."

"*Mon Dieu. Fils de putain!* Just fuckin' tell me." His head was going to explode.

"Trap. He did the surgery on you and he was worried about the wound in your chest. He said it was difficult and he didn't want the little ones jostling you. I figured if they couldn't, I couldn't."

She swept her hand through her hair, the action drawing his attention to her breasts. His cock jerked hard and her eyes dropped to the front of his jeans.

"You come to me when you're like this. Always. I don' give a damn what anyone else says. This is between us, no one else. They don' know what's right for us, what we both need." His gaze burned into hers. "Make no mistake, Pepper, both of us have needs, not just you."

"Because of *me*," she said, desperation in her voice.

She was making him crazy. Totally crazy. She still was thinking about running from him. Intellectually he understood. She blamed herself for his crass, idiotic behavior, that it had everything to do with her and not with him. Emotionally, he didn't understand at all. His cat DNA told him she belonged to him exclusively and she wasn't damn well going to leave him. The man, the hot-blooded Cajun, wasn't about to let the best thing he'd ever known walk out of his life.

He caught her wrist and turned, taking her with him down the hall. She tugged against his hold a couple of times, and he glared at her over his shoulder.

"Don'." It was all the warning he was going to give her. They'd had the conversation.

Once inside his room, he slammed the door shut and hit all three locks. Three, because the little ones seemed adept at getting through locks and he hadn't wanted any interruptions. He'd had Malichai install the locks the third day after he was knifed, expecting his woman to be sleeping in his bed.

He dropped her hand and leaned his back against the door. "You promised to talk to me. You gave me your word that we'd work things out. At the first sign of trouble—and we both know we'll clash at times—you're considerin' runnin' out on me." It was an accusation, plain and simple.

Her long lashes swept down. Yeah. She'd not only considered it, she'd planned it. He forced himself to take a breath. He shook his head. "You really are clueless, aren't you, Pepper? You have no idea of your own self-worth. You aren't a weapon to me. You're a woman. My woman. I'm going to act like a bastard sometimes. You need to learn how to defuse that shit."

She pressed her lips together. His heart reacted. Clenched hard.

"I can't make it stop. I tried everything. I tried staying as far away from the men as possible. I could see I was making them uncomfortable. They've all been good to me and they're your friends, but I couldn't make my body settle down. I noticed if I had physical contact of any kind, the most accidental, they winced and looked away from me. I can't make it go away, Wyatt. I'm not doing that to you."

"Damn it all, woman, *I* make it go away. That was the deal we had. You come to me when you even start to get uncomfortable and I handle it."

"You were incapacitated."

For the first time faint humor took hold. "Babe, I'm never gonna be that incapacitated. And if I am, I've still got a mouth and fingers and so do you. Don' listen to Trap, or anyone else when it comes to us. You share your concerns with me and no one else. And you don' run. You don' even think of runnin', not even when I'm bein' the biggest bastard in the world. You handle it."

"And when you're not here?"

"I told you, we'll find another way. But you stick with me. You stick with our girls. We're goin' to make a life for ourselves, and Braden and Whitney can go fuck themselves."

"Your mouth is terrible, Wyatt."

"And why do you think that is, Pepper?" he challenged, and folded his arms across his chest.

He didn't bother to hide his heavy erection from her. He was blatant about it. But even as he casually unzipped his fly and loosened his jeans to give his body a little relief, he knew she needed more. Something to hang on to when he was being a complete and utter bastard. Her eyes dropped to his groin as his cock sprang free. Her eyes shimmered with sadness when she looked up at him again.

"You don' know what you are to me, do you?" He dropped his voice even lower. Confessing should have been difficult. What man wanted a woman to know she held all the cards? It wasn't. He was asking a lot from her. He knew he was never going to be a picnic. Not ever. He'd try to tamp down his temper and learn not to let the monster loose. It was shameful and a little embarrassing to lose that kind of control. More, he didn't like hurting her.

"Here's the thing you should know and always hold in your head, especially when I'm being difficult," he said, his eyes on hers. "You're it for me, Pepper. You always will be. The air that goes in and out of my body, as necessary as that. My very breath. More even. You're my life. That's why I can't give you up or let you run away from this. I figure you're strong enough to live with me the way I am. I know I can live with you. I have to."

Her eyes went dark like the midnight sky. The look he loved, all soft and feminine. The starburst began to take form through all the dark purple.

"You're the reason I'm goin' to come home after I go out with my team into a hot zone. You're the one that's goin' to keep me safe, because I'll know you're here waitin' for me. I'll always know that when I'm not here to take care of you and the girls, you can kick serious ass if you need to. There are a thousand more reasons why you're necessary to me, and sex has nothin' to do with any of them." He flashed her a soft grin. "That's a bonus. A huge one, but still a bonus."

"I'm not running, Wyatt," she said quietly.

"Are you goin' to learn to handle the monster in me?" He slowly slid the buttons of his shirt open and pulled the

material from his body. The moment his shirt was gone, he
fisted his heavy, hungry cock.

She nodded slowly, her eyes on his chest, assessing. The
wound was far from healed, but it was healed enough.

"No matter what happens, it's you and me. Got that? No
matter how scared you get, or how worried about the things
you don' know, it's still you and me. When I say mean, hurt-
ful things, you're goin' to handle it. Hit me over the head,
yell at me, kick me or fuck my brains out, you handle it
because no matter what, it's you and me. You understand?"

She bit her lower lip, instantly centering his attention
there. He loved her mouth. He'd lain in bed—alone—
thinking about her mouth every minute of the day. Thinking about what her mouth did for him and how it led to
other tight, scorching hot places on her body that showed
him the way to paradise.

"I understand," she said, her gaze continually dropping
to his hand wrapped around his cock.

He let his fist glide over the shaft just to watch her eyes
change. Smolder. He loved that burn.

Her chin lifted and she gestured toward his groin with
it. "Do you think I want to have sex with you right now?
Especially after the way you acted? I've learned what
sugar and honey is, and Wyatt, I'm not feeling particularly
sweet right now."

He grinned at her. "I don' mind it when you're hot as
hell, baby, that's good too. And you want to have sex.
You're burnin up, I can feel that heat comin' from between
your legs from here."

"With you," she reiterated.

For one second he saw red. Actual red. His hormones
went crazy. He wanted to tackle her and take her right
there on the spot, show her she belonged with him, to him,
that the more she challenged him, the less she was going to
win. He breathed through the reaction, although the need
to dominate settled heavy on him.

"Who else, babe?"

"No one *else*, you idiot."

The crazy, insane monster striped in black and red settled back. "So this is your way of tamin' the beast, because, sugar, let me explain to you, it isn' workin'."

"This is my way of telling you that from the moment you walked into the room, the *moment*, I was wholly focused on you. It's always like that. I don't see other men. I don't want them. Only you. So, Wyatt, you tell me, why isn't it the same for you? Why don't you see *me* when you walk into a room? I don't want to be property that you possess and protect. I want you to see me, the person I am, the one who focuses on you and only you."

There was truth in what she said. He'd felt her there in his mind. She'd been spinning with the girls, helping to teach them to have fun, but he'd already been half out of his mind because the other men in the house were around her constantly, picking up and playing with his children. His woman. His.

"Pepper, just like you can't help bein' needy when that biochemical builds too high in your system, I need you when whatever monster is inside of me starts to break loose." He didn't have any explanation for her. She was right.

She stood there, across the room from him, looking so beautiful he ached inside. He'd hurt her. He didn't hurt women and he especially didn't hurt *his* woman.

"I don' think of you as a possession, honey, I think of you as my better half. My partner. And I need my lover before I go up in flames. So the biggest question I've got right now, sugar, is what are you wearin' under that skirt and camisole? You might want to show me."

Her eyebrow shot up. "After your mean comment on my clothes, do you think you deserve to know?"

Oh, yeah, she was his. Her eyes were soft and desire for him was there. She was wholly focused. On him. Wholly. That was another thing he loved about her.

"You're not a woman who holds a grudge, babe. And we both know you're wet for *me*, no other man, little darlin', just for me. And you're hot for me. I'm thinkin' right now you wouldn't mind my mouth between your legs. So show me the underwear." He crossed his arms over his chest, his eyes hooded, a little brooding, as he watched her. "And just so you know, that little attitude of yours only made me harder. You need to do somethin' about it, so show me the damn underwear."

Pepper tilted her head to one side, a small smile on her face. She unzipped the skirt and stepped out of it. The boots lovingly shaped her legs and did amazing things to her ass, just like he knew they would. She stayed across the room from him as she turned around and showed him the sexy French-cut red panties edged with white lace that framed her butt cheeks and showed a lot of magnificent bare skin. He'd picked those out himself and they were a particular favorite. All the time she'd been hiding them under her skirt.

He didn't bother to hide the desire flaring in his eyes. His hand dropped to his cock once again, because he needed something around all that heat. His fist was tight, but it wasn't hot, wet silk. "The top, baby, lose the top for me."

Both hands went up to the buttons on the front of the camisole. She took her time, slowly sliding them through the tiny enclosures. The sight of her, the time it took, mesmerized him. His mouth went dry and then just as suddenly he was flooded with the taste of her. Her scent permeated the room. Heady. Potent. Exotic. All his.

She kept her eyes on his face as she slowly unwrapped herself for him. A gift. A present. Her top slid away and there she was, her beautiful breasts, high and full, jutting out at him, nipples already taut with need. She wore only the red lace panties and those fuck-me high-heeled boots.

"I want your hair down." He loved her hair down. "I need your hair fallin' all around the pillow when I come inside you. I want to hear my name when you come hard. Every time you come hard."

She smiled at him and shook her head as her hands went to her hair and she unclipped the waterfall of black silk. He loved the little strange patterns in her hair. He always found himself intrigued by them when he sat beside her. Little rosettes, but so faint a man wasn't really certain they were there. Another thing he loved and found fascinating about her.

He crooked his finger at her. She came to him without hesitation. When she was close, she crouched down in front of him and unlaced his boots. He leaned against the wall, one hand on her bare shoulder and let her pull his boots off. The moment he touched her, heat flared between them. Electricity crackled.

Her hands slid up the columns of his thighs, sending streaks of fire straight to his groin. She hooked her fingers in his jeans and dragged them down, waiting until he stepped out of them before her hands got busy again, moving over his legs, up his calves and shins over his thighs. He felt the brush of her hair.

He slid his fist into all her glorious hair and tugged until her head came up. Her tongue had been sliding up his inner thigh and he nearly lost it. "On the bed, babe."

"Wyatt," she whispered, looking at his cock, disappointment in her eyes.

Who had a woman like her? How could he not want to keep her? To protect her? She *enjoyed* giving him pleasure. It was impossible not to love her just for that. She had a soft spot inside of her, the one he wanted to protect. She was the sexiest woman alive, but trained to be a deadly soldier. Major turn-on. And then she had that knife . . .

"You'll get your chance, woman. Right now, I'm so damned hungry I could eat you alive. Get on the bed. Take off the panties so I don' go crazy and rip them off of you. You can leave the boots on."

He reached down with one hand and helped her to her feet.

Graceful. Fluid. Her body moved like poetry. She walked across the room in front of him, her hips swaying, her long hair falling like a waterfall down her back to the curve of her very fine ass. She crawled onto the bed. Knees and hands, looking over her shoulder at him. Crawled. If it was possible, he got harder. He hadn't thought a woman could make him come just by crawling on a bed, but now he considered it.

She rolled over and lay down, the same graceful, fluid movement that robbed a man of both breath and sanity.

"Put your hands above your head and keep them there. Open your legs for me."

She did both without a word. No questions. Her face soft. Her eyes hot. Her breasts shifted and beckoned. He could see the moisture caught in the tight little curls at the junction of her legs. His mouth watered and he knelt at the end of the bed to move between her boots, and then her thighs.

She smelled like heaven. He licked up her thigh and plunged his tongue deep, hungry for her addicting taste. He'd been craving her honeyed spice for two weeks, going through withdrawals, and he devoured her like the starving man he was. She cried out, a mewling keen with his name on her breath. Her body thrashed, her head tossed and she came hard, spilling treasure in his mouth.

"More, damn it," he ordered. "Give me more." His tongue and fingers were ruthless, demanding, driving her up faster the second time, greedy for her orgasm, for the breathy sound of his name as she gave herself to him, trusted him with her body. With her mind. With her heart. *His.*

Pepper couldn't possibly stop herself, not when he was being so bossy and arrogant, not when his mouth was making her burn so hot she couldn't think of anything but him. She rarely thought of anything but him, unless it was the babies, but they were far from even the edges of her consciousness. Her body fragmented, came apart, and still he didn't stop, licking and sucking and using his teeth in a way that should have alarmed her but only made her want more.

She tried holding the sheet to anchor herself, bunching the material into her fists, but she flew apart and he didn't stop. Didn't slow down. Already, even as the aftershocks started, the next one was rolling up, harder and faster with far more power.

"Wyatt." She tried to call his name, but it came out a sob. A gasp. A plea. It came out a breathy moan and her body exploded a third time.

He was up and over her, slamming into her hard, his large cock driving through her hot folds like a jackhammer, an invasion that felt shocking. He was too big, her body too tight, but she unfolded for him, the friction making her sob and plead all over again. He lifted his head to watch her face as he pounded into her. She couldn't see that his injuries in any way had slowed him down.

God, he was beautiful. His face should have been carved in stone by a master, his body, hard and hot and purely masculine. His cock filled her. Completely. Beyond possible and still, she wanted more of him, all of him. She loved that he poured himself into her. That he was a little rough, and yet always caring of her.

She felt the pressure building and building, something powerful coiling tighter and tighter. The burn just got hotter and hotter. She closed her eyes, needing to let go.

"Don' you dare," he ordered, and leaned down to place a stinging bite on her left earlobe. "Open your eyes and look at me. I want you lookin' at me when you come. And you wait for me this time. Let it build, babe. Just look at me."

She loved that too. She shouldn't. He was too bossy in bed, but still, she reaped the benefits and his body never once stopped pounding into hers. She didn't see how she could stop the inevitable, but she tried, lifting her lashes, looking into his eyes. She loved his eyes, the way they began to glow like a great jungle cat's. She loved the way they focused on her, so predatory, so hungry and yet, she could see something else there. Something soft and exclusive, just for her.

"Wyatt." She whispered his name, brought her hand up to stroke her fingers down his face. "I can't . . ."

"You can. You will."

She was getting lost in him. Completely lost. In his face. In his eyes. In his relentless, almost brutal cock surging in and out of her. The flames were scorching hot and there was no way to breathe. To hang on. She clung to his shoulders, driving her fingernails into him. She clung to his eyes, drowning there, giving herself up to him. Waiting for him. Knowing it was worth the wait. Knowing he was worth whatever it would take to soothe the monster inside of him.

Satisfaction crossed his dark features. He leaned down and took her mouth. Hard. Savagely hard. *Now. Baby. Give me you.*

She did. The tsunami swept through her with hurricane force, her muscles clamped down like a vise and swept him up in the furious storm. A firestorm. A lightning storm. Flames licked over both of them. The hoarse sound of her name poured down her throat along with his breath as her sheath strangled him in silken fire. She could feel him so deep inside her she was afraid he would lodge in her stomach. It didn't matter. Just this. Wyatt in her arms, his body deep inside hers and the look on his face, in his eyes when he lifted his mouth from hers to stare down at her.

He didn't move. Didn't shift his weight from her. He covered her, his cock deep inside of her, still semihard as Wyatt seemed to always be. His hands framed her face.

"I love everythin' about you, Pepper. I love that you're the mother of my children. I'm sorry I'm an ass sometimes, and I wish I could promise you it won' happen again, but I think we have a better chance of it bein' the truth if I promised you it would happen again."

His confession made her toes want to curl. She loved that he was lying on top of her, pinning her beneath him, and when he looked at her, there was both a soft, special look in his eyes and a sheer male satisfaction. "I know that, Wyatt."

"You goin' to put up with me?"

"Yes. But I can't promise I won't kick you once in a while. Don't embarrass me in front of your friends. I don't know the rules of your world yet, Wyatt." She pushed at his hair, liking the way it fell around his face. "I don't always know what I'm supposed to wear or say or do. I'm just learning. Don't take my confidence away like that again."

"Pepper." He groaned her name and kissed her eyes. Her chin. Her throat. And then came to settle on her mouth. He knew how to kiss. How to pour fire down her throat. How to make her body go soft and melt, just like her heart. He knew how to give her the most delicious aftershocks possible. But still, "Pepper" was not an answer. Not even when he said it in that voice.

"If you feel the need to reprimand me, you can take me in another room, or talk to me telepathically. You don't have to be so . . . brutal about it."

She let him see the hurt. He'd struck deep. She didn't have a lot of confidence when it came to dealing with his friends and family. He'd stripped some of what had been hard won away from her. She let him see that as well.

"I'm sorry, baby. I'll do my best to see that when the monster comes, I hold on to some kind of control. You've been workin' hard to shield everybody, and I know that takes a toll on you. I can work just as hard to shield you when I get crazy mean."

She shifted, letting him know to roll them over. Wyatt took the hint immediately. "I'm not through with you yet, sugar," he whispered, and swept her hair out of the way so he could lick just behind her ear. It sent shivers up and down her body and quakes through it.

"I'm glad, but you got to have your fun, my love, let me have mine." She shifted, starting to go onto her knees to allow him to slide out of her. His arms snapped around her.

Hard. Tight. An unbreakable hold. Her gaze jumped to his. His eyes had gone liquid. Amazing. A dark chocolate that melted into an amazing pool she wanted to live in.

"You called me 'my love.' You never call me anything but Wyatt."

"You are my love. I'm learning about love. That's you. Only you."

His smile was slow. Lazy. Loving. "I like you callin' me that, honey. Whenever you want is good for me. Go ahead and get to doin' whatever it is you want and then I'll get to doin' what I want. Tonight, you're sleepin' in my bed and my cock is goin' to be buried deep inside your body. I want to sleep that close with you."

Something inside her, the last fear, broke away. She loved the gentleness in his voice, the way he looked at her so tenderly just after he'd been rough and crazy in her arms and body.

She moved back so she could take a look at him lying there naked and so alive. So hers. "I've got these boots, and I'm in the mood to ride you hard and long, Wyatt. But first . . ." She bent her head and took him deep into her mouth, watching his eyes. Watching his pleasure. She loved that.

CHAPTER 19

The night was warm. Rain fell softly and the scent of jasmine permeated the air. Wyatt could hear the snakes plopping into the water from the branches of the cypress trees. Alligators bellowed occasionally and insects droned. The music of the swamp. The moon was at half-mast, bathing the bayou in a soft bluish light—his favorite time of night.

A little hand brushed his jaw, tiny little fingers, softer than anything he'd ever felt in his life—other than Pepper's skin—walked their way to his lower lip. He smiled down into Thym's eyes. She snuggled closer to him. He loved rocking her, holding her close. His little shy Thym, already turning into a daddy's girl.

"Hey baby," he said softly, and kissed her little fingers.

I love when you do that. Pepper's voice filled his mind.

He felt her inside of him. He loved having her there, twisting him up into knots, soothing him, or just talking intimately, like now. She rocked Cannelle, a gentle rhythm of love, the small bundle curled up in her arms. Elle was a funny little girl, with the best sense of humor, always laughing and playing peek-a-boo or even trying to play a joke. She was good with the members of his team, but at night, she wanted Pepper. She cuddled with Wyatt and Nonny, but Pepper had to put her to bed.

Wyatt was still a little worried about her. She clung to Pepper, always wanted her in her sight. Sometimes she had nightmares. Wyatt wanted Braden to pay for those nightmares.

On his left side, Nonny rocked Ginger. Ginger was in her element now, comfortable in the house and with all members of their team. She chattered the most, learning English at a rapid rate. Ginger was definitely the leader of his little viper gang.

Pepper's soft little hiss had him turning his head to meet her eyes. His grin widened.

I'm in your head. Do not refer to our daughters as the viper gang.

He'd known she'd have that reaction. *Seriously? Who would pass up a chance at such a cool name? They'll kick ass in school. Trust me, sugar, they're goin' to love it. After all, their mama is the head viper . . .*

I have no viper in me whatsoever, Pepper denied. The rhythm of her rocking chair picked up, moving a little faster.

You're a snake snob. I had no idea.

He found he liked poking the tiger. The woman could get some serious attitude over the funniest things. He loved the flash of purple in her dark eyes when she glared at him. Especially now, when she held a baby in her arms and looked soft and beautiful. Even vulnerable and fragile. And then she had the attitude that always, *always*, turned him on.

Sprawled out on the porch was Ezekiel, lifting a bottle of beer to his mouth. Malichai lazily swung on the porch swing. Across from him, seated on the railing was Draden. Mordichai was up on the roof out of sight, and Trap was where Trap always was. In the laboratory, trying to solve the puzzle of why the caps weren't working on the girls' teeth and how to make the antivenom universal and less dangerous. Life was good.

"Trap really thinks we can set up shop here, Wyatt," Ezekiel said. "He's got his man looking for real estate, trying to buy up everything around this place and even right up to the plastics building."

"I can see him livin' in that monstrosity," Wyatt said. "He'd turn the entire second floor into a shooting range."

"He's a good boy," Nonny put in her two cents.

The men chuckled politely. Ezekiel raised his beer toward Nonny. "Grand-mere, you think we're all good boys."

"'Cept Wyatt," Nonny proclaimed.

Wyatt, busy playing with Thym's hand, swung his head around to look at his grandmother. He knew he should never have taken the rocker in between the two women. It was a dangerous spot.

"I don' think I want to know why even Trap is considered a good boy and I'm not. I'm not curious and I'm not askin'," he declared.

"You're goin' to find out. You got you a good woman, boy. And three beautiful daughters. If I'm readin' the tea leaves correctly, you're wastin' no time at all tryin' for a fourth. I don' see a ring on that girl's finger. I don' see her name is Fontenot. That's not right, Wyatt. I raised you better than that."

There was a stunned silence. Ezekiel was the first to break it. His snicker was loud in the stillness of the night. Malichai followed with a belly laugh. Draden broke into a coughing fit.

"Did I say somethin' funny, boys?" Nonny's voice cut like a lash. "Because I don' recall sayin' anythin' funny at all."

The men shut up instantly. Wyatt looked at Pepper for help. He didn't know why, but seriously, one didn't mess with Nonny when she spoke in that voice.

"Wyatt did mention getting married, Grand-mere," Pepper said softly. Instantly. Helping him out. *Mon Dieu,* but he loved his woman. "We thought it best to keep a low profile until we're certain the girls are out of danger. Marriage requires paperwork."

Wyatt thought her answer perfect. He sent her his warmest smile.

"These boys are mighty creative with paperwork," Nonny said. "I don' think that's any excuse. He puts another baby in your belly, girl, without marryin' you proper, I'm goin' to have to light candles for his soul at the church every day until I die. Since I'm hopin' to live a very long time, that's a lot of trips to the church just to save his soul."

Every one of the "boys" caught Draden's coughing fit. Pepper ducked her head and nuzzled Elle's thick pelt of dark, wavy hair.

"Well, then, Nonny, I expect you best start plannin' a weddin' because I'm goin' to make certain my woman is carryin' another little one as soon as possible," Wyatt announced.

Pepper's breath hissed out of her. *Are you crazy? Four children? I don't know what I'm doing yet.*

Babe. He grinned at her, his lazy, charming grin, the one he knew she liked. *Think of it as an experiment. I'll have to go sooner or later and I'll need to know you can get through the weeks without me. I don' want to come home and find out I have to kill some man because that fire burnin' between your legs was too much to bear without me.*

He saw her hand drop to her boot. He should have been warned, but the knife cut close to his shoulder—the one away from the baby—and lodged in the rocking chair.

There was a small silence.

"Wyatt, I expect you'd better apologize for whatever you jist did," Nonny said.

He laughed. He couldn't help it. "Woman, you know that just turns me on. Is that an invitation?"

"You're impossible," Pepper said. "It's time to put the girls to bed."

The rhythm of the bayou changed subtly. There was no way to explain it to anyone else, but Wyatt had grown up there, had sat on this very porch, hundreds of nights, listening to the music of the world around him. One moment it was natural. Perfect. The next there was a very small, but subtle difference. A new note had entered.

His smile faded, and he turned toward the water, scanning with his night vision. Everything in him went still. "They're comin'," he announced softly. "Right now. They're comin'. Get Trap. Put the others on alert. We need to be ready."

Nonny gasped. Made a single sound of distress. Wyatt frowned at her. She always kept her shotgun handy, always handled any crisis.

"We knew they'd come," Ezekiel said. "We're ready, Nonny."

"Not the safe room. It's not finished. If they get inside . . ." Nonny started.

"I'll kill them," Pepper said. "No one is going to get to the babies. I'll be in front of the door and you'll be inside with your shotgun with the girls. Let's put them to bed and do this, Grand-mere. I'm sick of waiting for them anyway."

There was steel in her voice. Absolute steel. Wyatt grinned at her. *First the knife and now this, sugar. You're makin' me hard all over again.* He jerked the knife from his rocking chair and shoved it down into the sheath in her boot. "Keep that handy, Pepper."

Wyatt stood up and reached out one hand for Pepper, drawing her up out of the rocker while holding Thym cradled against him with the other. He was getting very good at using one hand while cuddling a baby to him with the other. It felt natural and right.

Ezekiel was already helping Nonny from her chair. Ezekiel, Mordichai and Malichai hadn't known a family. They'd raised themselves in the streets. Nonny had taken them in, just like she'd taken Wyatt and his brothers in, and she'd turned her special brand of love on them. Wyatt suspected she was doing the same with Trap and Draden. In the meantime, Ezekiel was ever watchful with her. Looking out. Trying without saying a word to make her life better. Wyatt loved his grandmother all the more for her big heart and Ezekiel for his.

"Let's get you inside, Grand-mere," Ezekiel said, and then when she frowned at him, he added, "where you can stand in front of the girls with that shotgun of yours. We'll need to make certain you have plenty of ammo."

Nonny looked appeased at that. "Don' you worry none about me and my gun, Ezekiel, you go on out and do what you gotta do. And don' get shot or knifed like Wyatt did. We don' need any more grumpy men around here."

Wyatt stepped back to allow the women to get inside first. His mind was already working on how the attack would come at them. How much time they had. He kissed Thym and put her in her crib, drawing up a blanket around her. She looked so innocent. She even murmured "daddy," when he tucked the blanket closer. That earned her another kiss.

He felt Pepper's gaze on him and he glanced up to catch her look. That look. The one. Like he was the entire universe. Hot. Intense. Or maybe he wanted to see that look on her face because for him she was the center of his universe. He was hot and intense the moment he thought of her. He didn't have to actually see her to feel that way.

He kissed Ginger and then Cannelle before he took his grandmother's face between his hands and kissed her too. He didn't want to see the sheen of tears in her eyes, and she didn't want him to see them, so he let go immediately and jerked his head toward Pepper. She followed him out.

His arm swept behind her back and he pulled her close, right up against him, his body hard and tight against hers.

"You don' put yourself in harm's way unless you have to, Pepper," he said, pushing iron into his voice.

"I'm a soldier too, Wyatt. This is my family. I'll defend them, just like you."

He gave her a little shake, fingers biting into her shoulders. "I'm not sayin' you can' fight, baby, I'm just sayin' I need to know you're safe until you have to stand in front of Nonny and the girls. Anyone gets that far, I know you'll take them out. I have not a single doubt." He stared into her eyes so she could see the truth there. "I can' lose you, Pepper. Or the girls. Or Nonny. You're my fail-safe."

He saw understanding creep into the dark of her eyes. All the beautiful midnight purple sky. The sky above the bayou. Home. That was why he'd recognized her so fast, knew she was the one. Hell. Even the stars were there in her eyes.

"No one will get past me to hurt Nonny or our daughters. And nothing will happen to me. But you let me know what's going on, Wyatt," she demanded softly. "And you come back to me."

"That's a given, sugar," he drawled, and tilted her face toward his, thumb and finger holding her chin.

"In one piece," she added. "No bloody wounds."

He grinned at her. "Told you you'd be crazy about me."

"I'm just crazy. Kiss me. Right now before I can't let you go."

Her first real demand. His heart turned over. She was going to kill him before it was all said and done. A mixture of sultry, attitude, sex and vulnerability. What man wouldn't fall at her feet?

Wyatt got down to the business of kissing her, and he took it very seriously. She'd asked him, and he was going to give it his all so she made it a regular practice to ask him. Her mouth was hot and wild, and he devoured her, his tongue sliding deep, dancing with hers, pushing into her space to let her know she belonged. It was the kind of kiss that could move a mountain or send an earthquake through the lands. It did both.

"Yeah, babe," he whispered softly, his forehead pressed to hers so they could both catch air. "I'm comin' back to you always."

"Wyatt, just one more thing. I want you to listen to me. I've been giving this some thought and it's important. Just, can you hear me out?"

"I don' have a lot of time here, Pepper."

She nodded. "This is important. You told me that Whitney is behind this. Our getting together, the termination orders, all of it. What if he's not? What if this is about me and Braden, and Braden is messing up whatever plan Whitney had?"

Wyatt sucked in his breath. All the time nothing quite fit. He had the puzzle pieces but none of them actually snapped together—until that moment.

"I made him so angry, Wyatt. He called me into his office and he told me he would issue termination orders on the babies if I didn't give him what he wanted. He was very specific in his instructions. I told him to go to hell. I was so angry, and he was so smug. I think Whitney had already given him the heads-up that the babies might be taken to the States. To here."

Wyatt was still stuck on the specific instructions Braden had given to his woman. He breathed deep through his nose to try to keep the walls from undulating. "Keep goin', honey," he said softly. She was already alarmed by the look on his face. He didn't want his tone to make it worse.

Pepper moistened her lips with the tip of her tongue and avoided his eyes. "He tried to rip my clothes, and he was far stronger than I expected him to be. I went a little berserk. I'd already made it clear I didn't want another one of his men putting his hands on me without my consent. It took several of his soldiers to get me off of him and I wiped up the floor with them. I put seven of them down before they managed to knock me out. Seven, Wyatt. He was so angry."

He waited and he knew he wasn't going to like what came next. He heard his heart thundering in his ears, a roar of rage so loud he knew his team members caught it.

She continued to look down at the floor. "He retaliated of course. I was tied to the bed and gagged with this horrible piece of equipment so I couldn't use my teeth on him." Her voice dropped to a whisper. "He came several times a day for nearly a week."

"He's a dead man," Wyatt hissed.

He heard the echoes of his team. They didn't hear her soft voice, he hadn't built that bridge, but it didn't matter. They heard him. They felt him. The rage. The fury. It swept through them all until they were ice-cold and the flames had turned ice blue.

Pepper opened her mouth to continue, but Wyatt pulled her tighter against him and buried his face in her neck.

"You should have told me, honey. I would have been gentler with you. You should have told me."

Her arms slid around him. "I made my mind go blank. I told myself it was training. It didn't matter. He didn't matter. He was no different from my instructors, except he was a disgusting pig."

"Why didn' you tell me?" He pulled his head back to look at her, realizing she hadn't looked at him once. Not once while she was telling him.

She still didn't, but it wasn't hard to tell she struggled with tears.

Wyatt caught her chin. "Look at me, baby," he said softly. "Eyes right on mine. Tell me why you didn't say a word to me about this."

She swallowed hard and shook her head. "Please, Wyatt." Her hands curled into his shirt. "You don't have time for this. Just let me tell you about his soldiers. He beefed them up. He said if I could take them, Whitney's elite soldiers would wipe up the floor with them. So he really beefed them up. That soldier with the harder bone structure you encountered in the lab is one of several. Braden didn't bring very many with him, but he's had time to fly more here. He's doesn't stay at the plant, and neither did his personal soldiers."

He wanted more. He wanted reasons. He wanted to wipe that look off her face. The shame. It wasn't her shame. The humiliation. It wasn't her humiliation. He was going to kill Braden and never look back.

His hand went to the nape of her neck and curled there. He just held her. He needed it more than she did. He was only beginning to recognize what her life must have been like.

"So you think this is all Braden and he's goin' against Whitney."

She nodded her head, still not looking at him. Wyatt tipped her head up to his and bent to take her mouth. He was far gentler. Way more tender. It didn't matter, the flames poured over him and through him, a raging firestorm in spite of the blue flame burning hot in his belly.

He lifted his head and looked down into her eyes. "We good?"

She nodded her head. "We're good, Wyatt."

He turned and left her. He didn't look back. He didn't dare. When a man found the one woman who was his universe, he didn't want her in danger. And she sure as hell wouldn't be put in the fire ever again if he had anything to say about it.

He relayed the information about Braden's soldiers to his team. The skeletal structure was amazing protection, but they also had to have something else, something that revved them up. The soldier coming at him hadn't felt much in the way of pain. He should have stuck around and examined the man, but he'd lost too much of his own blood and there'd been no time.

Doesn't matter, Wyatt, Trap said. *Fucking Braden is dead and anyone we have to go through to get to him is dead as well.*

The rage didn't lessen. He would never forget the look on Pepper's face, or her quiet voice, so devoid of expression as she "confessed." She'd told him the truth for a reason. She blamed herself for Braden making his soldiers stronger. She'd taken down seven of his guards and kicked Braden's ass.

Man does that to a woman, he doesn't deserve to breathe the same air, Ezekiel added. *We've got company coming in from the south.* He didn't even change the tone of his voice.

He's not going to be with this bunch, bayou man, Malichai said. *Once we clean house here, I'll follow the bastard back to France if I have to. More coming in from the north.*

Wyatt was aware Braden wouldn't have had too much time to find his own soldiers. More than likely they weren't psychic, or even enhanced psychically. He recalled Pepper telling him Braden was more interested in physical enhancement. So the supersoldiers coming for them were going to be difficult to take down with bullets and knives. He said as much to his team.

Coming in from the east, Mordichai said. *I'll go with you, Malichai, all the way to ends of the earth to find this bastard and end him.*

Again, there was no inflection. Just a statement.

On the water, Trap reported. *They think they've got us surrounded. I'm fading into the night. Draden's already gone into the trees.*

We'll take the water, Ezekiel said. He was the logical one to go in, he could control reptiles better than any of the rest, although truthfully, Trap was best in water.

I'm with you, Wyatt said. *Malichai, don' let them near my family.*

Mind the alligators, Malichai cautioned. *No one's getting near your family. It's mine now too.*

Wyatt slipped from the porch into the shadows. He disappeared, just like most of his kind could do.

Braden built his supersoldiers to be men with muscles

and quick reflexes, but he left off other very important things. Wyatt, Trap and the rest of his team could outthink the soldiers coming for them. Braden already had proved he had no military background when he sent civilian guards in to look for Pepper and Ginger. He hadn't studied his enemy. He didn't know the first thing about Wyatt Fontenot. Braden had believed he was dealing with locals, and that meant Whitney hadn't told Braden about Wyatt.

Wyatt slipped under the pier into the murky water of the canal. He flinched a little thinking of the germs crawling into the mostly healed wounds on his body. Even a slight opening could mean infection. He made a mental note to give himself a hefty shot of antibiotics.

Braden had to know now he was dealing with more than local fishermen, but he still was not thinking like a soldier. He hadn't found their classified files and learned who he was dealing with; again, meaning Whitney wasn't giving him aid. Wyatt knew that because his sister-in-law, Flame, was hell on wheels with a computer and she would have warned him if his file had been compromised.

Keep talkin' so we know who needs help. Wyatt gave the standard order.

Two approaching from the south, Trap said. *They're moving through the trees, but they're not coming in stealthy. They have big guns and they're big boys.*

Remember the extra bone. I don' know what Braden mixed with it, but I shot that son of a bitch and knifed him. He kept gettin' back up, Wyatt reminded.

So aim for the Adam's apple, Draden said. *See how thick that armor plate is.*

The eye, the ear, Trap said. *Interesting to see what they're made of.*

If Wyatt could have rolled his eyes underwater, he would have. Of course Trap would want to autopsy one of the soldiers, dissect him and start figuring out just what Braden did to them.

They heal incredibly fast, Wyatt reiterated. *He's got them on some kind of supercharged drug to make that happen.*

I'll get blood samples, Trap said, meaning it.

Trap was a ghost moving through the woods. They'd never see him until he was on them. He went into camps alone and came out when everyone was dead. Wyatt had never figured out how a man who could heal the way Trap was able to could kill without repercussions. Trap never seemed to have any.

Don' let anyone get close to the house, Wyatt cautioned.

Ezekiel was already making his way along the bottom of the canal, straight for the boat coming silently toward them. Wyatt followed close, keeping at Ezekiel's left shoulder, feeling for creatures in the water and broadcasting strongly for them to stay away. The boat was being powered by oars, moving very slowly so as not to create noise.

The moment they were near the boat, Ezekiel went under it, hugging the bottom, Wyatt beside him. They both stood at the same time, using powerful thighs and enhanced muscles to upend the boat and send the two soldiers flying into the water. Zeke yanked the automatic out of the nearest soldier's hands and was on him immediately. He took a breath and dragged the soldier under.

Wyatt swept the legs out from under the other soldier as he turned toward his partner, trying to get a clear shot at his attacker. He went under, but kept his hold on the automatic. Wyatt hooked him with a vicious grip around his throat. At the same time, he brought his knife up and slammed it into the man's left eye.

Blood in the water, he warned.

The soldiers fought to get free. Neither had the ability to stay under anywhere near as long as Wyatt and Ezekiel, but they were strong and they used their bodies and legs to try to propel their attackers backward, to make them lose footing so they could rise to the surface for air.

Wyatt plunged the knife again, looking for any soft spot

he could think of. One where there might not be a covering of bone. *Go low with the knife, thigh, calves, crotch. Go for the soft parts, eyes, mouth, try the throat.*

Blood ran like a river and still both soldiers fought. In the end, it wasn't the loss of blood or the hideous wounds, it was the fact that neither could reach the surface for air. They simply drowned. Wyatt felt the soldier's frantic fight and then the last desperate heave for freedom before he seemed to succumb to the water filling his lungs.

Still, he didn't let go. He didn't dare. The last soldier he'd walked away from kept coming back. He wasn't making that mistake again. Ezekiel seemed to feel the same way. They stayed very still, holding the two soldiers in a choke hold beneath the surface of the water.

Alligator comin' in, Wyatt reported. *Stay still. He's goin' to bump you. Just checkin' you and then he'll go for the wounds.*

I'm holding him off, Wyatt, but we need to get these two in the boat and make it back to help the others, Ezekiel said. *You got a pulse there?*

I don' feel one. Let's do it. When we're in the boat, we'll search them, just to make sure they don' have any weapons they can get to if Braden found a way to resurrect them once they're dead.

He's probably got a shock collar on them, Ezekiel said. *You go first, Wyatt, dump the body in and climb in. I'll keep this guy at bay until you do.*

Wyatt knew enough to hurry. That much blood in the water was going to attract more than one alligator and it could get ugly fast. He went to the surface, trusting Ezekiel to keep the alligator from grabbing at his legs while he hoisted the soldier's body back into the boat and then pulled himself in.

Ezekiel was fast, dumping the second body while Wyatt was stripping the soldier of all weapons. Ezekiel followed suit and then took up an oar. Wyatt used the other one and they guided the boat back to the pier.

Wyatt took one last look at the dead soldiers. *They're not breathin'. No heartbeat. No pulse. Nothin' at all. That doesn' mean they'll stay that way. They could rise any minute, the new zombie warriors. Maybe it's Braden whose gonna be responsible for the zombie apocalypse.*

Ezekiel glanced at him, shook his head, his mouth twitching as he tied to the boat to the pier. *They look dead to me. I don't think they're getting back up, Wyatt.*

That's the point, Zeke. They rise after they're dead.

He heard Pepper's soft laughter, still betraying a little of her anxiety. Her face had been so strained. She'd looked so alone, so vulnerable when he'd left her. He kept her with him, bridging the gap so she could hear the conversations as the team reported in. He'd needed to hear her laughter even if it was tense.

They slipped out of the boat and onto the pier, two dark shadows reclaiming the night, moving into the trees to make their way around the house toward the east and Mordichai.

Mordichai heard the soldiers coming. With enhanced hearing, vision and smell, it wasn't that difficult to locate the exact position of each of them.

I've got my sights on a big bastard. He's got to be a good six-six, Malichai informed them from the rooftop. *Can't see his partner yet.*

Mordichai saw the big man's partner and for just one moment he stopped and shook his head. The man's entire body was distorted, bones so thick the skin stretched taut over them. He looked like a caricature of a man.

Whoever this Braden is, he's no Whitney, Mordichai informed the others. *I've got eyes on his partner, Malichai; it's going to take a bit to bring this one down.*

Wyatt didn't like the sound of that. He pushed his way through the grass and brush, moving fast, trying to swing around to get into a position to aid Mordichai. *Coming in from your right. Malichai, take the shot if you have it.*

Malichai didn't hesitate. He squeezed the trigger, once,

twice, a third time. Aiming for the eyes and throat. He didn't think the soldier's thickened bone armor was going to stop a high-velocity bullet from his sniper rifle, but still, Wyatt was worried about the zombie apocalypse and he didn't want to take the chance of helping the other side.

He watched the big soldier go down hard. He kept eyes on him, certain he wouldn't get back up again, but one never knew, not with enhancements and some kind of healing super drug. The soldier didn't so much as twitch.

A sound warned him. A soft footfall, or maybe the breeze switched directions for just one moment. He rolled fast, nearly going off the roof. *He's on me. They're diversions, Wyatt. I fucked up.*

He felt the bite of the knife sliding into him. The blade was razor-sharp and it cut through skin, muscle and everything else in its path without even slowing down. He knew he was going to die. The knowledge hit him even as the soldier withdrew the knife and came at him a second time.

The soldier's body jerked, his expression changing from satisfaction to shock. His eyes went wide. He staggered, recovered and turned. Behind him, Malichai saw Pepper, the knife in her hand dripping blood.

What the hell? Pepper, get out of here.

She backed away from the soldier, focused totally on the huge man. Malichai knew she was drawing the threat away from him in order for him to get on his feet. His wound was low, kidney low, and he couldn't exactly get back there to staunch the flow of blood, but she was so small and fragile, looking more vulnerable than ever.

Malichai's down. I've got one on the roof and three others in the yard getting close to the house.

Pepper didn't sound fragile and vulnerable. She sounded totally cool and in absolute control. She looked so small. He hadn't even been able to see her around the soldier. She was that small in comparison. Malichai was terrified for her. He had to get on his feet. He *had* to.

The soldier didn't so much as glance at him, already dismissing him as a threat. He smirked at Pepper. "I've been wanting to meet up with you again. This time it isn't going to end the way it did last time."

She kept gliding backward, drawing the soldier toward her and away from Malichai. "You mean when I wiped up the floor with you? Is that what this is, Pierre, revenge? You and the others? All seven of you?"

Pierre spit on the roof and kept walking toward her. "We agreed whichever got to you first got to keep you."

Pepper didn't so much as glance at Malichai when she reached for him. *Can you get off the roof? Slide down the side, if you can. I'll keep him busy until you're safely away.*

Wyatt will kill me if I leave you alone with that monster. He tried to move and nearly panicked. His body felt paralyzed. No matter what his brain said, he couldn't get on his feet.

Without warning, his brother was there, coming up over the side of the roof, one arm hooking around Malichai's chest, under his arms and then he was over Ezekiel's shoulder and Zeke was dragging him right off the roof. Leaving her. Pepper. Wyatt's woman. Alone with the hyped-up monster.

The moment Ezekiel had Malichai safe, Pepper moved with blurring speed, racing straight at Pierre, the man who would take her children, probably kill them and then do whatever he wanted to her. At the last minute, when he'd braced himself, ready for her, she took a dive, sliding under him, slamming her blade into him and continuing on to the other side of the roof and then over.

She heard him scream, a terrible, ugly sound she was certain she would never forget, but she landed softly, on the balls of her feet and raced around toward the back of the house where she knew the other three soldiers were working their way through Trap's intense security system.

Wyatt caught a glimpse of Pepper running fast, using

her crazy speed even he couldn't match, tearing around the corner of the house and out of his view. He sprinted after her and his speed wasn't anything to sneeze at. *Zeke, how bad?*

Nonny's helping me with him. It's bad. He's losing a lot of blood. I'm putting a line in him now.

They were all medics. Damn good medics, and Wyatt counted on the fact that Ezekiel had been looking out for his younger brothers his entire life. He rounded the corner of the building and skidded to a halt. Pepper was in the arms of one of the soldiers and she wasn't fighting. Her arms were around his neck, her face nestled into his shoulder.

What the fuck, Pepper? Fury shook him. What the hell was she playing at?

Pepper stepped back and removed the guns from the soldier's hands, still looking up into his eyes as if he was the only man in her world. The soldier's mouth opened wide. He put out his hand toward her. She took it. Wyatt's entire body stiffened. Coiled tight. He pulled out his knife.

Don't be a fool. That was Trap. *She's working. Get to work yourself.*

Trap moved past him, continued past Pepper, who never took her eyes from the soldier. Or dropped his hand. They just stared at each other. Wyatt realized Pepper's eyes could mesmerize, hypnotize. The eyes of the cobra, but more. The soldier was drowning in her eyes, lost in the stars in her night-filled gaze. His legs went out from under him and he went to his knees. She didn't let go. She stepped even closer and touched his face, holding his hand the entire time.

Movement to her left had Wyatt moving, shooting as he ran. The soldier coming toward Pepper, his semiautomatic in his arms, staggered back, the bullets spitting all around Pepper. She didn't move. Didn't acknowledge there was anyone but the man on his knees in front of her.

Wyatt kept shooting even when his target hit the ground.

He stood over the soldier, yanked his weapons away and sent up a silent prayer the man was really dead. It was nearly impossible to tell anymore.

Trap hit the nearest soldier with both feet, driving him back and away from Pepper. He hit him hard, with every bit of enhanced strength he had. The soldier went flying, and he heard an audible, satisfying crack. Still, every bone in his body was jarred on impact, as if he'd kicked a steel wall.

He fell heavily, the breath knocked out of him. Almost immediately the other soldier loomed over him, weapon out, pointed straight at his heart. Trap actually saw him squeezing the trigger. Time slowed so that every small detail was etched into his mind. He knew he'd die that way, seeing it coming without a damned thing he could do about it. He got his hands under him to launch himself in the air, but the finger was already squeezing.

Out of nowhere masses of silk rained down between Trap and the soldier. The silk spun in a tight cocoon, caging the soldier and his gun in the silken threads until the soldier couldn't move. The silk continued, spinning round and round so fast it made Trap dizzy. All the way up the body and neck to the mouth, the nose and eyes. The soldier fell hard, hitting the ground right beside Trap, but still the silk came, tighter and tighter, winding his enemy up until there was no possible way to move or breathe.

She came out of the night. She was more beautiful than he remembered. Her eyes were liquid, her skin perfect. She crouched down beside him and ran her hand over him. Gently. As if it mattered. It never mattered to anyone. Trap blinked at her. She'd killed a man in seconds. *Seconds.*

"We're even," she said softly.

"No we're not." He heard the words come out of his mouth and he meant them. "We're not even, woman. Don't think for one minute that we are."

Her eyes flashed at him. Liquid. Smoldering. She hissed

between her teeth, turned and leapt toward the side of the house, moving up and over it fast, heading around to the other side. He didn't know if spider woman was escaping or going to help Draden. Right then it didn't matter, because the soldier he kicked in the chest was slowly climbing to his feet and his eyes looked angry.

CHAPTER 20

Pepper felt bile rising in her throat at the sight of the soldier, his eyes locked on her with such hungry need. She'd killed him. She'd done it to save her children and Nonny, but not like this. The knife, the gun, was a far better way to die. She couldn't let him die alone, not when she'd caused this. She'd never killed this way before and she knew, the moment he was gone, when the paralysis hit his lungs and he no longer could breathe, she would vomit.

She'd killed the soldier on the roof to protect Malichai, but she'd done it cleanly. This man looked as if he idolized her. He had to know he was dying. She doubted that he even realized she was the one to kill him. He was enthralled with her. For a moment his face blurred and she felt tears on her face.

He crashed to the ground, still staring at her. Gasping for breath. She couldn't tear her eyes away from his, not even when his adoring gaze began to fog over. He looked so happy. So satisfied. She cursed herself. Hated herself. Hated what she was.

Pepper. Behind you. Damn it, behind you.

She heard Wyatt's voice as if it was far away. Wyatt. Everything good. How could she possibly have ever thought she belonged with him? Something hit her hard from behind and she slammed forward, falling, straight into the body of the soldier. She landed on the soldier, still staring into his eyes. She heard the rattle in his chest. Felt his last breath. She lay there on the man she killed, a weapon Braden and possibly Whitney had made her into. Maybe she killed him for the right reasons, but this was blasphemy.

A hard hand yanked her up. Wyatt stuck his face in hers. "Get movin'. Get back to the girls."

She looked at him. His face was hard. Carved of stone. His eyes flat and cold. A crushing weight descended onto her chest and just sat there. He'd seen this abomination. He knew what she was.

"*Now*, Pepper. *Get to the girls!*"

His commanding voice snapped her out of the daze she was in. She saw him turn, saw him meet another soldier, chest to chest, two combatants coming together with terrible force. She did what he said because she was trained as a soldier, and an order was an order.

Wyatt didn't have time to process the look on Pepper's face. He filed it away for the future. Right now he wanted her safe, inside where there were no supersoldiers to fight. The one swinging at his head with his gun was one tough bastard. Wyatt ducked, feeling a little as if his chest had been smashed into pieces when they'd come together. And truly, it might actually be the zombie apocalypse. The soldier he'd shot numerous times was moving, thrashing around, making hideous sounds—a serious Badboy, this one.

Wyatt ducked and made the mistake of trying to plant his fist in Badboy's throat. Badboy moved just enough that Wyatt's fist hit solid bone. He brought up his knee hard, needing room, shoving the soldier off of him. Fortunately, he was enhanced and that extra strength gave him the upper hand when it came to shoving. Badboy was lifted off his feet and sent flying.

I need you now, Wyatt, Ezekiel snapped. *Right now. Nonny's setting out your instruments, but you've got to get in here.*

Wyatt could have groaned, but he didn't have time. Badboy was charging, floundering a little without the weapons Wyatt had stripped from him.

Go, Draden snapped, firing from behind him. He punched numerous bullets into Badboy, a pattern, high and low, every soft spot and every major artery. *Get to Malichai. Ezekiel will get out here to help me.*

Watch zombie boy. He's goin' to come at you, Wyatt cautioned.

Draden turned the gun on the zombie, who was trying to get to his knees. He went back down when Draden added more holes to his chest.

Wyatt didn't wait to see what happened next. He raced back toward the front of the house, knowing if Ezekiel was calling for him, Malichai needed attention now. He tore into the house and headed down to the office he'd kept for the locals who needed a doctor. They'd moved his gear into the room and set up a surgery there, just in case.

The lights were blazing and he could see splashes of blood on the floor as he went inside. "Nonny!" She was steady. She'd always been steady, and like him, she was a natural healer. She didn't panic. Not ever.

She was there right away, assessing Malichai's condition as he lay on the operating table, facedown. He already had lines in. Ezekiel had worked fast to keep his brother alive, but he needed surgery.

"Pepper." Wyatt turned his head the moment he sensed her in the doorway. He was already at the sink, scrubbing. "You don' let anyone in the house. You understand me?" She was different. Distant. He couldn't quite reach her, not even through their connection. Her face was very pale, but her answering nod was firm. "Whatever it takes, babe. Just keep them off of us."

She nodded again and turned away, leaving him with Nonny and Malichai. Ezekiel had already raced outside to aid Draden. Wyatt looked at his grandmother. "Let's get it done. Zeke set everything up. Check and make certain Zeke has all my instruments, the gelfoam and coils."

Trap shot the big, burly soldier point-blank, and he didn't go down. The man was half covered in silk, but he'd somehow torn the sticky filament off his arms. The gun had gone flying, but he had Cayenne wrapped in his big, beefy arms. She looked tiny, but Trap could see she was a handful, much stronger than the soldier first thought. She used her legs and arms to gain wiggle room from his death hold on her.

The big, beefy soldier suddenly grunted, as if she'd scored a hit on him, held her away from him with one hand and punched her repeatedly with the other. That's when Trap shot him. Right in the face. Point-blank.

Trap wasn't a man who displayed emotion often. He often didn't recognize emotion in himself. Rage exploded through him, a rush of such proportions he followed up the bullets by kicking the soldier in the gut with both boots, using his forward momentum to gain even more strength.

He felt the jar through his body as he struck, but the beefy soldier dropped her and staggered back several feet. He turned his one working eye on Trap. There was malevolence there. A kind of distant boiling fury.

"Get up," he ordered Cayenne. The soldier was flying on something. Bullets and a kick that should have broken his insides to pieces hadn't even fazed him. "Damn it, get on your feet."

The malevolent eye hadn't stayed on Trap. It had gone to

Cayenne, who was moving slow, groaning, trying to push herself up off the ground. Trap caught her by the back of her shirt and yanked her to her feet, pushing her behind him.

"Get the hell out of here."

The soldier wiped at the blood running down his face, smearing it everywhere. Once more fixing his eye on Trap, he licked his fingers, smirking. Trap shot him again, a straight line of bullets up his body and back down, like a zipper. He heard the bullets thud into the man, but the soldier didn't do more than jerk with each strike.

I'll take him from the trees, see if I can drop silk around his neck like a noose while you distract him.

She was there. Moving in his head. No one moved inside his mind. No one. He spoke to his team telepathically, but they didn't get in his head. It was an invasion of privacy, and he would have broken her neck himself if they weren't in such a dangerous position. He was a man with too many secrets, and no one was allowed to ever get that close—or that intimate.

"Get the hell out of here," he snarled. Shocking himself. He didn't feel fear like the others. He didn't usually feel. Cayenne disturbed him in ways he didn't understand.

The soldier walked toward him. Walked. Not ran. He didn't stop to pick up the weapon he'd dropped, he just came at Trap as if he was out for a Sunday stroll. Trap swore between clenched teeth. He studied his opponent as the man came toward him, using the eye of scientist. He was good at finding weaknesses in everything around him—especially people. He catalogued and filed away the shambling walk. The blood draining from each hole in the man. The way he moved his arms and opened and closed his fists.

Trap's mind reduced the hulk to numbers, a stack of them shuffling through the dirt toward him. He calculated and calibrated and waited until the last possible moment, right before those big, beefy hands swung at him. He'd already figured the odds of the attack and exactly how the soldier would come at him. He had a few vulnerable spots, but not too many.

As the supersoldier reached with his large, ham-like hands, Trap ducked inside those arms and hit him full on the Adam's apple. It should have stunned him if not killed him. Trap had immense strength. It rocked the soldier, but those huge arms closed around him like a vise and began to squeeze. The thick skull slammed down into Trap's head. Stars burst behind his eyes.

Silken thread rained down, spinning fast around the soldier's head, covering his mouth and nose and eyes like a white mummy's hood. The soldier coughed, but he didn't let go.

Cayenne dropped from the tree above them, landing on the soldier's shoulders, wrapping her arm around his neck and sinking her teeth into the artery there. Instantly, the soldier flung Trap from him, reached back and ripped Cayenne off his back. Again he rained punches on her body while he held her in the air, fury and something close to hatred and revulsion in his eyes.

She didn't make a sound. Not a single one. As if she'd been punched like that before. Trap dragged himself up just as the soldier dropped her, aimed a kick and sent her flying. Trap was on him instantly, this time, ducking inside, but going for the kill, slamming his knife under the raised arm, directly into the armpit. He shoved it in, using every bit of strength he possessed.

The soldier didn't have any armor there. He screamed and went down, taking Trap with him. Trap ripped the blade loose and plunged it in a second time, this time, twisting it hard for maximum damage. The moment he had the blade out, he went for the throat, slicing through arteries to ensure this one wouldn't rise again.

He crawled backward like a crab away from the man and turned his head to find Cayenne. She was moving.

Slow. Again there was no sound. He hated that. Rage was there all over again.

"We can't stay down," he said, making his way to her. He wiped the blood from his blade on the grass and shoved the knife back down into his boot. "Can you walk?"

She lifted her head and looked at him. Looked at the hand he held out to get her on her feet. She made no move to take his hand. He actually felt the blast of distrust. No fear. Only that disdain. Contempt even.

"How bad is it? Can you get on your feet? I'm a medic, I can help."

He started to move his hands over her body and she rolled away fast, kicking out at him. Something wild crept into her eyes.

"Fine. Get the hell up." Trap was out of patience. "I've got men fighting these things and they need help. You like it better on your own, you've got it."

He stalked away from her, letting the fury have him for just a moment. Letting it consume him when he was always still inside. Always quiet. Emotions didn't figure in his world. They couldn't. He jogged. Then sprinted. Straight for hell. He knew hell and he belonged there. It was a world of kill or be killed. Black-and-white rules. He understood those rules and accepted them.

By the time he'd rounded the corner of the house, his mind was still again. She was gone as if she'd never been. Draden was down, under the weight of a sandy-haired soldier who would have looked more at home lifting weights on the beach than he did fighting. The muscles in his arms and back were so big, his head looked a little like a pin sitting atop a giant marshmallow.

Go for his armpit, Draden, Trap advised as he ran toward the two struggling men.

Draden's face was nearly purple as the soldier relentlessly clamped his hands around Draden's neck and squeezed.

Shoot, Mordichai. Take the shot, Draden ordered.

Still not clear, he's throwing you all around, Mordichai said.

Draden's boot heel smashed into his opponent's thigh repeatedly, but the soldier didn't so much as flinch.

Trap pulled a gun as he sprinted toward Draden. He knew Mordichai's approximate position and kept out of the line of fire, just in case, but truthfully, he was wholly focused on the soldier strangling Draden.

He shot him through the back of the neck, which should have instantly paralyzed the soldier, but Trap wasn't taking chances. He shot him again twice, and then as he got on top of him, he shoved the gun into the man's ear and squeezed the trigger. Blood sprayed over Draden's face and body. The grip seemed to tighten for a moment, and then the soldier slumped over. Trap tore his fingers from around Draden's throat.

Draden dragged air into his lungs. "Wyatt's right. Braden started the zombie apocalypse," he wheezed.

Trap shoved the soldier off his friend. "It's going to be a hell of a long night getting rid of bodies. We'll take them back to the crematorium when we go to visit Braden."

Draden nodded and allowed Trap to bring him to his feet. He wiped off the blood, spit, drew in more air and looked around.

Anyone left to fight, Mordichai?

Zeke's got two on him at the front door. I'm moving position to try to help him.

We'll come around.

One might have slipped inside, Mordichai advised. *Was three. Now two.*

Someone's *in the house,* Wyatt said, keeping his curses to himself. *Pepper, tell me you've got this.*

Both he and Nonny had weapons at hand, but killing any of the soldiers was clearly a difficult task. It took time he didn't have. Worse, stopping the bleeding and saving Malichai's kidney was proving to be more complicated than he wanted it to be. The knife had done considerable damage. He felt the presence of the soldier as he moved inside, a stealthy stalk, straight toward the operating room, drawn, Wyatt was certain, by the blazing lights.

Pepper braced herself. She didn't have the right angle on the soldier for a bullet to take him down. She had no choice. She knew that. She also knew what it meant for her. For Wyatt. Still, she wasn't about to let him kill Wyatt or take her children. Sacrificing her happiness for them was a no-brainer.

As the soldier yanked open the door to the operating room and thrust his gun inside, she flung herself at him, her hands sliding under his shirt, allowing the maximum of the biochemical to penetrate. His finger stilled on the trigger, just as she'd known it would. Just as she'd practiced a million times.

She moved around him, sliding her body against his so that he dropped the weapon and reached for her, ripping at the front of her shirt. That just exposed more skin, and she ripped at his shirt, allowing skin-to-skin contact. His mouth came down and she turned her head up, blocking out everything but what she had to do—what it would take to save her family. The very thing that would destroy her.

She kissed him. She kissed him and killed him, all in one bittersweet moment. She wasn't such a failure as a weapon as they'd thought her. Their weapon had worked perfectly twice now in a combat situation. Her heart beat fast as she stepped back from the man, knowing the cobra venom was fast acting. Was fatal.

The soldier's eyes clung to her as if she was his everything. As if she hadn't just injected him with enough venom to kill an elephant. Absolute adulation. Her heart stuttered in her chest. Bile rose in her throat. She didn't allow herself to look away from him, giving him that much, knowing he would die thinking she was his.

She despised herself. She couldn't look away from him, away from the blasphemy of biochemical love. She'd used something precious to kill. She'd been turned into such an abomination there was no saving her. She saw the knowledge in the soldier's eyes and it killed something in her.

She stepped closer to him, fighting tears. Her hand cupped the side of his face. He couldn't help being what he was any more than she could. "I'm sorry," she whispered. "So sorry."

His adoring gaze still clung to her. The venom was taking hold, his face drooping, but he still managed to turn his face toward her palm. She felt his tongue lick at her skin, seeking more of the addicting drug.

His knees gave out abruptly and she went to the floor with him, on her own knees, arm around his back, pushing the gun away from him, deeper into the room so if another came they had more protection.

Pepper was careful not to look at Wyatt or Nonny. The scent of blood and death permeated the air so that with every breath she drew into her lungs she brought the knowledge of who and what she was—what she would always be. There was no cure for a woman like her. And no living with a woman like her.

She watched him die slowly, his lungs paralyzed so that his death came inch by terrible inch, and she refused to look away from what she was.

"Pepper."

Wyatt's voice penetrated, but she didn't take her eyes off the dying soldier's eyes.

"Pepper, you're done. Get away from there."

She shook her head.

Honey, there's nothin' you can do. He would have killed us. He would have killed or taken our children.

She hated that Wyatt's voice was soft with tenderness. He didn't want to see the truth. He was too good of a man, but she was sitting on the floor with a man she'd killed, while he stared at her adoringly. What kind of a monster was she? How could Wyatt realistically live with her? Stay with her? Make a life with her? And her beautiful little daughters—*their*—daughters, they couldn't be like her. She couldn't let that happen.

The soldier's eyes were wide open, staring into hers, yet the muscles in his face drooped hideously. His eyes begged her. Pleaded with her. Not for life. Not that. That no longer mattered to him. Her stomach heaved. Her throat burned. She knew what mattered to him and he was dying.

She leaned into him and whispered into his ear. Let her skin rub along his. She gave him what he wanted more than life itself. The drug that was her.

Pepper! Get the hell away from him. He's killin' you. Can' you see that? You did your job. I've got my hands full and I can' get you away from him myself. Back off, go to the girls. Look at them, not at the enemy.

The tenderness was replaced by the commander. Ordinarily she would never have disobeyed an order—especially not if Wyatt gave it. This was different. She wasn't going to allow this man to die alone. She didn't have that in her.

Without warning, Wyatt stalked across the room and dragged her to her feet, yanking her blouse closed so that her full breasts were out of sight. Blood smeared the material—Malichai's blood—she could smell it. She refused to look up at Wyatt. She couldn't face him. Couldn't face the censure. Or the disgust.

"He's gone, Pepper. Get to the girls."

She already knew the soldier was gone. She'd never stopped looking into his eyes. She saw the life fade away, heard that last rattle as his body struggled against the venom. Without a word she stepped over him and hurried down the hall to stand in front of the door to the nursery where her daughters lay sleeping. She wouldn't go inside. She wouldn't contaminate them—bring something sick and evil into their sleeping place. She stood there with silent tears running down her face, but the gun was steady in her hands.

Ezekiel leapt into the air, ran up the side of the house and jumped onto the back of one of the soldiers attacking him. His powerful thighs closed like a vise around the man's neck while his knife bit deep into first the throat, then the ear and finally the artery along the neck. He stabbed dozens of times, trying for the soft places that might stop the soldier's forward momentum toward the door.

He'd already broken one blade, and his gun seemed useless. The soldiers barely paid attention to him, they were so fixated on the house. Every other soldier was used for distraction, for fodder. These three were meant to retrieve or kill the three girls or Pepper. Maybe all of them. One had already slipped inside. One was at the door. He had the biggest.

Dozens of stab wounds and the soldier wasn't even staggering yet. It made no sense. He didn't appear to feel pain at all. Whatever Braden had given his supersoldiers to kill the pain and exterminate the fear factor was working.

Another one getting into the house. I could use a little help here, Ezekiel said.

The soldier reached back at him, knife in fist, trying to plunge the blade in Ezekiel's thigh. Ezekiel was forced to catch the man's thick wrist and turn the knife away from him. He leapt from his back, landing low in a crouch.

Coming in now, Trap advised.

He shot through the columns, feet first, flying through the air to catch the soldier entering the house just as he was starting to pull open the door. The force of his flying double kick drove the soldier back to the rail. He teetered there for a moment and then fell over it headfirst. Unfortunately the drop wasn't that far, but he landed hard enough that it shook the ground.

Draden was waiting, crouched low on the other side of the railing, his gun out. As the soldier fell, he fired rapidly. Throat. Eyes. Ears. He got a lucky break and the soldier flung one arm out and he managed to fire three times into the exposed armpit. With each shot, he backed away, kicking the man's weapons away.

Trap landed in the middle of the porch on the balls of his feet and kept moving, straight toward Ezekiel and his monster of a soldier. At the last second, he hit the ground sliding, his momentum carrying him under the soldier, sweeping the big man's legs out from under him. The soldier went down hard, his gun pointed up in the air, bullets spitting loudly in the night.

Trap drove his knife deep into the soft parts of the body, and the bullets kept coming, although now the soldier was getting his weapon under control. Ezekiel went under the short automatic, his hands around the soldier's wrist, trying to gain some control. The bullets kept coming.

Trap swore, something rose in him, pouring ice into his veins, slowing time and allowing an absolute, utter calm so his brain could take over. He used his knife on the hand holding the gun, a ruthless, brutal act, and there wasn't a single cell in his body that even flinched.

Draden was there, shooting the man in all the soft parts of his face and neck, the only vulnerable spots on him. When he finally was still, the silence of the night took over.

All clear, Mordichai reported from above. *They're all down.*

Make certain, Trap directed. *Every last one of them. And then get them in the big boat. We're taking them back to Braden and using his own crematorium to get rid of them. I wouldn't mind five minutes alone with that bastard.*

Ezekiel took a deep breath. *Wyatt? Malichai?*

He's good, breathin'. He'll need to sleep off the anesthesia for some time. Nonny knows what to do. I'm gettin' ready to join you and I'm bringin' out another one.

One got in the house while you were operating? Ezekiel demanded.

No problem, Pepper took care of it. Malichai is fine. He'll be fine.

Trap moved away from the others and jogged around the corner to check on the woman. She was gone. He knew she'd be gone, but he had to check all the same. He went to the spot where she'd gone down, crouched and read the signs. She was hurt all right. It had taken her a few minutes to get up, but she'd done it. She'd dragged herself a good way before she was back on her feet. The tracks led straight toward the trees. She was heading for the swamp.

He shook his head. She had the right to live free. They all should, but still, banding together was far better than going it alone. He could have told her that. He turned back to the people who had become his family and joined in dragging the big soldiers to the boat.

Be careful, Wyatt, Ezekiel cautioned. *It bothers me we didn't come across one single civilian guard. The place looks deserted, but I'm getting a bad vibe.*

Got the same vibe, Zeke, Wyatt responded. *But Braden's goin' down tonight.*

Wyatt dropped down through the hole in the roof Braden hadn't even bothered to repair. The sheer arrogance of the man shocked him. Even Whitney didn't display that kind of contempt for the men and women he'd enhanced. He respected their skills and considered them worthy adversaries.

Clearly Braden thinks his brain is so much more superior that he hasn't bothered to step up the security here at his laboratory, Wyatt observed.

Braden found a way to give his soldiers more armor, but their speed and their thinking abilities were greatly impaired, Trap answered. *He's probably judging us the same way.*

Go easy, Wyatt, could be an ambush, Ezekiel cautioned again. He paused for a moment. *I got a bad vibe off your woman as well when we went in to secure the house.*

Wyatt sighed, checked the laboratory. It was empty. The entire compound seemed abandoned. Even the civilians and the dog. He pushed open the door and walked boldly in, scanning the dark room. He sighed. *Yeah. I caught that, Zeke. Whitney can definitely find psychics even when they're babies, but he can't tell who is goin' to make a good soldier. She isn' so good at handlin' the killin' part.*

She'll get over it, Trap declared.

No, Trap. She isn' like us, Wyatt contradicted. *She won'. She's goin' to have a difficult time with this one. All of you keep an eye on her.*

She's yours, Ezekiel said. *And ours. She's one of us. We'll watch her.*

They dropped down, one by one, and entered the laboratory.

Somethin's lyin' right out in the open. North side. On the table there, Wyatt said. *It looks like a man.*

He moved quickly between the rows of tables and desks to get to the one where the body lay spread out right on top of smashed beakers. Glass was everywhere, but Whitney had made a statement and it was a big one. Wyatt knew it was Whitney before he took the note off Braden's chest and glanced at the signature.

Four folders sat beside Braden's dead hand. The top one simply said *Pepper* in bold letters.

"He cleared everyone from this place. Any dead he must have had burned in the crematorium. He doesn't like anyone to go against him, and Braden must have branched out on his own." Wyatt frowned down at the paper in his hand, shaking his head.

"Braden died hard," Trap said. "They made certain he lived awhile before they gave him death."

"Whitney likes to make statements," Wyatt said. "He probably sent videos to his other little helpers to warn them what happens when someone messes with him."

"What's the note say?" Trap asked.

Wyatt handed it to him and looked at the others. "He says I owe him."

Ezekiel shook his head. "You don't owe that bastard anything."

Wyatt smiled at him and picked up Pepper's file, flipping it open. Yeah. He'd been right about her parents. They were famous in the field of studying snakes. Both had been killed in India, a break-in at their home. The newspaper articles were included in the file. Missing was their two-year-old daughter.

He closed his eyes. Whitney. He'd taken her. Killed her parents and taken her from a home filled with love straight into a nightmare. Wyatt flipped through his daughters' files. Pepper was definitely their mother, according to the file, and he was their father. They all had been split from the same egg. Whitney had wanted three of them exactly alike.

Pepper's parents had been highly intelligent, and Whitney had chosen her as the girls' mother and Wyatt as the father, hoping for superior intelligence. He had achieved that goal. He wasn't happy with the fact that Pepper demonstrated repeatedly that she didn't follow orders as well as he would have liked. She clashed with Braden and repeatedly refused assignments given to her. He'd ordered Braden to put her in charge of the three girls with the idea they could use the babies to keep her in line.

Whitney's notes were thorough. Everything. Including her training to be a sexual predator, taking her victims down with ease. Wyatt's stomach turned when he read what they'd done to train her. A girl not yet out of her teens with no protection from the men who refused to think of her as human—only as a weapon.

He found himself angry, and then it dissolved and he felt like putting his head down and crying. Around him, his men began the work of going through the laboratory, checking every floor and room for soldiers, but the place was deserted.

He sat and read Pepper's file, his heart aching for her. It disgusted him that Whitney felt no compunction about "sacrificing" her parents for the greater good. They had made the mistake of documenting their daughter's encounter with a cobra and how she seemed to have some kind of natural immunity. That had drawn Whitney's attention immediately. When he'd discovered Pepper's intelligence and her psychic abilities, there was no question in his mind the parents had to go so he could acquire her.

Wyatt pressed his fingers to his eyes. Whitney had coldly killed her parents and taken her, and then began his psychic enhancements of her. Pepper's mother had been a uniquely beautiful woman, and he was certain Pepper would be even more so. From the beginning he had the idea of using her as an assassin.

He turned over the typewritten note Trap had handed to him when the team went to take the bodies down to the crematorium. Whitney had left the keys and the handprints of the men who could open the elevators for his team. He'd thought of everything. Wyatt smoothed the note out and reread it.

Wyatt, you owe me for this. You have the woman and your daughters, although you don't get to keep them. You and Trap come up with the formula I need for our soldiers. Braden couldn't get the job done. He was so blinded by his need of Pepper he couldn't see straight. The fool lost sight of what we were trying to do. Stop

our soldiers from being killed. Give them every advan-
tage. This is a small thing I'm asking in return. I know
the two of you will figure it out. When you do, contact
me at this address.

There was an email address for him to send Whitney
the information.

I get what I want and you get what you want. The girls
I'll need back, but at least you will have spent time
with them while you're working this out. You can keep
the woman. She's useless to me. Pepper was never
going to do what we asked her to do. I'll cut my losses
and leave her alive, leave her to you.

Wyatt stared down at the note, anger roiling in his gut
all over again.

"Wyatt." Trap closed his hand around Wyatt's shoulder.
"He's not going to take your girls from you. None of us
will let that happen." He looked around the laboratory. "He
left behind good equipment. I'll make inquiries and see if
we can pick this place up ourselves. We'll make a fortress
around you. Stockpile weapons. He's not going to take
those children."

Wyatt looked up from the letter, and he tapped Pepper's
file. "I don' want anyone else readin' this, Trap. You have
to because we need to know everything he's done in order to
try to find a way to reverse it, or at least find something to
minimize it."

Trap carefully rolled his hand over Pepper's file. "He's
had years to work on her, developing that biochemical, and
we most likely aren't going to be able to remove it from her
system. You know that."

Wyatt nodded. "We may be able to counteract it, find a
way to give her some relief. I thought maybe pregnancy.

He must have considered that possibility. He wouldn't use her for missions if she was pregnant and he'd want more children from her."

"Maybe. That could happen. It's easy enough to test that theory. Still, Wyatt, her life isn't going to be easy and neither will yours if you keep her."

"I'm way past that, Trap, and you know it. I wake up in the mornin' feelin' alive. I do everythin' I can just to make her laugh. Her smile lights up the room—and my life. She's worth burnin' in hell if that's what I have to do every now and again."

"Then work the hell on that nasty temper of yours and your jealousy. She can't help what she is. They did that crap to her. You need to learn control. Control is the key to everything."

Wyatt found himself smiling. "Yes, Zen master. Your student hears and obeys."

Trap gathered up the files and smacked Wyatt over the head. "Let's get the hell out of here."

CHAPTER 21

***

Pepper held herself very still, looking down at Wyatt's sleeping face. He was beautiful. So beautiful. Everything about him. The home he'd made for their daughters. His grandmother. His sexy body and cocky grin. The rough way he dragged her to him, the tenderness in his eyes after sex, or when her mouth was on him. She loved that look, the way he watched her as she pleasured him. She loved the way he wanted to see her face when he gave her multiple orgasms and the way he wanted her to say his name. She just plain loved him.

The terrible weight that had been stomping on her chest ever since she'd killed the soldier using what she was, what they'd created in her, threatened to crush her. She had known the moment she'd first laid eyes on Wyatt, out there, in the swamp, when she should have been running for her life away from the compound with Ginger—when she should have been taking care of Ginger. She'd turned back and watched him casually beat the crap out of the guard. He'd looked beautiful then too, an avenging angel.

He'd walked into his grandmother's parlor, knowing she wasn't alone. He didn't care. He wasn't afraid, and he refused to back down. Pepper had known then. She'd known he was someone special. Someone who deserved far better than she could ever be.

She'd tried to be that woman for him, but as far back as she could remember, she'd been groomed for one thing—to tempt men. To lure them. It was in the way she walked. In the turn of her head. The sound of her voice. She couldn't stop those years of practice. She'd been taught to use sex as a weapon. She hadn't known sex could be something special or beautiful between a man and woman. Wyatt had taught her that.

Braden—or Whitney—had forced her body into a terrible, clawing, endless cycle of pure need. Her body turned on her. She worked hard to shield the others, but sometimes she just couldn't do it. Sometimes the clawing need and the burn between her legs was pure hell. Nothing helped but Wyatt. Only Wyatt.

She hated that he was affected by the vicious, unending cycle. It would never get better. He thought he could handle it, but when the months and the years went by, when he was angry with his friends and with hers, when jealousy got the best of him, he would feel different. He deserved better.

She knew the difference now. She knew women weren't trained from their teenage years to be sexual weapons. She remembered the men they'd brought in to instruct her. Her face burned. She'd hated it and then had begun to accept it as normal. It wasn't normal, and she would never be.

And then they had added the venom so she could lure her victim and then dispose of him. He would die, just as the soldier had died, looking at her as if she was the most beautiful, perfect woman in the world.

A sob tore up her chest and lodged in her throat. She hadn't told Wyatt what she'd done. She couldn't tell him.

She'd forced that soldier into a state of need, of addiction and made him think he loved her above all else. She didn't want Wyatt to know the worst of her. She couldn't bear it if he knew the worst of her. She couldn't bear it if he looked at her with disgust—which eventually would happen. She couldn't bear it if he walked out on her. All he saw that night was her saving them from certain death. He hadn't cared how. But he didn't see the soldier's face like she did.

She'd never known happiness. She didn't even know such a thing existed. Or families. But she could give those things to her daughters by leaving. They would never have to be ashamed of their mother and her highly sexual nature. They would never have to learn to kill with an intimate bite that was meant for love, not death.

She couldn't breathe. No air found its way into her lungs no matter how hard she tried to drag it in. She truly was afraid she might vomit, her stomach roiling and churning, knots so hard she wasn't certain she could ever get them loose again. Her chest was the worst. A horrible, heavy weight pressing and pressing until she was certain her heart would implode from the sheer pressure.

She had to get out of there. Now. That minute. She couldn't stay another second or she would break down completely and lose her nerve. He didn't deserve that either. She turned away from the bed and lifted the small bag she'd packed. She'd kept it under the bed in preparation for him falling asleep. She hadn't taken much. She didn't need much.

She had nowhere to go. No skills. No paperwork. She was nothing. She wouldn't allow Wyatt Fontenot to tie himself to nothing—to trouble that would eventually get him or someone else killed. She loved him too much for that. She loved her daughters and Nonny too much for that.

A hand slapped hard around her wrist, tightening like a vise, yanking her back to the edge of the bed. "Just where the fuck do you think you're goin'?"

She closed her eyes at the pure rage in his voice. She did

that to him a lot. There was no way to explain this to him, no way that wouldn't put him in a position of having to try to talk her out of it.

She refused to turn around and look into his eyes. She couldn't. "Let go, Wyatt. I don't want to have to fight you, but I will. Just let go."

"Fight me?" A hint of amusement slid through the rage. "You think you're capable of winnin' a physical fight with me, babe?"

He yanked her hard, and she sprawled across the bed. Sprawled on top of him. Her gaze jumped to his face, to the eyes she knew better than to look into. There was no amusement there whatsoever. He was furious.

"Wyatt, I'm leaving. I can't do this. There's nothing more to say." She fought to keep her voice low. Controlled. Firm.

She still couldn't breathe, her lungs burning for air. Her chest felt like it might explode. Fear skittered down her spine and the terrible knots in her belly rose to her chest to add to the weight threatening to crush her.

"You're not leavin' me, Pepper."

She actually saw the glitter of the cat as the dominant male rose in him. The need to meet every challenge. She wasn't trying to challenge him, she was trying to save him. She couldn't stand this. Couldn't do this. She was such a coward to try to run in the middle of the night from him, but she knew this would happen. Knew he would fight her, and she couldn't bear that either.

It hurt. It hurt to breathe, to think. She tried getting her wrist back, dropping the bag and using her other hand to try to pry his fingers loose.

"Wyatt, stop it. Let go of me."

"No."

Just like that. No. That was Wyatt.

"*Mon Dieu*, Wyatt, just let go. I have to leave. We both know it. Stop acting like you don't. It just makes it worse."

It burst out of her. Unexpected. Frightening in that she couldn't contain it.

He went still. His eyes changed. His entire demeanor. The anger slipped, but his grip on her wrist didn't. "You're stayin' right here, Pepper, and we're goin' to figure out just what's wrong and fix it."

Something inside her, the terrible, frightening, *explosive* knot in her chest expanded and contracted, radiating such pain she thought her heart might have actually burst. There was no containment. No way to stop the volcano from erupting. She felt it rising like a tide, a mad insanity she couldn't escape.

"Wyatt. *Mon Dieu!*" She scraped one hand through her hair. "How can you not see I have to do this for you. To protect you. You won't protect yourself. What's wrong with you that you don't see someone has to protect both you and the girls from me? From what I am? You're such a good man. Clean and decent. You have a family who loves you. You came from that, Wyatt. I don't even have a last name. I can't unmake what I am. No matter what I do, I'll always be this."

She swept her hand down her body, tears spilling, lungs burning, throat raw. "What I do is so vile, so disgusting, entrapping men with sex and then killing them. Watching them adore me as the life goes out of them. I won't have that for you. Or the girls. I have to leave. I *have* to."

She couldn't stand it one more second; she began to fight, swinging at him, trying to break his unbreakable grip. He rolled fast, forcing her onto her back, and he was over her in an instant, his thigh coming down over the top of hers, pinning her while his hands caught both her wrists, stretching her arms above her head and pinning them to the mattress. She thrashed, trying to dislodge him, desperation setting in.

"Wyatt. Please. You aren't thinking this through."

"Stop fighting." His voice went soft. Smoky. Drawling. A sexy Cajun drawl.

She felt the heat of his body and tried to buck him off of her. She was strong, but not in comparison to him. And she would never, ever hurt him. Never use venom to escape. He seemed immune to the biochemical spilling from her body, so she couldn't even use that weapon against him.

"Baby, focus here. Look at me." He waited until her gaze reluctantly met his. "Even if you got loose, which you won't, did you think I wouldn' recognize the signs of my woman sayin' good-bye when we have sex? A man like me knows his woman. I know how you breathe when you come for me, how your eyes change, that dazed, sweet look of confusion and bliss. I gave the boys the heads-up and told them to stop you if you managed to slip away from me."

Wyatt lifted his head, and something in his eyes made her shiver. "That's not goin' to happen. I'm not givin' you up, so lie still and let's talk this out."

She shook her head, the crushing weight in her chest settling over her heart. "You aren't thinking straight, Wyatt. You're a rescuer. You think I need to be rescued. When there's no let up, you'll see I'm right. This won't work. Do you really think I can get pregnant every single time you leave? That's the solution? Years will go by and something terrible will happen because this isn't going to stop."

She was pleading with him. She'd worked up the courage to leave, but she was leaving behind every single thing that was good. Everything that meant anything to her. She knew it was a form of suicide; once she was away from him, from the children and Nonny, she'd be dead inside. But this was Wyatt and her children and she was—unclean.

"First, babe, we're workin' on the problem, and there are birth control pills that simulate pregnancy. If that works, it's an easy solution. If not, we'll come up with an answer. And second, more importantly, you did what you needed to do to save Malichai. To save me. To save Nonny. Braden's soldiers weren't particularly fast, but they didn't have many vulnerable spots on them. They weren't smart, but they kept comin'. You did what you had to do, Pepper."

"You didn't see their faces, Wyatt. You didn't see what I did to them. Just skin-to-skin contact. Mouth to mouth." She said it deliberately to rile him.

Wyatt didn't even wince when she told him. He didn't even blink, nor did his eyes move from hers. "That was combat, baby. You weren't doin' anythin' wrong. I'm not upset with you. I know that hurt to look at them, it *should* hurt. When it doesn', that's when we know we're in trouble."

Wyatt watched her face. Her eyes. She was breaking his heart. She thought so little of herself. She didn't see her own courage. She had known when she'd taken that soldier out what it was going to cost her and she'd done it anyway. For him. The girls. Nonny. Malichai. Hell, for the entire team.

"I know what you had to do, babe, but you did it for us. To save us. That's what people who love one another do. They save each other by any means available to them. You weren' goin' to bring that soldier down with a bullet or a knife, not and keep him from sprayin' the operatin' room with bullets. I didn' have an assistant other than Nonny and I was havin' a hell of a time keepin' Malichai alive. Without you, all of us would have been dead."

She shook her head, looking so sad his heart stuttered in his chest. He held her there, the strong column of his thigh pinning her down while he blanketed her body with his own. He was careful not to crush her, but he took no chances. She was well trained and skilled in hand-to-hand combat. She just didn't want to hurt him.

"Talk to me, sugar." He bent his head and pressed a kiss to her throat. "You have to talk this out with me. We have an agreement and I'm holdin' you to it."

She ran her fingers through his hair. Gently. Lovingly. He felt love for her, rising like a tide deep inside of him. She had no clue, and he only had words and his body to show her what she meant to him. He didn't blame her that she didn't trust that he knew for certain what he wanted. She'd had so little time with him.

He brushed his mouth down her throat to her sternum, pressed more kisses there. One hand slid up to her blouse with those little buttons he liked so much. Her hand caught at his as he slid them open.

"Wyatt, think about this. Think with your brain. You're so smart. You know how this is going to end."

"It's goin' to end with you underneath me and my cock inside of you. That's how it's goin' to end, baby. But I want to hear everythin' you've got to say so I can put those fears to rest. I just prefer you sayin' it when you have no clothes on." He slid three more buttons free before her hands stopped him. He settled his mouth on her skin, his tongue sliding down to taste the sweet curve of the tops of her breasts.

"Wyatt, why can't you just let me go? You're making this so hard for me."

"Babe." He swept aside the last of the buttons and pulled her blouse open. "You're wearin' my favorite bra." He bent his head to her right breast and sucked at her nipple through the fine lace. She gasped. Her body trembled beneath his.

He lifted his head and smiled at her. "I'm never goin' to make it easy for you to leave me. If I have to keep you tied to my bed, then that's what I'm goin' to do. The thing is, Pepper, I love you the way you are. You think you're flawed, but I know you're perfect for me. We fit. We're supposed to be together."

"It was *wrong*. What I did to that soldier was wrong," she burst out. "An abomination of what this is."

The tears and guilt in her voice wrenched at his heart. He kept his gaze steady on hers. "What we have between us is love, Pepper. There's no way that what you did can fuck that up. This is love. When I'm kissin' you. When I've got my mouth or my cock between your legs. That's love. That's me showin' you love. I'm lovin' you right now, sugar, keepin' you from doin' anythin' stupid because your heart is so big, you're thinkin' of everyone but yourself."

"Wyatt . . ."

He took her mouth. Gently. Tenderly. Because he'd read her file and he knew there was no gentleness or tenderness *ever* in her life. His hands brushed away lace and silk and settled over her breasts. He kissed her over and over, not giving her a chance to breathe. To protest. To do anything but hang on to him. He knew how to kiss, and this was his woman. He used his skills shamelessly.

She tasted like heaven to him. He wanted her to know that. He lifted his head and looked down into her eyes. Her beautiful, unusual eyes a man could get lost in forever.

"The thin' is baby, you have to understand, I wasn' alive until you came into my life. I went through the motions, but I didn' feel the things I was supposed to. I saw you there in the parlor, your hair all over the place, your eyes wild, almost feral. The mother in you watchin' over that baby. And then you did the one thing that sealed your fate. You threw yourself in between me and that child. You took her bite. You knew there was a tremendous risk, and you knew how sick you were goin' to be, but you still did it."

He brushed at the tears on her face with his thumbs, leaned down to sip and then lick one away. "You were never meant to be a soldier, babe. That's not in your makeup. You protect people. You nurture. You weren' trained for it, but that's what's inside of you. That's why it hurts so bad when you have to take a life."

His hand slid between their bodies and he dragged down the zipper of her jeans. "Whitney knew it, that's why he sent you to the children. You're not flawed, woman, you don' want to kill people. That's a good thin'."

His hand slipped inside her jeans to the sweet French-cut

lace panties he'd chosen himself. He curled his fingers into her, found damp heat, just as he knew he would. His mouth found her left breast as he pressed deep inside her.

Her body moved under his. Not to fight this time. Melted, just like she did whenever he touched her. He lifted his head again. "Tonight, after I make love to you, baby, I'm goin' to fall asleep with my cock buried deep inside you. You lyin' on top of me. I want you that close." It was his favorite way to go to sleep. He'd done it several times, her on top of him like a blanket, him buried inside her. He loved that.

Her fingers stroked through his hair as she took a deep, shuddering breath. "You're sure, Wyatt? Because it will break me if I stay and then somewhere down the line you won't be able to look at me anymore because of what I am."

"I've never been more certain of anything in my life. I was born for you. I was born to keep you safe. To love and protect you. To keep your body from burnin' you up from the inside out. That was why I was born, baby, no other reason. I intend to do my job."

His tongue licked at the nipple of her right breast. His teeth scraped gently, a little rough, just the way she liked it. She arched her back and a moan escaped.

"You're seducing me again and it isn't fair. Not just your mouth and hands, but your words as well," she accused.

"I don' play fair, sugar. You have to know that by now. And Whitney's goin' to come for our children. He actually had the balls to tell me that in his note to me. He's lettin' me borrow them. We need you. All of us."

He turned his attention to her other breast, waited until she was panting and squirming, before he lifted his head again.

"You've got too many clothes on, honey. Let's get them off of you. Shoes first, although I like those boots on you. But we need to go to bed."

He shifted his weight, keeping his arm around her

waist, still leery that she might try to run. She sat up grace-fully and bent to reach for her boots. He couldn't help him-self. He pulled the clip from her hair and tossed it across the room. His hands came up to cover her breasts.

"We're already workin' on turnin' this entire area into a fortress."

"If he's as wealthy as you say he is and has friends in high places . . ."

"So do we. The thing is, honey, we don' have to worry about money all that much. I'm not even talkin' about the money Trap will donate to the cause. I work with Trap all the time. I've been doin' it for years. We didn' meet up in the teams, we met in college. He was wicked smart. I mean I'm smart, but he's fuckin' off the charts. He's been comin' up with solutions to problems for years and he was smart enough to patent everythin' and either develop it himself or sell it to a company for big bucks. I started helpin' him in college. That means my name is on those patents and half the money goes to me. Later, when we worked with Joe, Zeke and the others, we offered them shares in what-ever we were workin' on."

He skimmed his hand down her body, her rib cage and belly, feeling the helpless shiver run through her. He lifted her hair and swung it around to the front over her left shoulder so he could kiss the nape of her neck.

"Lift up, honey. Slide your jeans and panties off." He whispered the command in her ear, kissing that too. "You're so beautiful. Everythin' about you is beautiful to me."

She did what he said and that was beautiful to him too. She rarely got upset at his personality. She smiled at him sometimes with a look that said maybe he was skating the boundaries, but she rarely complained, and never in bed. In bed she always accommodated anything he wanted. Once, when he'd talked to her, asked her if there was any-thing she wanted different, she just smiled, shook her head and told him she trusted him to take care of her.

That had meant the world to him. She trusted him when she had no good reason to trust anyone.

"Crawl up on the bed, babe, on all fours. I want to be in you so deep you feel me in your throat. And don' ever do this again. I mean it, Pepper." He smoothed his hand over her hip. He loved her ass. The shape of it. The way she swayed when she walked. "The next time I might just put you bare-ass naked over my knee and whale on you."

She turned in his arms, sliding her hands up his chest and then her mouth was on him. She poured fire and honey down his throat. Into his belly. Into his groin. Filling him with her. His cock was so full for her, so drunk on her, he feared he wouldn't last long once he was inside her furnace.

When she lifted her head, her eyes searched his. For the first time since the soldiers had attacked them, he could see the beginning of amusement there.

"Why is it I hear that note in your voice, Wyatt? The one that tells me you like the idea of me over your knee."

She crawled up on the bed, straight to the center.

"Widen your legs, baby, you know what I like." He kissed the small of her back and then wrapped his hand around the nape of her neck, pushing her head down to the mattress so her bottom was up even higher. His hand reached between her legs, stroking and caressing, making certain she was ready for him.

"I'd better like the idea. You'd better like it as well. I have the feelin' you're goin' to be there a lot over the next few years. But babe, if you are across my knee bare-assed naked, it had better not be for tryin' to run off on me." He let a warning growl into his voice, meaning it.

"I won't do it again," she said in a low voice.

He plunged two fingers deep and she cried out. "You told me that before. You said you'd come to me, talk first." He smacked her bottom, once, twice, and felt the answering heat surrounding his fingers.

"You feel that, Pepper? All that heat running right

where you need it? Scorchin' hot. You'll like it when you need to. I'll make certain of that."

"I won't do it again, Wyatt," she repeated, her voice shaking. "Please. I need you inside me."

He pushed his fingers deeper, drew them out and licked at the honey there, that secret, wonderful taste he never wanted another man to know. "No, you won', honey, because I'm not goin' to be so nice the next time. We've had this conversation before. You get scared, you come talk to me. I know you don' have that experience, but you know me now. You know I'm goin' to listen and then we're goin' to take care of the problem."

Her breathing had changed. Ragged little gasps were interspersed with those beautiful little sounds she made in the back of her throat.

"Tell me you understand that, Pepper. You understand you need to talk to me." He knelt up behind her. Close. He pressed the tip of his throbbing erection into her hot furnace. It took his breath away, but he refused to let her see it.

She pressed back into him. So hot. So needy. She never held anything back. She always wanted him. She would always want him. It would never matter the time of day, or what was going on around them, she would want his body just the way he wanted hers.

He rubbed her bottom. "So beautiful, baby. You're just so damned beautiful."

"Wyatt." Her voice was demanding now.

"I'm waitin' on you," he pointed out.

The breath hissed out of her. She turned her head and looked at him over her shoulder. "I understand and I'll talk to you, but not now."

"So demandin'." He took her hard. He took her fast, and he went so deep he might have actually made it to her throat. His hands settled around her hips and he pounded into her, telling her in no uncertain terms how much she meant to him. Telling her without words, knowing if there was one woman in the world who got it, it would be her. Still, she needed the words. His woman deserved them.

I'm in love with you, Pepper. I always will be.

She was there. In his mind. Filling him with her, just as he filled her body with him. He was damned glad he'd done a stupid thing and followed his brother into Whitney's demented program. And maybe, whether he liked it or not, he owed Whitney in a weird, roundabout way. None of it mattered to him except his woman and the fierce way she loved him back.

Keep reading for an excerpt from
the next Leopard novel
by Christine Feehan

CAT'S
LAIR

Available May 2015
from Jove Books

Catarina Benoit woke to screams. Terrible, frightening screams that echoed through her bedroom. Her heart pounded and sweat beaded on her body. Her long hair hung around her face in damp strands. She clapped a hand over her mouth to still the cries, her throat raw even as her eyes darted around the room. Searching. Always searching.

She searched the high places first—anywhere he could be crouched. Watching. Waiting to strike. She searched the windows. The glass was covered with bars, but she knew that wouldn't stop him if he found her. *Nothing* ever stopped him. He could get inside any house, any building. Anywhere. Rafe Cordeau, the thing of nightmares.

She was safe. She had to be. She lived completely off the grid. Underground. She only came out at night. Her one exception to her night rule was her hour of running just before sunset. She worked in a quiet part of town, in a store no one would ever consider she would work in. Rafe would never figure it out, not in a million years. He couldn't find her this time. She'd planned too carefully. She'd even stolen enough money to get herself a start. Right out of his safe. The one no one could crack. She'd done that. He wasn't going to get his hands on her again. Never again.

She fell back against the pillows, drawing her knees into her chest, making herself into a small, protected ball, rocking gently to try to calm herself, to push the terror of the nightmare away. She could taste bile in her mouth.

Drawing in great, deep breaths to try to control her wild heart, she felt something else, something inside unfurl and stretch. It terrified her too. There was something in her, biding its time, waiting for a chance to get out, and she feared it was a monster. She feared *he'd* put it there, he'd somehow made her like him.

She knew she wouldn't go back to sleep. Every window was covered with heavy drapes to block out the sun, but still, she would never be able to go back to sleep. She forced her legs to straighten. That hurt. Every muscle was sore from the terrible coiling in her body. She knew from experience it would be like that all day, her body feeling as if someone had beaten her up with a baseball bat.

She sat up and scooted to the side of the bed, first, as she always did, feeling for the gun hidden beneath her pillow. The solid weight of it always made her feel better. She worked out, trained hard, even when she knew she still wouldn't have a chance against him if he found her. Even so, she lived her life. Held herself still. Kept to herself. Reduced his odds.

She took a shower in the small cubicle. It was a rigged hose with a spray nozzle over the top of a tiny booth with a drain. It didn't matter. She was safe. She lived in a warehouse and not in her car. Mostly the warehouse was empty, but her martial arts instructor owned the property and he'd allowed her to rent the space when he realized she was living out of her car. He had barred the windows for her. She had put in the double locks herself.

She had done everything necessary to make herself safe, but then she'd made a vow. She would be happy every single second she was living free and alive. She wouldn't hide in the warehouse, shut away from the world; she would *live*. She'd be smart and careful about it, but this time she wouldn't be a mouse hiding. It hadn't done her much good the last time, and she'd wasted that little bit of freedom she'd had. The price definitely hadn't been worth it then. She was going to make certain it was this time.

Catarina pressed her fingers hard against her temples, unwilling to revisit the moment when he'd last found her and his terrible punishment. Her entire body shuddered. She'd paid dearly, but that had only made her all the more determined to escape permanently. She'd been terrified, and he thought that terror would work to his advantage. She let him think that and then she'd escaped again.

Her life had really started with her martial arts instructor. Malcom Hardy was in his late sixties, and from the moment she'd entered his class, he'd seemed to know something was wrong. He didn't exactly ask questions, but somehow he found out she was living out of her car and he casually mentioned his empty warehouse. That had been the start of their strange friendship.

Catarina had never had a friendship with anyone before, and at first she was distrustful of his motives. It had taken Malcom months to gain her trust enough that she stayed and had a few words privately with him after each class. She hadn't told him her past, only that she was looking for a job and needed a safe home. She'd used the word *safe* in the hope that he would understand without an explanation— and he had.

When she'd escaped, she hadn't taken tons of money from the safe because she didn't want Rafe to have more reason to come after her if by chance he'd given up on her. That meant she didn't have a lot of money. It also meant that if he had given up on her, he'd send his kill squad after her. Either way she wasn't safe and she needed to be very careful with her money.

Malcom slowly won her over with his many simple kindnesses. He casually dropped by to put the bars on the windows when she'd mentioned she was a little nervous. He'd also been the one to find her the job after she told him what her dream job would be.

Catarina loved her job. The coffee-house-slash-bookstore was old, the kind where poets and writers came and read their work every Friday. It was a throwback world that suited her. Books were everywhere, and people gathered to talk and read and show off their work. She liked that the place was a tribute to a bygone era and the regulars who occupied it were loyal and definitely different.

She made certain never to stand out. She dressed in loose-fitting jeans. A loose-fitting shirt. Her hair had always grown thick and fast and got worse the more she cut it. She'd given up on short hair, so she pulled it back in a ponytail or braid and often wore hats. Since everyone who came to the coffee-house wore berets or felt hats, she wasn't out of place. Most wore sunglasses, even at night as well, so she did that too, hiding her unusually colored cobalt eyes.

The coffee-house stayed open nearly twenty-four hours, and she had the shift that ran from seven in the evening until three in the morning, when she closed the shop. They got a large influx of people looking to wind down from drinking, dancing and clubbing at the bars that closed at two. She wasn't fond of that particular crowd, but she'd grown used to it.

She spent an hour on working the heavy bag Malcom had hung for her and another hour doing sit-ups and crunches and push-ups. She dressed in baggy sweats and went running. That killed another hour and put her to sunset. Another shower and she headed for the coffee-house.

She tried hard not to allow her heart to do a little stutter, wondering if the new instructor Malcom had hired would drop by again. She liked looking at him. He was a bonus at the dojo as well as the coffee-house. She'd never found herself looking at a man before—she'd never dared to. But he was special. Everything about him was special.

He'd been at the dojo a month and she'd watched him with the same distrust she had for anyone new who came into her world. He was absolutely the most beautiful man she'd ever seen in her life. He was brutal when he fought, and yet at the same time, graceful and fluid. Sheer poetry. He was light on his feet, very fast, so smooth. He was always, always utterly calm. She couldn't imagine him ruffled over anything. He embodied the world of martial arts—he lived that way, not just in the dojo but out of it.

Still, she kept her distance, even when he'd noticed her in the dojo and smiled at her a time or two. She didn't smile back. She didn't encourage any kind of a relationship, nor did she want one. Not because she didn't ever talk to people, but because he made her feel something she'd never felt before. But she liked looking at him. Maybe a little too much.

She didn't have flights of erotic fantasy or dreams. Her body had never awakened, on fire, burning with need and hunger. Her breasts hadn't felt swollen and achy, desperate for a man's touch. Not until she laid eyes on Malcom's new instructor. Something moved in her. Something took over and unexpectedly, at night, when she wasn't having nightmares, she had erotic dreams that burned through her body until she couldn't breathe. Abruptly they'd leave her, and once they were gone, her body would settle and she'd be perfectly fine again. He was definitely someone she needed to stay away from, but looking at him was acceptable.

He'd sauntered into the coffee-house two weeks after starting with Malcom. She'd noticed him immediately. How could she not? When he moved, the roped muscles of his body, even beneath his tight black shirt, did a delicious kind of rippling that drew every feminine eye in the place. Ridley Cromer. The name was as strange and unique as the man.

Catarina stood outside the coffee-house just staring into

the windows, feeling happy. She always made certain she acknowledged being happy. That was important. She woke up in the morning and always, *always* told herself she would be happy that day.

"Hey, beautiful."

She froze, the smile fading. The other thing strange about Ridley Cromer was the fact that she never heard him when he came near her. He didn't make a sound. She heard everyone. She always knew when someone was close to her. The reason why she excelled in martial arts was because she always anticipated her opponent's move. It was as if she had a kind of radar telling her where everyone was at all times within her space. Everyone but Ridley Cromer.

She turned her head, holding her breath, her smile fading. Her eyes met Ridley's and the impact was so strong the air rushed from her lungs as if she'd been punched. He had beautiful eyes. Intense. The way he looked at her was intense. Everything about him was intense. And zen. Very zen.

She forced herself to nod out of politeness. She knew if she tried to speak she would squeak like a mouse and nothing else would emerge. Ridley Cromer was fine to look at. Daydream about. Even have night fantasies over, but there was no talking. No interaction. Not ever. If all the rest of the world of women were smart, they'd adopt her steadfast rules with him.

"You working tonight or just looking for company?"

His voice was low and sexy. Her pulse beat hard in her throat. She swallowed hard. She'd never had a crush on anyone in her life, but he was standing right in front of her. Towering over her. His eyes smiled and his white teeth flashed. He should be locked up to preserve all women's virtues.

She shook her head and reached for the door handle. He reached at the same time, his hand settling around hers as she grasped the knob. A shiver of absolute awareness slid down her spine. Curled in her belly. There was a sudden tingle in her breasts, and she felt heat gathering in her very core. Not like her night fantasies, where her body burned up, but still . . .

He didn't let go of her hand, and she couldn't remove hers from the doorknob. His touch was light. Gentle. She should have pulled her hand way but she was frozen to the spot. He stepped closer, so close she could feel the heat of his body seeping into hers. He was hot. He radiated heat. His breath was warm on the nape of her neck, and for the first time she wished she'd left her hair down to protect herself.

"It's Cat, right? Malcom calls you Cat. You're his favorite student. I've never known him to have a favorite. I'm Ridley Cromer."

She closed her eyes briefly. Thunder roared in her ears. Her brain short-circuited. His voice was pitched so low that it seemed to slide beneath her skin and find its way directly into her bloodstream like some strange new drug. No one touched her. No one dared. He had broken that taboo. She didn't know how to feel about it.

"You're quick. Very fast," he went on, as if she wasn't the rudest person in the world for not answering him. "I couldn't help but watch you sparring the other day. You were wiping up the floor with men ranked much higher than you. Men with a lot more experience. It was a thing of beauty."

A thing of beauty. She would hold that close to her and think about it when she was alone. A compliment. Coming from someone who clearly could best anyone in the dojo, probably including Malcom, it was very high praise. Still, she couldn't stand there being an absolute idiot.

She finally found her wits and gave the doorknob a desperate twist, flashing what she hoped was a careless smile of thanks over her shoulder at him. She yanked open the door, but found when she stepped back she stepped right into him. *Right* into him.

His body was as hard as a rock. It was rather like smashing herself against an oak tree. His arms came around her automatically to steady her. The heat radiating from him nearly burned right through her clothes.

To her absolute horror, she banged the door closed again as she threw herself forward and away from him. She nearly ran into the heavy glass, but his hands were suddenly at her waist, gently moving her away from the door.

One moment she was heading for danger, the next he had literally lifted her and put her a foot away from the door.

"Kitten, you'd better let me get that."

Color rushed up her neck into her face. To her everlasting mortification, she could hear male amusement in his voice. She was an idiot—a tongue-tied idiot—and he'd think she was crazy. Still—she gulped air—that was for the best. He'd just dismiss her, hopefully never look at her again. Not with those eyes. Those beautiful, antique gold eyes. Who had eyes that color?

He pulled the door open and held it, waiting for her to go through. Thankfully she found her legs and moved past him, once again throwing a small, hopefully thankful smile at him over her shoulder. She walked stiffly to the counter and shoved her things beneath it on the other side.

She was absolutely certain someone needed her to file away books in the back where no one could see her. Someone else could make the coffee tonight and she'd just go hide.

"Cat, great, you're here." David Belmont, the owner of Poetry Slam, threw her an apron. "Get to it, hon. Everyone's been complaining because apparently my coffee doesn't taste like yours. I've watched you a million times and I do exactly the same thing, but it never comes out like yours."

"You don't like making coffee, David," Catarina replied and put on her apron. Which she found hilarious because he owned the coffee-house.

The moment she was behind the coffee machine, David moved into position to take orders and money. Clearly there he was in his element, chatting up the customers, remembering their names, talking them into some of the bakery goods sold with the coffee. He even remembered the poetry or short stories they wrote. He was awesome with the customers, and she was awesome with the coffee. They made a great team.

She didn't look up when anyone ordered. It was part of her strategy to keep in the background. The mouse in the coffee-house. Unfortunately, because she was *great* at making any type of coffee drink, the customers were aware of her. She was the reigning barista, and the customers had begun to fill the coffee-house nightly.

She had worked hard to learn what she needed to in secret. She read, watched countless videos and committed coffee books to memory. Before that, she'd had to learn to read. She was a little smug about it. Rafe would never, ever think to find her in a bookstore/coffee-house. *Never.* She was poor little illiterate Catarina.

She kept her eyes on the espresso machine when she heard Ridley give his order in a soft, low tone that set a million butterflies winging in her stomach. She already knew exactly what he wanted, just as she did with most of the regulars. He hadn't been coming in all that long, but she was aware of every breath he took—just as the other women were. She certainly remembered what he liked for coffee.

She knew exactly where he sat without looking up. He always pulled out a book, usually on meditation or essays from a zen master, while he drank his coffee. He savored coffee. She'd watched him, sneaking looks, of course, and he always had the same expression on his face. She knew she put it there. She might not be a conversationalist, but she made spectacular coffee.

She forced herself to make fifteen more coffees before she looked up. Her gaze collided with his. All that beautiful, perfect, molten gold. She almost fell right into his eyes. She blushed. She knew she did. There was no stopping the color rising into her cheeks. He gave her a faint, sexy smile. She looked down without smiling back, concentrating on her work.

One look and her stomach did a crazy roll. What was wrong with her? She didn't have physical reactions to men. It was just not okay. She couldn't ever be stupid enough to wish for a relationship. She'd get someone killed that way. In any case, she'd be too afraid. She didn't even know what a relationship was.

But he was darned good to look at, she acknowledged with a secret smile. *Darned* good. The familiar rhythm of the coffeehouse settled her nerves. The aroma of coffee and fresh-baked goods swept her up into the easy atmosphere. Once the poetry slam started, darkness descended. There was usually little joy in the poems, but she enjoyed them all the same.

Bernard Casey, a regular who was usually first up at the microphone, accepted his caramel macchiato from David, took one sip, and pushed his head over the counter the way he did each evening.

"Hey, coffee woman. Heaven again."

She shot him a smile. It was safe to smile at Bernard. He loved coffee, his poems and little else. "Hey, coffee man, glad you think so." He only looked at her once a day and that was when he gave her the nightly compliment.

It was their standard greeting. Bernard waved and settled at his usual table right in front of the microphone, making certain he would be the first and last poet of the night.

Ridley observed Catarina over the top of the book he no longer had any interest in. She was beautiful and she was scared. Very scared. She thought she'd managed to downplay her looks, but a man would have to be blind not to see through her baggy clothes and attempts to tame her wild hair.

Her sunglasses didn't hide the perfection of her skin, and when she took them off and looked at a man with her exotic cobalt blue eyes, the color a deep intense violet at times, ringed with those long dark lashes . . . well, the punch was low and it was just plain sinful.

And then there was her mouth. Full lips like a cupid's bow. Turned up at the corners just slightly. Her lower lip could make a man go to his knees and fill his nights with erotic fantasies. When her lips parted and she gave a small, distracted smile, the one that meant she wasn't seeing you, any man worth his salt couldn't help but take on that challenge. When she smiled, like she'd just done to Bernard, the strange poet who poured out his feelings for her through his poems, Ridley knew a man would kill for her.

She was nothing at all like he expected her to be. He watched her at the dojo with Malcom during her lessons and training sessions. She was focused. Intelligent, which, when fighting, was important. She was quick, her reflexes good, and she moved with a fluid grace that took his breath away. He wasn't the only man in the dojo who stopped what he was doing to watch.

He expected her to be a man-killer. She should have been. She had the face and the body. She had the voice. She had a soft drawl, barely there, the kind of drawl that reminded him of drifting down the bayou on a lazy summer night with the sky above him dark and a thousand stars shining overhead and a woman naked in his arms.

She should have had all the confidence in the world. She had confidence when she sparred with any man Malcom put her against, and so far she'd wiped up the floor with them no matter their rank. She was that fast. She had confidence behind the espresso machines and she had every reason to. She had confidence when she walked home at three o'clock in the morning and she shouldn't.

But she didn't look at men. She didn't talk to them. There was no flirting. He'd never seen her flirt with anyone. Not a man or a woman. She was definitely a puzzle, and one he wanted to solve.

He'd deliberately stepped up close to her, crowded her space, to see what she'd do. She hadn't defended herself. She hadn't told him to get the hell away from her. She froze. Breathless. Terrified. She'd confused the hell out of him, and that didn't happen very often. She'd intrigued him, and that happened even less often. She'd also done something insane to his body.

He was a man always in control. Always. Control defined him. He was a man and he lived his life as a man. He was tough and liked things his way, and he always got what he wanted. He was single-minded that way. Women, especially man-killers, didn't do a thing for him. But Catarina . . . The moment her soft body had come up against his, the moment he'd touched bare skin, everything hot and wild and hungry in him responded. He wanted her. And he wanted her for himself. Exclusively. That had *never* happened before.

He looked down at his arms, at the tattoos he'd acquired so painstakingly over the years. He looked rough and mean. He knew that. It served him well to look that way. He deliberately wore his hair longer than most. He served notice to other men just who he was and what he was capable of. Men got the hell out of his way when he was after something. Especially a woman.

Women were easy for him. He didn't have to work hard at all and that was okay, but it never lasted more than a night or two—not for him anyway. But this woman . . . She'd burn up in his arms, and it wouldn't be enough. He got that already just by looking at her. So did every other man who came near her. The difference was, most of them would step back and wait for a signal that was never going to come. That was definitely not the way to handle a woman like Catarina. A man had to take over and be decisive about it.

Catarina felt the weight of Ridley's gaze on her. She knew he was watching her without even looking up. Her body responded just as if he were standing in front of her. For one moment she felt restless, achy, in need even. That something wild crouched inside of her stretched. Her skin itched. She couldn't breathe and her skull felt too tight. For one terrible moment, her skin went hot and that terrible burn began between her legs. She could barely breathe with the need and hunger.

Horrified, she dragged off the apron and tossed it to David. "I need a break, just a short one."

Even here in her sanctuary, the one place she could go and be around others, her past tried hard to drag her down. She was aware of Ridley's attention settling on her instantly, alertly, but she didn't so much as glance at him. Her past was too close. Even from a thousand miles away, *he* was controlling her. She couldn't look at another man without something inside of her turning ugly.

The book aisles were narrow, the stacks rising from floor to ceiling. She wound her way through them to the back door and pushed it open. The night air hit her face, cool and refreshing, enfolding her in its blanket of darkness. She drew in several deep breaths and stepped outside. The cool air felt good on her skin. She dragged the hat from her hair and sank down onto the steps leading to the back door.

Strangely, she'd always had great night vision, and this past month she'd noticed it had gotten even better. She liked that she could see in the dark. She loved the night. There was an entirely different world going on at night and she was part of it. That made her part of something. And Rafe couldn't take that away from her.

"Kitten?"

She had to stifle a scream as she twisted, nearly throwing herself off the stairs. Ridley stood behind her, in the doorway, his tall body solid, both terrifying and safe. He stepped next to her and closed the door, sinking down onto the step beside her.

"Are you all right? You went very pale in there."

His voice could mesmerize. At least it was mesmerizing her. She nodded, because his eyes refused to leave her face, drifting over her intently.

He frowned suddenly. "Are you afraid of me? All this time I just thought you were shy, but you're afraid of me." He made the last a statement.

She looked away from him. Thankfully whatever was inside of her, threatening to burst free, had subsided along with the terrible need to feel Ridley's hands and mouth on her body.

His fingers settled gently on her chin and he turned her face toward him. "I wouldn't hurt you. You don't know me, but I would never harm a woman. I'm not like that. I'm new in town and you're at the dojo and make fantastic coffee, that's all. I wanted a little company. Just to talk to, Cat. That's all. End of story."

It was impossible to look into his eyes and not believe him. Up close she could smell him, and he smelled nice. Very nice. Very masculine. His lashes were long and thick, framing his incredible golden eyes. His tattoos were just as intricate and intriguing as he was. They crawled up his arms, drawing attention to his amazing and very defined muscles.

He was still looking at her and hadn't blinked once. His fingers remained firm but gentle on her chin. She'd forgotten that she'd been so mesmerized by his eyes. Catarina forced air into her lungs and smiled. Before she could speak, he shook his head.

"I saw the genuine thing, Cat. You smiled at Bernard.

You gave him the real smile, the high-voltage one that can knock a man off his feet at two hundred yards. I don't want a pretend smile. Give me the real thing or don't smile at me at all. I'm telling you again, I don't hurt women."

His voice was pure velvet. She shivered, his tone smoothing over her skin. "I'm sorry. I'm not afraid of you." A blatant lie. "I just don't talk much." That was lame. More than lame. She was a total idiot, but maybe that would save her.

Ridley's fingers slid from her chin. He didn't move, his thigh tight against hers on the narrow steps. "Unfortunately for you, Kitten, I am very adept at knowing a lie when I hear one. I've done my best to reassure you, but talk is cheap. I guess I'll just have to show you I'm a nice guy."

She was certain he was not. Oh, not like Rafe Cordeau. Not like that. But he was dangerous. She knew dangerous men, and this one sitting beside her was no domestic kitty cat. He was a tiger, all raw power and razor-sharp focus. But he wasn't *bad* dangerous. He was just plain scary dangerous. And a heartbreaker.

She sighed, hating that she actually felt the loss of his fingers on her skin—hating that every single cell in her body was aware of him. He was a good ten years older in years and experience. There were scars. There were the tats. There was the cool confidence and the lines in his face that only seemed to add to his masculine beauty.

She knew what he saw when he looked at her. She'd always looked young, and she was barely twenty-one. He would consider her someone he had to look after, just as Malcom did. That was safe. She needed safe, especially around this man.

"Maybe I am a little afraid of you," she forced herself to admit. "I've seen you in the dojo and you're rather terrifying." That much was true, and if he really was as adept at reading lies, then he'd have to hear the sincerity in her voice.

"That's a place of practice. This is a coffee-house. Unless

you're going to stand up in front of that mic and read off some really bad poetry, I don't think you have a thing to worry about," he assured.

There was a drawling amusement in his voice, one that made her want to laugh with him, but it was as sexy as all get-out, and she couldn't make a noise. Not a single sound for a few seconds. She cleared her throat. "I'm not good at talking to people."

"You talk just fine to Malcom. In fact, you laugh when you're with him. It's the only time I've seen you actually laugh."

Her heart jumped. She tensed and knew he felt it. Still, as hard as she tried, she couldn't relax. Had he been watching her? Why? What did that mean? She bit down on her lower lip, a little afraid that she was so paranoid even such a simple statement could make her want to run.

"Malcom isn't people."

"I know he's your friend," Ridley conceded. "He's very closed-mouthed about you, and protective."

She turned her eyes on him. Fixed. Focused. Alert. "Were you asking him questions about me?"

"Of course I was. You're beautiful. Mysterious. A turn-on in the dojo. When you move, honestly, Kitten, I've never seen anything like it. You're fast and fluid and hot as hell. You put James Marley down with one punch. One. You hit him exactly on his weak spot and dropped him like a ton of bricks. Your eyes are amazing and so is your hair. You have the most beautiful face I've ever seen. Are you telling me Malcom doesn't get asked about you regularly? Women like you don't walk the streets alone at night. That's just asking for trouble."

Her breath slammed out of her lungs. "You followed me?" That couldn't be. She would have known.

"Every night that you lock up and walk back to the warehouse. Did you really think I'd let a woman walk alone at that time of night? *Any* woman? But especially a woman like you? No fuckin' way."

Something in his eyes made her shiver. Hot. Angry. A flash, no more, and then quickly suppressed. He really didn't like her walking alone at night.

He had been at the coffee-house every night the past two weeks until three a.m. But she hadn't seen him or heard him or even felt him following her. And that was bad. She couldn't afford to miss a tail. She had a sixth sense about that kind of thing, and yet he had followed her every single night.

"I can take care of myself."

"Cat, even Malcom will tell you that you aren't being realistic. You're good, there's no question about it, but you're small. A man gets his hands on you and you're done. You're smart enough to know that. You can defend from a distance, but if he knows what he's doing, he's going to get past that guard and tie you up. Why don't you drive your car? That would be much safer."

She wasn't about to tell him gas cost the earth. He didn't need to know her personal finances, but she wasn't wasting precious gas when she could walk to and from work. It just wasn't that far.

"It isn't any of your business," she said, and knew she sounded uptight and stiff. Well, she was uptight and stiff. *And* it *wasn't* any of his business.

The same flash was there in his eyes. Hot. Angry. Pure steel. Her stomach did another flip. He was both scary and sexy at the same time, a combination she wanted no part of.

"I'm making it my business, Kitten, whether you like it or not. After hours, half the men in here are drunk. Why do you think they're in here?"

"I make a mean cup of coffee and word has gotten around. It sobers them up a little. Coming to Poetry Slam gives them some time to wind down."

He made a sound in the back of his throat that alarmed her. A rumble. A growl. The sound found its way to her heart, kick-starting her into flight mode.

"You can't possibly be that naïve, woman. Just in the two weeks I've been coming, the traffic between midnight and three has doubled. Mostly men. They come here because they're hoping to get lucky. They spend the entire time staring at you and trying to think of ways to get you in their beds. A few of them may have figured out that you walk home and they may make plans you aren't going to like and can't do anything about on your own."

She jumped up fast, but he was faster, his long fingers settling around her wrist, shackling her to him. He stood too, towering over her. His fierce golden eyes stared down into her blue ones, just as intense as she remembered, more so even. His gaze cut right through her until she feared every secret she had was laid bare in front of him.

"Don't run from me. I'm telling you the truth. Clearly you're living in a dream world when it comes to men and their intentions."

She tilted her head to one side, forgetting to keep her attitude in check. "Would you like to tell me what *your* intentions are?" she challenged.

His eyes changed and she knew immediately she'd made a terrible mistake. His eyes went liquid gold, focused and unblinking, locked onto her, and this time there was interest. Real interest. Before she'd been the one locked onto him, playing in her head with silly fantasies, but his motivation for following her had been actually watching out for her—she could see that now, at least she thought she could. Until that moment. That second.

She'd put too much sass into her tone. There was no backtracking from that, not with the stark speculation in his eyes. She forced air through her burning lungs and tugged at her hand to try to get him to release her.

His thumb slid over her wrist, right over her pounding

pulse, a mere brush, but the stroke sent hot blood rushing through her veins. She wanted to look away, but there was no getting away from the piercing stare of his eyes.

"Now I'm seeing you, Kitten. And you've got a little bite to you."

"Enough to handle myself if someone decides to attack me on my way home."

"I disagree."

"That doesn't matter," she said, and tugged at her hand again.

His hold didn't loosen. He wasn't hurting her; in fact, the pad of his thumb sent waves of heat curling through her body as it continued to brush little strokes over her pulse.

"It matters to me."

"It isn't your business." Now he was back to scaring her. He couldn't follow her around. Especially not to her home.

She was usually adept at spotting and shaking a tail. She practiced. He couldn't see her practicing. He'd wonder what she was doing and why. She desperately tried to remember if she'd done such a thing in the last two weeks. Usually, after working a full shift, she was exhausted and didn't take the extra time.

"I've decided to make it my business."

His voice was so low she could barely catch the sound, but the tone vibrated right through her body, disturbing her balance. She almost felt as if she was caught in a dream, waking up for the first time, suddenly aware of what real chemistry between a man and a woman was. She was certain she'd been the only one to feel it, and even then, it was just an awareness, not in the least harmful—like her silly daydreams of him.

This was altogether different. Her awareness of him, her reaction, was so strong, almost feral, female reacting to a male on the hunt, wanting him, yet wanting to run. Maybe needing the chase to prove something to both of them. She saw the answering challenge in his eyes. It was impossible not to see.

She shook her head and took two steps back, trying to put distance between them despite his fingers around her wrist. In spite of the fact that she couldn't look away from him. *What was wrong with her?* Her lack of control was frightening. She couldn't blow this. She didn't dare.

"I have no interest whatsoever in a relationship with anyone. I don't do one-night stands and I don't date. I don't want attention from you or any other man. I'm asking you politely to let go of my wrist."

She could barely get the words out. There was something, a part of her she'd never known existed, a part of her that didn't want to walk away from this man. He was beautiful. Sexy. Intelligent. And dangerous. Everything a woman might find attractive in a man. Everything *she* found attractive when she hadn't even known she could be attracted.

He didn't release her right away. His amazing eyes searched hers for a long moment. His face softened, and the male challenge was gone from his hard features as if it had never been there. Instead, he looked gentle. Still holding her wrist with one hand, he retrieved her hat with the other and gave it to her.

"You really are afraid of me, aren't you? I'm not going to hurt you, Cat. No matter what you think, I won't do that to you." His voice was pure velvet, stroking over her skin, low and vibrant and all male, almost a purr. His eyes hypnotized her all over again. They hadn't blinked. Not once. She was watching to see. He was absolutely, entirely focused on her and her alone.

Her belly did a slow roll and her breasts ached. Each separate spot where the pads of his fingers touched her bare skin felt as if he burned a brand right through her skin to her bones.

She hated that she was so susceptible to his voice. To his eyes. She retreated back to the character that always served her so well. She let her eyelashes fall, and nodded as if she understood. She couldn't handle a man like

Ridley. She knew that. She didn't dare chance becoming his friend. She wouldn't know what to do with him.

He let her go. The moment she was free of his grip, she pulled her arm to her, pushing her wrist up against her body as if she could hold in the heat from his touch. She sent him one look from under her lashes and hurried past him back inside.